Wild IN TEXAS

CHARLENE SANDS

KATHERINE GARBERA

ALI OLSON

MILLS & BOON

First Published 2019
Second Australian Paperback Edition 2023
ISBN 978 1 867 29832 8

First Published 2018
Third Australian Paperback Edition 2023
ISBN 978 1 867 29832 8

First Published 2017
Third Australian Paperback Edition 2023
ISBN 978 1 867 29832 8

MIX
Paper | Supporting responsible forestry
FSC® C001695
FSC www.fsc.org

Published by
Mills & Boon
An imprint of Harlequin Enterprises (Australia) Pty Limited (ABN 47 001 180 918), a subsidiary of HarperCollins Publishers Australia Pty Limited (ABN 36 009 913 517)
Level 19, 201 Elizabeth Street
SYDNEY NSW 2000
AUSTRALIA

Printed and bound in Australia by McPherson's Printing Group

CONTENTS

Texan For The Taking

Charlene Sands

Charlene Sands is a *USA TODAY* bestselling author of more than forty romance novels. She writes sensual contemporary romances and stories of the Old West. When not writing, Charlene enjoys sunny Pacific beaches, great coffee, reading books from her favorite authors and spending time with her family. You can find her on Facebook and Twitter, write her at PO Box 4883, West Hills, CA 91308, or sign up for her newsletter for fun blogs and ongoing contests at charlenesands.com.

Books by Charlene Sands

Harlequin Desire

The Slades of Sunset Ranch

Sunset Surrender
Sunset Seduction
The Secret Heir of Sunset Ranch
Redeeming the CEO Cowboy

Heart of Stone

The Texan's Wedding Escape
Heart of a Texan

Boone Brothers of Texas

Texan for the Taking

Visit her Author Profile page at
millsandboon.com.au,
or charlenesands.com, for more titles.

You can find Charlene Sands on Facebook,
along with other Harlequin Desire authors, at
Facebook.com/harlequindesireauthors!

Dear Reader,

Welcome to Boone Springs, Texas! Here you'll meet all three of the Boone brothers: Mason, Risk and Lucas. Each one of these hunky guys has their own story of love, loss, redemption and inspiration.

We start off with widower Mason Boone, who lives on Rising Springs Ranch and runs the megacompany Boone Incorporated. In this ranching town his ancestors founded, Mason butts heads with his onetime family friend, Andrea "Drea" MacDonald, a woman who blames him for the destruction of her father's ranching business. A woman who has secrets and a more personal reason to fight off any attraction she has for Mason.

My inspiration in creating Boone Springs and the widespread ranching community came from visiting our Texas family members in towns very similar to Boone Springs. These proud, dedicated and hardworking people are also fun and free-spirited, as you'll witness in Mason and Drea.

I hope you enjoy all three of these tall Texas tales of love!

Until next time, happy reading!

Charlene

To my sister, Carol, and her hubby, Bill,
two of the nicest people on earth.
Thanks for your love and support and
always being there for us!

And to Eric, Whitney, Reese and Quinn,
and Angi and Zane, my nieces and nephews
who make our family even more special!

One

Of course *he* had to be here.

Mason Boone.

Drea MacDonald had avoided him all these years, but there was no hope for it now. She had to deal with him on a strictly professional level. She liked to think she'd moved beyond what had happened, had moved way beyond *him*, but how could that be? Something that profound in her life, something that had scarred her so permanently, wasn't easily forgotten.

Mason pressed his tall frame against the back wall of the hospital conference room, arms folded, watching her through intense coal-black eyes. She couldn't ignore him. He was a presence in the room; a tall, dreadfully handsome man, dressed impeccably in a dark suit, who commanded respect and exuded confidence.

As a young girl, all those traits had lured her in. But he'd rejected her without a second thought.

Her best bet would be to treat him with indifference, to give him a nod and get on with her business. He didn't have to know the pain he'd caused her. He didn't have to see the hurt look in her eyes or the flush of her skin. It would take an award-winning performance, but she was up to the task. After all, she'd imagined this moment in her head fifty times, if not more.

Her heart sat heavy in her chest because she wasn't the only one who had lost something precious. She wasn't the only one who'd been deeply scarred. Mason had, too. He'd lost his wife and unborn child nearly two years ago. His loss and grief only contributed to the tremendous guilt she felt for disliking him so. He had the town's support. Everyone was sympathetic to his loss. It was hard to hate a guy everyone else rallied around. Guilt ate away at her even though she had every right to hold a grudge.

She stood at the head of the conference table, just finishing up her presentation. "And thanks to the generosity of Mason Boone and his family," she said, grinding her teeth as she gave him praise, "we'll hold our multifaceted weekend fund-raiser at Rising Springs Ranch. Our goal, two million dollars."

The doctors, hospital administrators and committee members overseeing the fund-raiser gazed at each other, raising skeptical brows. It was a tall order, true, but she had always banked her reputation on fulfilling her goals. And this part of Texas was rich with donors of cold hard cash.

"It's doable," said an assured voice from the back of the room.

All heads swiveled to Mason Boone. His family had founded the Texas town of Boone Springs decades ago, and the hospital had recently changed names from County Memorial to Boone County Memorial. The Boone family and their kin practically owned the entire town. Well, they owned the best parts, so when a Boone spoke, people listened.

"It's very doable, if we're smart," Drea persisted, again avoiding Mason's dark eyes. "And I intend to be…very smart."

"Thatta girl," gray-haired Dr. Keystone said. "We trust you, Andrea. You're one of our own."

"Thank you, Doctor. I appreciate your support. Together, we'll make this work."

She smiled, feeling powerful in her black suit and three-inch cherry-red heels. She wore her long, dark cocoa hair up in a sleek, practical style. She meant business.

Landing this job at the hospital served many purposes. Nailing it would all but guarantee her promotion to vice president at Solutions Inc., the consulting and events planning firm she worked for in New York. But more importantly, she wanted to help the community where she'd grown up by raising funds for a much-needed cardiac wing, to honor her mother, who'd died of heart failure. And she also wanted to reconnect with her ailing father. Unfortunately, that meant living in the cottage the Boones had gifted Drew MacDonald after practically stealing Thundering Hills Ranch out from under him. Her father's acceptance of the living arrangements irritated her to this day. How could he be okay with their charity, while Drea's life had been snatched right out from under her as a young girl when the Boones took over Thundering Hills? She'd lost her home, too, but her father hadn't seemed to notice how much that had disrupted her life.

After the meeting, as Drea collected her papers, carefully placing them in her briefcase, she heard footsteps approaching and held her breath.

"Nice job, Drea."

That deep confident voice unsettled her. The timbre, the tone, the way Mason said her name—memories came rushing back, tilting her world upside down. *God.* Why was he heading this committee? Deep in her belly, she knew. He'd lost his pregnant wife to heart disease. Drea couldn't really fault him for wanting to be involved; she had similar reasons for being here. Yet, even knowing the pain he'd recently endured, seeing him in the flesh for the first time in years curdled her stomach. She resented the Boones, but him most of all.

Mason stood facing her, his eyes boring in, and finally, because she felt defiant and fearless, she stared back and gave him her best aloof smile. "Thank you."

Twelve years had only given his good looks a more rugged edge. She took in the sharp angle of his jaw, the facial scruff that hadn't been there before, the length of his hair, whipped back and shining like black ink. None of it mattered. She was merely observing. She'd turned off all her buttons, leaving him none to push anymore.

"You look good," he said.

The compliment slid off her back.

"Drew will be glad to have you home."

"It's temporary," she said, closing the clasp on her briefcase.

"Still, it'll be good for him."

She looked away. What about what was good for her? What about all those days and nights when she'd had to be the adult because her father was passed out drunk on the floor? What about the dinners he'd never cooked, the clothes he'd never washed? What about a twelve-year-old kid having to baby her own father? And what about the heartsick motherless girl who'd desperately needed…love?

"We'll see."

"You haven't been home yet?"

She shook her head. "No, I came here straight from the airport."

"Drea?"

She couldn't look at him, even though there was something pleading in the way he'd said her name. Instead, she continued fiddling with the closure on her case.

"It's good to have you home," he said finally.

Chin down, she nodded. "I have a job to do."

"Yeah, about that. We should probably coordinate on the events you have planned. We could look at them over dinner one night or—"

"No." Her voice was sharper than she'd intended. So much for being professional. He was staring at her like she'd lost her mind. Maybe she had, thinking she could come home in hopes of doing something good for the community, something to honor her deceased mother, even if it meant working alongside Mason. Were her emotions so tangled up that she couldn't separate her professional life from her private one?

Goodness, but she had to. She'd committed to this fund-raising campaign. She was being paid to see it through. And she had to remind herself over and over that she was doing this to honor her mother. It was time she came home. At least temporarily.

"No?" Mason narrowed his eyes.

"I mean, I'll email you. I really am very busy, Mason. I have a lot on my mind today."

She gave him a plastic smile, one he immediately picked up on as bullshit. He nodded. "Yeah, I get it." His mouth curled in a frown and there was an edge of annoyance in his voice now. *Ha!* He had no right being annoyed with her. Not when the last time she'd been with him, he'd treated her like dirt.

He slipped a business card into her hand, his long lean fingers skimming over her knuckles. Immediately her heart beat faster, her nerves jumped. The shock of his brief, warm touch strummed through her body. "Email me when you find time. We have exactly one month to pull this off."

His urgency wasn't lost on her. This was as important to him as it was to her. They had that in common. Both wanted a special cardiac wing of the hospital built in Boone Springs. But all of a sudden one month in Texas seemed like an eternity.

Not to mention she'd be living at the cottage on Rising Springs Ranch again.

On Mason's home turf.

"Yum, this is just as delish as I remembered." Drea swallowed a big hunk of her Chocolate Explosion cupcake. Unladylike, but Katie Rodgers, her bestie from childhood and owner of the bakery, would expect no less.

Her friend laughed and removed her apron. She put the Katie's Kupcakes is Klosed sign on the door and joined Drea at the café table.

"You do not disappoint," Drea said. "And you remembered my favorite."

"Of course I did. Can't forget all those times you'd come over and we'd bake up a batch. We were what, ten at the time?"

"Yeah, but ours never came close to these marvels you crank out at four in the morning. Gosh, you always knew what you wanted to do with your life. I'm so proud of everything you've accomplished, Katie. I bet you've got all of Boone Springs wrapped around your sugary fingers, with lines out the door in the morning."

"I have no complaints," she replied. "Business is good." She sighed sweetly. "It's great to have you back in town. I've missed you."

Drea grabbed Katie's hand and squeezed. "I've missed you, too. I couldn't drive out to Rising Springs without seeing you first."

"I'm glad you did. Only I wish it wasn't temporary. I kinda like seeing you in person instead of on Facetime."

"Well, let's try to make the most of my stay here. We're gonna both be busy, but we have to make a pact to see each other a few times a week," Drea said.

"Pinkie promise?" Katie curled her last digit, and they linked fingers just like they had when they were kids.

"Pinkie promise."

"Good, then it's settled." Katie began to rise. "Would you like a cup of coffee to wash down the cupcake? I could brew up a fresh pot."

"When did your cupcakes ever need washing down?" She smiled. "No thanks. Any more coffee today and I swear I'll float away. Let's just talk."

Katie smiled and plunked back into her seat. "Okay. So, you're working on the hospital fund-raiser."

She nodded.

"With Mason?"

"Yeah, which is the major drawback to my coming home. I

have to make the fund-raiser my high priority, so I'm enduring the Boones for as long as it takes."

"I get that it's hard for you, Drea. I really do. It was hard on Mason, too, losing Larissa and the baby. From what I hear, he's only just starting to come out of his grief."

"It's a tragedy. But let's not talk about the Boones. Because if we do, then I'll have to ask you about Lucas."

Katie's eyes rounded. "Lucas? We're just friends. If that anymore."

"Uh-huh. So you say."

"For heaven's sake, he was engaged to my sister. And he broke Shelly's heart when he went off and joined the Marines."

"But I hear he's back now." Drea took another bite of cupcake, certain she'd die from an overdose of decadence.

"Don't remind me. Shelly still hasn't healed from him running out on her like that. It was such a shock. Luke seemed true blue. After the breakup, Shelly hit some rough patches. Mom's convinced it's all Luke's fault. I mean, it sounded more like something Risk would do. Not Luke."

River "Risk" Boone, heartthrob and one-time famous rodeo rider, was the player in the Boone family.

"Yeah, well, we can't forget he's a Boone. It's part of his DNA," Drea said.

Katie's right brow rose and she shook her head. "So, after all these years you haven't gotten over it, either?"

"Over what? The fact that the Boones preyed on my father's grief and then stole Thundering Hills out from under him? Our families had been friends for years, but as soon as my dad hit a rough patch, the Boones swooped in, stole our ranch and we were reduced to living at the cottage on Boone property. They gave Dad a pity job as caretaker. Then there's Mason and all that he put me through... Oh, never mind. I don't want to rehash it." She waved her hand, ending her rant.

Katie gave her a serious knowing look. But Katie didn't know everything. Drea hadn't told her best friend what had happened after her debacle with Mason. How she ran into the arms of the first willing man and gave up her virginity. How she'd gotten pregnant and lost her baby. It had been the worst time of her life.

"I guess we need to put the past behind us, Drea. That's what I keep telling my sister."

"Yeah, easier said than done sometimes."

She was through talking about the Boones. She polished off the cupcake and licked the frosting from her fingers, closing her eyes as she relished every last morsel of goodness. "Mmm."

"So, I hear your dad is struggling a bit. The fall he took last week was pretty bad. When I heard about it, I stopped by his place with a batch of apricot thumbprints and half a dozen cupcakes."

"Ahh, you're the best. He loves your thumbprint cookies. Thanks for checking in on him."

"He's very excited to have you home."

"I know." She couldn't say too much; her emotions were curled up in a knot about going home to Drew MacDonald. Maybe that's why she was procrastinating. She'd missed her father, and she loved him. But she was a realist. Her dad would never win a Father of the Year award. Hard fact, but true.

"He's changed, Drea. He's trying very hard."

She sighed. "I'll believe it when I see it." She glanced at her watch. "Which is what I should do just about now. I hate to go, but I've really gotta get on the road."

"Will you text me later?"

"Of course."

They both stood and then Katie went behind the counter. "Just a sec. I'm not sending you home empty-handed." She packed up a white box with goodies and sealed it with a pastel pink Katie's Kupcakes sticker. "Here you go," she said, handing over the box. "Welcome home."

"Thanks, friend. My hips will never be the same."

"Your hips and my thighs. We're all doomed."

Drea chuckled and kissed Katie on the cheek. "At least we'll both go down together."

After she excited the shop, a sense of real doom flashed through her system.

She couldn't procrastinate any longer.

It was time to go to the place she'd never considered home.

Drea parked her car in front of her father's house just as the autumn sun was setting. Splashes of deep pink and purple painted the sky overhead. She'd forgotten the stunning sunsets in this part of Texas. How many years had it been since she'd seen a horizon so rich and vibrant? These wide-open spaces were tailor-made for such amazing spectacles. Texas was known for doing things large and the sight brought a little peace to her jittery heart.

Lordy be.

She chuckled at the slang that had come back to her after crossing state lines.

But she wasn't that Texas girl any longer.

She gazed toward the cornflower-blue cottage trimmed in white, and saw her father sitting in a rocking chair on the front deck. As soon as he spotted her, he made an attempt to rise. His face turned a shade of red, not from pain, she assumed, but from frustration as he faltered and slid back down onto the seat. On his next try, he pulled himself up and leaned against a post. His hair was lighter gray than she remembered, his body chunkier, but he was still a handsome man, and there was a spark in his green eyes as he waved to her.

She waved back, holding her breath. She reminded herself this wasn't the same drunken man who'd given up on life after her mother died. He was trying to be a good father. He'd honed his skills on a smartphone so he could send her text messages. He called her every week to talk. He never once made her feel guilty for not coming to visit. He never once asked her to give up her adult life to be with him. But she'd felt bad anyway.

She got out of the car and retrieved her luggage from the trunk. As she approached, wheeling her suitcase behind her, a big smile surfaced on his ruddy face, making him look ten years younger than his sixty-five years.

"Hi, Daddy," she said. *Wow.* Whatever possessed her to call him that? She hadn't referred to him that way since she was a kid.

"Hey there, my girl. Welcome home."

As far as she was concerned, Thundering Hills, a large parcel of land to the west that was now incorporated into Rising Springs, had been her true home. Before the Boones got their hands on it. "Thank you."

She climbed the steps to come face-to-face with her father. He was pale and moving slowly but the light in his eyes was bright with excitement.

He opened his arms and took a step toward her, a shadow of fear crossing his face for a moment. He didn't trust that she'd embrace him. There'd been so many times in her young life when she'd needed a hug from him or a kind word, and he hadn't been there. For right now, she put that behind her. Well, as much as she could hope to. That kind of rejection was hard to forget.

She stepped into his arms and gave him a brief hug before backing away.

"It's good to see you, Drea. You look so pretty, just like your mama. You've been well?"

"Yes, I've been well. How about you, Dad?"

"Ah, I'm doing just fine."

She didn't believe him. He'd taken a fall and had downplayed it to her when she'd questioned him over the phone. He'd blamed it on a bad case of arthritis, but according to Katie he'd refused to go to the doctor for a health screening.

Back in the day, her father would lose his balance and crumble in a drunken stupor a few times a day. Now he probably feared she wouldn't believe he was clean and sober if he admitted to falling down the steps.

God, she hoped he wasn't backsliding. Not after all this time.

"We have a lot to catch up on, girl."

"Yes, we do. Let's go inside. I'll make us some dinner."

Her father's eyes brightened. "It's already done. I made your favorite, pot roast and red potatoes. I even attempted your mama's special biscuits."

"You did?" Nobody made homemade biscuits like her mother. Maybe Katie was right. Maybe her father was really trying. She could count on her fingers and toes how many meals her father had actually cooked for her as a child.

"Well, let's go inside and try them out," she said. "I'm starving."

"Sounds good to me. My stomach's been growling. But mostly I'm just pleased to have my little girl back home."

She was twenty-nine years old, hardly a little girl anymore, but she was here now and she'd have to deal with old memories and the pain those reminders evoked.

She forged into the house, wheeling her suitcase easily as her father followed behind her.

The next evening, Drea breathed a sigh of relief as she arrived back at the cottage after a very productive Mason-free day at the hospital. All day long she'd held her breath, thinking she'd run into him and have to make nice for appearance's sake, but he was a no-show and she was glad of the things she'd accomplished without having to deal with him. She'd gone over some important aspects of the fund-raiser with the supervisors of various departments and had called to confirm donors for the art sale. The rest of the event details involved the Boones and she had no other option than to deal with Mason on that.

She walked into her bedroom, left untouched since she'd lived here, and shed her business suit and high heels for a comfy pair of washed out jeans and an I ♥ New York T-shirt she'd received for running a 5K race. After pulling her hair up in a ponytail, she washed her face and brushed her teeth. Man oh man, she thought, glancing in the mirror. There was no denying she looked like a schoolgirl again. It was amazing how a little makeup and a sleek hairstyle could transform her appearance. But inside, she was still that unsure, guarded little girl.

At least it wasn't horrible living here, and her father was making a gold-star effort on her behalf. She was trying like hell to keep an open mind, trying to put the past behind her, but her scars ran deep and it wasn't easy to forgive and forget all she'd gone through here in Boone Springs. Not a day went by that she didn't think about the baby she'd lost, about the child she would never know. It wasn't Mason's baby, yet she'd blamed him for rejecting her, destroying her confidence and causing her to run into the arms of the first man who'd showed interest in her.

A knock at her bedroom door shook her out of her thoughts. "Drea, can I speak to you?"

She opened the door and glanced at her father. Beyond him, down the hall, she saw four men standing in the parlor. What were Mason and Risk Boone doing here? The ranch foreman, Joe Buckley, and Dwayne, one of the crew, were also there. "Sure. What's going on?"

Her father shook his head, his expression contrite. "I forgot about the poker game. We, uh, the boys usually come here on Tuesday nights. I'm sorry, Drea. I guess I've been so wrapped up in you being home, it slipped my mind. Should I send them away?"

"No, Dad. Of course not. I don't want my being here disrupting your routine." The irony was that as a kid, she'd always felt like a disruption in his life. She got in the way of his drinking.

"They brought dinner. Pizza from Villa Antonio. Will you come out and eat with us?"

What could she say? She liked Joe; he'd always been decent to her, and Dwayne was her age. They'd gone to school together. She didn't like breaking bread with the Boones, but she was hungry and she couldn't hide out in her room all night. "I suppose I can do that."

She walked into the parlor with her father and the men took off their hats. Everyone said hello but Mason. Hat in hand, he gave her a long stare and nodded.

"You still breaking hearts in New York, Drea?" Risk asked, his wide smile almost infectious. Risk was a charmer and she'd always been a little wary of him. He was too smooth for her liking.

"I don't know about that, but I like to think I'm killing it in other ways."

"I bet you are."

"Good to see you, Drea. You're looking well," Joe said. "It's been a while."

"Yeah, it has," she said. "How's Mary Lou?"

"Doing fine."

"Please tell her hello for me."

"Will do," he said, smiling.

"Hey, Drea," Dwayne said. "Missed you at the ten-year reunion."

"I know. I just couldn't get away, but Katie caught me up to speed on everyone. Congrats, I heard you just had a baby."

"We did. Heather and I named him Benjamin, after my father." He took out his phone and showed her a picture of his son.

"He's precious."

"We think so, too. Thanks."

"So you and Mason are gonna work together on the fundraiser." Risk shifted his glance from her to his brother, a twinkle in his eye. Was he trying to cause trouble, or just being Risk? She didn't know how much his family knew about her history with Mason. True, it was old news. But not for her.

"That's the plan," Mason said, eyeballing her. "After the game tonight, I'd like to talk to you about it."

"We don't usually finish up too late," her father interjected. "It's a workday for everyone tomorrow."

"Okay, fine." She'd just have to put on her big girl panties.

She couldn't postpone it any longer. She'd gotten herself into this and she had a job to do.

Mason gave her a nod and they all sat down at the dining room table. As she chewed her pizza and drank iced tea, every so often she'd steal a glance Mason's way, and each time, his coal-black eyes were on her, as if she was the only person in the room. He made her jumpy. She didn't like it one bit, and she fought the feeling.

But there'd always been *something* between her and Mason. Well, maybe it was all one-sided. At age seventeen her feelings had started out as hero worship for a guy six years older than her and had grown from there. Until he'd shot her down and humiliated her.

After dinner, the men got serious about poker, and Drea busied herself cleaning the kitchen, collecting and trashing pizza boxes and setting the coffeemaker timer to brew a dark rich roast in two hours. The guys had brought beer, something Drea knew her father had insisted upon. He wasn't going to spoil their night because he had a drinking problem. A tall glass of iced tea sat in front of her dad and he seemed fine with it.

Three years clean and sober.

God, she hoped the worst was behind him now. But there was always doubt in her mind, and maybe her father was trying to make a point by showing her he was a changed man.

During the game, she disappeared into her room and flipped open her laptop. She stared at the screensaver, a golden Hawaiian sunrise, wishing she could jump right into the picture.

But no, that wasn't going to ever happen. Was that kind of serenity even real?

She clicked open her spreadsheet and calendar and got busy working on items for the fund-raiser. There were dozens of moving parts for the big push and she was beginning to make headway.

After twenty minutes or so, she was totally engrossed in

her work. A knock at her door broke her concentration and she jumped.

It wasn't her father's light rapping. No, she knew who it was. *Ugh.* She got up and yanked open the door, ready to face Mason.

Immediately the woodsy scent of his cologne wafted to her as she looked into his dark eyes. It was hard to miss the broad expanse of his chest as he braced his arms against her doorjamb, making her feel slightly trapped. "Hi," he said.

She'd expected him to be demanding, to insist they get to work, to pressure her. But that one word, spoken softly, surprised her and her defenses went up. "Mason."

"I, uh, I know it's late, but we should probably talk. If that's okay with you?"

It wasn't late. It was barely nine thirty. On really busy days, she'd often work until midnight. But things in Boone Springs were different than the big city. The pace was slower, the nights shorter, and the mornings came earlier. "It's fine."

"It's a nice night. Why don't you grab a jacket and meet me out back?"

She blinked. She didn't want to be alone with Mason on a moonlit night, but she wasn't about to show fear.

"Your dad's probably tired. I wouldn't want to keep him up with our chatter," he explained.

"Right," she said. "Give me a minute and I'll meet you outside."

Mason nodded and took his leave.

Drea shut the door and leaned against it, her pulse pounding in her ears.

Memories flashed through her mind, but she halted them in their tracks. She had a job to do. She was vying for a vice president position at Solutions Inc. A lot was riding on her communication and marketing skills with this fund-raiser.

And she couldn't allow Mason Boone to get in her way.

* * *

The screen door opened and Drea stepped outside. Mason shot up from his seat the second he glimpsed her. Her boots clicked on the deck as she approached. She was wearing jeans and a pretty pink blouse underneath a black leather jacket. Her hair was pulled back in a ponytail, with a few wavy strands falling loose, caressing her cheeks. She looked soft and pretty, so different than the uptight, buttoned-to-the-neck woman he'd met in the committee room yesterday.

Years ago, he'd been attracted to her for a short time, until rational sense had kicked in and he'd backed off from the hell storm it would create. At seventeen, Andrea MacDonald had looked at him with adoring eyes and his ego had taken flight. But she was Drew's daughter, a mixed-up girl yearning for affection. Affection that couldn't come from Mason. He'd been twenty-three, six years older than her, and supposedly wiser. He would've only screwed her up more.

Now, he wanted to tell her she had nothing to fear from him, that he was dead inside and had been for a couple years, ever since Larissa died. But that was assuming too much. Maybe her coolness wasn't necessarily aimed at him. Maybe she'd changed from that sweet, caring, innocent girl she'd been to someone he didn't know, didn't recognize. Lord knew, he'd changed over the years as well, and he was simply here to work alongside her. The past was the past and maybe it was better to let it alone.

"Brought you some coffee," he said, grabbing for the cup on the wicker table beside him.

She smiled, apparently surprised at the gesture. "Thanks."

"I didn't know how you like it."

"Black is fine."

He handed it to her, their fingers brushing in the transfer, and he gazed into her pretty eyes. She lowered her lids and looked away. Those sage-green eyes were the same as Drew's, and her long, lustrous dark hair and olive skin were all her mother, Maria. Drea was a striking mix of Irish and Latina.

"You want to have a seat?" He gestured toward the bench he'd been sitting on. He could feel her reluctance, sensing she'd rather have a root canal than sit with him, but she finally perched on one end. He sat as far away from her as possible, which was all of twenty-four inches, if that.

"So, you still resent all the Boones?" he asked on impulse. The question had been bugging him since he'd laid eyes on her yesterday.

Her head snapped up and coffee sloshed in her cup. Luckily, it didn't spill onto her hand. He would've never forgiven himself for that.

"Some more than others." Her eyes narrowed on him and suddenly she wasn't looking quite so pretty anymore.

"We tried to help your father, Drea. He was in desperate need and—"

"I know the story your family tells. I don't need to hear it from you."

"Maybe you do. Maybe that's the only way this is going to work between me and you."

"So, I'm supposed to forget all about the fact that when my father came to yours, asking for help with Thundering Hills, asking for a loan to tide us over for a few months, he was flat-out refused. Our families had been friends for years. And then, the next thing I know our land was bought out from under us and all we got were crumbs. Dad had to swallow his pride and take a job on Rising Springs. I had to move off our land to come live in this little cottage. We lost everything."

"That's not the way it happened, Drea."

"That's the way I see it, Mason. Total betrayal."

"Your dad..."

"What? What about my dad? He took to drinking heavily after mom died and...he's never been the same."

Mason didn't have the heart to tell Drea the truth. If Drew hadn't after all these years, then it wasn't his place to tell her that her little girl's perception of what happened had been all wrong. Drew had made Mason's father promise not to reveal details of the deal. Since both of Mason's folks were gone now, victims of a small plane crash years ago, he felt it was up to him to see that vow was upheld. If Drew wasn't willing to set his daughter straight, Mason surely wasn't going to do it.

"Drew's doing real good now." It was all he would say on the matter.

"So everyone in Boone Springs is telling me."

Mason didn't understand her. He was just barely coming out of his own grief, and related to how Drew MacDonald had been in the same situation, losing his wife the way he had, so unexpectedly. Mason hadn't taken to drinking the way Drew had, but everyone coped with heartache differently. He wasn't excusing Drew's bad behavior, but he knew what the man had been feeling.

Mason shook his head. "Aren't you glad he's getting better?"

"Of course I am. If it's the real thing this time." Her voice lowered to a whisper. "I've been disappointed before."

Mason ran his hand down his face. "I know it wasn't easy on you, Drea."

She shook her head, and he took in how her long hair flowed in natural waves down her back. "You know nothing about me, Mason."

He met her sad green eyes and something shifted in his heart. She tried to talk tough, but she wore her pain on her sleeve and her vulnerability grabbed him. "I know more than you think."

"That's a Boone for you, claiming to know every—"

He pressed two fingers to her lips, quieting her tirade. "Shh, Drea."

Her eyes snapped to his.

He couldn't believe he'd done it, touched her this way. But grazing her soft lips, looking into those defiant eyes was like a live wire sparking and jolting inside the dead parts of him. He felt alive for the first time in years. It was heady and he wanted more. He wanted to hold on to that spark that told him he was a living, breathing man.

Sliding his fingers off her mouth, he cradled her face, his thumb circling her cheek, strands of her hair caressing the back of his hand.

"Mason, are you crazy?" she whispered, yet the look in her eyes told him she was thinking something different.

"Maybe."

"You're not going to—"

"Yes, I think I am."

He put his mouth to hers and tasted her sweetness, the plump ripe lips that were meant to be kissed. Sensation flooded him. He remembered her. As a teen. A girl who'd needed affection, and he'd given it to her without question, until the night that she'd bared her soul to him and offered her body.

He'd had to turn her away.

Any decent man would have.

But she wasn't a kid anymore. And it was good, so damn good that instant guilt flooded him. His heart belonged to another and always would. That jolt of life he felt worried him and scared him silly. It was as if he was losing his wife all over again. He hadn't done anything this impulsive in years, much less with Drea, the very last woman on earth he should be kissing.

Two

Drea's mouth trembled as Mason brushed his lips over hers. She couldn't believe this was happening. She didn't want this. She didn't want him, even though his lips were firm and delicious, scented by coffee and the fresh night air.

He grabbed her upper arms, demanding more of the kiss. Her heartbeats raced, her body warmed and a sudden realization dawned. Whatever she and Mason had between them hadn't completely disappeared. It was real and hot and almost too out of control, but no, she couldn't do this. In the past, he'd caused her to do crazy, impulsive things. Her infatuation with him had almost ruined her life and she couldn't forget that. Ever. She squeezed her eyes tight, laid her hand flat on his chest and pushed as hard as she could.

He reared back, startled. "Damn, Drea."

"Mason, I don't know what you think you were doing—"

"The same thing you were. Kissing."

"I didn't w*ant* to kiss you." She'd wanted to slap his face, but…she wasn't a drama queen. The push sent the same message.

"I didn't want to kiss you, either. Okay, I did, but only in the moment."

"I thought you were a grieving widower." Her hand flew to her mouth, but the damage was done. She couldn't take it back.

He stared at her, his eyes losing their brightness. "I am," he said quietly.

Then why kiss her? "I'm…confused, trying to make sense of this. It was…unexpected."

"I know. For me, too."

She folded her arms over her chest, her lips slightly bruised from his kiss. "You had no right."

"I know that, too."

"Why did you?" She searched his eyes, saw raw emotion there.

"I, uh… You want honesty?"

"Always."

He ran his hand down his face again, stroked his chin. "I felt something. Something that wasn't dead inside me. Something that came to life the second I touched you, and I wanted to continue feeling it, even for a few more seconds."

"Oh, wow." She understood. Sort of. He'd been happily married with a baby on the way. And suddenly, it had all been taken away. She'd known that kind of loss, too, impetuously running into the arms of the first man she'd met after Mason rejected her, and getting pregnant. She'd lost that child in a miscarriage and walked away from Brad Williamson, the man who'd loved her. That year had been the hardest in her life.

And now what shocked her the most about all this was that *she'd* been the one to make Mason feel something. How was that possible? "Why…me?"

He smiled crookedly and shook his head. "I have no idea."

"Well, that's honest."

"Why did you kiss me back?"

She wasn't going there. She wouldn't tell him how much he'd once meant to her. How painful it had been when she was seventeen. And how much she resented him now because he'd made her feel something, too. "You're a good kisser."

"That's it?"

"Of course that's it. I haven't dated in a while and…"

"Okay, I get it." He blew out a breath and jammed his fingers into his hair. He seemed frustrated and a little bit angry. "Listen, let's forget this ever happened."

"Amen to that. So what now?"

"Now we do what we came out here to do. Talk about the fund-raiser."

"Okay, I guess we have no choice."

Mason frowned and she felt a little triumphant. At least he wouldn't try to kiss her again. That would be a big mistake on his part, and an even a bigger mistake for her. As long as he kept his hands off her, she'd be fine. She took a big breath, willing her racing heart to calm down.

"So, where do we begin?" he asked.

"With me telling you my ideas and you thinking they're all incredible."

Half an hour later, Mason said good-night to Drea in the kitchen and waited until she headed off to her room, before grabbing another cup of coffee.

"You having more?" Drew said, coming in from the parlor.

"Yeah, if that's okay. We didn't disturb you. Did we?"

"Nah, not tired enough to sleep. Thought I'd get some coffee and sit for a while. I think I'll join you."

Mason knew how the older man liked his coffee. He poured him a cup, stirred in two lumps of sugar and handed it to him. Drew had a sweet tooth but it was harmless enough, a substitute for alcohol perhaps. "Actually, I was hoping to talk to you for a bit," Mason said. "If you're up to it."

"Winning always perks me right up. I figure I'm good for a few more minutes while I drink this mud. You and Drea were out there awhile. Everything good between you two?" he asked.

Mason had kissed Drea. He wasn't sure if he'd ever forget the spark that had lit him up inside like fireworks on the Fourth of July. So no, everything was not good. Drea didn't like him much, and he, well, he was feeling a hefty dose of guilt now, like he'd cheated on his wife. That gnawing ache wasn't going away and he doubted he'd get much sleep tonight. "Yeah, everything's fine. She's a smart woman. She's focused on the fund-raiser."

"She tell you all her ideas then?"

"She did. They're right on target. She seems to know how put on an event and build momentum."

They'd kick off the weekend on Friday evening with the HeART Auction of Boone Springs, garnering donations from local and not so local artists to sell on-site. For Saturday, she was planning a Family FUNd-raiser Festival, full of games and pony rides and raffles for children. Saturday night was reserved for a dinner-dance and she was in negotiations with a Grammy-nominated young country band to provide the entertainment. She'd managed to enlist a talented designer to create a website and was in the process of soliciting volunteers for the event.

Mason would be in charge of logistics and overseeing the big picture, while Drea and her committees would work on the details.

Their thirty-minute talk after they'd locked lips had managed to get his mind off her pretty green eyes and sweet body, and back on track.

"I'm sure proud of her, but I wish she'd let up a little bit."

"She only has a short time to make it all happen, Drew."

"I know, but is it selfish of me to want her to myself? I mean, I know I don't deserve it, and Lord knows, I'll spend the rest of my days trying to make up for being a lousy father to her when she needed me the most."

"She'll come around. She loves you, Drew."

"Yeah, but she doesn't always like me so very much."

Mason rubbed his jaw. Drea didn't like him, either, and maybe that was a good thing. It would keep him from making the mistake of kissing her again. But he wasn't one to give advice to Drew or anyone on matters of the heart, so he kept his mouth shut. "Aunt Lottie's back home. She arrived last night from her trip to Africa and she's thrilled that Drea's here. I think you can expect her to come for a visit."

"Lottie, huh? What the hell was she doing in Africa for all those months?"

Mason grinned. He suspected Drew was sweet on his aunt, but the two were like oil and water. And they had history: Lottie and Drew's late wife, Maria, had been best friends until the day she'd died. "Don't know. Maybe you should ask her when she stops by."

Drew looked away and grumbled something about her not wanting to see him.

"What?"

"Nothin'."

"Aunt Lottie wants to surprise Drea, so don't say anything to her, okay?"

"I won't say a thing. My lips are sealed."

"Dad, are you talking to yourself?" Drea wandered into the kitchen and stopped short when she spotted Mason. "You're still here?"

He nodded, speechless. Drea was in her pajamas, a pair of soft pink cotton pants and a matching top that clung to her breasts, hiding little. His mouth was suddenly dry, but Mason kept his composure, even while that *alive feeling* bombarded him. "I was just going."

She folded her arms around her middle. If she thought that shielded her, she was mistaken. The material only pulled tighter across her chest.

Mason turned and brought his coffee mug to the sink. He couldn't look at her another second without showing her—and her *father*—how much she affected him.

He could hardly believe it. Drea had poked the sleeping bear and he needed to get out of here, pronto. He headed for the front door, keeping his back to the MacDonalds. "Thanks for the game tonight, Drew. Good night, Drea." Then he exited the cottage without giving either of them a parting glance.

The next day, Drea must've put a good one hundred miles on the car making stops all over the county, checking items off the to-do list on her cell phone. She'd be lost without her list. It was sort of scary thinking how if anything happened to her phone or tablet, her entire life would be erased. Lately, for this project, she'd been taking pen to paper, jotting notes as a backup, too. But her mind was crowded just the same with all the details for the event.

As she parked the car in the driveway of her father's cottage, she closed her eyes, thoughts running rampant through her head.

Check in with the caterers.

Make the rounds at local art galleries.

Double-check with Katie regarding the children's cupcake-decorating booth.

Plead with The Band Blue to donate an evening of entertainment.

Stop thinking about Mason.

Darn it. The more she tried, the harder it was. She'd be right in the middle of planning her next move with the fund-raiser when her mind would flash to Mason. His fingers softly touching her, the immediate red-hot spark that baffled them both and then the determination in his eyes when he'd finally bent his head and made exquisite contact with her lips. He'd stirred something deep inside her, more than curiosity, more than bravado, and she'd had to see the kiss through.

He'd said she made him feel alive. Now if that wasn't an ego boost. And she hadn't lied; it had been the best kiss she'd had in a long time. That was where it got confusing. She resented Mason. For how he'd humiliated her. For how he'd dismissed her so easily and broken her heart. She'd lost so much of herself then and had run into the arms of the first man who'd paid her attention, giving him her body, but not her heart.

A knock on the car window snapped her out of her thoughts. She opened her eyes and focused on the woman smiling in at her.

"Drea, sweetheart. I couldn't wait another second to see you. I hope I didn't startle you."

"Lottie?"

"It's me. I'm back and I'm dying to talk to you."

Drea couldn't get out fast enough to give her "aunt" a long, lingering hug. "Oh, Lottie. It's so good to see you!" Because Drea's mom and Lottie had been BFF all their lives, she'd been in Drea's life, too. After her mother died, Lottie had given her the love and attention Maria couldn't any longer.

Drea pulled back to look into Lottie's eyes. They still held sparkle and spunk. At sixty, Lottie was no wilting flower. She'd kept up her appearance, wearing trendy clothes, staying slender and coloring her gray a honey-blond shade, her silky locks reaching her shoulders. "You look beautiful, Lottie. I swear you never age."

"Age is just a number, sweetie. And that's so kind of you to say." Lottie smiled again, giving her the once-over. "You're the one who's beautiful, Drea. You're all grown up. I know I say that every time I see you, but it's true. You look more and more like your mama every day."

"I'll take that as a compliment."

"As well you should. Gosh, what has it been? Two years since I've seen you?"

"Yeah, two years. You came to visit me in New York."

"We had a great time, going to shows, shopping."

"It means a lot to me that we stay in touch." They'd made an effort to call or text every month or so whenever Lottie wasn't traipsing around the globe.

"I promised I would."

"Hey, what's all the fuss about?" Drew came ambling out of the house.

Lottie rolled her eyes and whispered, "Your father has turned into an old man."

"I heard that, Lottie," Drew said with a scowl.

"I don't care if you did, Drew. It's true. You're not ready for the grave yet. Lose a few of those extra pounds you're carrying and see if you don't feel like a new man."

"Well, now you're my doctor, too. Did you learn all that in Africa?"

Lottie grinned. "Actually, I learned a lot of things on my trip. I spent a good deal of time on the tour bus with a homeopathic doctor, as it happens."

"Oh, yeah? Did he cure your ailments?"

"If I had any," Lottie said softly, "I'm sure Jonathan would've cured them."

Drew's eye twitched and just for a second his face grew pale. "Well, come in. You girls can jabber all you want inside the house."

Drew held the front door open for Lottie and Drea and they marched into the parlor. Lottie had brought them all a home-cooked dinner, Cajun chicken and shrimp pasta, her signature dish and one of Drea's favorites. It was warming on the stove.

Drew took a seat and listened to his daughter and Lottie chat about Broadway plays, clothes and music. Whenever Lottie was around, Drew felt old. Her vibrancy and zest for life looked darn good on her. She was a pain in his rear end, but she was also a lifelong friend. One who never ceased to speak her mind. Whenever she was gone, he missed her. And whenever she was home, he wished she'd keep her opinions of him to herself. He was tired, his bones ached, but listening to his daughter and Lottie chat lightened his mood.

"Dad, did Lottie tell you she went on safari?"

"She did."

"Sounds exciting, doesn't it?"

"Well… I suppose."

"It was a grand adventure," Lottie said, her soft brown eyes gleaming. "I loved every minute of it."

"But now you're home for a while, right?" Drea asked.

"Lord above, yes. I'm home for a good long time. Texas is in my blood. I missed it and my nephews."

The relief Drew felt gave him pause. Why was he so darn happy to have her home? Hell, whenever Lottie was around, his head became jumbled up with all sorts of mixed emotions.

"And I'm especially glad I'm back in time to see you." She took Drea's hand. She'd been more a mother to Drea than he'd been a father.

"How long are you here, honey?"

"I'll be staying for several weeks, putting together the fund-raiser for the hospital."

"Mason told me about it. You two are working together, so I know it'll be successful."

"I think dinner's just about ready," Drew announced.

"Gosh, I smell something delicious cooking," Drea said.

"It's Lottie's Cajun supper."

"Your favorite, Dad." Drea gave him a big smile, her eyes twinkling.

"As I recall, it's your favorite, too. And Lord knows, she wouldn't be fixin' anything so delicious if it was just me."

Lottie whipped her head his way. "Drew MacDonald, why are you always so disagreeable?"

"You saying you fixed that special meal on my account?"

Lottie rolled her eyes. She did that a lot and he found it annoyingly cute. "I'm saying we all like the dish, so why not dig in."

"Sounds great to me. I missed lunch and I'm starving." Drea stood and gave them both a quick glance.

"I've got the table set," Drew said. Well, Lottie had helped. She'd arrived just a few minutes before Drea got home and they'd worked quickly together. His heart flipped over the second he'd laid eyes on Lottie, after her being gone for so long, and he'd been a bit flustered ever since.

"Sounds good to me. I only hope the meal's as good as you two remember it."

"If you made it, Lottie, we're gonna love it." Drea eyed him, sending him a message to give Lottie his assurances, as well. But she didn't need any more encouragement, he decided. She was the strongest woman he knew.

As Lottie walked past him, arm in arm with his daughter, the woman's sweet, fruity scent teased his nostrils, reminding him of freshly picked strawberries. Oh man, it was going to be a long night.

The autumn sun arced over the horizon, shedding light and warmth on the morning. Drea squatted in the dirt and gave a good hard pull on one of the many weeds, gripping the base near the root with her gloved hands. The darn thing wouldn't budge. She'd be damned if it would get the better of her. She stared at it, as if hoping it would wilt under her intense scrutiny.

No such luck.

While she was here in Boone Springs she'd vowed to tidy up her father's neglected yard. Since her meetings didn't begin until eleven, today was a good day to get started.

"Okay, you monster, you're not getting the better of me." On her knees now, she tightened her grip and pulled with all her might. "You're going...down."

The weed popped from the earth and the momentum sent her flying back. She landed on her butt in a pile of wilted petunias. "Ow."

"Looks like the weed wasn't the only one going down."

She stared up, straight into Mason's face, and saw a smirk twitching the corners of his mouth. "Are you kidding me? Where did you come from?"

He put out his hand to help her up.

She ignored it, bracing her hands on the ground and shooting to her feet, then dusting the dirt off her jeans. Why was this man always catching her in embarrassing situations?

"I usually run this way in the morning."

She took in his black jogging pants and snug white T-shirt. His arms were two blocks of muscle straining against the cotton material. It was sigh-worthy how good he looked this early in the morning. The whole package smacked of good health and vitality and…sexy man.

The truth was the truth. Mason was still handsome, but that one kiss the other night meant nothing to her. She clung to her resentment, because the alternative—getting hurt again—wasn't an option.

"I'll remember that," she said. She would make sure not to bump into him again at this hour.

"You're up early."

"Gardening, as you can see. My dad's been neglecting the grounds and I'm hoping to make a dent in all this."

"If I know you, you'll fix up this garden and make it shine." His words came with an approving gleam in his dark eyes.

"You sound so sure of yourself."

"I am."

"And you know that about me how?"

"I can see how hard you're working on the fund-raiser. You won't stop until you reach your goal."

He was right. She was a woman on a mission. She'd never had much approval in her life, having to fight for everything she'd attained, without much recognition. Not that she'd needed constant glory, but a compliment now and then was always welcome. "Thank you."

He pushed his hand through his hair and gave her a solemn look. "Listen, we've sort of hit a snag with The Band Blue. I spoke with their agent last night and it doesn't look like it's going to happen for us."

"What? How can that be? They seemed interested last time we spoke."

"Yeah, about that. You spoke with Sean Manfred, the lead singer, and apparently the kid has a soft spot for our cause. His mother is a heart attack survivor and he wants to help, but their agent isn't onboard. He says the band couldn't possibly come until his demands are met."

"What are his demands?"

"He wouldn't say. He wants a sit-down to go over everything."

"That's fine. I can do that. I think when he hears how much good—"

"The thing is they've got a gig at the Hollywood Bowl in LA this weekend and their manager will only agree to a face-to-face meeting. I suppose he's trying to appease Sean, while making it harder on us. Frankly, we can't afford to waste any more time on this. If we can't get them to agree, we're dead in the water as far as entertainment goes on such short notice."

"We?"

"Yeah, we."

"I can handle it on my own, Mason."

"Showing up as a team will help persuade him. We can take my company plane, and besides, it'd give me a chance to check out a piece of property I've had my eye on."

"In Los Angeles?"

"Yeah, on the beach."

"I didn't know you were a beach kind of guy," she said matter-of-factly, while her heart pumped overtime. She'd have to spend a lot of time with Mason on the trip. It was business, but still…

"I'm not really, but maybe it's time for me to branch out a little. I mean, Larissa always loved the beach. Claimed it soothed her, gave her peace."

"And you can use a little of that?"

He shrugged. "Yeah, I guess."

He gazed down at Drea as if puzzling something out. Perhaps he was looking for inner peace, while his body craved vitality. She could understand that.

"So it's settled? We'll leave Saturday morning."

"Uh, sure. We'll be home Saturday night, right?"

Mason eyed her and she saw him calculating what they needed to accomplish in one day. It was a three-hour trip to Los Angeles. That meant six hours of flying in one day. "If the agent isn't being an asshole, we should be able to make it back in time." His eyes twinkled. "Do you have a hot date on Saturday?"

"Me? I have no time for dating. I'm concentrating all my efforts on the fund-raiser."

"Okay, then. I'll make the arrangements and let you get back to fighting weeds."

"Sounds…good." It didn't. She nibbled on her lip, battling emotions. On the one hand, she really needed to nail down the entertainment for the night. She'd hit a brick wall on getting a band to agree, until she'd spoken with Sean. He'd made it seem as if there wouldn't be a problem; all they had to do was iron out a few details. But she should've gotten the okay from their agent first. Her mistake. Now she had to do some fast talking to secure their commitment. But on the other hand, traveling with Mason meant they'd be spending a full day together. She vowed not to let her ill feelings about him get in her way. "And I wish you'd stop doing that."

His brows pulled together. "Doing what?"

"Catching me in embarrassing situations." First the pajama thing and today her ungraceful battle with a weed.

His smirk spread into a wide smile. "Just lucky I guess." He took off jogging down the road and she stood there watching him slice through the wind with those long strides. An unwanted thrill ran through her body and she chewed on her lip, silently cursing the warmth filling her up inside.

Three

Saturday morning, Drea rose and double-checked her luggage making sure she packed her usual change of clothes just in case of an accidental spill or a delay, along with the necessary paperwork for the deal with The Band Blue.

Almost as important, she brought along her notes on her top five reasons it would be advantageous for the band to join in their fund-raising event. No one would ever call her lazy or doubt her determination. She'd done extensive research on the group and was prepared to use all the tools in her arsenal to get them to sign on the dotted line.

She showered and dressed in black slacks and a white bell-sleeve blouse, all the while going over her business strategy in her head. She'd wear her blazer during the meeting, but for now, a comfy cardigan would do for the plane ride. A pair of short beige boots completed the outfit.

She tiptoed into the kitchen and found her father up and dressed already. "Dad, you're up early." It was barely seven o'clock.

"That I am."

He tied the laces on a pair of walking shoes that looked brand-new.

"What's going on?"

"Lottie wants me to walk with her. Claims I need to get in shape."

"Oh, uh…"

He glanced at her and frowned. "I'm not so old I can't still get around, you know."

"But…you haven't been exercising. Maybe you should take it slow."

"If I don't go, Lottie's gonna keep pestering me."

"Dad, I think you're darn glad Lottie's here to pester you."

"I don't know. Maybe." He shrugged. "I'm meeting her at the main house in half an hour."

"Is it like a date?"

Her dad groaned as if she was insane. "It's a walk, period."

"Dad, I'm going out of town. What if…" She bit her tongue. She knew what he was going to say and couldn't very well stop him.

Her father finished tying his shoes and looked up at her. "I've been on my own a long time, Drea. Don't worry about me. I've gotten along all this time without you."

Bingo. It was true, so she couldn't argue with him on that.

"Okay, well, I'll probably be home late tonight. I'm going to California with Mason. We have hospital business."

"You need a suitcase for that?" Drew eyed her momentarily and she mentally cringed. She didn't want to think about spending the night with Mason, yet it was a possibility. But that didn't mean she had to pack her prettiest lingerie, a light sage nightie that barely covered her thighs. Why had she done that?

"I have papers in there, mostly. And a change of clothes, just in case, Dad."

Her father's pale green eyes lit up. "I bet Mason's hoping for *just in case*."

"What? Don't be silly, Dad. He's the last man on earth…"

"He's hurting and you two go way back, Drea."

"It's business, Dad. You know I don't like the Boones, Mason most of all."

"All right, honey. If you say so."

She felt like she was ten years old again. "I say so. I'll text you before we take off."

"To make sure I survived the walk around the ranch?"

She smiled. "Making sure you survived Lottie's well-intentioned nagging."

That made her father grin. "That woman is a pain in my rear end."

"She's a sweetheart and you know it. You just give her grief."

"Turn that around, and it'd be true." But there was a lightness in his voice she hadn't heard in a long time.

There was a knock at the front door. "Sounds like Mason's here," her father said.

"I'll get it." Drea headed there through the parlor.

She found Mason dressed in a pair of crisp jeans and a snap-down shirt under a black jacket. Business casual. At least they were in tune in the apparel department. "Mornin'," he said in his sexy Texas drawl.

"Mason, I'll be right with you. Unless," she began, her manners getting the best of her, "you'd like to come in?"

"Come in, boy," her father called from the kitchen. "I've got a fresh pot of coffee going."

Mason eyed her outfit and hairdo. Maybe she should've put it up, instead of leaving her hair free to drape down her back. "Man, right about now, I'd kill for a cup." He glanced at his watch. "I think there's time. Our flight leaves at eight."

"Thank goodness," she said. "I'd kill for a cup, too." She let him in.

"A quick one. We'll have breakfast on the plane, so no worries there."

Drea bit back a snide comment. His company plane was just another classic reminder of losing Thundering Hills to the

Boones. Mason spoke of it casually, as if normal everyday people could fly around in their own airplanes. The Boone empire had flourished, while her legacy, the land she'd loved, had been swept away.

Hastily, she poured them each a cup and listened while Mason and her father spoke about the weather, cattle prices and Lottie. "I'm afraid she's on a crusade," Mason said, grinning. "She spent some time with that doctor and now she thinks she can cure the world."

"Well, I'm gonna give it a go."

"Exercise never hurts. But be warned, next she might tackle your diet."

"That'd be the day."

"Mason," Drea said, slurping the last sip of her coffee. "We should probably go."

"Yeah, I've gotta get a move on, too," her dad said. "You be sure to take good care of my girl while you're gone. Okay, son?"

"Dad!" She sucked in a quick breath. "I don't need Mason or anyone else taking care of me. I'm perfectly cap—"

"Yes, sir," Mason interrupted. "I'll be sure to keep her safe."

Drea shook her head and kissed her father on the cheek. "Don't strain yourself today."

"I'll be just fine. You have a good trip now."

Mason grabbed her luggage in the parlor and then held the door for her. "All set?"

As much as she was going to be. "Yes."

He put his hand to her lower back and guided her to a shiny black limousine in the driveway. The warm contact felt too good. She stiffened up and focused her gaze on the uniformed driver standing at attention beside the car.

"I've got this," Mason said to him. He put her luggage in the back and then gestured to the open door. "After you."

She slid inside and he followed. His presence seemed to fill the lush leather interior, and she was surprised at how little physical space there was on the seat between them.

She'd seen the inside of a limousine exactly four times. The first had been during her mother's funeral. That had tainted her perception of limos for life. The ride had been the hardest she'd ever taken. She hadn't been able to look at her father's ashen face another second, so during the drive she'd stared out the window in utter silence, her young heart breaking.

Who ever said limos were fun?

"Let's head to the airport," Mason told the driver.

She glanced over at him, noting how he seemed to be in total control of his environment. She could really respect the business side of Mason. He was focused and driven. She'd dwell on that aspect during her time with him and not think about his pleasing musky scent. Or how the sunlight seemed to catch the inky strands of his hair in just the right way. Or how intense his dark brown eyes were. No, she'd concentrate on her newly thought up theme, *Business with Mason.*

"Just so you know, I can keep myself safe. I don't need you protecting me."

He grinned. "I know that. I was humoring your father."

"Oh." She sank back in her seat. Should she believe him? It didn't matter. She knew the truth. She'd been taking care of herself for a very long time now.

She spared him another glance. His eyes were twinkling, as if he found her amusing.

She tried to drum up anger or resentment, but neither emotion surfaced. She hated to admit it, but he'd been sweet to consider her father's feelings.

And who would've thought she'd ever associate the word *sweet* with Mason's name?

"Comfortable?" Mason asked, sitting down across from her on the plane.

The white leather seats were wide and luxurious. A small table separated them. She was aware of the stocked liquor bar behind her and a television screen on the opposite wall. The flight attendant had just taken her order for breakfast.

"Yes."

"Okay, we'll be taking off soon."

"At your command," she said.

He stared at her and put a finger to his eye, struggling not to frown. "Drea, what?"

"Nothing."

She smiled. She was a master at hiding her demons, but somehow being with Mason made them all come out again. "I'm fine."

"Fear of flying?"

Fear of Boone. "No, nothing like that. I think I'm just hungry."

"Breakfast is coming right up."

The pilot's voice came over the speaker. He explained the flight route and weather conditions and asked them to put on their seat belts. Shortly after, the plane began to taxi on the runway.

She and Mason were quiet until they were airborne.

"Here you go. I hope you enjoy this. It's one of Mr. Boone's favorites." The flight attendant presented her with a vegetable egg white scramble and a cup of coffee. Mason had the same.

"Looks wonderful, thank you," Drea said.

The stewardess walked off and Mason began digging in.

"So, you really think we can get The Band Blue to sign on the dotted line?" he asked her.

"With my people skills, yeah, I do."

"You have people skills? You mean the way you charmed me?"

He was teasing, but he'd caught her red-handed. "I'm not a phony."

"You mean if you liked me a little more, I'd know it? Never mind," he said, dropping the subject. "So how did you come upon fund-raising as a career?"

"It was accidental, actually. My college roommate came down with a rare type of lung disease in our senior year. It was pretty serious and she needed treatments that required hundreds of thousands of dollars, treatments that her insurance didn't cover. I knew I had to help her. I gathered up a bunch of her friends and fellow students and started a fund-raising page on social media. I wrote articles for the local newspapers and even did a morning show with Sandra's parents to bring awareness and raise funds. Within a matter of weeks, we had more than enough money for her procedures."

"Impressive. How is your friend now?"

"She's doing well. There's no cure for her condition, but she has a good quality of life and I was just invited to her wedding."

"Nice. You saved her life."

"Not me, the doctors."

"You're being modest."

"I wish there was something I could've done for my mother, though. I know I was just a kid, but I always think that maybe my father and I missed something. Her heart attack came on so suddenly and we never had a clue she had heart disease. She had no symptoms and, well, after that first attack there was so much damage…"

Drea lowered her head as emotions whipped through her system. Her mother had lasted only three days after the attack. And Drea wished she'd said more to her, wished she'd realized that she was losing her, wished she'd told her how much she loved her. Instead, everyone had tried to protect her, to make it seem that Maria MacDonald was going to be fine, when they'd probably all known differently.

Drea didn't know why she'd exposed herself to Mason this way. She never talked about her mother's illness, much less confided in a man she thought of as the enemy. She lifted her eyes and found pain in Mason's expression.

"Yeah, I know what you mean," he replied.

"Mason, I'm sorry." His pain had to be more raw. More fresh.

He'd lost his wife and unborn child to heart failure just two years ago.

Drea reached out to him, put her hand over his. It was instinctive, a move she'd afford anyone in pain. The connection flowed between them, strong, powerful, sorrowful. She resented the hell out of him, hated what his family had done to hers, but in a moment of shared grief, she'd forgotten all that. And then she pulled her hand away. *Business with Mason.*

"All through here?" The stewardess appeared, ready to remove the plates.

"Yes, all through," she said.

"Would either of you like more coffee?"

"No," they answered simultaneously.

"Okay, if I can get you anything else, Mr. Boone, please let me know."

He nodded. "Thank you."

The flight attendant went back to her station and Drea was left alone with Mason once again. "You know, I think I'll stretch my legs."

Why not? The plane was roomy enough to move around in and she needed space.

When she stood, Mason stood, too, his Southern manners on full display. As she started to walk past him, the plane lurched and she was tossed against his chest. Immediately, he wrapped his arms around her. Even after the quick bout of turbulence was over, Mason didn't let go.

"You okay?" he whispered in her ear.

"Uh-huh."

From where she was nestled in his arms, the slightest hint of his masculine cologne teased her nose. She closed her eyes, enjoying a few seconds of comfort. "Thanks for the catch."

"My baseball days come in handy."

"Tee-ball?"

"College. All Star."

"Of course. You wouldn't be anything else."

Her snarky remark brought a chuckle. "You make me laugh, Drea."

He skimmed his hands over her back, stroking her ever so gently, bringing her closer. His legs pressed against hers. She didn't want to know what a brush against his groin would bring. She didn't want this. But her heart was pounding and the strength of him, his *maleness*, sent thrills careening through her body.

The plane lurched again, this time breaking them apart. Mason reached for her, but she was too far from his grasp. It seemed the stratosphere had more sense than either of them.

"Sorry about that, folks," the pilot said over the loudspeaker. "There shouldn't be any further turbulence. You can relax and enjoy the rest of the flight."

"Good news," Mason said, but his words belied the dangerous gleam in his eyes.

Drea grabbed her bag from where she'd been sitting and pointed to a sofa a few feet away. "I think I'll just sit over there for a while. I…have some work to go over."

While Mason watched, she moved as gracefully as she could down the aisle and then plopped onto the sofa and avoided him for the rest of the trip.

A few hours later, as she and Mason were driving down the highway in a rented Cadillac SUV, breathing California air and enjoying West Coast sunshine, his cell phone rang. He tossed her the device. "Can you get that for me, please?"

Drea picked it up and glanced at the screen. "It's the agent," she said to Mason before answering. "Hello, this is Drea MacDonald."

"Hello, Drea. Alan Nesbitt here."

"Yes, Mr. Nesbitt. We've just landed and we're on our way."

"That's why I'm calling. I'm afraid I can't do lunch today. Something's come up that I have to deal with. I hate to do this to you, but it can't be helped."

"But we've flown in from Texas. And we need to speak with you."

"Yes, yes. That's fine. I don't have a spare minute until after the show."

"You mean tonight?"

"Yes, the band goes on right before the headliner. We can talk then. I'm afraid that's all that I can do. I'm swamped today."

"Okay, we'll come to the show."

"I'll leave VIP tickets and backstage passes for you. We'll have a good hour to talk then."

"I guess that will have to do. We'll be there. This is important."

"I understand. I'll see you tonight."

Drea pushed the off button and faced Mason. "He's canceled lunch."

"I heard."

"He claims he has time to see us tonight at the show."

Mason frowned. "We have to give it a try. What else can we do? We're here already."

"I agree. But now we have a lot of time to kill. What are we going to do for eight hours?" Drea was not happy about this. She and Mason would be spending the entire day together. And after what almost happened between them on the plane, she had to be on guard.

"I can think of a few things," he said cryptically. Yet there was no villainous arch of his brows or twitch of his lips. When she didn't respond, he asked, "Are you hungry?"

"I'm not starving, but I could eat."

He nodded. "Me, too. Do you like seafood?"

"Who doesn't?" She actually loved it. When she was in college, she'd go for Friday night fish frys with her friends. It was always something she'd looked forward to.

"Great." At the next signal, Mason whipped the car around. "I know this little place on the beach I think you'd like."

And soon they were on Pacific Coast Highway, the ocean to

her left and the cliffs to her right. The homes on both sides of the road had amazing views of the sea. "Have you have been to LA before?" Mason asked.

"Yes, once, but I never saw the outside of my hotel."

His brows arched and he glanced at her.

"I was attending a conference," she explained. Not that it was any of his business how she'd spent her time here. "So yes, technically I've been here, but not enough to get a West Coast vibe."

"I think I can remedy that."

It didn't sound awful so she nodded. "Okay."

A few minutes later, Mason pulled into the parking lot of an outdoor café. Big Fish was a small take-out restaurant with picnic tables and café chairs facing the water. "Not fancy," he said, "but the fish are fresh and everything is delicious."

After being on the plane for three hours and then in the car this past hour, sitting outside in the autumn sunshine sounded pretty good. "I'm game."

They got out of the car, Drea stepping down before Mason could open the door for her. She wasn't a feminist really, and understood he was just displaying his ingrained Southern manners, but she was perfectly capable of getting out of a vehicle without his assistance. Still, he put his hand to her back and guided her through the parking lot to the take-out window. She glanced at the chalkboard menu on the wall. "What do you recommend?"

"If you love shrimp and scallops, their Big Fish Special is pretty good. Everything comes with fries and coleslaw."

There wasn't a salad on the menu. Or a fruit plate. She decided to throw caution to the wind today and go for broke. "I'll have the Big Fish Special then, thank you."

"Make that two," Mason said to the lady behind the window.

When the food was ready, they walked over to a picnic table near the water. Drea took a seat and Mason slid in next to her. Both wore their sunglasses and silly bibs around their necks while they enjoyed the food. She had to admit Mason didn't look intimidating now; his body was relaxed, his hair swept back by the slight breeze, his usual glower gone.

"This was a good idea," she said, plucking up the last of her French fries.

"You mean I did something right for a change?"

She caught the twinkle in his eye. "All I mean is you have good taste in food, period."

"I figured."

"So, what's the plan now?"

Mason glanced at his watch. "It's a little after one." They still had several hours before the meeting. "How do you feel about carnivals?"

"Carnivals?"

"Santa Monica-style. We'll hit the pier next. It's not far from here. If you've never been, it's worth seeing. And I promise you, they have the best ice cream on the beach."

"It's your nickel," she said. "I'm going along for the ride."

A short time later, Drea had settled on a cup of strawberry ice cream and was spooning small bites into her mouth as they relaxed on the Santa Monica pier.

Mason shook his head at her choice of dessert. "You're no fun."

"I'm a lot of fun," she said, "when I want to be."

He held a mouthwatering double-fudge-brownie ice cream waffle cone in his hand. They stood against the guardrail overlooking the ocean, listening to the lapping waves hitting the shore. It was something they didn't get in their part of Texas.

"Oh yeah? When do you want to be?"

His eyes were on her, watching her lick the cream from her spoon. It unsettled her, the gleam in his eyes, the sudden flirty tone in his voice. "When I..."

"When you what?"

He seemed intent on her answer. "Well, not now. Today is all about business." At least it should be.

"We're taking a business break…out of necessity."

She blinked.

"This is a no-business zone," he continued. "Look at the people here. Think they're worried about numbers, spreadsheets, their boss's latest tirade? No, ma'am. I don't think so."

He did have a point. "So if this is a no-business zone, do you mind sharing some of your double-fudge-brownie ice cream?"

"It depends," he said. "What do I get in return?"

"What do you…uh, what do you want?" A memory flashed of being nearly naked in his bedroom, craving his kisses, wanting his touch. She didn't allow those recollections often, but today they came easily, and for a second she was reminded of the good parts of that memory. How it felt when he'd released her hair from her braid. He'd weaved his fingers through it, as if the strands mesmerized him. And how it felt to be in his arms, his lips on hers, his body hot and demanding. She'd never known a greater desire in her young life than anticipating making love with him. But it had ended there. Mason had put a stop to it, and she was left with only rejection and humiliation.

"A ride."

She blinked, pulling herself back to the present. "What kind of ride?" Back then, there was only one she'd wanted from Mason.

"Take your pick." He nodded toward the amusement park attractions behind them. The hum of laughter, mechanical noises and screams merged in her head. It was the sound of good, honest fun.

"But I get my ice cream first?"

"Fine."

She went in with her spoon and he backed away. "You can't eat a cone with a spoon. Take a big bite and enjoy it."

He offered her the side he hadn't licked yet. But still, wasn't it too intimate to be sharing ice cream this way?

The I-dare-you look in Mason's eyes sparked a desire to prove something to him. She grabbed the cone out of his hand

and dug in, taking a bite of the waffle and the dreamy chocolate ice cream in one big mouthful. She'd literally bitten off more than she could chew and Mason's eyes were on her, watching her deal with it, watching her mouth move inelegantly. Then he laughed and his well-hidden dimples appeared. There was a brightness in his expression she hadn't seen since they were much younger. He lifted a napkin to her lips, catching a drop of ice cream.

Their eyes connected then, and there was a moment of intense awareness.

He was touching her face again, standing close enough for her to see the coal-black rim around his deep dark eyes. Close enough to see his jaw tighten suddenly, to see his expression change. She felt it, too. Every time he touched her, she felt desire. Here, with dozens of people milling about on the pier, it was as if they were the only two people on the beach. If he bent his head and leaned in, would she allow him to kiss her again?

"Excuse me, miss. Would you mind taking our picture?" A woman stepped up, unaware that her interruption had just prevented them from making another mistake. Drea should have been relieved. Instead she didn't know how she felt. Let down, maybe. The woman waited patiently, holding a cell phone in her hand. Adorable twin boys stood beside her.

"Of course. I'd be happy to," Drea answered, handing Mason back his cone.

With the beach at her back, the woman ushered her two boys in front of her and Drea snapped the picture.

"Thank you," she told Drea, then took off with the children.

Mason stepped up. "Let's take that ride now."

Getting chummy with Mason put her nerves on edge. She didn't want to enjoy the day so much, and in the back of her mind she was second-guessing all her decisions. While she wanted to stick to her *Business with Mason resolution*, he was trying his hardest to change it into a no-business zone.

"Well?" he asked, watching her closely. "Have you decided?"

She turned around to peer at the rides and made a decision. "I'd like to try the Pacific Wheel. I overheard someone saying it's the only solar-powered Ferris wheel in the world."

He shook his head. "Boring."

"Boring? But you said it was my choice?"

"That's before you slurped up half my ice cream cone. I figure you owe me."

Of course Mason wouldn't play fair. She knew that about him. "I do, do I? Why don't I like the sound of that?"

He led the way. "C'mon. Let's see what the Pacific Plunge is all about."

Mason drove down Pacific Coast Highway with Drea beside him in the passenger seat. Her hand was braced on her midsection, which she rubbed every so often. She hadn't wanted to go on that ride; he'd seen it on her face, the fear, the doubt. Yet she'd been a trouper, bravely getting on the contraption that lifted them up ninety feet over the water. He'd wanted her to see the view from the highest point of the pier, and it had been amazing. But then, as promised, once they'd reached the top, they'd plunged. Other people had screamed and laughed as they went down. But not Drea. She'd turned the same shade of green as her pretty eyes. Once they'd touched ground he'd helped her off the ride as she'd clutched her queasy stomach.

"Feeling any better?" he asked, taking his eyes off the road to look her way.

"A little." She adjusted herself in her seat. "I'll be fine. The fresh air is helping. Even if it didn't end well, I'm okay with taking the plunge."

"I'm glad. It was fun."

"For you, maybe."

He sighed. Drea wasn't giving an inch, but he knew darn well she had enjoyed getting a little taste of the beach town. "I meant, I'd hoped it was fun for you, too. I'm glad you're feeling better."

"Thanks," she said simply.

Hell, Mason couldn't remember the last time he'd felt so carefree, but he focused on the drive now, since Drea seemed to be lost in thought.

Ten minutes later, she asked, "So, are you meeting a Realtor at the beach house?"

He shook his head. "No. I have the keys."

"Is that a privilege of the rich and famous? You get keys to homes you're thinking of buying?"

"I'm not famous."

"Gee, I don't know too many people who have whole towns named after them."

"My family settled Boone Springs decades ago," he told her. "*They* built the town, not me. I'm not going to apologize for them." He couldn't hide the pride in his voice or miss the pout forming on Drea's mouth.

Right now that pouty mouth looked very kissable. Ever since he'd kissed her that night, he'd had mental flashes of how wonderful it had been to touch his lips to hers, to taste her sweetness.

Yet, every night, his heart ached for his wife. He missed her like crazy and so these unexpected thoughts of Drea were confusing the hell out of him. Part of him wanted to hold on to the guilt and sadness, but another part was trying to break free. It was all so new to him and he could only go with what felt right in the moment.

She remained silent. He knew what she thought about his family. She had no warm feelings for any of them, with the exception of Aunt Lottie. Drea had misconceptions and so much hurt buried deep inside, he didn't know if she'd ever find resolution or peace. So he let the subject drop. Today wasn't the day to be on a Boone family soapbox.

"Actually, the beach house belongs to a business associate of mine. She was nice enough to overnight me the keys so I could look the place over at my leisure."

"Have you been here before?"

He almost heard the "with her" in her question.

"Yeah, I have been. Once. Missy coaxed me to come out and stay here shortly after Larissa passed."

"Missy? I see. So you stayed with her?"

"I did."

He glanced at Drea and she immediately looked away, concealing her expression from him. But her face had turned that green shade again. Was it disapproval? Disappointment? Jealousy?

Thinking of her being jealous made him smile inside. Maybe she'd been fantasizing about him a little bit, too.

"For a few days, yeah. Missy needed me almost as much as I needed her."

Slowly, Drea nodded, as she fiddled with straightening her blouse. She wouldn't look him in the eye.

"Missy's husband had passed, just about the same time my wife… Uh, anyway, after her grandchildren showed up to the beach house, I went home."

"Grandchildren?"

Mason grinned. "Yeah, she has five of them, as I recall. Did I mention Missy's in her seventies?"

"No," Drea said, then cleared her throat. "You left that part out."

"Well, she's an incredible woman."

Drea's eyes narrowed on him. Had he deliberately led her down a merry path? Maybe. He sort of liked thinking she'd been jealous.

"You know, you're a—"

He gave his head a shake. "Uh-uh, Drea. Don't say it."

Her shoulders slumped. "You're right. I won't."

Mason kept a straight face, but inside he was actually grinning.

Four

The beach house, two stories of gorgeous space, smart styling and incredible views, was set on a shelf of land just above the ocean. Drea looked out on the waves as the fall sun began to lower to the horizon. Ten steps led down to the sandy shore, where the water foamed only thirty feet away.

"It's perfect," Drea mumbled.

Mason placed a glass of white wine in her hand as he came up behind her. "Now it's perfect," he said.

Both of them watched the waves hit the shore, and quietly sipped wine.

After several minutes, Mason asked, "I take it you like this place?"

She turned to look into his eyes. He seemed genuinely interested in her opinion. "What's not to like?"

He shrugged. "It's different than Texas."

"Isn't that the point? You'd use it as a getaway, right?"

He shrugged again. "I'm…not sure."

"Then why are we here? I mean, why are you considering

buying this house, if you don't think you'll be comfortable here?"

Mason finished his wine and set his glass down on the white wooden railing. Both floors had a wraparound veranda.

"It's hard to explain. I feel as if I need to do something to move forward with my life. I thought a change of pace, something new, might help me figure it out."

He stared at her, as if wondering why he'd told her something so intimate. Most of the men she'd known weren't forthright in sharing their innermost thoughts. Was he sorry he'd confessed this to her?

"It's weird, right?" he asked, doubt evident in his eyes.

"No. Not weird at all." She didn't want to sympathize with Mason. It was crucial to hold on to her anger and indignation and never let it go. Because her life hadn't been peachy, either. Not only had she lost her home, her mother, and her father to alcohol, she'd lost something even more precious.

A baby.

"Hey, are you okay?" Mason tipped her chin up so he could meet her eyes.

Sincere concern washed over his features, frightening her. She didn't want to be friends with Mason. She didn't want his concern. Quickly, she snapped out of her musings. "Sure, I'm fine."

She faked a smile and turned to walk into the house, but he grabbed her hand, halting her retreat. "Would you look at that." He pointed to the ocean. Following his gaze, she glanced at the water and saw a frolicking school of dolphins close to the shore, their smooth, silvery forms rising up from the water and then diving back down, making perfectly shaped arches. Up and down, up and down.

"Wow, I've never seen this in person."

Mason tugged on her hand. "Let's go get a better look. You game?"

"I'm game."

Once they were both barefoot, Mason led the way down to the beach, where sand squished between her toes. The air was cooler by the ocean and beaming sunlight cast a beautiful sheen on the water. Breezes kicked up as she kept her eyes trained on the dolphins swimming by. She stood stock-still, watching them until they faded from sight. "That was something."

"It's pretty incredible." Mason glanced along the empty beach. "I'd like to take a walk before we have to leave. Care to join me?"

She wanted to say no, to put some time and space between them, but when would she ever get another chance to stroll a Pacific beach? "I think I'll tag along."

They walked along the shore, with the foamy waves inching up the sand and teasing their feet. She'd never been a beach-goer, but this little game of keep-away was fun.

Until she stepped on something sharp. It jabbed at her right foot, catching her off guard. "Ow!"

She stumbled, and Mason rescued her midway before she fell, grabbing her waist and righting her. "You okay?"

"I think so. I stepped on a seashell or something buried in the sand."

Mason looked around. "You're right. It was a seashell."

He held her still, his hands clamped around her waist. Ocean breezes swept his hair back and ruffled his shirt. As they stood facing each other for a moment, a monumental thrill scurried down her spine. He was incredibly handsome like this, appealing in a way she didn't really want to admit.

She was about to tell him that maybe the cowboy was also a beachcomber, but her lips parted and nothing came out. When Mason's gaze slid to her mouth, a little gasp escaped her throat. Before she could utter a word, he pulled her closer, bent his head and delivered a gift to her lips. It was so pure, so natural a gesture, with them standing on the deserted beach, the sun lowering on the horizon and all the planets aligning, that she didn't think to stop the kiss. Or him.

He pressed his mouth more firmly now, and she parted her lips in a gasp of pure pleasure. He wasted no time inserting his tongue and tasting her, shocking her senses in the very best way. His kiss shot hot beams of pleasure straight through her, and if that wasn't enough, his arm snaked around to bring her even closer. Her legs were touching his, with her hips against his groin and her breasts pressed to his chest, She was willing and at his mercy.

Yes, Mason knew how to kiss.

He knew where to touch her to elicit a needy response, too.

He wove his free hand through her hair.

His other hand dropped from her waist, his long fingers inching down to graze her rear end. *Oh God.* She craved his touch, wanted more, wanted to stay like this a good long time.

His masterful kiss did that to her.

They were molded together, lip-locked and fully engaged. She felt his shaft, thick and hard, pressing against her. It didn't surprise her to feel it, but what did surprise her was her total acceptance of the situation.

She sighed deeply, majorly turned on but confused all the same.

"Don't think," Mason whispered, as if reading her thoughts. "I'm not."

He nipped at her lower lip and then drove his tongue into her mouth again.

I'm not thinking. I'm not thinking.

When the kiss finally ended, Mason's dark eyes probed hers. He reached out to touch the side of her face, his fingers a gentle caress on her cheek. "Thank you," he said softly.

She blinked. Instead of saying *that was amazing*, or *you're beautiful* or *wow*, Mason was thanking her?

And then it hit her like a ton of bricks. She made him feel "alive." He'd already admitted she'd been the only woman to make him feel that way. *So far.*

She could turn him on. Make him hard. Get his juices flowing.

Yet she couldn't help feeling used. Slightly. It pissed her off a bit.

She didn't want to be Mason's *test kitchen.*

She didn't want to be Mason's anything.

His phone alarm buzzed and he reached into his pocket and pushed a button on his cell to shut it off. "It's time to go. There could be traffic."

She nodded, speechless, and when he grabbed for her hand, she pretended not to see it and jogged up to the house. Once she was on the veranda, she turned to him as he approached the steps.

"Just so you know, thanking me wasn't necessary. You're a good kisser, Mason. And like I've said before, it's been a long time since I've been kissed."

His eyes narrowed. She whirled around before she had to acknowledge the deep frown surfacing on his face.

It was definitely safer to harbor resentment for Mason.

But it sure wasn't as easy as it had once been.

Electricity charged the air at the Hollywood Bowl that night. The iconic outdoor stadium in the Hollywood Hills held a huge crowd of country music fans. A person might think she was back in Texas for all the cowboy hats, silver belt buckles and snakeskin boots filling the arena. Drea's sour mood lifted the second she entered the place and they were shown to their center stage seats. She had to hand it to Mr. Nesbitt.

They'd arrived just in time to see The Band Blue walk onstage amid a roar of cheers. To be the opening act at the Hollywood Bowl was huge. Landing a commitment from the band would almost surely guarantee the fund-raiser's success. She understood that Nesbitt was just doing his job; she understood his hesitation. From this point on, their careers depended on visibility. Drea just had to make sure Nesbitt would see it her way. At least she had Sean Manfred, the lead vocalist, in her corner. The kid had an amazing voice.

During the performance, she found Mason's eyes on her. Too often. It was as if he was puzzling her out. But her puzzle pieces didn't fit with his and it was time she made that clear to him.

No more hand holding. No more kisses. No more intimate conversations.

Business with Mason.

She sat with her hands in her lap, swaying to the music and applauding when the songs ended. The Band Blue drew a noisy crowd bordering on rowdy. But it was all in good fun and she found herself really enjoying the music.

Thirty minutes in, Sean angled his guitar to his side and spoke into the mic. "Thank y'all for coming. The band and I, well, we sure do appreciate your support."

"We love you," a woman shouted from behind Drea.

Sean chuckled. "We love you guys, too. And now, if you're ready, we're gonna end our night with a song I think you'll recognize. Recently, my mama took sick with her heart, but she's one of the lucky ones. She survived."

Drea drew a deep breath. Mason glanced at her, his eyes soft, and for a second—okay maybe more than a second—she connected with him emotionally.

Sean went on. "So tonight I'm dedicating this here song to my mama. Love you, Bethy Manfred," he said. The crowd shouted words of support and adoration, and then quieted as the band began to play.

When the sweet love ballad called "Your Heart Is Mine" was over, Sean thanked the crowd again before the lights dimmed and the band walked off.

"Time to get backstage," Mason said.

Drea rose and Mason ushered her down the aisle and over to the backstage door. They showed their VIP passes and were immediately let into a special room. A buffet table lined one wall and they were told to help themselves. Drea grabbed a bottle of water and took occasional sips.

Finally, the band entered the room, led by a guy who couldn't have been more than thirty years old. He actually looked like he belonged in the band, with his wispy blond hair and casual dress. He took a look at Drea and Mason, then immediately walked over, while the band members hit the refreshment table. "I'm Alan Nesbitt," he said, no smile, all business.

"I'm Drea Macdonald."

"Mason Boone." The two men shook hands.

"The show was spectacular," she said.

Alan shook his head. "It's always a challenge with outdoor acoustics, but yeah, the boys did real good. Would you like to sit down?" He gestured to a group of tables. "We have a bit of time before they go on for an encore performance with Rusty Bonner."

The conversation was stilted and one-sided, and Alan didn't seem to want to make any allowances. He called the band a hot property and said that right now they needed to keep their options open.

"I understand all that," Drea said. "But what if we promised you they'd get a ton of exposure? And don't forget the goodwill this charity would invoke."

"Listen, I'm not hard-hearted, but there are costs involved. We'd need a place to stay, since traveling with a band is expensive. These boys have played for pennies, and now's their big chance. We're just gaining momentum."

"Okay, so you'd need a place to stay and travel expenses." She glanced at Mason and he nodded. "Got that covered. What else?"

"We need maximum exposure. This is a small-ass town, right? Who's gonna see them perform?"

"We can accommodate about five hundred people on the grounds."

"Did you see the size of the Bowl? Try five thousand for starters."

"Yeah, but Boone County is full of larger-than-life Texas donors. These are people who have connections all over the globe. Isn't it all about networking?"

Alan's brows lifted. "Keep talking."

"This fund-raiser is a big deal for the community. There'd be a lot of local news coverage."

"Understood."

"So what if we auctioned off one of the band members for a date with a fan? We could start promoting it now, and by the time the event rolled around, you'd have a ton of exposure, and the fund-raiser would get an added boost, as well."

"I'm volunteering to do it," Sean said, walking over to the table. "I think it's a great idea. And… I'm single at the moment." A crooked grin spread across his face. He was probably twenty at best.

He put out his hand to Mason first. "Hi, I'm Sean." They shook and then he turned to her. "You must be Drea MacDonald. Nice meeting you in person, ma'am."

Drea smiled. "Same here."

"Yeah, uh, I'm sorry about what happened to your mom, Miss MacDonald. Losing her like you did must've been very hard."

"It was. Still is," she said honestly.

"I like the date idea," Alan said quietly, considering it. "It's a good marketing ploy."

"If you agree, I promise no one will work harder to get the coverage you want than I will," Drea declared. "I'll write up a press release tomorrow."

"I'd like to help your cause." Sean looked at his agent. "I've been telling Alan that we should do this. It's important. Chances are my mother wouldn't be here today if she hadn't had excellent cardiac care. I spent a lot of time in the hospital chapel praying for her recovery. I think this is a way I can give back and make good on the promises I made that day."

If Drea had liked this young man before, now she adored him. "Thank you, Sean. And it *is* important." She glanced at Mason. "Many of us have lost loved ones."

Mason's expression softened, his gaze touching hers. She hated the effect he had on her. Tonight she wanted no distractions.

"My family owns a hotel in Boone Springs," Mason said to Alan. "We'd be happy to put you all up. And I can make sure the company plane is available to fly the band in."

Alan Nesbitt's expression changed, his skepticism replaced with consideration. She'd done all she could to address his main concerns, and luckily, the group had that weekend free. This might work out, after all.

The rest of the band members walked over and stood around the table. "It's a good gig," the drummer said. "I'm in."

The others nodded.

"We've got the details covered," Drea said. "Now we just need an agreement. And I happen to have something written up here in my briefcase."

Drea felt as if she was floating on air, spreading her arms like wings and gliding through the parking lot. She'd signed the deal with the band. "Can you believe it?"

Mason grinned. "You were amazing in there. You had a comeback for every single one of Nesbitt's demands. I'm impressed."

"Now we can go back to Texas with clear heads."

"Yeah, we can." Mason glanced at his watch. "But not tonight."

"What?" Drea stopped in her tracks.

"I told my pilot if we didn't need him by 10:00 p.m. to go to bed and rest up. It's only fair. We'll have to take off in the morning."

"What time is it?"

"Eleven thirty."

"Oh, wow. I didn't realize how late it was." Sean had asked them to stay for the final song of the night, when the band joined the headliner, Rusty Bonner, and Drea had been happy to agree. "Can we get a hotel at this hour?"

"We could try. But the beach house is twenty minutes from here. We could be there faster than trying to find rooms on a Saturday night."

Drea eyed him carefully.

"There's five bedrooms, Drea. You can sleep downstairs and I'll—"

"I get it." She wasn't worried. The house was enormous, and all she wanted to do was plop her head on a pillow and get some sleep. It had been a long day. "It would be cool to wake up in the morning at the beach."

Mason nodded and they took off immediately. The drive to the house was traffic free. When they got there, he parked the car and grabbed their bags. They entered the house quietly; the gentle roar of the ocean was the only sound in Drea's ears. She welcomed the peace and quiet.

"Pick a room down here," he said. "I'll check things out before turning in upstairs." Their eyes met. Mason hesitated briefly, as if he wanted to say something, but then thought better of it. "Good night, Drea."

"Night," she said. "See you in the morning."

Drea entered a bedroom decorated in dove blues and grays, the furniture sleek and modern with sharp lines. The contemporary feel of the place was so different from anything Mason Boone was accustomed to in Texas. She had a hard time picturing him being happy here. There was too much Texan in his bones.

She unpacked her bag, taking out fresh underwear and her nightie, and walked into the bathroom. What had she been thinking, bringing her finest lingerie on this business trip? She chuckled at the absurdity. After that kiss today on this very beach, Drea knew better. The kiss had only reinforced her resolve to steer clear of Mason. As soon as she was back on Texas soil, her focus would be on the fund-raiser, and not on Mason's swoon-worthy body and masterful kisses.

After undressing, she showered quickly. Then she dabbed herself dry with an ultrasoft towel, donned her sage nightie and crawled into bed.

Pure heaven.

Closing her eyes, she sank down into the comfy mattress and settled in.

Minutes later, a piercing alarm brought her head up from a sound sleep. She glanced at her surroundings, disoriented, until she finally remembered where she was. The alarm rang louder, more urgently.

"It's okay, Drea," she heard Mason call over the deafening noise.

She rose and opened her door just as she heard a crash in the other room. "Ow! Damn it."

"Mason?" She ran into the living room and found a shadowy form pushing up from the floor, then hopping on one foot. "What on earth?"

"Hang on a second," he shouted above the blaring alarm. He limped over to the hallway wall and punched a code into the security system. The harsh ringing immediately stopped. Turning, he explained. "Sorry. I, uh, couldn't sleep and decided to get some air. I forgot I'd set the alarm and when I ran inside to shut it off, I knocked over a lamp."

"Are you hurt?" she whispered.

"Just my pride," he said.

In the darkness she could barely make him out.

"Let me take a look." She found a light switch and clicked it on. When she turned back to Mason, the expression on his face faltered as he looked her up and down. His mouth dropped open and a fiery heat filled his eyes.

"Holy hell, Drea," he rasped.

Oh yeah, her slinky nightie.

He cleared his throat. "Is that what you wear to bed?"

His chest was bare, his pants dipping well below his waist. She swallowed, her heart racing, his hard body disturbing her sanity.

"No, I, uh…yes. Sometimes."

"Sometimes, meaning when you're on a business trip with me?"

"Don't flatter yourself."

"I'm not. I'm…*grateful*."

"I just grabbed the first thing I found." What a lie. "Let's just forget about this."

"Don't think I'll ever forget it."

She closed her eyes. She was drawn to him in inexplicable ways, and right now her body was calling the shots. Seeing that look in his eyes wrecked her good sense. She spun around. She couldn't submit to him. She hated him. She…she didn't want him or anything to do with the Boones.

"Don't go, Drea."

She squeezed her eyes tighter. Her feet wouldn't move. "This isn't going to work," she murmured. She couldn't possibly cave, not after all that had happened—or rather, hadn't happened—between them years ago, all that had changed the path of her life.

"We have the night. One night, Drea. Here. You and me."

"There is no you and me."

"There could be."

"Mason, we can't do this. There are things you don't know. Things that make this impossible." Why was he being so persistent? Why wouldn't he just let her go? Maybe for the same reason she'd packed her sexiest nightie for this trip. Maybe there was something that needed finishing.

"All I see are possibilities tonight."

He was pleading his case, countering every one of her refusals. It was hard saying no to him. Not when her body cried out for him. To know Mason that way one time. Would that be a punishable crime?

She pivoted around slowly and Mason was there, in front of

her, his eyes raking her in as if he'd already touched her. As if he was making love to her with his deep dark gaze.

Just once. Just once. Maybe she needed to finish this.

Yet she wanted to scream at the injustice. She hated him more because she *wanted* him.

Mason knew the exact moment Drea decided their destiny tonight. It was in the sudden release of tension in her shoulders, the parting of her sweet lips, the tiny, almost imperceptible nod of her head.

He reached for her hand. "Come with me."

"Where?" she whispered.

"Upstairs."

Without another word, she took his hand and he led her up the staircase to the room he'd chosen to sleep in. The bed was massive, but that wasn't why this space spoke to him. He'd slept in big beds before, but never one with a wall-to-wall window looking out to the ocean and a big beautiful moon. It was as exquisite as a painting. And to have Drea here, set against this stunning backdrop, only heightened the moment, heightened his arousal, made him ache for her. "You're beautiful, Drea."

She looked away, out the window to the seascape. She was still unsure.

"Just one night," he promised. He couldn't take anything more. His heart wasn't healed yet and he didn't know if it would ever be. But Drea woke something in him and he couldn't let it go. He couldn't stop what was about to happen between them.

Taking her hand, he placed it flat on his chest, right over his heart. Her body trembled and her lips quivered.

Was she remembering the last time they'd been like this? Ready to make love, until his brain finally clicked in. It seemed like a lifetime ago. He'd wanted her then, but she'd been young and pure, a virgin, and Drew's daughter.

Tonight was different. She was no longer that young, insecure girl who'd needed affection, who'd needed to feel loved. Drea was all woman, decisive, someone who knew what she wanted. Even though she was reluctant, she would have walked out the door if she truly didn't want to be here with him.

Right now her sweet palm was on his skin and he burned for her touch. He had been empty for so long, but Drea was filling him up, making him overflow with need.

No other woman had done that to him. Not since Larissa.

Tomorrow he might regret this encounter. Tomorrow they'd have to forget all about this and go back to working on the fundraiser. But not now. Tonight was about the two of them finally coming together.

Just once.

Her fingers glided over his chest. He sucked in oxygen and moved closer to her, giving her better access to his body. "Oh man, Drea."

She put her lips to his chest and her lustrous black hair fell forward. He spread his fingers through the strands as Drea's mouth skimmed over him, licking, kissing, gently, timidly.

She was driving him insane.

He tipped her chin up and brought his mouth down, tasting her sweetness. Her lips were soft and plump, and deserved to be ravaged.

A tiny moan escaped her throat, proof that she wanted things to move faster. His body was on fire and each kiss brought them closer and closer to…more.

All he could think about was getting her naked and touching every single part of her. "I'm glad you wore this," he murmured, slipping a finger under one strap of her sexy gown.

"Why?" she asked, sounding innocent.

"Because I'm dying to take it off you."

"Mason?"

He lowered the strap all the way down her arm, then did the same to the other, allowing. her gorgeous, perfectly rounded breasts to pop free. It was suddenly hard for him to breathe. "Wow."

She smiled and wrapped her arms around his neck, causing all that beautiful softness to crash into his chest. His skin burned hot where her nipples pressed against him, and he struggled for control. He kissed her once more, then moved her back against the window and undressed her, removing the flimsy garment carefully.

"You've got it off me," she whispered. "Now what are you going to do with me?"

"Are you kidding me, sweetheart? What am I not gonna do with you?"

"Hmm. I like the sound of—"

He brushed his mouth over hers again, impatient and yearning to touch her. Then he whipped her around so that she faced the window, her back to him, and cupped her breasts in his palms, stroking her again and again. He kissed the nape of her neck and watched her reflection in the window as she opened her mouth to gasp, to smile, then squeezed her eyes shut at the pleasure. His thumb flicked one rosy peak, then the other, and she squirmed in his tight hold. "Drea, open your eyes and look out. It's—"

"Stunning." She gazed out at the glistening water, and then her eyes met his in the reflection from the window. "You're a devil," she whispered, fully aware now that he'd been watching her. "I've never…" She didn't finish her thought, but she wasn't backing off, wasn't angry. Instead, there was awe in her voice.

"Don't close your eyes, Drea. Try to keep them open."

She nodded, the back of her head gently knocking into him.

He rained kisses along her shoulder blade and then slid his palm down her torso, leaving the comfort of her beautiful breasts, seeking another comfort below her waist.

She jumped when he touched her there. "You okay?" he asked.

"Oh, I'm perfect," she murmured, meeting his gaze again in the window, her eyes smoky.

"I can't disagree, darlin'."

And then he began a slow deliberate stroking, eliciting whimpering moans from her. She was so ready, so willing, and he wanted to go on making love to her this way.

In just a matter of minutes, she came apart, and he witnessed the pleasure on her face, knowing full well he'd given that to her.

She turned around and fell into his arms. He clasped her to him and held on tight. It seemed so natural with her, like it was meant to be.

Then he lifted her up and carried her to the bed.

The night was just beginning.

Five

Drea lay on the bed, not quite believing what had just happened with Mason. It was so much more than she'd expected. Now she had to face her new reality: she'd just given in to the enemy and liked it. How monumental was that? And how did she feel about Mason now?

He stood by the bed, his eyes dark, bold and dangerous, totally wiping out her long-ago fantasies of him. He was better than anything her young mind could've conjured up. But back then, it had been about more than sex. Then, it had been about love.

Mason unzipped his pants and pulled them down, never once looking away from her.

A lump formed in her throat. Her body immediately revved up again when she saw him fully unclothed for the first time. All that bronzed skin and muscle. Below the waist, he was pretty awesome, too. He caught her eyeballing him and smiled, but she didn't care. She wasn't a kid anymore. She knew lust and desire, and if this was her only night with Mason Boone, she wasn't going to hold back. "Come to bed," she demanded.

"Bossy," he said with a wide, gorgeous grin. "Are you always like this in bed?"

She chewed on her lower lip and went for the truth. "I'm never this way…in bed."

"Then I think I like it."

He placed one knee on the bed and the mattress dipped. The reality of what was happening hit her, but she focused her attention on him, his masculine beauty, this drop-dead handsome guy covering her body with his.

Every touch, every caress was thought out, meant to bring them both the greatest amount of pleasure. He played the boss game with her, asking her what next, what did she want from him, and he obliged, but deep down she knew Mason wasn't a pushover. He was in full control at all times. And secretly, it turned her on even more.

She wanted to think of this as an impulsive, quick encounter, one they'd both probably come to regret later on, but there was nothing impulsive about the way Mason made love to her. He was slow and deliberate and knew exactly how to make her cry out, how to make her want more, how to make her forget everything but what was happening right now.

"Tell me when you're ready," he murmured against her throat.

"I'm ready," she blurted.

He pressed a kiss to her mouth. His face was a picture of sheer lust and promise.

"Hang on, darlin'," he said, leaning over the bed. He rummaged through his pants pocket and came up with protection.

"Do you always bring those with you?" she teased, watching him rip open the packet.

"I grabbed them at the last minute," he said. "Sorta like how you brought along that slinky piece of fluff you were wearing tonight."

She smiled. Wasn't he clever. "How many *did* you bring?"

"Three." And then he was settling over her body, laying claim, joining them together in a hot flurry of lust and craving.

* * *

Drea lay in the crook of Mason's arm, her head resting on his shoulder, her body drained, all her energy spent. She didn't know how long she'd been resting against him. She must've dozed off for a time. Clouds partially covered the moon now and through light and shadows she saw the steady rise and fall of his chest.

She considered going downstairs to sleep in her designated bed, because somehow, sleeping like this with him seemed far too intimate. Yes, they'd taken liberties with each other tonight, but that was about sex. And this was about intimacy and closeness.

She still didn't know Mason any better than she had before.

Except to say he was better than good in the sack.

Her decision made, she slowly backed off, slinking away from the warmth of his arms.

But he pulled her closer. "Drea, where are you going?"

"To…to my own bed."

He sat up then, and urged her to do the same. She kept a sheet around her nude body, covering her to the neck. His eyes dipped there and he frowned slightly.

"Why?"

"Because…it's for the best."

"You know what's best? Getting something to eat. I'm starving," he said. "You must be hungry, too."

Now that she thought about it, they really hadn't had much of anything to eat since having lunch at Big Fish. "I am a little bit hungry."

"Missy keeps the fridge semistocked."

"We can't just eat her food."

"Sure we can. I'll replace everything. I owe her for the busted lamp, too."

Mason swung his legs over the bed and stood up. He wasn't shy, that was for sure. She had a great view of his backside as he slipped on his pants. He grabbed his shirt and stepped around her side of the bed to hand it to her. "Come on, Drea. The night's not over yet. Let's raid the fridge."

According to the digital clock on the nightstand, it was 2:15, the middle of the night, for heaven's sake. But Mason bent his head and kissed her softly on the lips, and her arguments dissolved. There was still some time left before this magical night would end. "Turn around."

His brows shot up. "You're kidding, right?"

He had a point. There wasn't any part of her body he hadn't caressed or kissed, so she shouldn't be shy with him. "I'm not kidding."

He didn't argue as he turned away from her, which gained him a brownie point. She rose and slipped on his shirt; it almost reached her knees. Her fingers quickly worked the buttons all the way up to her throat. "Okay."

He turned and nodded. "Cute." He took her hand in his and they went down the stairs together, bumping bodies in the dark and chuckling about it.

Once in the kitchen, they set the dimmer switch to soft lighting. Mason opened the fridge and she peeked around him to see inside.

"Eggs, bacon, bread, milk," he said.

"Do you like French toast?"

He looked back at her. "You willing to make it?"

"I am. I might cook up some bacon, too."

"I didn't think this night could get any better," he said. He sounded serious and his tone sent shivers through her body. He wasn't teasing. He wasn't making a joke. So far it had been a pretty spectacular day *and* night, yet everything about it scared her silly.

She reached past him and grabbed the bacon. "I'll get this started."

When she turned, he was there, smiling. "Drea, you're an amazing woman."

"Tell me that after you try my French toast."

He curled his hand around her neck and kissed her, hard. When he finally let her go, she rocked back on her heels, her heart hammering.

"You could burn the damn toast and you'd still be amazing."

She felt a blush coming on. Was she that good in bed, or was it that she was the first woman he'd been with since his wife? Could that be true?

Had he been celibate for two years?

She was getting too deep inside her head. That wasn't good. This was a one-time thing and in the morning she'd go back to being cranky Drea from New York and he'd be the man she loved to hate.

Things would get back to normal.

"Uh, thanks," she said, then set about searching for a pan to fry the bacon.

Ten minutes later, she flipped the French toast on the griddle while the bacon cooled on a plate. Mason came up behind her, lifted her long hair and planted tiny kisses behind her ear and along her neckline. Ever since they'd come downstairs, he'd found ways to touch and kiss her while she cooked. And each time, her heart raced and her mind flashed on how he'd made her feel upstairs in the bedroom.

"Did you set the table?" she asked softly.

"All done," he said.

She dished up a platter of brioche French toast halves and bacon, and turned toward the table. "You're only halfway done, Mason. You only set out one plate."

He took the platter out of her hand, set it down and then sat in front of that one place setting. "One plate is all we're gonna need, darlin'."

"What are you—"

"Come here." He grabbed her hand and guided her down onto his lap.

Her body nestled into his easily and he placed a hand on her thighs. "Comfy?"

She laughed. "Are you serious? You want me to feed you?"

"My stomach's growling, but you get the first bite." He lifted a strip of bacon to her mouth.

She hesitated half a second, looking into his eager eyes, then took a small bite. After chewing and swallowing, she offered a piece to him. He gobbled a big mouthful chewing with gusto like a little boy getting his first taste of candy.

"Mmm."

"You like my bacon?" she asked.

His mouth twitched, a wicked gleam entering his eyes. "Very much."

She caught his meaning and shook her head.

They took turns feeding each other in the dimly lit kitchen, munching on French toast and bacon in between sweet kisses until most of the food was gone. Mason's body reacted every time she moved on his lap. His large hand held her in place as he stroked her thighs with the flat of his other palm. Her skin prickled and moisture pooled at the apex of her legs. Beneath her, Mason's body was hard, his shaft nudging her side. Her breaths came faster now, and he caught her mouth and kissed her thoroughly until they were both breathless.

"Drea, sweetheart," he whispered hastily, lifting her body and turning her so she straddled him on the chair.

His hands worked underneath her shirt and he tormented her unmercifully.

There was no hope for it. She gave him everything she had, and when he joined their bodies again, her release was instantaneous and damn near glorious.

And when they were through in the kitchen, Mason carried her upstairs to the bed. "The night's not over yet," he promised.

They still had two hours before the dawn of a new day.

Drea doodled on a pad, drawing irregular circles and juvenile-looking flowers, her mind a million miles away from her fund-raising update that would begin in ten minutes in the hospital boardroom. Her lists were all prepared, but it hadn't been easy concentrating on the task. She had Mason Boone on the brain and she kept reliving the magical night they'd shared in California. She would probably never top those twenty-four hours. She and Mason had allowed themselves a brief interlude and made the most of it.

One night.

That's what they'd agreed on.

She'd reminded Mason of that as they'd left the beach house two days ago. Two days of not seeing Mason by her request. She'd insisted on delegating duties and carrying them out separately. He hadn't argued, but her gut told her Mason didn't like it much.

It had made for a long, tense plane ride home. No touching, no teasing, no easy conversation.

And now her body ached, yearning for what was forbidden.

"Good morning, Miss MacDonald. Am I too early for the meeting?"

Her head snapped up at the sound of the female voice. She faced a pretty blonde woman dressed impeccably in a pencil skirt similar to the one she was wearing. "No, not at all. Please call me Drea. We're all working toward the same goal here."

"All right, Drea. Nice to meet you. I'm Linda Sullivan. I missed the initial meeting, but I've been briefed. I'll be your go-to publicity person."

"Great, we're gonna need you. Our financial goal is lofty, but I think we can do it. Are you on the hospital staff?"

"Oh no. I don't have a medical background. I work for Boone Inc. Mason Boone sent me over to help out."

"Oh, so he's not coming?" A dose of relief washed over her.

"That I don't know. He told me about your incredible idea to raffle off a date with the singer from The Band Blue. I've been working behind the scenes and have already contacted their agent. We're putting our heads together on some ideas."

"Okay, great. Sean is a great kid and so are the other band

members. We're lucky to have them. So I'm hoping we can make this happen seamlessly."

"I'll do my best," she said.

"Is Mason your boss?"

"I work for all three of the Boones, but mostly for Mason. Risk does some traveling for the company and Lucas was just recently discharged from the military. He's working his way back into the family business, I guess. Mason is pretty awesome to work for."

Drea tilted her head. "How so?"

Linda shrugged. "He's…nice. Not just to me, but to everyone in the office. You know, he seems to really care about his employees."

"Does he?" She sounded skeptical and Linda gave her a funny look.

"Sure he does. When my mama took ill, he gave me all the time off I needed and then called me once a week to make sure I was okay."

Drea didn't want to hear this. She didn't want Linda's hero-worship of her boss to sway her opinion of the Boones. Especially Mason. "I'm sorry to hear your mom was ill."

"She's recovered now and living a good life again."

"I'm glad."

The committee members and volunteers began filing into the conference room, greeting Drea as they took their seats. Once they were settled, she rose to address them.

"Hello, ladies and gentlemen. Thank you for coming. I'm pleased to say that because of all of your hard work, the fundraising event is shaping up nicely. We're right on target and things are really coming together. I'm thrilled that The Band Blue has agreed to be a part of the festivities, with an added bonus. We'll be raffling off a dream date with Sean Manfred, the lead singer of the band, to one lucky fan. We're hoping this will spark more interest and bring in more revenue for the hospital."

She spoke to the volunteers in charge of the game booths and the art auction, and introduced Linda Sullivan to everyone. Linda stood up and spoke about her ideas, all of which were right on target, and then Drea took the floor again. She went over her to-do lists and was just finishing up when Mason walked through the door, holding a poster board.

Their eyes met, and she froze inside. He smiled at her, a dazzler that revealed his dimples, then apologized to everyone for being late and interrupting. Mason took a place beside her at the front of the room, and the slight hint of his cologne immediately filled her personal space. Breathing it in jarred a memory of being naked with him, losing her inhibitions and giving herself so freely. My goodness, she'd never done anything as wildly erotic as making love to a man on a kitchen chair before. It had been thrilling. Her body heated at the memory and she reined herself in from the rampant thoughts totally unfit for the boardroom.

"It appears Mr. Boone has something to share with us, so I'll let him have the floor now."

Mason turned to her, but she couldn't bring herself to meet his eyes again for fear the entire boardroom would see something she was dead set on concealing. She immediately took her seat.

"Thank you, Miss MacDonald."

She only half listened as he showed the volunteers a detailed mock-up of the grounds at Rising Springs, where everything would take place, from the pony rides and game booths to the art auction and dinner. He was impressive, but she already knew that firsthand.

When he was done with his presentation, he answered questions about the ranch and how it would all work. The dream date raffle also drew enthusiastic praise from the group.

Once the meeting concluded, Drea made quick work of gathering up her notes. When she heard laughter coming from the other side of the room, she looked up. Mason and Linda were chuckling about something they thought dreadfully funny, and sudden sharp pangs stole into her heart. It wasn't easy seeing the two of them smiling at each other, seeing Linda's gleaming eyes fixed on Mason. It was obvious she thought the world of him.

Drea grabbed her briefcase and moved toward the door.

"Drea, hang on a sec. I need to discuss something with you," Mason called out in his deep baritone.

She turned to find both of them looking at her. "I'll be in touch, Drea. Bye for now," Linda said, giving her a little wave.

"Goodbye, Linda."

When the woman exited and closed the door behind her, Drea was left alone in the room with Mason. He walked over to her. "Where are you running off to?" he asked.

"I'm a little busy today," she said.

"Too busy to say hello?"

"Hello," she said softly.

He didn't find her joke funny. His eyes were on her, that dreamy, deep dark gaze latching on. He smelled delicious and looked even more so. She backed up a step.

"I've been thinking about you," he said. "How are you?"

"Fine. Busy, like I said," she blurted.

"Actually, I can't stop thinking about you. Have you been thinking about me, Drea?"

"No."

He gave her a crooked smile. "Liar."

Mason was so confident; he would never believe he hadn't left an impression. And she would have a difficult time denying it. "This isn't the place," she said, as forcefully as she could.

"Name the place, Drea. And I'll be there."

Oh God. No. No. "We can't, Mason. We said one night."

"Maybe we were wrong. Maybe we need more than one night."

His hand came up to her face and he stroked her cheek. His touch warmed everything cold inside and now she couldn't look away, couldn't stop staring at him. "Go away," she whispered.

"I can't," he said, stepping closer, cupping her face in his palm.

"I don't like you," she said, so quietly she could barely hear herself.

"I know. But you like the way I make you feel."

And he liked how she made him feel alive and vital again. Though he hadn't mentioned it since the very first kiss, she understood his attraction to her. He'd been dead inside, deeply grieving the loss of his family, a heartbroken man in pain. She'd been the one to wake him up to pleasure again, and of course he wanted more. His body was obviously craving life and lust again.

But could the same be true of her? Was having a satisfying sexual relationship good for her, too?

It sure felt that way when she was with him.

"Drea, you're thinking about it."

"I'm…not. I need to go."

He dropped his hand from her face and immediate disappointment set in. What was wrong with her? Deep down she understood this wouldn't end well, so shouldn't she be relieved that he let her go?

He was messing with her head, confusing her.

"You can't avoid me forever," he said.

"I know that. We've got a common work goal. It's important to remember that."

"I haven't forgotten the good we can do for the community." He focused on her mouth and then quickly swept his gaze over the rest of her body. It was enough to send shivers along her spine and quicken her pulse. "We're capable of separating the two, Drea."

"I'm not so sure of that." He had no idea what he was asking of her. He had no idea of her pain and suffering. She had too much pride to tell him what she'd gone through. She hadn't trusted anyone with her secret, and Mason was the last person on earth she'd tell.

"Maybe I'm sure enough for both of us."

She glanced at his mouth, recalling what those lips had done to her, how expertly he'd kissed her, and the memory caught her off guard. Her mask of indifference crumbled and she felt completely exposed.

"Drea, sweetheart." He took her hand and pulled gently until she was encircled in his arms, pressed against his chest. Then he kissed her thoroughly, devouring her lips as if he were starving. The kiss ended too quickly, yet both of them were completely breathless. Mason smiled at her, satisfaction in his expression as if to say he'd been right. They needed more time, more nights.

Maybe they did. Maybe Mason *was* right but it scared her and she had to end it now. "I'd better go." This was not what she'd expected when she'd come home to Boone Springs. Mason was changing all the rules and confusing her. It wasn't fair.

"I'll see you soon, Drea," Mason said confidently.

Oh no, he wouldn't. Not if she could help it.

"Dad, next time please ask me before you accept a dinner invitation from the Boones. I was planning on working late tonight." And the last person she wanted to see socially was Mason. They'd had their day and night, and now it was over, but she couldn't tell her father that.

Drea muttered under her breath as she and her father walked up the path to the Boone mansion. When she'd seen Mason as the hospital earlier, he didn't say a word about dinner, yet he must've known.

"I thought you'd want to spend more time with Lottie. Lord above, Drea. Can't I do anything right?"

Drea's shoulders fell. She had been hard on her dad for years, and she'd never accepted his *acceptance* of losing Thundering Hills to the Boones. Why hadn't he fought harder to save their home? "Yeah, Dad, you can. You do." He'd made a supreme effort to win her over since she'd been home. She shouldn't take out her bad mood on him. He had no idea what Mason had put her through, back then and…now.

She couldn't fault Mason for *now;* she took full responsibility for spending the night with him. It had been her own once-in-a-lifetime guilty pleasure, and now she was trying desperately, and without much success, to put that all behind her. "I'm just… Never mind."

"For what it's worth, I'm sorry…about everything," her dad said.

His tone was heart-wrenching.

She didn't mean to sound like a scrooge. And none of this was really his fault. It was hers, for caving in and letting Mason upend her life the way he had. "No, I'm sorry, Dad. I guess I'm stressed about the job. And yes, of course I want to spend time with Lottie. Let's just go and have a nice time tonight." She slipped her arm through his and smiled. "Okay?"

He hesitated a moment, then gave her a nod and a smile back. He seemed relieved and that was all she could ask for at the moment. "Sounds good to me."

Her father looked really nice tonight. He'd never had a smoother shave, his silvery hair was newly cut and tidy, and he'd put on a crisp button-down shirt and pair of slacks for the occasion. On his head was his ever present tan Stetson.

He rang the doorbell and a few moments later Lottie appeared, wearing an apron tied around her waist over a lovely rose silk blouse and skirt, her blond hair touching her shoulders. Drea heard a sudden noise: a quiet intake of breath from her father as he removed his hat.

"Welcome, you two," Lottie said, opening her arms to Drea. "You come here and let me give you a big hug."

Drea laughed and stepped forward, immediately cocooned in Lottie's brand of motherly love. She closed her eyes and hugged back. Only Lottie could make her feel this way, as if she was loved unconditionally. "So good to see you again, Lottie. You look wonderful."

"Thank you. Same here, sweetheart."

Her father remained stonily quiet.

"Hello, Drew."

"Lottie."

Drea wanted to roll her eyes at the two of them, but whatever it was between them they'd have to work out on their own.

"Please come in. Everyone is here."

Lottie led them into the main drawing room, where all three Boone brothers were conversing. Lucas and Risk leaned against the river rock fireplace mantel, and Mason immediately stood up from his chair as they walked in.

His gaze latched on to her and she felt the burn from across the room. Suddenly all the intimate things they'd done to each other were up front and center in her mind. It was as if Mason owned her, at least a little bit, because of what they'd shared. How they'd been with each other.

But she'd had too many years of crushing on him as a young girl and then too many years of hating him as an adult. She was tired of being owned by Mason. Tired of letting him have that much power over her.

She aimed her greeting at Mason's brothers, the other culprits of the Boone clan.

"Hey, Drea," Lucas said, giving her a smile. He'd grown into a handsome man, with his military haircut and piercing eyes. Risk gave her a wave.

"Lucas. Risk." She wasn't exactly on friendly terms with them, but had to be cordial since she'd been invited to dine with them, and they'd be helping with the fund-raiser.

Lottie made a good effort to engage them all in conversation, the topic being fund-raising. It was a good ice-breaker; Drea could speak for hours on the subject. Mason chimed in, too, adding his insights as Lottie poured wine for everyone but Drew. She handed him a tall glass of iced tea.

Five minutes into their discussion, the doorbell rang. "We've given Jessica the night off, so please excuse me while I get the door," Lottie said.

A short time later, Lottie led Katie into the room. She held a big pastry box in her hands. "Look who was kind enough to deliver our dessert to us. I've invited her to stay for dinner, but I think Katie needs some arm-twisting."

Katie scanned the room, her gaze stopping for a heartbeat on Lucas. He put down his wineglass and faced her squarely, giving her a look that smoldered, before catching himself. Everyone else spoke up. Drea especially wanted her friend to stay. With Mason here, she could really use reinforcements. "Please join us, Katie."

She glanced at Drea's form-fitting black dress, silver jewelry and high heels. "I'm, ah, I don't think so," she said. Clearly, Katie thought she was out of place in her work clothes. "Thank you, though."

Katie had shoulder-length blond hair and the softest blue eyes, and she could wear a pair of jeans like nobody's business. More importantly, she was a good person, through and through.

Mason stepped up. "Why not stay and have a bite with us? We have a new foal in the stable you'd just about fall in love with. I'm sure Luke would love to show it to you."

Katie was a horse lover from way back and this sparked a light in her gaze, though she avoided eye contact with Luke, staring at Mason instead.

"He's a beauty, too," Risk chimed in.

"Looks like the decision's made, Katie," Lottie said. "You're staying."

Katie forced a smile and nodded. "Okay, thank you. I would…love to."

Lottie took the box out of her hands and replaced it with a glass of wine. "Here you go. You all talk while I put these away and check on dinner."

"Want some help?" Drea's father asked Lottie.

Lottie's brows rose. She couldn't recall the last time Drew had offered her any help with anything. "Well now, that would be nice."

Lottie entered the kitchen, Drew a few steps behind her as she mulled over her confusing feelings. She'd known him forever, it seemed, but he'd always been Maria's guy.

He'd started off being a good provider for his family, a good father to young Drea and a pretty good husband to her best friend. But after tragedy struck, he'd simply given up…on everything. He'd let his ranch go to ruin, he'd stopped fathering Drea, and worst of all, he'd sought comfort in a bottle. How many years had he wasted? Lottie had promised Maria that she'd watch out for Drew and Drea when the time came. And she had, as much as she could without being a thorn in their sides. But Drew had been so dang hard to deal with. There was no reasoning with an alcoholic. Drew had had to come out of it on his own. He had, but not before causing a lot of damage.

Lottie put the cupcakes on the kitchen counter and turned to find Drew's soft green eyes on her.

"You look real nice tonight, Lottie."

"I bet it killed you to say that," she said, giving him a brief smile. There was truth to her words, but Lottie also had trouble accepting compliments from him. They were rare and made her uncomfortable.

"Well, no. It didn't, actually. That shade of pink suits you."

He looked good tonight, too, better than she'd seen him in a long while. "So do you. Look nice, I mean."

He cleared his throat and stared at her. When they weren't bickering, as they were prone to do, Lottie didn't know how to react. "Here, make yourself useful." She handed him a bowl of fresh greens.

"What's this?" He gave the dish a horrified look, as if weeds were growing inside it.

"Quinoa and kale salad."

Drew's face wrinkled up, but even that couldn't detract from his good looks. "Why?"

She laughed. He was so predictable. She knew he'd rebel

against her nourishing meal. "So you can get used to eating healthy foods."

"Oh, the devil. Mason said you might try to change my eating habits. What else do you have planned for supper?"

"All good things, I assure you."

"That's what I'm afraid of. You got dressing for this *salad*?"

"Yep, right here. Lemon vinaigrette."

She handed him the carafe and their fingers brushed.

His gaze shot to hers and she paused for a second, taken by unfamiliar sensations of warmth. She didn't know where to stash those feelings. And Drew wouldn't stop staring at her, the moment seemingly suspended in time. Finally, she snapped out of it. "You go on, bring in the salad. I'll get the rolls."

"Rolls? Now we're talking," he said eagerly.

"Don't get too excited. They're gluten free."

As he marched out of the kitchen, Drew muttered something about how a man could starve to death from good intentions. Lottie braced her hands on the edge of the counter and smiled. She was trying to do right by Drea and Maria, and Drew giving her grief about it wasn't unexpected.

What was unexpected was how much she enjoyed ringing his bell.

Six

Drea finished her meal. She had to admit the dinner hadn't been uncomfortable at all. Lottie had made sure of it. She could talk endlessly about her adventures. She'd traveled the world, and had led a really intriguing life. The woman wasn't the least bit shy about telling everyone about the ups and downs of living large. The one thing she didn't have was a husband and children of her own. Oddly, she'd never married. Drea had always thought the Boones were Lottie's fill-in family. Whenever she decided to stop and rest up a spell before heading out again, she'd spend time with her nephews. Lord knew, the boys loved and respected her to pieces.

"Mason, you haven't touched your broccoli." Lottie narrowed her eyes at him.

"You know I'm not a fan, Aunt."

"And Risk, that poached chicken isn't going to eat itself."

"Yes, ma'am," Risk said, eyeing his brothers for mercy.

"And—"

"I had a late lunch, Aunt Lottie." Lucas rubbed his stomach. "I'm about to bust."

Lottie pursed her lips. The boys were not helping her cause in the least and Drea wasn't going to let her go down without a fight, especially since her father had a big smug smile on his face. All the woman was trying to do was to get her dad to eat a healthier diet. Apparently, none of her nephews were in her corner.

"Lottie, this is a wonderful meal. I think I'll have seconds," Drea said, and right away Mason lifted the dish of chicken and passed it to her. His smirk was nothing short of daring. "Thank you," she said, tipping up her chin as she helped herself to another piece.

"Me, too," Katie said. "I love how you made the salad, Lottie. It's light and delicious."

Lottie nodded at Drew before passing over the salad bowl. "Here you go, Katie. I can tell you girls have a good palate."

Drea's father put his head down, concealing his amusement. Well, at least Lottie could make him smile. It was a good distraction from having to deal with Mason.

His eyes were forever on her and it rattled her nerves. As much as she was at ease during dinner, thanks to Lottie, every time she stole a glance at Mason he was watching her. Not only did his eyes burn straight through to her unguarded heart, he looked devastatingly handsome tonight in a pair of dark pants and a caramel-brown snap-down shirt. What was under that shirt made her head spin; she was reminded of the ripped chest with just enough wisps of hair to weave her fingers through as she'd kissed the hot skin there. His face was chiseled perfection, made even sexier by the dark stubble on his jaw.

Why did he have to appeal to her so much? Why couldn't she forget about the night they'd shared? She'd promised herself it would be only that. *One night.* She wasn't foolish enough to think that she could totally forgive Mason and his family, or to believe that he was over the loss of his wife.

They'd agreed on one night and now Mason wasn't playing fair. He wasn't letting it be. He was pursuing her, and Lord, if all he had to do was aim some scorching looks her way to get her to rethink her resolve, she was in deep trouble.

"How about you all take a look at that adorable new colt in the stable," Lottie said. "I'll get some coffee brewing and set out Katie's scrumptious cupcakes."

Katie rose. "I'll help you, Lottie."

"Don't be silly. You need to see that colt. Luke, take Katie on up to the stable, will you?"

Luke tossed his napkin onto the table and rose. "Okay, sure. Katie?"

Her friend's tight smile only confirmed to Drea that she didn't want to be alone with Luke. He'd been engaged to Shelly, Katie's older sister, and had walked out on her right before their wedding. He'd joined the Marines and had been gone a while, but Katie's family still hadn't forgiven him. "Will the rest of you be joining us?" Katie asked.

"I'd like to see it," Drea said, coming to her friend's aid. Katie and Luke had once been easy friends. Now things were strained between them.

"I'll stay behind," Risk said. "I've already seen the colt."

"I think I'll just sit a spell on the porch, if you all don't mind," her father said.

Mason didn't say a word, but as Luke ushered Katie out the door, Mason waited for Drea on the threshold. "Haven't you seen the colt?" she asked him.

"Not since Trinket gave birth."

He gestured for her to exit, and when she did, he followed. She did her best to catch up with Luke and Katie, and she was making ground until Mason took her hand from behind, slowing her down.

"Let the two of them talk," he said quietly. "I think Luke needs to repair some of the damage."

She stopped and looked at him. "You think Lucas can do that?"

"He can try. They were pretty close friends."

"Yeah, well. Things change. People change. I'm not sure Katie wants to be alone with Luke."

"What you really mean is you don't want to be alone with me. Isn't that right?"

She sighed and all the fight went out of her. "Maybe."

"Why?"

"You know why! We made a deal and now you're going back on it."

Once Luke and Katie were way up ahead, Drea and Mason began slowly walking toward the stable. "I just think the deal was a mistake."

"Taking that trip to Los Angeles together was the mistake," she said.

"It's killing you that you're starting to like me."

"I don't...like you."

Mason grinned. Oh, he was infuriating. He had enough confidence to fill up a football stadium. Normally, she liked that trait in a man. She'd never been attracted to weak-kneed men who were wishy-washy about themselves. Mason seemed so sure of everything, except when it came to his own heart. He'd been broken, and he was just coming out of that. He was starting to rebuild himself again, but she had no place in his life. Correction: she wanted no place in his life.

When they were in LA, it had all seemed so easy. They were far away from Texas, away from family and friends, away from reality, sharing the night on a beautiful beach. It had almost been as if she were a different woman and Mason a different man. She'd fully expected things to get back to normal once they'd touched down on Texas soil again.

"You don't like me, even a little?"

"Well, maybe I see some redeeming qualities in you." She was being honest.

"Like what? I'm curious."

"You're decisive. You get things done. I admire that."

He nodded. "Anything else?"

"Well..." She stared at him for a long moment. The sun was setting, and only a glimmer of light touched his face now. "You're good—"

"In bed?" He was smiling, and those hidden dimples popped out underneath his sexy day-old beard.

She shook her head. "You have a tremendous..."

His brows lifted wickedly.

"Ego."

"I thought you were going to say—"

"Mason," she warned. "Don't."

"We had a good time in LA."

"It's going nowhere."

"Do you want it to go somewhere?" he asked.

"Of course not. But I can't forget certain things."

"I can't forget certain things, either. Like the way you tremble when I touch you. Or the way your body responds to mine, or the feel of your silky hair or—"

"Mason, please...that's not what I meant."

They reached the stable and Mason glanced inside. "Let's give the two of them some privacy." He took her hand and tugged her toward the back of the structure. She followed his lead, not putting up any resistance. Why didn't she? She had no answer to that question. She could've just as easily held her ground and walked inside the building to meet up with Katie and Lucas.

Now her back was to the wall, literally, and Mason's big body blocked her vision of anything else. All she saw was one gorgeous man, staring at her like she held the answers to the universe in the palm of her hand. "What are you doing?" *To me?* she really wanted to ask.

"I'm spending time with you. I've thought about little else these past few days."

She had to admit that Mason was getting to her. What she liked about him was his determination to never give up. But that trait could also be her downfall.

"I'm leaving when the fund-raiser is over."

He lifted a strand of her long hair and twirled it around his finger. "It's not like we both don't know that, sweetheart."

Sweetheart. There it was again. She wasn't his sweet anything. She really wasn't, but his soft tone made her think otherwise. And it confused her to no end. "This isn't good."

"You're right. It isn't good. It's pretty great."

He leaned in, his face coming inches from hers, his mouth, that delectable expert mouth, so close.

"I—I make you…feel things," she stuttered.

His lips lifted in a smile. "So true."

"That's all this is."

"I make you feel things, too," he whispered, cradling her face in his hands. "Tell me it's not so and I'll back off, Drea."

She opened her mouth to deny it. To deny him. But the words wouldn't come. What was wrong with her? Why couldn't she say no to him and mean it? The look on his face, the hunger in his eyes spoke to her. He smelled of lime and musk, something expensive and rare that was drawing her to him, making her want, making her crave. All she could do was feel his approach, leaning closer until his hips touched hers and her breasts were crushed against his chest.

Memories flooded in. Of unparalleled kisses. Of being naked with him. Of their two bodies completely in sync with each other. A whimper escaped her mouth as she surrendered totally.

And then his lips were on hers, his mouth taking claim, his kiss a beautiful reminder of how much she'd missed…this. Not *him.* She wasn't missing him so much as she missed the womanly way he made her feel. Desirable and attractive. She had his total approval and that was something she hadn't often felt while growing up. To be honest, her adult life hadn't been all that glorious, either. So naturally, she would take what Mason offered. That had to be it. That had to be the reason his kisses made her legs weak and her heart flutter wildly.

At least that's what she told herself as Mason's mouth demanded more of her, as his body went rigid. It was heady knowing she made him come alive. A true boost to her morale, she had to admit.

As he pressed his hard body home, her lips parted in a moan of pure delight. Everything tingled. Every sensation was heightened.

Voices and then footsteps reached her ears. "Oh no," she whispered.

"Shush." Mason kissed her quiet.

Lucas and Katie were leaving the stable and heading back to the house. It was dark now. Drea and Mason stood still and waited until the sound of their footsteps receded.

"We need to go back," she whispered. An owl hooted and leaves of surrounding trees rustled in the night breeze. The fall air grew crisp but Drea's body was still heated, her heart still raced.

Mason released a deep sigh. A houseful of people waited for them and they couldn't do this any longer. He took her hand. "Let's go see the foal for a minute," he said.

"Okay, yes. We should." So that they could say they had. So that no one would get suspicious.

Once in the stable, they watched mama with her new babe. It was a thing of beauty and grace, and Drea was struck by deep yearning. Remembering her loss, the child she would never know, only compounded the feeling.

Mason stared into the paddock filled with a layer of straw to cushion the horses from the wooden walls and hard ground. Drea had grown up on a ranch, too, and welcomed the pungent scents, the smell of leather and earth.

"Meet me later tonight," he said, his voice firm, determined.

She squeezed her eyes closed. Not because it was a ridiculous idea, but because it was an enticing one. "I…can't."

Mason turned to her and his eyes spoke of promises he would fulfill.

Her body still hummed from his kisses. He wanted more. So did she. But it was impossible.

"Why can't you?" he asked. "And I'd like the truth."

She drew breath into her lungs. "Aside from the obvious reasons—"

"Like you hate me for hurting you, for taking away your family land? You blame me for all the woes of the world?"

"Mason."

He pressed closer to her. Wrapping his hand around her neck, he pulled her in and kissed her thoroughly, without pause, softening up all her hard, unsettled edges.

"Now tell me the truth," he whispered over her lips.

"Where would we meet? I mean, you live here, and it's not exactly private. And my dad's place is off-limits."

Perhaps she'd revealed too much of her thoughts. She should be denying him this, outright refusing his suggestion. But she couldn't. Maybe she wanted to see what he had in mind. Maybe she was more than a little bit intrigued by a secret rendezvous.

Mason stroked a finger across her cheek, his tender touch creating tingles down to her toes. "At The Baron. I keep a room there, for when I work in town."

"Your hotel?"

He nodded. "I'll be there at eleven. Waiting for you."

A dozen questions filled her head. She wasn't a teenager, sneaking out for a date. She wasn't a woman who liked lying. But she'd have to do one or the other in order to meet Mason.

"I don't know."

"Think about it, sweetheart. And you do know. You just can't face it yet."

Face what? That she wanted him? That after their time in LA she'd been thinking about Mason in a purely unbusinesslike way.

So much for *Business with Mason.* That had lasted as long as a snowball in hell.

He kissed her again, then took her hand and led her out of the stable.

Already she felt like a fraud, entering the Boone home pretending that nothing monumental was happening between them. Pretending that they weren't crazily attracted to each other.

Back at the house, Katie pulled her into the kitchen as the others were drinking coffee. Her friend whispered, "What happened to you two out there?"

"You mean, when we didn't show in the stable?"

"Yes, that's what I mean. You were supposed to be my cover. I didn't want to be alone with Lucas."

"I know. Sorry. I let you down. Was it horrible?"

"What? No, not really. We're just distant friends now, is all."

"Okay, good. That's what I was hoping. But he was sort of ogling you at dinner tonight."

Katie giggled. "I was just going to say the same thing about Mason. He wasn't letting up. His eyes were all for you. So, what happened out behind the stable tonight?"

Drea gasped, partly in shock. Not about Katie knowing something was going on, but the idea that maybe the others were piecing things together, as well. "You know?"

"I don't think Luke gave it a thought, but I figured something was up."

"It's complicated," Drea said, keeping her voice down. "I can't go into detail, but something happened between me and Mason when we were in LA and now he wants to see me again. Like, later tonight."

"Go."

Drea blinked. "What do you mean, go?"

"Drea, you haven't been with a man in a long while. And maybe...well, maybe you just need to get Mason out of your system. Geesh, I sound like a guy, don't I? But it's true. How can you move on with your life until this part of it is satisfied? See what happens with Mason. I mean, if you didn't want to meet him, if you thought it ridiculous, you wouldn't have told me. You would've shot him down immediately. But you didn't do that. You want to go."

"I don't like sneaking around."

"Sounds kind of exciting, if you ask me." Katie's voice got animated, making Drea smile and shake her head.

Her decision now made, she gave Katie her best stern look. "If this goes south, I'll come after you, Katie girl."

Her friend kissed her cheek. "Go, and have a good time on my behalf. Heaven knows, I've been a safe little mouse all my life, so at least let me enjoy a bit of intrigue through my bestie."

"So glad I'm a source of your entertainment."

Katie shoved a bunch of extra napkins into Drea's hands while she grabbed the plate of cupcakes, "Come on, let's get back out there before someone comes looking for us."

"Yeah, Luke might come searching for you."

"That would be a no-can-ever-do," Katie said.

"Yeah, and that's what I thought about Mason Boone for all of my grown-up life. Just goes to show, never say never."

Drea stood outside the door of The Baron Hotel's top floor suite, ready to knock. That she was here at all still shocked the stuffing out of her. But Katie had been right. Drea had unfinished business to settle with Mason and so his proposed midnight interlude might not go exactly as he'd planned.

Getting away hadn't been hard at all. She'd waited until her father was sawing logs, before quietly stepping out of the house. She'd left him a note saying that she had trouble sleeping and had gone for a drive, just in case he woke and didn't find her home. All that was true, so she hadn't really lied. At least that was what she told herself.

She knocked on the door softly and heard footsteps approach.

Swallowing hard, she braced herself. When Mason opened the door, his shoulders relaxed, a small smile surfaced and she read great relief in his expression. This wasn't the confident man she'd expected to find. Instead, Mason's vulnerability had shone through, touching something deep and precious in her heart. He hadn't been sure she'd show up. And he'd been worried, perhaps even saddened, to think she'd let him down.

It wasn't fair. She had Mason pegged as an arrogant pain in her side, and he was proving her wrong.

"Drea." There was a wistful tone in his voice. So different than the man who ran an empire, the man who commanded respect at all times. Mason Boone was full of surprises.

"I'm…here." She lifted her shoulders, then let them fall.

He took her hand and gently pulled her into the room. "I'm happy to see that."

He let her hand go and she walked into the suite taking in the living area, with its fireplace and twin sofas facing each other, the dining area and the hallway that led to the other rooms. It was luxurious and grand, something she'd expect from a Boone. But it was also homey in a way that said Mason spent a lot of time here, from the scattering of square, embroidered pillows on the floor, to the sports magazines on the coffee table to a giant screen TV on the wall. She recognized the pillows as being Lottie's handiwork. Peaches, oranges and apples filled a bowl on the kitchen counter and photos of Rising Springs Ranch graced the hallway walls. Soft classical music played in the background, perhaps the biggest surprise of all.

"Is this your Zen place?" she asked turning to find him watching her from the middle of the living room.

"Or my man cave."

His gaze was forever on her, as if to say he couldn't believe she was really here.

"No, it's definitely Zen." She walked to the window and stared out at the town Mason's ancestors had established. How must that feel? To know your family had built this town from the ground up. To have streets, a hospital, an entire town named after the Boones. To have that entitlement.

She looked at Mason, standing there, curiosity on his beautiful face. "You didn't think I'd come, did you?"

He sighed and walked over to her. “I’m…a little surprised.”

“No one is more surprised than me, Mason.”

He stood at arm’s length from her and his presence consumed her. He was that type of man, one who could overpower with just one glance. Usually he loomed large, but tonight she was seeing a different side of him. “Do you still resent me and all the Boones?”

“My feelings about you are…complicated.”

He stepped closer and entwined his fingers with hers. “Can we try to uncomplicate things? Can we just talk about it, Drea? About that night so long ago?”

His question made her jittery. She wanted to yank her hand away, to turn her back on him, to walk out the door if necessary. She’d lost her baby and a big part of herself, after all. How could she possibly explain the damage that was done after that night? She’d struggled for years with all of it.

But as Katie had said, she needed to be able to get on with her life. To move past this. And maybe there was no better way than to talk it through. “At one point in my life, you were my everything, Mason.” God, it was hard to admit that.

“Come here,” he said, leading her to the sofa. She sank down and he sat beside her. They faced each other, still holding hands. “You were saying?”

“You heard what I said. I was halfway in love with you, Mason.”

“And I shouldn’t have let it go that far. I was attracted to you. I’d always liked you. We used to play together, if you remember.”

“Of course I remember. We were friends once.”

“And then, when you were bucked from your horse and took a hard fall, I found you in the meadow. Your ankle was bruised and you couldn’t put any pressure on it.”

“You were wonderful that day,” she said, remembering how gallant he’d been. He’d stayed with her, helping remove her shoe and using a cold can of soda pop he’d been drinking to keep the swelling down on her ankle. He'd missed a baseball game with his friends to stay with her. And then, when she was able to stand up, he'd lifted her and carried her to an old carriage house on their property. The chemistry between them had been off the charts. She'd never looked at Mason that way before, but having him tend her, having his dark concerned eyes on her, having him touch and care for her, had made her dizzy. From that moment on, she'd set her sights on him.

"And you were seventeen."

"A month away from my eighteenth birthday, Mason. I wasn't a kid."

"I didn't think so, either. But you were a virgin and I was going for my final semester at Texas A&M."

"I was willing, Mason. That night, up in your bedroom. We were all alone."

He heaved a big sigh. "I know. It was so hard to say no to you. But I had to. You were Drew's daughter, for one. And he was a family friend, even if you didn't want to think so at the time."

"But we'd been seeing each other every day for a full month and I knew my heart. I told you I was ready."

"Look at me, Drea," he commanded, and she lifted her chin to meet his gaze. "You also said one other thing to me. Do you remember what that was?"

She thought back and couldn't really recall what else she'd said. For all these years, she'd blocked out the hurtful memory of that night, the exact words spoken, but the humiliation had lingered on. She shook her head. "No."

He squeezed her hand gently. "You said…you needed me. Not wanted, not loved, but needed me."

She pulled back, wrenching her hand from his in utter shock. "Oh, so you thought I was this needy kid, starving for affection. You thought you'd get stuck with me, the pathetic daughter of a widower drunk, a girl so confused about her feelings that she'd give up her virginity to you. What you did to me that night was cruel."

Tears stung her eyes. This was horrific. She didn't think she could ever be more humiliated than when she'd bared her body to Mason and he'd rejected her. But this was just as bad, if not worse.

"No, that's not what I'm saying." Mason's voice sharpened immediately. "I wanted you, Drea. But there were too many obstacles blocking us and I had to be the grown-up. I had to deny you and myself. It was for the best. And I'm sorry that I hurt you, but I had to be firm. I had to make sure not to leave any doubt in your mind, because…because there was doubt in mine. So yes, I spoke harshly to you and I've regretted it every day since. But we did the right thing, Drea. We did."

She got up and walked to the window, staring at the lights of the town. "You wanted me to hate you. Well, you succeeded. You have no idea what your rejection did to me."

Mason came up behind her. "I did what I thought best for you at the time. I cared about you too much to use you, to have you for one night and then take off. My conscience wouldn't allow it, but no, I didn't want you to hate me."

"But I did. Especially after what your family had already done to mine. I thought you heartless and mean, and wondered if I'd ever meant anything to you."

"Drea, listen to me. The Boones aren't as bad as you seem to think. We're not greedy robber barons after people's land. My family tried to help yours."

He wasn't convincing her.

Mason clasped her shoulders, his hands gentle, as if testing to see if she'd flinch. But his touch, like always, comforted her instead, giving her solace and peace. She'd spent so much time hating him that now there wasn't much hatred left. Only regret. She had so many regrets.

"If it's any consolation to you, I didn't date for nearly a year after that. Every time I looked at a woman, I thought of you. I swear it, Drea. It's hard to admit, but I have second-guessed that night in my head many times."

If she could believe him, it helped knowing that he'd suffered a little bit, too. That he'd had doubts about letting her go. It helped her ego and her pride and also helped put things in perspective. She'd never heard his side of the story before. She'd never known his motivation for breaking things off and breaking her heart.

Yet there was more to her story, but she couldn't reveal it to him. It would only serve to prove he'd been right. She had been needy, a girl craving love and affection.

She'd done a stupid thing and maybe now she could put the past behind her. Her hatred depleted, maybe now she could move on with her life, just like Katie had said. For the first time in a long time, she would be free of that burden. Her feelings about the Boones in general were a different story. Her resentment about Thundering Hills was still there, but no longer was she driven by contempt and anger. "It does help knowing that."

Mason kissed the back of her neck, then nibbled along her collarbone. She arched her head, giving him more access. The skin where he kissed her burned.

"If you want to leave, I'd understand. But I don't want you to, sweetheart. I want you to stay."

She turned around and he immediately wrapped her in his arms. His head came down and his lips brushed hers gently, sweetly. Mason pulled back and smiled at her, and there was that vulnerability in his eyes again. When he was like that, she was even more attracted to him. The look on his face as he waited for her answer had her melting inside.

"I want to stay."

A wide grin spread across his face. He squeezed her tightly and kissed her again, but briefly. "Would you like something to drink? Eat?"

"After eating Katie's Molten Ganache cupcake, I don't think I'll ever eat again. But I would like a drink."

"A drink it is. What can I get you?"

"White wine?"

He nodded and headed toward the kitchen. "Have a seat. I'll get it for you."

She settled on the sofa, and while she waited, made note of the fact that Mason didn't have one photo of his wife in any of the rooms she'd been in. No wedding pictures, no pictures of the two of them lounging around, riding horses or sitting on a fence at Rising Springs Ranch.

Were the memories too hard for him?

She'd heard people say Larissa was the love of his life. He'd been crushed when she died.

Yet Mason almost never brought her up.

And so now here Drea was, hardly a replacement for his dead wife. No, she was a brief interlude, and she had to remember that. After the fund-raiser, she'd head home to her pretty, cool apartment and life in New York, and Mason would move on, too.

"Here you go," he said, handing her a glass of wine. He sat down beside her with his own drink, something golden-brown, bourbon probably.

"Thank you." She sipped her drink and breathed in Mason. She should never mix alcohol and the scent of a gorgeous man. Or maybe she should. She smiled.

"What's going on in your head?"

"Nothing."

She took another sip.

"You smiled. What were you thinking?"

"Okay," she said. "I'm thinking that I'm here with you without..."

"Without hating me?"

She nodded.

"So you like me now?"

"Well," she said, bringing the glass to her mouth. "Let's not go that far."

There was a gleam in Mason's eyes. He wasn't vulnerable anymore, far from it. His expression meant danger and pleasure and promise.

He took the glass out of her hand and set it down. "Actually, let's go as far as we can tonight," he whispered. He took a last gulp of alcohol and then kissed her hard on the lips.

Her body reacted to the potent taste of whiskey, to the scent, the kiss, the man.

"You look amazing. I wanted to tell you earlier. That dress is—"

"Coming off?" She loved the look the surprise on his face.

He chuckled deep in his throat. "That, too, but it's gorgeous on you."

And five minutes later, after skillfully undressing each other, piece by piece, kiss after kiss, Mason lifted her up in his arms and carried her to the bedroom.

The bedroom was low-key but luxurious, with large dark furnishings. The windows looked out over the other side of town, toward the quiet suburbs of Boone Springs. The drapes were pulled back, and the light of the half-moon filtered in through nearly sheer curtains, splashing over Mason's body as he lowered her onto the bed. She felt the cool, silky sheets on her back.

Mason stared at her a moment, something dark flickering in his eyes before he joined her on the bed. That look frightened her. Was it guilt? Or doubt? Was he second-guessing all this? Had he lost his desire for her? "What?" she asked softly.

He didn't hesitate. "I'm thinking how beautiful you are."

His words sent a thrill through her body. Yet she had never wanted this. To be his experiment, to have him want her solely due to a crazy chemical attraction he had for her. But here she was, also lured by that undeniable chemistry, waiting and wanting to be dazzled by him again. It would all be okay as long as she recognized this for what it was. As long as she didn't let him in, the way she had as a teen.

"But are you okay with all of this?" he asked her.

"He asks as I'm naked in bed with him."

"Just making sure, sweetheart."

His next kiss wiped away any doubt.

Mason was a thorough lover, from his mind-numbing kisses to his attention to her body. He caressed her lovingly, gently massaging her breasts until her nipples ripened to tiny hard pebbles. His tongue did wonderful things, making her whimper in a way that couldn't be mistaken for anything other than pure sexual pleasure.

Her skin prickled as sizzling, sweeping heat poured into every crevice, and when he paid deep attention to the sweet spot below her navel, she cried out. His mouth was relentless, his hands were masterful. Her back arched off the bed as an earth-shattering release tore through her. She panted his name.

"I'm right here, darlin'."

And he *was* right there, now sheathed with protection and rolling onto his back so he lay next to her. She was still coming down from her high and Mason waited for her patiently.

Then he whispered, "Come to me, Drea."

He guided her so that she was on top, her legs straddling him. He circled her waist with his big hands and helped her, fitting her body to his. She sank onto him and her eyes shuttered closed. It was a beautiful joining.

"You are incredible like this." His voice was a husky mixture of awe and gratitude. "Your hair, your skin. You feel like heaven, Drea."

His words brought her joy. And her skin prickled again, the heat from before magnified. She didn't wait for him to move, but began a slow, steady gyration, sinking farther down, giving Mason a reason to grit his teeth and groan.

He touched her all over, his thumbs flicking across her breasts, his hand working magic below her waist. She sped up her pace, cementing that look of awe on his face. Her second release was intense, stronger than before, her voice at a higher pitch as she called out Mason's name.

Her completion couldn't be compared to anything she'd experienced before. Not that she was an expert. She'd had exactly three relationships in her life, and yes, Mason topped them all. But if she'd had a hundred, he would still come out the winner. She knew that for a fact.

She fell into his arms and he kissed her silly. And then he rolled them both over, so that he towered above her on the bed. She gazed up into his handsome face filled with hunger and lust.

"I want you, Mason," she said softly.

"You've got me," he said.

Then he drove his point home, telling her yes, indeed, she had him.

Mason's phone alarm woke him from a deep sleep. Normally, he liked waking up to Larissa's favorite song, Faith Hill's "Breathe." It was a humbling reminder of his wife, and the child he'd never know, and somehow it made him feel closer to them. He'd never thought to change it. If he did, it would be like losing another piece of Larissa. Another soul-emptying piece of her.

But today, he shut off the alarm quickly and hinged up to a sitting position.

"Hell." He ran his hand down his face. He didn't have to see the empty place beside him on the bed or look around the suite to know that Drea was gone. He should've been more considerate. He shouldn't have fallen asleep. At the very least he wanted to make sure she'd gotten home safely last night.

He would have gladly driven her home. He would've kissed her goodbye in the wee hours of the night and watched as she entered the cottage.

He rose and dressed then wandered over to the window. Boone Springs was just rising, too, and the autumn sun was warming everything up.

He craved a cup of coffee to clear his head. Right now, his thoughts were on two women.

His wife, for one. Dead and buried two years ago next week. He didn't need a calendar under his nose to remember the date. He still saw her pretty face and the silky cinnamon hair that bounced off her shoulders when she walked. And those light blue eyes that lit like fireworks every time he smiled at her.

She'd moved to Boone Springs seven years ago, and he'd met her at his friend Trace Burrows's wedding. She'd been a college friend of the bride, just visiting town and looking for work. Mason had fallen hard for her immediately and was desperate for her to stay on in Boone Springs. Without her knowing it, he'd pulled some strings and she'd been hired as a television anchor for the local news station, WBN. She'd been great on camera and off.

After they were married, he'd fessed up about his desperation to keep her in town, hoping she wouldn't go ballistic. She'd only smiled. "I would've gotten the job without your help. I nailed that audition." That was Larissa. She'd been fierce and smart and wonderful.

Mason grabbed his phone and walked into the kitchen. He set up the coffeemaker to brew. Later, at the ranch, he'd get breakfast. For now, the steady drip, drip, drip of dark roast was enough to satisfy him.

That's when something shimmery on the hardwood floor caught his eye. He walked over and bent to pick it up. It was a long strand of looped silver, the necklace Drea had worn last night. As he stared at it, memories rushed in, of him removing her black dress, taking off her shoes and every other pretty little thing she wore. Man, he'd wanted her so badly last night.

He'd been struck that she'd shown up at all. And that they'd finally cleared the air about their past.

That's when his doubts had rushed in. He'd had a moment, a panic attack of emotion. Drea's resentment about him and his family had always been misguided, yet it had provided protection he could count on, a barrier she wouldn't allow to be broken. Because he was never going to fall in love again. He'd never have another permanent relationship. His wife was still in his heart.

"So now what, idiot?" he murmured, holding Drea's necklace in his hand. It was warm, like her. And sleek and beautiful. Also like her.

Mason picked up his phone and texted Drea. I have something of yours.

He waited a minute, poured his coffee and then received her answer. Did I lose my panties?

He laughed so hard coffee sloshed from his cup, just missing his hand. If you had, I wouldn't be giving them back.

Ha! What then?

Wait and see. I'll bring it by your place this morning.

I'll be at Katie's Kupcakes.

Great, save one for me. I'll see you there.

Mason put away his phone before she could text him not to come over. He was going to see her. To tell her he'd wanted to take her home last night. Any man of honor would do the same.

And that's where it got confusing. Because he had a sinking feeling that even if she hadn't lost her necklace and slipped out of his place quietly last night, he would've found a reason to see her again today.

Seven

Drea didn't have to try another cupcake. She'd chosen her favorite and that was that. When she set her sights on something, usually there was no changing her mind. "This one, Katie. This has got to be one of them."

In the back work area of the bakery, Drea leaned over the stainless-steel countertop and took another big lick of raspberry cream cheese frosting. The cupcake was so pretty, a lemon rosemary cake infused with raspberry filling and covered with delicious icing. "I love your idea, by the way."

Katie had offered to come up with two signature cupcakes for the fund-raiser, one that appealed to adults and one for the kids. Of course, her other cupcakes would be for sale, too, and Katie was donating all the proceeds she earned to the cause. She was also overseeing the cupcake decorating booth.

"Thanks. And I agree. I love the combination of flavors in this one. So now we've got one for the adults. What about the kids?"

"Kids love all cupcakes." Drea continued to devour hers.

Great sex had a way of making her hungry. Her heart sped as

she thought about the incredible night she'd shared with Mason. After he'd fallen asleep, she'd quickly dressed and driven home, making as little noise as possible as she entered the cottage. Luckily, her father had been sound asleep. She'd tiptoed to her room, undressed quietly and gotten into bed.

Sleep hadn't come easily. She'd missed Mason, missed waking up with him like she had at the beach house, breathing in his after-sex scent and snuggling up tight. But it was best this way. At least she didn't have to answer questions from her dad. That would've been awkward for sure.

"I want to make it special for the kids—a cupcake they can't pass up," Katie said.

Drea tapped a finger to her lips. "Well, what do kids love more than anything?"

"Christmas?"

She laughed. "So true, but not Christmas this time. I know… they love parties. Can you conjure up a party cupcake?"

"Confetti cake isn't new."

"No, but what about…a rainbow cupcake?"

Katie's eyes widened, and Drea could just see the wheels of invention turning in her head. "I think I can do that. We'll have three flavors on the inside, and then I'll do a rainbow frosting on top. I don't know a single child who doesn't like rainbows."

"That sounds wonderful," Drea admitted, but then as an afterthought said, "But isn't it a lot of work?"

Katie grinned. "Not if you're helping me."

"Are you serious? I can't…bake. I'm so not a baker, and definitely not one of your caliber."

"You are a baker. It's not that hard. But I was teasing. I'll get extra help from Lori, my assistant, and it'll all work out. Besides, you'll be running the entire show at Rising Springs. You're gonna have your hands full that weekend."

"I know. It's hard to believe it's less than two weeks away."

"I'm looking forward to having the kids learn how to frost a cupcake. I've got all these ideas for decorating. Some moms and dads from Park Avenue Elementary School are going to run the booth with me."

"I think that's going to be a hit. Kids love that sort of thing."

The overhead bell on the shop door chimed. Katie took a peek out front. "Speaking of having your hands full. There's a gorgeous hunk of a guy out there, and I don't think he wants a cupcake."

"Mason?"

Katie nodded. "He looks impatient. He must be dying to see you."

"Don't be silly. He's only returning something of mine."

"That you left at his place last night?"

Drea opened her mouth, but nothing came out. She straightened out her dress, slipped her feet back into her heels and fluffed her hair a bit.

"You look great. Go. And remember, I want deets later. You owe me."

"Okay," she answered breathlessly.

She walked into the café, coming around the corner of the glass display case to face Mason. "Hi."

His eyes filled with warmth. She tried not to notice, not to make a big deal of the way he was looking at her. But her heart swelled and she was absolutely certain she was eyeing him with that very same look.

"Hi." His voice was husky and deep. He wore a tan shirt under an ink-black suit, no tie, his collar open at the throat. He removed his hat, smiled and then gave her a kiss on the cheek. "You ran out on me last night."

"Shh," she said, glancing out the window. It was midmorning and the bakery café was empty yet someone could walk in at any moment. "I didn't run out. You knew I had to get home before I turned into a pumpkin."

"Well then, Cinderella, I came to see if this fits." He dug into his pocket and came up with her silver loop necklace.

She smiled. "Not exactly a glass slipper."

"And I'm hardly a prince. But let's see if it fits."

Mason walked behind her, his body so close, his memorable scent teasing her nostrils. He lifted her ponytail out of the way, and his warm breath caressed the back of her neck. "You're trembling," he said as he secured the clasp.

"It's a little cold in here." It wasn't.

He nibbled on her nape, planting delicious kisses behind her ear. Her breathing hitched and she felt a hot tingling in her belly. "I can keep you warm."

"I know." Heat flushed her cheeks. She didn't often blush, but Mason was capable of bringing out new sides of her personality.

When he came around to face her, he noticed her pink cheeks, which should've embarrassed her. But there was an incredible softness in his eyes. Then he glanced at the necklace and his brows furrowed, his expression turning serious. "I would've driven you home last night."

"I had my car."

"Still, I should've made sure you got safely home."

"Thank you. But I didn't want to wake you."

"I missed you when I woke up."

Her breath caught in her throat. She didn't have a response for him. He was too devastatingly handsome and honest for her peace of mind. She'd felt the same way; leaving him asleep in his bed had made her feel terribly lonely. She hadn't felt that way in a long time.

When she didn't reply, he sighed. "What are you doing for lunch?"

"Lunch? I'm working through lunch. In case you don't realize it, the fund-raiser is less than two weeks away."

"And look at all the progress we've made. It's all gonna come together. Linda is working her buns off on promo for The Band Blue and the date with Sean. You've got a handle on the art auction. I heard you managed to get donations from several art galleries. That's huge."

"Yes, I'm excited about that. More than twenty-five paintings and five bronze sculptures, and some wood sculptures, as well. It should bring in a good deal of revenue. Is everything going well at the ranch?"

"Yeah, but I need your advice. There's things we need to go over."

"I'm happy to. When?"

"We can discuss it over lunch." His eyes twinkled. He'd caught her and all she could do was smile.

"You are persistent."

"It's for the cause, Drea. We both have to eat. Can't afford to run our bodies down."

As if the man had ever been sick a day in his life. He was fit and she knew that firsthand. "So *survival* is your new pickup line?"

"Do I need a pickup line?"

No. Never. But she wasn't going to admit that to him. "Where should I meet you?"

"At the ranch…in about an hour and a half?"

"Okay, I'll finish up here with Katie and meet you."

He nodded and turned to leave, then pivoted around, strode over to her and landed a kiss on her mouth that literally rocked her back on her heels. *Wow.*

He grinned, plopped his hat back on his head and then took his leave.

"Bye, Katie," Drea said, giving her friend a peck on the cheek. "I'm off now. Got a few errands to run before I head back to the ranch."

Katie shook her head. "To meet Mason. Boy, oh boy. You sure do lead an exciting life."

Drea slung her handbag over her shoulder. "We're discussing business over lunch, is all."

"Didn't sound like the two of you discussed much business last night. Don't get me wrong, I'm glad you two hooked up. It's about time."

Drea stood on the threshold of the bakery kitchen, grateful Lori was busy serving customers and no one was within earshot of their conversation. Katie had pried some deets, as she called them, out of her about last night's trip to The Baron as Drea helped bake an experimental batch of rainbow cupcakes. Katie sure knew her stuff; the cupcakes had turned out perfect. And now she was matchmaking, which wasn't allowed between close friends. Or at least it shouldn't be.

"I bet you two don't get much work done this afternoon, either. I bet he takes you somewhere really nice."

"You do have a crazy imagination."

"Just go. You don't want to leave his hunkiness waiting."

"I'm going, I'm going."

Drea left Katie in the bakery kitchen and had reached the front door when it opened suddenly and she bumped into the man walking in.

"Excuse me. Sorry," he said.

"No, no. It was my fault, too. I wasn't looking where I was…" She glanced up and found the man's eyes on her. It wasn't just any man, it was Brad. Dr. Brad Williamson, the taker of her virginity, the man who'd offered to marry her. The man she'd had to walk away from because it wouldn't be fair, since she didn't love him.

"Drea, is that you?"

She bit her lip and nodded. Too many emotions stirred inside, pain and regret being at the top. She hadn't seen Brad in ten years. But he looked the same, if a bit fuller in the face, more solid all the way around. He was in his early thirties, an age when men flourished, showing a certain mature confidence and grace. He had intelligent blue eyes, a nice tan, and his longish hair was the same sandy-blond color she remembered.

"W-what are you doing here, Brad?" she blurted. He was a blast from her past and not necessarily a welcome one. Immediately, her nerves jumped. It wasn't him, but the memory of the entire ordeal that rattled her. "I mean, I never thought I'd see you in Boone Springs."

"You and me both," he said, smiling at her as if he was really glad to see her. "But I had the opportunity to give a few interviews and lectures on my book tour not far from here, and well, when I read about the hospital fund-raiser and your part in it, I thought I'd come by and see for myself."

"You've written a book?" After college, Brad had gone on to med school and had become a pediatrician. She knew this only because he'd texted her occasionally after the breakup, updating her, though she'd never replied. She'd just wanted that part of her life to be over. After a time, he'd stopped texting her.

"Yes, on the trials of raising a toddler."

"Do you..." She swallowed hard. "Do you have children?"

His blue eyes softened immediately and he nodded. "Two. Meggie is three, Charlie is five. Living with their mother now, but we have joint custody."

"Must be hard," Drea said.

"The kids are well-adjusted. My ex and I try our best to make sure of that. That's one reason I wrote the book. It's called *The See-Saw Effect of Parenting*."

She nodded. Brad had been destined to be a leader in his field. He was superintelligent, determined and, well, very handsome. Not that it had anything to do with anything, but she couldn't help noticing that about the man she'd singled out and seduced her first week of college, just to get back at Mason, just to prove that she was desirable. Mason's rejection that summer had her running into a stranger's arms, and lucky for her, Brad had turned out to be a decent guy. A guy who'd fallen for her, a guy who'd planned on marrying her to give their child security.

God, she'd been so confused, so scared and so damn naive.

The door chimed again and a few customers walked in and. Drea and Brad had to move over to continue the conversation. "Guess we're in the way," he said. "Do you have a few minutes...for an old friend? Just to catch up?"

She glanced at her watch. "I have a few minutes before my meeting." With Mason.

"Here?"

No, not here. Not where people might overhear their conversation. "There's a park just a few streets down. We could walk there. Did you want coffee? Or a cupcake?" she asked, figuring it was the reason he'd come.

"No, I'm good. How about you?"

She shook her head. "Katie's a friend and I've been tasting cupcakes all morning, so no. I'm definitely good."

"Well, then. Let's go." He opened the door for her and she walked out onto the busy sunny street. Donning her sunglasses, she waited for Brad. Once he caught up, after holding the door for a few more customers walking in, they headed south toward the park.

The tree-lined street looked so smalltown compared to New York, with its skyscrapers blocking the sun so that some streets were in shadow most of the time.

"How have you been?" he asked, keeping stride with her.

"I've been really good. This project is very special to me, since it'll fund a cardiac wing at the hospital in my hometown. I'm here for a few more weeks."

"Are you okay with me looking you up?"

"Sure. It's…good to see you, Brad."

"Same here. I, uh, think about you and what you've taken on here. Because of your mom?"

She stopped and stared into his blue eyes. "You remember?"

"Of course I remember, Drea. When we met, your mother's death and your helplessness over it were a big part of who you were. And now you're doing something to make a difference. I remember you'd always wanted that."

She looked away for a second, tears misting her eyes. She was touched that he remembered what made her tick, how vulnerable she'd been when they'd met. "You're right. It was."

When he smiled at her, her spirits lifted a bit. She hadn't been thrilled to bump into him, but now, after talking with him a few minutes, she began to relax.

When they reached the park, they took a seat on a bench facing the playground. A few toddlers were giving their moms a merry chase around the slide.

"How about you?" he asked. "Did you ever marry? Do you have a family?"

"No and no. I'm married to my job right now."

"I hear that." He didn't criticize her for not settling down, like so many others had. If a woman closing in on thirty wasn't married, well then, either there was something wrong with her or she was too ambitious for her own good.

They spent the next hour catching up on news, keeping the conversation light without mentioning the heartache they'd both endured. Brad seemed to hold no grudge toward her. Even though he'd been in love with her and would've married her, baby or not, she'd broken up with him after she'd miscarried. She'd made one mistake after another, but marrying Brad when she didn't love him would've been cruel.

Drea had learned a valuable lesson. Love is only right when it's two-sided and equal. There could be no imbalance.

Brad told her about himself, his years in med school and how he'd opened a pediatric practice in Manhattan and gotten married shortly after that. When she asked about his children, his face lit up and he spent a good deal of time on his little Meg and Charlie.

"I'll be in town until your fund-raiser," he said. "I plan on making a donation."

She smiled. "That's wonderful. We have lofty goals, so it will really be appreciated."

"Drea, do you mind if I ask you a personal question?"

Her heart stopped. *Oh no. Here it comes.* She braced herself. "What would you like to know?"

"Are you seeing anyone right now?"

That was totally unexpected. She fidgeted with her blouse,

her head down. So he wasn't going to dredge up the past, or excoriate her for breaking his heart. "No, not really." It wasn't as if she was dating Mason or anything. *Just sleeping with him.*

Brad's face broke out in a big smile. It was almost laughable how obvious he was. "Well then, I'd like to ask you to dinner one night."

Why? She wanted to know, but she held her tongue.

"As a friend," he added. "I'm staying close by and have the book signing in a few days, but I'd love to catch up more over a nice relaxing dinner."

She hadn't expected a dinner invitation. Sure, she could tell him she was too busy, but he was looking at her earnestly and what would it hurt? Maybe it would actually be therapeutic to spend time with him. How odd, but just being with him this past hour had helped relieve some of the remorse she felt over the whole situation.

"I think, maybe…" She tilted her head. "Yes."

"Great, I'll give you a call. Are you at the same number?"

"Let me give you my new one."

After they traded phone numbers, she stood up and he rose, too, though a bit reluctantly. "I really should get on with my errands," she said, excusing herself.

"Okay. Thanks for today," he replied, taking her hand in what was definitely not a shake but a touch of reconnection. "I should be going, too."

And that's when she realized…

Holy crap! She was late for her meeting with Mason.

Mason glanced at his watch for the third time as he paced up and down along the wraparound veranda at his house. He got out his phone, debating whether to text Drea. She was late, but only by fifteen minutes, and though he was anxious to see her again, to spend time with her, he didn't want to come off as… what? Pushy? Needy? Worried?

Because he was worried about her. She wasn't one to be late.

She was usually professional and prompt. He didn't know where it was coming from, but it gave him hives thinking something might've happened to her.

Risk stepped onto the porch, a beer in his hand. He lifted the bottle to his lips and took a swig before turning to Mason. "You're pacing? Bro, that's not like you. You must be waiting on someone." His brother had a penchant for stating the obvious.

Mason gave him a look.

Risk grinned. "You're waiting on Drea. Well, isn't that something."

"We have an appointment, about work."

"Right..." Risk smirked before taking another swig. "I wouldn't worry overly much, Mase. She's fine. When I was in town, I drove right past her. She was sitting on a park bench with some guy. The two looked pretty cozy, if you ask me. She probably lost track of time is all."

Mason eyed him. "Some guy? Who was he?"

"I have no idea. Never saw the man before. But he was all buttoned up in a suit and tie, and looked like he wasn't from around here. Just my observation."

Mason cleared his throat. "Okay, thanks."

Just then Mason's phone buzzed. It was an incoming text from Drea.

Sorry, my errands ran long. I'll be there soon.

Mason stared at the message a few seconds, relieved and curious.

"That her?" Risk asked.

"Yeah, she's running late."

Risk put a hand on his shoulder. "You care about her? And give me the truth, because lying to your brother is punishable by a swift kick in the ass."

"Like to see you try." It was an old joke between them. Risk had always stood his ground, no matter that Mason was older and stronger. But that was Risk, always snarky, always trying to defy the odds. He was the last one to give relationship advice. He went through women like a cat licking up bowls of sweet milk: quick and none too pretty.

"I'm serious," he said.

"Of course I care about Drea. She's Drew's daughter and I've known her most of my life. That's all there is to it."

"Okay, bro. Just thinking it would be pretty cool if you did. You've sorta been *not living* these past two years, you know what I mean?"

He knew. He just didn't like the idea that his whole family was worried about him. They didn't understand how grief had to work its way out of you, and there was no speeding the process. "Yeah, I do know."

And now, just the thought of Drea on her way to meet him sent a jolt of adrenaline speeding through his system. She'd been the only woman to break through the wall of his grief, and he would welcome that relief for the time she had left in Texas.

Thirty minutes later, Drea pulled up to the house and dashed up the steps. He was waiting on the porch for her, reading local news on his phone. It had been hard to focus, and as soon as he laid eyes on her, his body jerked to attention as if Drea had defibrillated him with paddles to his chest.

"So sorry I'm late," she said, her face flushed.

"It's okay. What happened?"

"I lost track of time running errands. I have a lot on my mind these days. I hope I didn't mess up your schedule for the day."

So she wasn't going to tell him about the guy. It was probably nothing, maybe a meeting with someone related to the project. And little did she know he'd cleared his schedule this afternoon to be with her. "Not at all. But I am hungry. How about you?"

"Yes."

"Okay, let's get going."

"Where?"

"You'll see."

Mason led her to his truck, opened the door for her and watched as she slid onto the seat. Her dress hiked up her thighs, giving him a clear view of her long tanned legs. Legs that had driven him insane wrapped around him last night.

When he was with Drea the world seemed right, but he was taking this one day at a time and living in the moment. Because it would end. It had to end. He was counting on it ending. That was the only way he could justify this brief interlude with her. He wasn't ready for anything permanent, anything that could go awry and scar him deeply. He hadn't healed from his first heartache. He didn't need another. Drea was leaving soon, and they would part ways. But for now, he wanted to spend as much time with her as he could.

A few minutes later, he parked the truck and helped Drea climb out. Holding her in his arms, he bent his head and kissed her lightly.

Her eyelids fluttered and he wanted more, but he held back, straining his willpower. "Close your eyes and come with me."

"What?"

He put his fingertip to her nose. "Just do it."

She closed her eyes, a big smile on her face. "I don't like surprises, just so you know."

"Trust me, you'll like this one."

He took her hand and guided her down a grassy pathway that led to the spot he'd picked out just for her. "Okay, open your eyes."

The sound of ducks quacking reached Drea's ears first, and then came a noisy flutter of wings. But when she popped her eyes open, the first thing she spotted was a café table dressed with a white tablecloth and two chairs set up on the bank of a small, secluded lake she'd never been to. A cut-crystal vase filled with pearl-white roses served as the centerpiece and wine was chilling in a bucket. The whole scene looked too good to be true.

A family of ducks glided across the water just at the right moment, as if it their swim was choreographed. She smiled at the sight they made. "Wow. What's going on?" She hadn't expected anything like this.

"Lunch."

"I know, silly." She turned to Mason, noting a gleam of satisfaction in his eyes. "But why?"

He shrugged, a myriad of emotions flowing through his expression. She didn't know if she'd get the truth out of him by the look on his face.

"You've been working hard. I thought you'd like a quiet lunch out here where it's open and peaceful."

"You went to a lot of trouble," she said, truly touched. Her heart warmed every time Mason did something nice for her like this. And to think she'd nearly canceled lunch with him today. But she knew she was treading dangerous ground. "Thank you."

He smiled. "You're welcome."

"Are we still on Boone land?" she asked, although she was pretty sure of the answer.

"Yep. This is Hidden Lake. I named it myself."

"You did? When?"

"Just now." He laughed and so did she. "Seems appropriate, doesn't it?"

"You have a knack," she said. "But I never knew this lake existed."

"It's been here the entire time, but through years of drought it had nearly dried up, the water level too low for it to be considered anything but a big puddle. We've had some good rainfall the past few years. And now Hidden Lake is once more."

"It's beautiful."

"Yeah, it's a nice spot." He held out a chair for her. "Ready?"

"I am." She took a seat and Mason served her one dish after another. The food was catered by Bountiful, the best restaurant in town.

She feasted on lemon chicken, shrimp risotto and roasted

vegetables. There were three kinds of bread and a nice bottle of white wine. She nibbled on her meal, enjoying the ambience, but the best thing of all about the scenery was the tall, handsome man in front of her.

Mason's gaze never strayed from hers. He chewed his food and looked at her. He sipped his wine and watched her sip hers. The conversation was light and fun, and he smiled a lot, which made her smile a lot, too.

Peace surrounded her and she squeezed her eyes closed, soaking it all in. It was truly what she'd needed today. "Thank you," she said. "I almost don't want to spoil this by talking about work."

"Work?" he asked.

"You said you needed advice. What was that all about?"

"I do need advice, but it's not about work."

She chewed on her lower lip a moment. "Then what is it about?"

"The beach house in Los Angeles. Missy has a potential buyer for it, but she wanted to give me the first option to purchase. I really don't know what I want to do."

"And you think I can help with your decision?"

He nodded. But she wasn't sure she wanted to be included in such a major decision in his life.

"You've seen it. What do you think?" he asked.

"I love it. I mean, what's not to love? But it's not up to me. Would you actually use it as a second home? It's definitely a big change from Boone Springs. Do you think you'd be comfortable there?"

Mason shrugged. "I was, when I was with you."

Oh... Her heart did a little flip at his unguarded reply. She'd had a great time while she'd been there, too, but she couldn't make a big deal about it. Mason was talking past history. He had to think about the future, and that didn't include her. "That was a one-time thing," she said softly.

Mason stared at her for several seconds and nodded slowly, conceding the point. "Yeah."

Then he rose from his seat. "Take a walk with me along the lake."

"That sounds nice," she said, rising in turn.

He took her hand and led her down to the lake's grassy edge. He pointed at the cute duck family still swimming nearby, and they laughed together as Mason took her into his arms. Her heart nearly stopped when he kissed her fully, thoroughly, as only he could do. "Meet me tonight, Drea. Be with me."

Drea murmured her agreement.

Because she just couldn't help herself.

Eight

Drea didn't know where the time had gone. There were only six days left before the big event. In the days since their lunch by Hidden Lake, she'd mostly been holed up with Mason, working. But when they weren't working, they were playing. Mason had retaught her the art of horseback riding and they'd gone riding several times on Rising Springs land. It *was* just like riding a bike. She'd never really forgotten. Once the reins were in her hands, it had all clicked again. She was thankful to him for making her take that first ride, and for the long walks, the meals they shared and especially for their secret nights at The Baron.

Tonight, she had dinner plans with her father. It would be just the two of them. As she walked up the steps of the cottage, she realized how full her life was right now. Family, friends and the attention of her fantasy man all put a smile on her face.

She no longer counted the days before she would return to New York and resume her life there. She was falling in love with Boone Springs again, something she thought would never happen. She questioned it every day, tried to find fault in her thought patterns, but that was just it. It wasn't so much what she was thinking, but more what she was feeling. And those emotions were getting stronger every day.

"Daddy, I'm home." She entered the house and found her father at the kitchen table, going through a big wooden box she'd never seen before.

"Hi, dear girl." He quickly closed the box and latched it.

"What do you have there?" she asked, more than mildly curious now that he'd seemed so secretive about it.

"Just some things from the past."

"Mom's things?"

He nodded and shrugged. "Yeah, there's some of your mama's stuff in here."

"Can I see?"

She sat down next to him, watching him carefully. Fear entered his eyes, followed by a look of resignation. Or was she mistaken? Maybe the box just held mementos. When her mother died, her father had given her keepsakes of her mom that she would always treasure, including a birthstone ring, her wedding ring, a favorite silver locket and a pair of diamond earrings.

"It's just some old stuff. I haven't gone through this box in a long time."

"Why now?"

"Maybe because you're here visiting." Her father opened it and revealed a treasure trove of clippings and old ticket stubs to concerts, movies and dances. "I saved all this. I don't know why."

"I do, Dad. It's a testament to your life with Mom. It's like your history together." She picked up a photo she'd never seen before, of a very young couple standing in front of a diner, obviously crazy about each other. "When's this from?"

"Oh, sweet girl. That's one of our first dates. I took your mama to some fancy restaurant and she took one look at the prices and said she'd rather have burgers and fries. Back then, I was working for my daddy and he was harder on me than on his crew. Said I had to work my way up the ladder if I wanted a piece of Thundering Hills one day, so money was tight and your mama, even then, had my back. She wasn't going to have me break the bank to impress her. I think I fell in love with her that night, Drea. She was something."

Tears welled in Drea's eyes. But she wasn't sad, not at all. She was truly amazed at the beautiful love the two of them had for each other. Clearly, her father had adored his Maria.

Drew shared several more memories with her and showed her a couple trinkets that made her smile. And then he brought out an unsealed envelope. He tapped it against his other hand a few times and turned to her. "Tell me, Drea," he said, his gravelly voice sharper than usual. "You and Mason are getting close, right? I see the way he looks at you."

What? Goodness, she wasn't prepared for a question like that. "Dad, we're working on the fund-raiser together. We both have a vested interest. And no, I could never get seriously involved with a Boone. You know why. I can never forgive them for what they did to our family."

"Drea, my brain hasn't gone to seed yet. I know you're going out at night. I'm assuming you're meeting with Mason. You're a grown woman and it's none of my business, but I got a reason to be asking."

She felt heat rising to her face; she was probably turning the shade of a ripe tomato. "Dad, you know?"

"I do now," he said without sarcasm.

"It's… Mason and I…we're just casual."

Her father's bushy brows rose. "Doesn't matter. I've been talking to Lottie and she thinks I've been doing you an injustice. Maybe I have. Maybe I was just making myself look better in your eyes by putting the blame on the Boones all these years. I'm sorry, Drea."

"For what, Dad? What are you talking about?" Her heart began to pound as dread overtook her. She'd never heard such remorse in her father's tone.

"All those years ago, after your mama died, I let the ranch go to ruin. I couldn't deal with the loss, the pressure and raising you. I was a terrible father, Drea. I know that, and I'm making amends now, by telling you the truth. I didn't go to the Boones for a loan like I told you. They didn't deny me. The fact is, I didn't ask them to help me save my ranch. I practically begged them to take it off my hands. I knew they'd give me a fair price. I made the deal with them, specifically stipulating that the money would go into a fund for your college education. I didn't trust myself with the money. I knew I'd drink it away. That's at least one good thing I did. I wanted to protect you, from myself."

Bile rose in her throat and she felt dizzy. "Dad…are you saying that they didn't steal Thundering Hills out from under you? Are you saying the Boones paid for my education?"

He ran a hand down his face. "Yeah, darlin' girl. That's the truth. It's all here in this personal agreement I made with Henry Boone."

Drea snatched the envelope out of his hands, opened it and took out the written agreement. She scanned the contents quickly, her eyes keying in on words that verified her father's claims until there was no doubt. "Oh my God. Why? Why didn't you just tell me the truth?"

"And admit yet another failure to my only daughter? I was a coward. It was easier to let the Boones take the blame. To let you think they'd robbed you of your birthright, when actually, I was guilty of that myself. It's eaten at me all these years. And now, Drea, I see you and Mason together, and if there's a chance for the two of you, well, I couldn't let that get in the way of your happiness. I couldn't bear it, not again. Lottie said it's about time."

"Lottie?" It was the second time he'd mentioned her. "So everyone knew the truth but me?"

Her father shook his head. "Not everyone. We kept the terms of the agreement private. Let people come to their own conclusions. But the Boone brothers know, yes."

"And you let me berate them, hate them, think the very worst of the people who actually saved your hide?"

"I'm sorry, Drea. Truly sorry."

"Sorry's not enough, Dad. Not nearly...enough."

Limbs shaking, tears spilling down her cheeks, she dashed out of the room. When she got to her bedroom, she slammed the door and then slumped against it, slowly sinking into a heap on the floor. She'd been betrayed and lied to one too many times. Everything she thought she knew about her life had just been whisked away. Was she overreacting? Maybe, but why did she always have to be the grownup? Why couldn't she be the kid, the one who needed tending, the one who needed comfort? She wanted to fall apart. She needed to. It was her right, something she'd been deprived of for too many years. She didn't care if this episode would send her father back to the bottle. She'd lived with that fear for too long.

This was her time to grieve and she wasn't holding back.

"Drea, please. I'm sorry," her father said from the other side of the door.

"Go away, Dad. Leave me alone."

It was a while before she heard him sigh heavily and walk away, his footfalls receding until there was no sound.

No sound but the deep, stabbing sobs racking her body.

It was after eleven when Mason got the text from Drea.

I need to see you tonight. Can we meet?

Mason was at home at Rising Springs, already in bed, going over the final details of the fund-raiser. It was hard to believe the event was coming up so quickly and he'd wanted to make sure he had everything covered. He didn't like leaving things to chance. That's what he and Drea had in common: they paid attention to details. She was having dinner with her dad tonight and they hadn't planned on seeing each other, so getting this text message from her this late surprised him.

What's going on? he typed.

Please, I need to see you.

At The Baron?

Yes, in thirty minutes?

I'll be there.

Mason wasn't going to pass up an opportunity to see Drea. The nights when they weren't together felt strange to him and he didn't much like analyzing why that was, especially after the conversation he'd had with Larissa's mother earlier in the day. She'd let him know she and Larissa's father were driving to town, coming all the way from Arizona, and they wanted to see him. He knew why. They were coming to lay flowers on Larissa's grave on the second anniversary of her death. Two years had gone by. Two. In one respect, the time had seemed to crawl by as he relived his wife's final days and the singeing loss he felt even before she'd taken her last breaths. But it also seemed as if the past two years had flown by. How could it be both? And how could he have lived two full years without Larissa by his side?

Now, as he headed to the hotel to meet Drea, he was conflicted and guilt-ridden. His in-laws were coming to town. They were coming to help him grieve, to honor their daughter's memory, to feel closer to her. But all he could think about was Drea.

Yet her ominous text message made him nervous. She'd never been cryptic before. She'd never initiated their meeting. So he pressed his foot down on the gas pedal and sped through the relatively empty roads leading to town. He made it in quick time and entered his suite before Drea got there.

He was just removing his jacket when he heard her knock.

He opened the door and she flew into his arms. He stood there stunned for a second, until her warm breath caressed his face and she planted a kiss on him that had him forgetting his first name. Hell, she didn't come up for air, just kept kissing him, tearing at the buttons of his shirt, splaying her soft palms on his skin, making him sizzle, making him want.

He slammed the door shut behind her. He didn't know where the hell this was coming from, but he wasn't about to question it. Or her. His body reacted, as it always did from Drea's touch, and he was immediately caught up in the urgency, the intensity. He tore away at her clothes, too, pulling her blouse out of her jeans, unbuttoning it between kisses. She removed her bra without his help and her beautiful breasts sprang free.

He was hard and ready. This aggressive, wild Drea was a big, big turn-on.

He held her long hair away from her chest and bent his head, moistening one rosy areola with his mouth, his tongue, causing the tip to perk up. She was gorgeous, too damn beautiful for his sanity. She whimpered, a cry of need that pierced his soul. She was on fire, hot and frenzied, and he wasn't far behind. He removed the rest of her clothes, then his. But when he stopped kissing her to lead her into the bedroom, she shook her head and kept him right there, as if even the slightest separation would be too much for her.

After pressing her against the door, he had just enough time to grab a condom and sheath himself before lifting her back into his arms. Instinctively, she wrapped her legs around his waist and her kisses became softer, slower, as if she were savoring him, as if she were committing this to memory. Her soft mewling nearly killed him. He was too far gone to play games. His need to join their bodies was intense, ferocious. He picked up the pace, taking charge now, kissing her thoroughly, nipping at her swollen lips, tasting her hot skin and trailing a path down her throat.

He positioned her over him, his hands cupping her butt, and then guided her down onto his shaft. She was warm and wet and the look of pure pleasure on her face was so damn perfect.

It was fast, fiery, frenzied and about the most incredible thing he'd ever done with a woman. When she cried out, her throaty sounds of pure bliss sent him over the edge.

He tightened his hold on her, feverishly moving, his body desperately seeking the ultimate prize. Then, making one deep, long, final thrust with his hips, he let out a groan of contentment that shattered him.

He was done.

Totally destroyed.

He held on to Drea and carried her to the bedroom.

That was when he got a good look at her face. Her pretty green eyes were rimmed with red.

She'd been crying.

Mason lay with Drea nestled in his arms, her head resting on his shoulder. He stroked her arm, absorbing the softness of her skin. She was quiet now, seemingly drained of energy. Why had she been crying? He had no clue. She'd come here like a woman on a mission, and it was only afterward that he took note of her distress. "Are you okay?" he asked quietly.

"No," she replied. "I'm not okay. I haven't been okay for a long time, Mason."

The sadness in her voice nearly broke him. "Why?"

She sighed deeply, her voice brittle. "I found out the truth about Thundering Hills tonight. My father told me...everything." She nibbled on her lip a moment and then continued. "At first I didn't believe it. My entire life I was led to believe one thing, only to learn that none of it was true."

She lifted her head from his chest and those sad, sad eyes touched something deep inside him. "I've misjudged you, Mason. I've been awful to you."

He rubbed her shoulder and smiled. "What are you talking about, sweetheart?"

"I hated and resented you for years."

"I know."

"Why didn't you tell me the truth? Why did you let me go on hating you? Why did you lie to me all those times? It wasn't fair, Mason. It wasn't fair to let me go on believing the worst about your family."

"It was the way your father wanted it. He made a pact with my dad to keep the terms of their agreement a secret. He must've had his reasons for keeping you in the dark. And as far as we're concerned, I always thought you'd figure out on your own that you didn't hate me."

She frowned. "Because you're so darn irresistible?"

"Because you're a smart woman and eventually you would see me for the man I really am."

"To think I've blamed your entire family, I've had terrible thoughts of them all this time. I thought you were all greedy and now I find that it wasn't anything but kindness and generosity. The Boones are responsible for me getting my college degree, for heaven's sake."

"Your father did right by you, Drea. At least in that way, he put your needs above his own."

"He didn't want me to see him as a complete failure. He told me so tonight, how he put the blame for our loss on the Boones. It wasn't right or fair of him and I let him know it. I was really hard on him tonight."

"Is that why you're so upset?"

"Yes, it's a lot to take in." She ran her hand down her face, then gently tapped her cheek. "Do I look terrible?"

"You look beautiful, Drea."

He sat up on the bed, drawing her with him, and wrapped his arms around her. "Did he say why he chose tonight to tell you?"

"It was your aunt Lottie. She told him it was time for me to know the truth. Gosh, I wish one of you would've told me before now. I'm feeling betrayed…by everyone. But I also think the two of them were conspiring about…"

"About?"

"About us… They think—no, my father knows I've been seeing you. He said he didn't want my feelings about the Boones to stand in our way."

"Our way?" Mason wasn't sure what she was getting at. She was leaving after this weekend. She had a life to go back to.

"I think he meant just in case we fall for each other," she said, so softly he could barely hear her.

Mason bit down, keeping his mouth clamped shut. Drea had to know going in he wasn't available. Not emotionally. Not in any way. Just the thought of a permanent relationship made him shudder. He wasn't ready for anything like that. He didn't know if he ever would be. The thought of loving someone again, and losing her, scared the hell out of him. Yes, if it was going to be any woman, he'd want it to be Drea. But he just couldn't…go there again. Call him a coward, but his head and his gut told him no, no, no.

"I mean," she said quietly, "we aren't falling for each other, are we?"

There was such hope in her voice, such tenderness, as if the answer could break her.

He shifted away from her on the bed. Here they were, stark naked after a blistering night of wild sex. He felt closer to Drea than any woman he'd met in the past two years. He liked her, admired her and cared deeply for her. Yet he didn't have an answer for her. He didn't know what to say. She'd already been hurt enough.

All he could do was speak the truth. He stared into the distance, keeping his back to her. "You're leaving in a few days, Drea."

He hoped like hell the words came off gentle, kind. It was a statement of fact. Not a yes, not a no. Well, maybe a no. He'd made it clear he wasn't committing to anything.

He turned to her finally and stared into her eyes, hoping to see understanding, a note of agreement. But all he saw was her attempt to mask pain.

It hurt like hell seeing the emotions pass over her face, one after another, as she tried to conceal what she was really feeling. At this moment, she didn't have to hate him; he was doing a pretty good job of hating himself.

"Right," she said quietly. "I… This has been great. But it's… nothing."

The *nothing* stung. She hadn't meant it to, she'd merely been searching for words, and he hated that he'd put her in that position.

She rose then and headed for the living room, where she'd left her clothes. "I'd better get home. It's very late and we have a big day tomorrow. Sean and the band are coming."

"Drea?" Mason got up and followed her. "Let me drive you home."

"Really, Mason. I have to go. Just know I don't h-hate you anymore."

With her clothes thrown on haphazardly, she picked up her bag, slung it over her shoulder and took her leave.

Last night, after learning the truth, Drea had finally been free to open her heart and let her emotions fly. Now what she felt for Mason was love. She *loved* him. She loved him so much the burn of his rejection seared her heart. After the last time he'd rejected her, she should've learned her lesson. She should have known it would never work out between the two of them. She'd been a fool, a silly fool for falling in love with a man who was still painfully in love with his dead wife.

He wasn't a bad man. He wasn't horrible. He was loyal and true blue. For some reason, she'd been the woman to wake his sexual senses after two years of hibernation. She'd made him come alive and sparked something in him he thought long dead. She would always have that. She'd gotten over Mason once before, and would just have to find a way to do it again.

While her heart bled for a love that would go nowhere, she had to forge on. She had a job to do and that meant dealing with Mason. Her wounds were raw and open, but this project was too important to her. She couldn't fall apart. She had to maintain, to keep up, appearances.

Drea poured tea into her mother's favorite hand-painted floral teapot and walked into the dining room to rejoin Lottie. She'd invited the older woman over after Drew left to visit a friend earlier this morning.

Drea's relationship with her father was still on rocky ground. She hadn't had a chance to speak to him yet, to clear the air and perhaps try to forgive him. She'd put that on the very long list of things she needed to do.

"Lottie, would you care for more tea?"

"Sure, thank you. It's delicious. I'm so glad you invited me over. We don't see enough of each other."

"I know. I'm sorry. I've been superbusy."

"Mason tells me you've been doing a fantastic job."

At the mention of Mason's name, she frowned. It was automatic, and she righted herself, but she didn't fool Lottie. Her eyes softened and she gave Drea a knowing look. "Something tells me this is more than a social visit. You need to talk to me, don't you, sweetheart?"

Drea nodded, sinking down in the chair. Tears welled in her eyes. "I do."

"Is it your dad or Mason?"

She smiled halfheartedly. "Both."

"What is it?"

"I need some direction, Lottie, and I need to tell someone the whole truth. I thought I could tell Mason last night when we were together. Instead we ended up...well, breaking up. Which is so dumb because you actually have to be a couple in order to break up. But we never were, not really."

"Oh, sweetheart...you love him."

She nodded. "I do. But he isn't over Larissa, and maybe he never will be."

Drea spent the next half hour pouring her heart out. She explained how she knew the truth about Thundering Hills now, and the Boones' part in all of it. She told Lottie how she'd fought with her father, unable to see the logic in what he'd done, the lies he'd told.

She told Lottie everything, from her infatuation with Mason and his abrupt rejection years ago to how she'd run into the arms of Brad Williamson, conceived a child with him and miscarried. Her scars were finally exposed, and it was brutal revealing all the secrets she'd held inside. All the pain and injury she'd suffered through the years.

Lottie held her hand through most of it, and wiped Drea's cheeks when tears flooded her face. "I've loved Mason, hated him, and now I'm so terribly out of my element I don't know what to do. Brad is a doctor now and he's here in Boone Springs for a short time. I've spoken to him. He's a really good guy. I hate that I hurt him. He was ready to marry me, and that would've been a big mistake. I didn't love him. So how can I fault Mason for not loving me, and easing out of our relationship, when I did the same thing to Brad?"

"You know what I think?" Lottie said. "My nephew has been living in the past for far too long. He's got to get over it."

Drea sucked in a sob to steady her breath. "No one can make him do that, Lottie."

"Don't be so sure about that." Lottie's voice took on a mischievous tone. "Will you be joining us for dinner tonight, sweetheart?"

"I have to be there," she said. She wouldn't let her queasy stomach stop her from doing her job. The Boones were hosting a dinner for The Band Blue. "It's the band's first night in town."

"Good."

Drea dabbed at her face with a napkin. She was too busy for any more crying jags. And shedding her burden to Lottie had been the best therapy. At least now someone knew the entire truth. At least Drea had someone to confide in.

Lottie finished her tea and rose. "Don't you worry about a thing."

Drea wished she had her confidence. Her life was a total mess. And perhaps most of it was her own fault. That's what stung the worst.

When Lottie put out her arms, Drea got up and flowed into them. Lottie was warm and soft and welcoming, all the things Drea's life had been missing. She closed her eyes and absorbed the comfort, missing her mother so very much, but grateful for this woman who had loved them both.

They hugged a good long time, and then Lottie spoke softly. "You're an amazing woman, Drea. I love you with all of my heart."

It was the best thing she could've said to her. "I love you too, Lottie."

Lottie pulled away and looked into Drea's eyes. "Thanks for the tea, sweetheart. I'll see you tonight."

"Yes, I'll be there." Suddenly Drea felt stronger, a bit more like herself. She had a job to do, and she'd focus on that for the next three days.

As Lottie exited the cottage, she heard noises coming from the back woodshed. In the past, when Drew had been up to it, he'd built things there. Of course, those days had been few and far between. Now, letting her curiosity get the better of her, Lottie went behind the house to investigate.

She found Drew at a worktable, his jacket slung over an old chair. He must've just been dropped off by his friend. She thought it odd that he hadn't come right into the cottage.

Then she saw him lift a bottle of Jack Daniels from the table, the amber liquid swishing around inside. She had only a moment to react. Only a moment to stop the foolish man from doing something he'd regret later on. "Drew, don't you dare take a swig of that bottle."

He jumped and turned around quickly, still clutching the bottle in his hand. "Geesh, woman. You nearly scared me half to death. What are you—" Then he blinked and his eyes darkened as her words finally sank in. He looked from her to the bottle. Then back at her again.

His shoulders slumped and his eyes hardened. "Why in hell would I take a swig of shellac, Lottie Sue Brown?"

Lottie took a better look at the bottle. It said Jack Daniels on the label, but there was a thin strip of masking tape around the center spelling out SHELLAC. "I, uh, it's just that I know you and Drea had some issues to deal with and I, uh…couldn't see too well with the morning shadows and all."

"You think a spat with my daughter would've turned me to drink again?" His voice was quiet. "You have no faith in me, Lottie. None at all, and that's not about to change, is it? Don't answer. I won't believe anything you say right now. You want to know what I'm doing with this bottle, which I borrowed, by the way, from my friend Rusty? I'm trying to shine up Drea's softball trophies to give to her. I never made it to many of the games back then, and these things mean a lot to me now. I'm always looking for ways to make amends with my daughter."

Lottie had stepped in it now. She'd been quite effectively told off. Oh boy, she'd let preconceived notions about Drew influence her judgment. If only she'd kept her trap shut. If only she'd had more faith in him. He'd been trying to prove to her he was a changed man, but now she feared she'd destroyed any trust they had between them. "Oh, Drew. Forgive me. I'm sorry, very sorry."

He turned away from her. "Lottie, just let me get back to this."

"But Drew—"

"Go, Lottie. You've said enough this morning."

And suddenly, her heart ached and her stomach burned. Had one incident of mistrust ruined things with him forever?

Nine

Drea straightened her snow-white, curve-hugging dress and knocked on the front door of the Boone mansion. She was flying solo tonight, her father opting to stay home. They'd had a good long talk this afternoon and had agreed to put the past behind them. She could forgive him for past mistakes, but it would be a long time before she would truly be over it. She loved her dad and he loved her. All they could do was go from there.

She wore red high heel pumps and the silver jewelry she loved so much. The Boones' housekeeper, Jessica, opened the door and greeted her. It appeared the entire staff was on call tonight. Drea had no idea of the scope of the dinner, but apparently the Boones had invited more than family. The sheriff of Boone County and several hospital administrators were in attendance, as well as the mayor. Mason's cousins, Rafe, Nash and Cord, were also in attendance. They were part-time cattle ranchers, among other things, and obviously big country and western fans. So of course they were invited to meet the band.

"Drea, you look drop-dead gorgeous," Risk said, being the

first to grab her hand and lead her into the fray. The house was hopping with laughter and music.

"Thank you. Are Sean and the band here yet?"

"Yep, they're out back. Come with me." Risk kept a tight hold of her hand as he led her to the poolside area. It was quieter out here and cooler.

"Wow, this is quite a welcome for the band."

She shivered a bit and Risk took note. "You need a drink to warm you up."

"I won't refuse. Just one."

They wandered over to a bar set up under a pillared deck. "What'll it be?"

"White wine, please."

Risk shook his head. "Make that two whiskey sours," he told the bartender.

"Risk!" She laughed, finally able to let loose with the Boones, finally able to see them for the good men they were. "Why'd you bother to ask me?"

He shrugged. "White wine won't warm you up, sweetheart. Take it from me. You need something stronger."

"I do, do I? And why is that?"

He was charming and quite a player.

"Baby, that dress you're wearing exposes more skin than it covers. Don't get me wrong, I'm digging it, and I would offer to keep you snuggled tight tonight, but I think my brother would have me hung from the highest rafter."

She tilted her head and stared at him. Risk handed her the drink, and took his own as he pointed toward Mason, who was standing alone by the side of the house, watching her. She shivered again and glanced away. She couldn't give in to Mason's penetrating stares. He'd made up his mind and that was that.

"What's going on between you two?" Risk asked.

"As of tonight, not a thing," she answered, drinking deep from her glass.

"Well, in that case," he said, bending his head and kissing her cheek, "do I get a chance at keeping you warm tonight?"

She smiled at him. "I think the drink you fixed me up with is doing the job."

"Damn. Should've gotten you the white wine, after all," he replied, and both of them laughed.

After finishing her drink, she walked over to a group conversing with the band. Sean spotted her and broke away from the others. "Hey, Drea. Good to see you."

"Sean, it's good to see you, too."

He hugged her, a shy kind of hug that tickled her to death. She gave him a hug back.

"This is great. The Boones sure know how to do it up, don't they?"

"Yes, they sure do. I take it you got in okay today? All set up in your hotel?"

"Yep, the hotel is really cool. Alan has no complaints and we're all happy to be doing this gig."

"I'm happy, too. Listen, about the Dream Date event, we have it all set. Do you have any questions or concerns? I hope you'll let me know, since I was the one who kinda got you involved with it."

"Nope. I have no concerns."

"That's fantastic."

Mason approached, eyeing her before greeting Sean. It was *Business with Mason* all over again. It didn't matter that he looked fine, in a form-fitting charcoal suit with no tie, or that his hair was just as she liked it, brushed back with the very tips curling up at the collar. She could do this. She could. She entered into the conversation, smiling, and enjoyed getting to know Sean a little better.

A few minutes later, Sean was pulled away and she was left standing with Mason. "I think everything is ready for the big day," she said brightly. "I'm confident that, as long as the weather holds, we'll be able to pull it off."

Mason eyes were dark and serious, and when he opened his mouth to speak she shook her head immediately. If it wasn't going to be work talk, she wanted no part of it. "Don't, Mason. There's nothing more to say."

Lottie approached then, looking dazzling in a blue floral chiffon dress, on the arm of… Brad Williamson. Drea was too stunned to utter a word. Brad was smiling at her, looking a little sheepish, as well.

"Hello, you two," Lottie said. "Mason, I'd like you to meet Dr. Brad Williamson. Brad's visiting here from the East Coast. He's a dear friend of Drea's and so I thought it fitting that he join us tonight. They've known each other since college, right, Drea?"

She nodded. "Yes, that's right." Wasn't it just a few hours ago she'd been pouring out her heart to Lottie about Brad, Mason, her father? Goodness, Lottie didn't let up.

While the two men shook hands, Lottie's eyes met hers.

"Nice to meet you," Brad said to Mason. "Drea's told me all about the fund-raiser. I'm on board. It's an important thing you're doing."

"Thank you. We think so, too," Mason said. Then he clamped his mouth shut, glancing at her with a question in his eyes.

"Lottie, may I have a word with you?" Drea didn't know what exactly Lottie had hoped would happen by inviting Brad to the dinner party.

"Oh, uh, I can't right now. Chef needs me in the kitchen. You three have a nice talk and I'll see you all later."

An awkward moment passed. Mason remained tight-lipped.

"Brad, how did you meet Lottie?" Drea asked. It was the question of the day.

Brad looked handsome tonight, dressed in a casual gray suit. His eyes were mesmerizing, almost a transparent blue. "Well, we met at the local bookstore. I was signing copies of my book and we got to talking about the fund-raiser. So when she found out I was a country fan and that I knew you, she invited me.

I'm sorry I didn't run it by you first. You're okay with this, aren't you? Since we never did get to have dinner together, I was hoping—"

"It's perfectly fine, Brad. I'm glad you're here."

"Then I'm glad I am, too." He smiled. "You look...*amazing*."

She didn't dare glance at Mason, but she sensed him stiffening up. "Thank you."

Drea's nerves were shot. She was standing between the two men who'd had a major impact in her life and she had no idea what was going on in either of their minds.

Lucky for her, one of the hospital administrators joined the conversation and she was able to slip away leaving the men behind. She walked out the front door and kept on walking. She was on the path to her father's house, her mind all mixed up. She wasn't sure where she belonged. Or whom she belonged with. It was dark and the path she traveled was lit only by moonlight, so when she heard footsteps behind her, she sucked in a breath and turned around. "What are you doing here?" she asked, seeing it was Mason.

"Walking you home," he said casually, as if he hadn't just broken her heart last night. As if he had a right to walk her anywhere.

"Not necessary. I'm capable of seeing myself home."

"You left early."

"Go away, Mason." She turned her back on him and resumed walking.

He caught up with her. "Why'd you leave?"

"Maybe because you didn't." Oh, that was cruel. She was better than that. She didn't want to lash out at him. She just wanted some peace.

"Who is he to you?"

So that was it. His ego was bruised. "A friend."

"Not just a friend. I get the feeling it's more than that."

"It's none of your business, Mason."

"I say it is."

She stopped and shook her head, looking into his troubled eyes. It hurt to still feel something for him, to care that he was as frustrated as she was. "You can't have it both ways."

He looked puzzled. "Is that what I'm doing?"

"I have no idea what you're doing. It doesn't matter anymore. Once the fund-raiser is over, I'll be leaving, as you already mentioned."

She pivoted and continued walking. She'd gotten as far as three steps when he looped his arm around her waist, stopping her. He stood behind her, his body inches from hers, his breath at the nape of her neck, and for a minute she allowed herself to remember him, his touch, his kiss, the way he could make her feel unglued, yet whole at the same time. It wasn't to be. She had to accept it. She untangled herself from his grasp and turned to stare at him.

His arms dropped to his sides, a defeated look on his face. "Drea."

"I know you still love Larissa. I know you can't commit, so why don't we just move on and not torture ourselves this way?"

"Are you moving on with the doctor?"

She rolled her eyes. Then a fissure of anger opened up quickly becoming one giant sinkhole of incensed emotion. "No. I'm not, but not because Brad isn't wonderful. I just can't get involved with him again. I did that last time after you scarred me with your brutal rejection. I ran into the arms of the first man who'd have me. It was Brad. I shamelessly seduced him the first week of college and gave him my virginity. I gave him what I'd wanted to give you. I gave him my body, because you didn't want me and because I'd been unwanted since my mother died. And weeks later, when I turned up pregnant, the clichéd virgin too stupid to use protection, Brad was there for me. He loved me and offered to marry me."

Mason's throat was working, as though he was taking a big gulp. He stood there in stony silence.

"I almost went through with it, almost married him. But then

I lost the baby, Mason. I lost my child and I was devastated. I broke up with Brad. I couldn't marry a man I didn't love. I hurt him badly, when all he wanted to do was take care of me. But you see, I couldn't love Brad. Not when I was still in love with you."

"Drea, I didn't know. I'm sorry." And she believed he was truly sorry—the emotion in his eyes was inescapable. "I never wanted to hurt you. Ever. You have to believe that."

Mason reached for her. Trembling, she moved out of his grasp, her heart breaking again. Yet it felt good to finally get the truth out, to lighten her heavy load.

"I loved you, even though I hated you, too. It doesn't make any sense, but it's true. I've never stopped loving you, Mason Boone. And all I want from you now is to leave me alone. Please. Let's get through the weekend, do our jobs, honor the people we've loved the most and then be done with it. Can you do that for me, Mason? Can you leave me alone?"

Mason's eyes grew wide; she could almost swear he was tearing up. His expression was raw, full of sympathy.

He reached out for her again and once again she backed away. She didn't want to be his friend. She didn't want to see him after this weekend. It was too hard.

"Please."

Mason finally relented, giving the smallest nod of agreement.

This time when Drea walked away, he didn't follow.

But she knew that Mason was probably still standing there, unable to move. Unable to register all that she'd confessed. She'd shocked him and worried him and made him ache with the pain he'd put her through. He probably thought she hated him again.

But that wasn't true.

She couldn't hate him.

She would probably go to her grave loving him.

Mason woke with an intense headache. He'd drunk half a bottle of bourbon last night, but even with all that mind-numbing alcohol, he couldn't forget the pain on Drea's face, the words spoken straight from her heart. He couldn't believe what she'd gone through at seventeen years of age. He'd been responsible for that. He knew that now. He thought he'd been doing right by her by turning her away, but the honest truth was he should've never let his fascination with the olive-skinned beauty mar his judgment. He'd known she was a mixed-up kid, missing her mother, having to deal with an alcoholic father. If Mason hadn't gotten involved with her in the first place, none of it would've happened.

He pushed his hand through his hair. Just thinking about how alone Drea must've felt when she'd learned of her pregnancy, how scared she must've been, filled him with guilt. And then to lose her child…well, he knew something about that. The pain never really went away. It lingered under the surface and every time you saw a child on the street, whether laughing or crying, happy or sad, you wondered. What would your child be like had he or she lived?

It deadened a part of you and you hurt quietly, without anyone ever knowing.

A sudden knock at his door sounded more like a fire alarm going off. "What?"

"It's Aunt Lottie, Mason. Are you all right? We thought you'd be down by now."

"Who's we?" he asked, trying to sort through the cobwebs in his head.

"Larissa's parents are here."

"Holy hell." He jolted up from the bed. What time was it?

Within ten minutes, he was showered and dressed, his head still hurting like a son of a bitch as he walked into the parlor to greet his in-laws. He was in a fog, but there was one thing he was crystal-clear about this morning.

Drea had said she loved him.

And he couldn't get that out of his head.

"Paul and Wendy, good to see you." Mason shook hands with

Paul Landon and then gave Wendy an embrace. She was a petite woman, much smaller than Larissa had been, but her hug was fierce and affectionate. He hugged her back with equal intensity. They'd all been through hell, and that tended to bring people closer.

They drank coffee and ate pastries, catching up on news. The Landons would stay in town for the all-important fund-raiser, which started tonight with the HeART auction.

Mason had a thousand things to oversee today, but this morning was reserved for Larissa and her parents. The time had finally come for him to drive them all to the site of Larissa's grave.

Mason visited monthly, taking a bouquet of flowers for his wife and unborn child. He grieved silently, and today, on the anniversary of Larissa's death, he'd grieve along with her parents.

They paid their respects on grounds that were impeccably groomed. It was a serene resting place. There were wrought-iron-and-wood benches under old mesquite trees; bold, beautiful statues; water stations and two chapels on the property. Mason had donated the benches; Larissa's name was engraved on the one closest to her grave.

They all stood together, laying down flowers, saying prayers, and then he walked away to give the Landons a bit of privacy.

A short time later, he felt a hand on his arm and turned to find Wendy's soft, caring eyes on him. "Mason, this is a hard day for you."

He nodded. "For you, too."

"Yes, it is. But what you're doing this weekend is a good thing. It's something that will make a difference. Paul and I feel that it takes some of the pain away. I think it's time to move forward, hard as it is. Building a cardiac wing at the hospital is a great testament to Larissa's memory. And to so many others. We can't look back anymore, Mason. We have to look ahead."

He nodded, though he felt pulled in two directions. He'd

clung to his grief for so long, he almost didn't know himself without it.

"You should give yourself a break. You've mourned a long time. Maybe it's time to start a new life," she said. "Guilt-free. You deserve that, Mason. No one has honored a love more than you have."

"Thank you, Wendy."

She slipped an envelope into his hand. He thought it was a donation for the fund-raiser until he recognized the handwriting as Larissa's. "What's this?"

"I don't know. It's sealed. But when Larissa was sick she gave it to me, trusting me to give it to you. She said specifically to give it to you in two years."

Two years? "You've had it all this time."

She nodded. "It was her wish."

"Okay, thank you," he said, not knowing what to make of it. But he wouldn't open the letter now. No, he needed privacy...and *courage*. It had taken him an entire year before he could dream about her at night without breaking down, eighteen months before he could watch videos of the two of them together. But to read words written by her when she'd been alive... That would require something he didn't know he had. Just holding the letter in his hand unsettled him. He slipped it into his jacket pocket.

Wendy seemed to understand his need to read it alone, to keep this last moment between them private.

An hour later, with the Landons promising to return this evening for the auction, Mason climbed the steps of his home. But he turned when he heard Drea's sweet laughter. She was walking with Sean Manfred, and they were obviously enjoying each other's company.

After the way they'd left off last night, he didn't think she'd want to see him. But the sound of her voice beckoned him and he turned and walked toward them.

"Hey, Mason." Sean's tone was friendly. "We were just going

over the plans for the concert and dance tomorrow. The stage looks great. Drea's got everything under control."

"She always does," Mason said, meaning it.

Drea didn't hesitate to smile, and that smile reached down deep and battered the heck out of him. Apparently, she was still the grown-up of the two of them, forging ahead for the sake of the event.

"Thank you. I think we're all set for the art auction tonight. The tent is up and the committee is busting their buns to have everything in place. The art has all come in, and it's impressive."

"Can't wait to see it," Mason told Drea.

"It's just a precursor to tomorrow. That's our big, big day," she stated, more to Sean than to him. "We have a dozen wheels turning, and hopefully, there will be no glitches. I'm happy to say the tickets for both the Fun Day and the Dinner-Dance and Dream Date are sold out. Thanks to you, Sean. I think all the high school girls in three counties bought up every raffle ticket."

"Somebody save me," he joked, his eyes wide.

"Not to fear, your date will be chaperoned."

"By you?" he asked in a hopeful tone of voice.

"No, sorry. I'll be gone by then. But I promise you'll have a good time."

"Are you leaving right after the event?" Sean asked. Mason wanted to know, too.

"My flight leaves on Sunday night."

Mason's throat tightened up. His chest hurt like hell.

"Hey, Drea, can I have a word with you?" It was Brad Williamson. He'd walked up from the festival area, his eyes only on Drea. Mason clenched his teeth. Sure, he'd tied one on last night, but his sour stomach had nothing to do with bourbon right now. Why wouldn't wonderful Brad Williamson, the guy who'd loved Drea and probably still did, get lost?

"Hi, Brad," Drea said. "I didn't expect to see you until tonight."

He scratched his head, looking too conveniently perplexed.

"Lottie had a good idea, something that would help the cause, and I wanted to run it by you."

"What is it?"

"I could give away free signed copies of my book during the festival tomorrow, if you can squeeze me in at the last minute. I have author copies I'd like to donate."

Drea's face lit up. "That's a great idea. Excuse us a minute," she said, looking at Sean.

She walked off with Brad, practically rubbing shoulders with the guy.

Sean watched her go. "She's really amazing," he said to Mason. The kid had a bad case of hero worship.

Mason nodded. "Yeah."

"Are you two…a couple?"

Mason looked at Sean. "No, we're not a couple. Why do you ask?"

He shrugged. "Back in LA, I thought you were. You seemed kinda flawless together."

Flawless… That word struck him. They *had* been flawless together, two parts of a whole. But that was back at the beach, when everything seemed surreal.

"We just work well together." Mason said, feeling the lie down to his snakeskin boots.

"Yeah… I guess," Sean said.

He wasn't sure the kid believed him.

He wasn't sure of anything anymore.

Ten

Standing inside Katie's Kupcakes' decorating booth, Drea nibbled at the raspberry cream cheese frosting, then took a giant bite of Katie's signature cupcake. "Mmm, this is the best, my friend." She licked frosting off her finger and dabbed at her mouth with a napkin. "You have outdone yourself."

Katie shook her head, her eyes bright. "You're the one who's outdone herself. Look around. This was your brainchild. Whatever money is raised, you're the one behind it."

"I had help. The volunteers have really come through," she said, thinking about Mason and how on board he'd been from the get-go. He'd been instrumental in donating his property, his time and his support to get this project off the ground in a month.

She was putting on a good show for everyone, hoping to keep the spirit of the event alive, while inside, her heart was broken. Totally, sadly broken. Tomorrow afternoon would be here before she knew it and she'd be leaving behind people she loved. Her father, her friends and… Mason. Her pain was very real, very frustrating.

The festival was in full swing and she was thankful to see the vendors' booths crowded with paying customers. Almost all the businesses in town had either made donations or offered to sell their goods at no cost to raise money for the cause. Children were taking pony rides, food and beverages were being sold, and pretty soon Katie would be swamped with young cupcake makers.

Last night's auction had been successful. Every item had been purchased. Drea wouldn't know the final weekend tally for some time, but all in all, things were going smoothly.

Her father walked up and kissed her cheek, wrapping his arm around her waist. "Hi, sweetheart," he said.

"Hi, Daddy. Glad you made it out today."

"You're looking good, Mr. M," Katie said. "Want a cupcake?"

"Ah, thank you, Katie. But actually, I came to see if I can help you girls today."

Katie glanced at Drea and then back at him. "Sure. I could use a hand in here. Gonna need to keep the cupcakes and frosting flowing when the booth opens for decorating."

"Glad to help," he said.

Drea and her father had come to terms with the past, and ever since then, their relationship had flourished. He was back to being her dad, the man she'd known before her mother died, the man who was a loving father and sound businessman. She'd have days and days in New York to get over it, but now was a time for healing between them. She wanted to leave on a good note.

She glanced across the field to where Brad was setting up his booth. Luckily, they'd had extra room for him. "If you two have it covered, I need to check on something."

Katie gave her a nod. "Go. Your dad and I will handle the kids."

"Thanks. I won't be long."

Drea walked through the crowds of people having a great time. When she arrived at Brad's booth, she said hello.

"Hi, yourself, pretty lady. This festival is really something."

"It is. Thanks. And thanks for donating your time and books. There are a lot of families here, and I'm sure many parents are in need of advice about their toddlers."

"Uh, Drea? May I have a word with you?"

"Of course," she said, curious about what Brad wanted to discuss.

He took her hand and walked her to the back of the booth. "I know you're leaving tomorrow, and I'll be back in New York in a month. I was wondering if you…and me. Well, if I can call you sometime."

Drea paused, trying to hide her indecision, and not doing a very good job, judging by the wary expression on Brad's face.

"We've been through a lot together, Drea. I know there's painful history between us, but I care very much about you. I never stopped."

If he had anything but friendship in mind, she'd have to come clean. She didn't want to use Brad, to run to him just because things got rough and lonely when she got back home. And she didn't want to hurt him again.

"I know you do. And I care very much about you," she said, as sincerely as she knew how. "But the truth is, I'm in love with someone."

Brad let a beat go by. "It's Mason, isn't it?"

She gave him a long look and nodded. "Is it that obvious?"

Brad smiled. "Ever since you walked over here, Mason's had his eyes on you. He's like a hawk, that guy. And I think he'd like to kill me where I stand for talking to you."

She rolled her eyes. "Please."

They laughed, but when she turned around she found Mason's deep, smoky eyes on her, and her heart skittered to a halt. He was leaning against a tree, his hat tipped low, cowboy-style, his jeans and black boots dusty. He'd been helping out with the ponies making sure the riders were safely on their mounts.

It wasn't fair that he had the ability to turn her life upside down like this. Their eyes connected for a moment and it was as if his heat traveled across the twenty feet of space between them. He was all she saw through the crowd and her insides immediately warmed up.

She dropped her head and sighed. "It's impossible." Then she brushed a chaste kiss on Brad's cheek. "I'd better go. Good luck today. I'll be sure to talk to you later."

Drea walked away, getting as far from Mason as possible, heading toward the Boone kitchen, where the caterers were prepping for tonight's dinner and dance.

Hours later, the sun set in a brilliant orange blaze. All the festival goers who'd filled up on fun, cupcakes, rides and games, were gone. On another part of the grounds, a stage was ready for The Band Blue. Fifty round tables with elegant white tablecloths and short pillar candles surrounded the parquet dance floor.

People were arriving for the dinner and concert. Women were dressed in classic Western wear, jean skirts and leather boots or elegant gowns or somewhere in between. Drea, being the co-master of ceremonies had put her best foot forward, treating herself to a form-fitting gold gown. Shimmering sequins covered the crisscross back straps. Her hair was held away from her face with two rhinestone clips, allowing it to flow softly down her back.

Mason walked up behind her, putting a hand on her shoulder. "Are you ready for this?"

She glanced at him, felt his familiar mind-numbing touch, and for a moment her breath stuck in her throat. He wore his suit well, a dark three-piece with a gold brocade vest. In another lifetime she would've grabbed him by his bolo tie and dragged him behind the stage to have her way with him.

What a dream that would be. "I think so."

He leaned in close and whispered, "You look like a goddess."

"Th-thank you." She absorbed the compliment and they stood

there together, in the background, watching the donors taking their seats.

When everything was in place, Mason took her hand. "Let's do this," he said.

They walked up on the stage together. Mason gave her the floor first. She went to the podium and spoke from the heart, thanking everyone for coming, thanking all the volunteers and thanking The Band Blue for donating their time. "This is a project near and dear to so many of us, but as you know, both my family and the Boones have lost someone to heart disease. We hope, with all of your generous donations, we will make our ambitious goal of raising two million dollars for the cardiac wing. I hear we've come close, as donations have been pouring in from citizens who couldn't attend the festivities this weekend." Drea put her fist over her heart, tears welling in her eyes. "This means so much to me, personally. Thank you all."

She turned to find Mason's eyes on her, filled with pride. There was a moment between them, something sacred, something that went beyond their personal relationship issues, something that connected them. Nothing could ever take that away. "And now Mason Boone will say a few words."

As he sidled up to the podium she began to walk away, but he discreetly curled his hand around her waist, drawing her close. They stood beside each other, and Mason took over the microphone. "Once again let me thank everyone who helped put this fund-raiser together. All of you have done a great job and we can't thank you enough. I have to give most of the credit to the woman standing beside me, Andrea MacDonald. She has been absolutely dedicated to the cause.

"Our goal was to break ground on the new wing in two years, but the Boone family hopes to make that a reality even sooner. To that end, our family is pledging an additional one million dollars to the cause."

Applause broke out. Drea opened her mouth to speak, but words wouldn't come. She stared at Mason as he continued.

"The only stipulation I have is to be able to name the new cardiac wing. It will be called the Maria MacDonald Heart Center."

He turned to Drea then, his dark eyes full of emotion, and she'd never loved him more.

"Th-thank you," she mouthed, still unable to speak aloud.

"And there'll be a garden on the grounds named for my late wife. It'll be called Larissa's Blooms."

Mason paused a second, struggling a bit. Then he went on. "Miss MacDonald and I hope you have a wonderful evening, starting off with a concert from Grammy nominees The Band Blue. Feel free to come up onto the dance floor and swing your partner around. Oh, and after dinner, be warned, we'll be raffling off a Dream Date with Sean Manfred. You girls on the back lawn there will just have to be patient."

There were hundreds of girls sitting beyond the tables, under the twinkling lights strung from the trees. Their raffle tickets had also admitted them to the concert.

Drea and Mason walked off the stage just as the band stepped up to take their places.

Her mind swirling, she heard Sean give the guests a warm welcome. But just as she turned to speak to Mason about his generosity, a local news reporter with a film crew nabbed him.

"Mr. Boone, do you have time for that interview now?"

Mason sighed. "Sure thing. Give me one second, okay?"

Of course they'd want to speak with Mason. After his announcement and personal donation to the cause, he was newsworthy.

He looked into her eyes. "Save some time for me later. Maybe a dance?"

She didn't want to dance with him. She didn't want to suffer any more than necessary. Her scars were too raw right now. Mason had impacted her life in too many ways to name, and she would never forget him. But the sad fact remained, that he'd had many opportunities this month to sort out his feelings for her. To allow himself a fresh start and get over his guilt and pain.

To allow someone else in. He, too, was scarred. He, too, had endured great loss. And it was extremely hard for him. It was hard for her, as well, but at least she was willing to take the chance.

It was obvious he wasn't.

"I…c-can't, Mason. I'll always remember you and this." She spread her arms out to encompass the festival. "We did a wonderful thing here. And…well, naming the wing in my mother's honor was…"

Once again stung by his generosity, she felt her eyes begin to burn. She didn't want to cry in front of him. "Thank you." It was all she could say. "You'd better get on with that interview."

She turned away from him then and headed for her dad who was standing off to one side looking a bit overwhelmed and misty-eyed after the announcement honoring her mother Maria. He needed her as much as she needed him right now.

Her heartache aside, she and Mason pulled this weekend off, and with the Boone's charitable donation, they may have far exceeded their goals. She had to feel good about that.

Evening turned into night as the band played, wowing the guests. Dinner was served when the band took their first break, and then as they began to play their second set, Sean encouraged everyone to get up on the dance floor.

Drea found Lottie sitting at the Boone table off to the side, and took a seat next to her. Lottie gave her a big hug. "Drea, this has been a fantastic evening. I'm so proud of what you have accomplished."

"Thanks. I'm really thrilled with the outcome."

"Thrilled?" Lottie's eyes narrowed a bit and she took both Drea's hands in hers. "I don't see thrill on your face, sweetheart. I see sadness and regret."

"I'm leaving tomorrow afternoon. I didn't think I'd say this, but I'm going to miss Boone Springs. And my dad."

Lottie stiffened at the mention of Drew. "I understand. This place is your true home, Drea. You've got roots here. And friends."

"I do. I promised Dad I'll come visit often. We're doing pretty well now and I've forgiven him for what he did. But Lottie, what's up between the two of you? I've noticed you haven't spent a minute together this entire weekend."

"Oh, um..." Lottie shook her head and glanced away. "I'm afraid he's very angry with me. He's been avoiding me for days. You know us. We've always had a rocky relationship."

"Yes, but... I thought this time things were different."

They were interrupted by the sound of Mason's voice coming from the microphone onstage. "And now it's time to announce the winner of the Dream Date with Sean raffle. To do the honors, our own publicity pro, Linda Sullivan, will come up here and pull the winning ticket. As you know, Linda was instrumental in putting this part of the event together."

When Linda reached the stage, Mason turned the mic over to her. She made a few jokes about the girls languishing on the back lawn, waiting for this moment. Then she had Sean come up to a big Plexiglass cube filled with raffle tickets. "It's only fitting that Sean pick the winner. Don't you think so, girls?"

Shouts and giddy laughter broke out as Linda gestured for Sean to dig deep into the cube and grab a ticket. Everyone at the tables and on the lawn quieted.

"And the dream date with Sean goes to... Regina Clayborne!"

Lofty sighs of disappointment filled the back lawn, except for where the winner was standing, surrounded by her friends. She began jumping for joy, her blond hair bouncing in the breeze. Linda brought her up onstage to meet Sean and the girl couldn't stop crying happy tears.

"Well, I guess my part is officially over," Drea said to Lottie. "I think the committee can finish up tomorrow."

"What are your plans then?"

"I want to spend the entire morning with my father. My flight leaves in the late afternoon."

Lottie folded her arms around her middle, looking none too pleased. "And here I was hoping that you and Mason would have worked it out by now."

"I can't fight a ghost, Lottie. I can't make Mason feel things he doesn't."

"You're hurting."

"Love hurts sometimes."

Lottie's eyes glistened with moisture. "Yeah, sweetheart, sometimes it does."

As the guests filed out of the concert area and the band packed up to go back to their hotel, Mason walked over to the Boone family table and found Lottie sitting with Risk and Lucas.

"Well done, brother," Risk said.

Luke nodded in agreement.

"Thanks, guys." Mason should be flying high. After this past month of hard work, their fund-raiser had achieved its goals. The new cardiac wing of the hospital was destined to break ground, but one important thing was missing. Or one person, rather. "Didn't I see Drea sitting here a few minutes ago?"

"You did," Luke said. "But she's gone now. I grabbed a dance with her earlier this evening."

"Yeah. Me, too," Risk said. "She's pretty light on her feet."

Mason gave his brothers a good-natured frown. They liked busting his chops. "So where did she go?"

"Home, I think," Lottie said.

Mason swallowed hard. "Already?"

"She said she was tired and had some packing to do."

Risk sipped from his glass of wine. "She promised to come back to Boone Springs soon, though. I made a date to take her to dinner."

"Yeah. Me, too," Lucas added.

"All right, boys," Aunt Lottie said to Mason's pain-in-the-ass brothers. "You've made your point. Let me have a chat with Mason."

The guys got up, and both gave him a conciliatory pat on the back before walking off.

"Mason, what's going on?" Aunt Lottie asked.

He slumped into the seat next to her. "I just need to talk to Drea."

"No, you don't. The time for talking is over between you two. You have to act. And if you can't, then it's best you leave that girl alone."

"Are you saying I've been taking advantage of her, Aunt Lottie?"

"That's not what I'm saying, my thickheaded nephew. What I am saying is that you have less than twenty-four hours to figure out what you truly want. If it's not her, then let her leave town. And you should resume your life."

Resume his dreary life? Go back to all that emptiness? Go back to dwelling on his loss, dwelling on the pain? Go back to life before Drea? What in hell was wrong with him? He couldn't do that.

Aunt Lottie was right.

He needed to act.

Wearing daisy-yellow gardening gloves, Drea inserted the last vinca plant in the landscaped border surrounding the cottage and then gave the soil a loving pat. The garden was finished, returned to its former glory. That had been her goal.

Her father watched from the front porch. "Drea, don't you tire yourself out now."

"I'm not. It feels good to finish this. Doesn't it look great?" She stood up to gaze at her handiwork. Flowers and shrubs adorned the land once overrun by weeds.

Drew came down the steps, his eyes sharper than she'd seen them in a long time. "Yeah, it's beautiful."

"You have to promise to keep the weeds at bay and water the plants."

"After all your hard work, you know I will." He looked at his watch. She had only a few hours left at home with him.

"You ready for breakfast now, sweetheart? I made you pancakes with chocolate chips and apple bacon and—"

"Whoa, Dad. You had me at chocolate chip pancakes."

He laughed and hugged her shoulders. "Go shower and I'll get the meal on the table."

She kissed his cheek. "You're on."

Half an hour later, Drea patted her stomach and pushed her plate away. She'd dressed in the clothes she'd wear later when she boarded her plane, a soft pink, lightweight sweater and a pair of designer jeans that were feeling a little snug about now. "I ate too much."

Her dad grinned. "Me, too. How about we take a little walk, burn off some of those pancakes."

Whatever he wanted to do, she was game. This was their last morning together for a while and she was happy just being with him. Walking in the morning air would help keep her mind off leaving town. "That's a great idea."

"I'm ready." Her father glanced at his watch again. "Let's go."

They walked down the road a bit, taking sure but slow steps, just enjoying the scenery and weather this autumn morning. Drew MacDonald was healthier than when she'd come. He'd been eating better and had lost some weight, and his daily walking rituals were really helping build his strength.

About a quarter mile into the walk, after rounding a turn, she spotted a black SUV parked on the side of the road just a few feet away. A man climbed out, long legs in fitted black jeans, silver belt buckle gleaming, with a familiar Stetson atop his head. Mason. Her heart began to pound. "Dad, what's going on?"

Her father's eyes grew soft and he smiled. "Hear him out, darlin' girl."

"What?"

"Mason needs to speak with you."

Her mind clicked away. "But I don't want… Is this a trap?"

Her father grinned. "God, I hope so." He kissed her cheek and gave her a big hug. "Don't be mad, and listen to your heart." With that, he turned around and began walking back toward the cottage, leaving her dumbfounded in the middle of the road.

It took only four long strides for Mason to reach her. He gave her a warm smile, as if he hadn't just hijacked her. "Mornin'."

She clamped her mouth closed. She didn't like surprises. At least not like this, especially when Mason was looking all casual and gorgeous. But his eyes, those dark, dark eyes, weren't filled with his usual confidence. He had that vulnerable look on his face that always got to her.

"Good to see you." His gaze flowed over her intently as if… as if he was… No. She wasn't going to think it. She wasn't going to hope. Mason had made his choice and it wasn't her.

"What's this all about, Mason?"

"It's about me and you. I want to show you something."

"I don't think so. I'm supposed to—"

"Please," he said. "It won't take long and I'll bring you back to Drew's quickly." He extended his hand, palm up, and waited.

She gestured to the car. "Are you driving me somewhere?"

"That's the plan. It's not far."

Listen to your heart. Listen to your heart. Her father's advice helped her make the choice.

She began slowly walking to the SUV, ignoring Mason's outstretched hand. She wasn't going to make this easy on him, whatever it was. But her reluctance didn't faze him. Instead, he raced to open the car door for her and she climbed in.

Mason got in and didn't look at her, didn't say anything. They drove in silence down the road and then Mason took a cutoff that led to the west end of the property that was once Thundering Hills.

He stopped the car and they both got out, her heart hammering in her chest. At one time, this had been MacDonald land, her home. She hadn't come here in a long, long time.

Mason leaned against the grill of his car and grabbed her hand so she landed next to him.

"Sean said something to me the other day that made a lot of sense," he said softly, his eyes touching hers. "He said you and I were flawless together."

She blinked. "Sean said that?"

"Yeah. The kid's pretty damn smart."

"Unlike you."

He laughed and it was so hearty, she had to smile, too. "When you're right, you're right."

"Excuse me, did I hear correctly?"

"You did. You heard me right. And I got to thinking that when we were first together, some weeks back, I thought you were good for me. There was something about you that jump-started my life again. You were the catalyst I needed, the fire under my ass, whatever you want to call it. I don't know, maybe it was because we had history together, but you came to Rising Springs and saved me from drowning in my own grief. After that one kiss, I was suddenly filled with light and energy and I wanted more. I wanted to feel again. But I was afraid, too, because I'd clung to Larissa's memory for so long and I didn't know if I could go through something like that again. I didn't know if my emotions were all screwed up."

"What are you saying, Mason?"

"I'm saying that after I learned about what happened to you in college, I freaked out a little bit. I blamed myself for getting involved with you, for taking advantage of a much younger woman."

"But you didn't. I wanted you, Mason. It was your rejection that hurt me. I wasn't a very secure girl back then, and I guess I understand now why you did what you did."

He squeezed her hands and looked solemnly into her eyes. "We've both been hurt in the past, and it's time to put that behind us, Drea. Sweetheart, I realize now that all those sparks you ignited in me weren't just sexual. It was love, Drea. I love you. You're the only woman for me. We are meant for each other and I can't stand the thought of you leaving. We belong together."

It was a stunning declaration that left her breathless. But she wasn't sure she could truly trust it. "Mason, are you sure you're ready? I know you care about me, but love?"

"Believe me when I say I am ready. Granted, I'm a late bloomer, but last night, after you left the event, it finally hit me how much I love you. I'm never afraid when I'm with you, Drea. Just the opposite. When I'm with you, I am the man I'm supposed to be. I was so sure of myself last night at our event that I asked your father for his blessing, and he gave it to me. Drea, I want to do it again, I want to marry you. I want a family with as many kids as you'd like. I want it all, as long as it's with you."

She smiled at the notion. It was a precious thought. She wanted babies with Mason. Lots and lots of them. All week long, she'd been dreading going back to New York, dreading leaving this place that now felt so much like home, her true home. In her heart of hearts, here with Mason was where she really wanted to be.

Mason got down on one knee and presented her with a brilliant square-cut diamond ring. It was so beautiful her breath caught in a big gasp.

"Andrea MacDonald, I promise to love and honor you for the rest of our lives. Will you marry me?"

She took his upturned face in her hands, gazing into those dark, sincere, beautiful eyes. "Yes, Mason. My dream, my heart. I'll marry you."

He grinned widely and placed the ring on her finger. "My grandmother would have been happy to see her ring on your finger, Drea. She would've welcomed you and loved you almost as much as I do."

He stood then and claimed her lips in a kiss that sealed their love. A kiss that meant forever. And they stayed cradled in each other's arms for long, sweet moments, Mason stroking her hair as she gazed out onto the hills.

"When you brought me out here, you said you wanted to show me something?" she finally asked, looking at him curiously.

"I wanted to propose to you here, on the land you've always loved. We can build a place of our own here, if you'd like. We can design a house you'll love overlooking the hills."

"I'd like that. I guess I'm moving back to Rising Springs."

Mason pulled away slightly. "I know your career is important to you and I'll support whatever you want to do about it. You don't have to decide now, sweetheart."

Her job had once been the only thing she'd actually had in her life. And since coming home, she realized that there was so much more she wanted. She loved Boone Springs. She loved her father and her friends. And she loved Mason Boone, more than she'd thought possible. "Actually, I think I'd like to do volunteer work in Boone Springs. I can donate my time and hope to continue to make a difference here."

"That sounds like a good plan."

"It's the best plan as long as we're together," she said.

"It is," he agreed, placing a light kiss on her forehead. "Missy isn't selling the beach house, after all. She decided to keep it for family and friends. And I was thinking it's a good place for our honeymoon. Shall I book it, say, for the spring?"

"You want to get married that quickly?" Drea asked, liking the idea of being Mason's wife.

"I do. As soon as we can plan the wedding."

She leaned against him, looking out at the place she'd once called home, the place she would finally return to. It was uncanny, something she never would have believed possible.

"And there's one more thing," he said quietly. "Larissa's parents gave me a letter she wrote to me two years ago, right before she passed. It's her last words to me. I haven't opened it yet."

"Why not?"

Mason drew a deep breath and pulled an envelope out of his pocket. "I didn't realize the reason I've been holding on to this letter until last night. It's because I wanted you by my side when I read it. Larissa was my past, and I loved her deeply, but you… you are my future. And I needed you to know that no matter what's inside this letter, it won't change my love for you. You need to know how much I love you."

"I think I do now," she said, her eyes filling with tears. "I love you very much, Mason. If you're ready, go ahead, read the letter privately." She squeezed his forearm, holding on to him. "I'm right here and I always will be."

Mason unsealed the envelope and pulled out the piece of paper. He took a few moments to read Larissa's words and then faced Drea. He swallowed hard, his eyes glistening. "Larissa knew me so well. She knew I'd grieve a long time. She said she wanted me to be happy, to find someone to share my life with. She wanted me to move on."

He sighed and then kissed Drea's lips gently, sweetly, and she felt his love all the way down to her toes. "And I have, Drea. I am moving on. I've found happiness with you. I promise you'll never doubt my love. We'll have a good life."

"Yes we will, Mason. I believe it, too. After all, together the two of us are absolutely *flawless*."

* * * * *

Rancher Untamed

Katherine Garbera

USA TODAY bestselling author **Katherine Garbera** writes emotional, sexy contemporary romances. An Amazon, Barnes & Noble and iBooks bestselling author, she is also a two-time Maggie Award winner and has sold more than seven million copies of her books worldwide. She loves to hear from readers via her website, www.katherinegarbera.com.

Books by Katherine Garbera

Harlequin Desire

Sons of Privilege

The Greek Tycoon's Secret Heir
The Wealthy Frenchman's Proposition
The Spanish Aristocrat's Woman
His Baby Agenda
His Seduction Game Plan

The Wild Caruthers Bachelors

Tycoon Cowboy's Baby Surprise
The Tycoon's Fiancée Deal
Craving His Best Friend's Ex

Cole's Hill Bachelors

Rancher Untamed

Visit her Author Profile page at
millsandboon.com.au,
or katherinegarbera.com, for more titles.

Dear Reader,

I'm really excited to be telling Pippa's story at last! From the moment she showed up on the page in *Tycoon Cowboy's Baby Surprise* I was intrigued. I knew she'd run away from her family, but I didn't know all the details at first. Her bond with Kinley and with Penny showed me how compassionate she was, and in each book since then I've been learning more about her. After I finished *Craving Her Best Friend's Ex*, it made sense to tell Pippa's story as I knew her pretty well by that point.

If you've been reading my Wild Caruthers Bachelors series, you'll also recognize Diego Velasquez. He's one of Bianca's four brothers, and as the eldest has always felt a sense of legacy and heritage. He has taken over running his family's horse ranch in Cole's Hill. He is intrigued with Pippa from running into her around town, but it's not until she bids on him in the annual Cole's Hill charity bachelor auction that he gets a chance to really know her.

Neither of them intends for their night together to be anything more than that. Both of them have complicated lives, but you know how it is with love—we have no control over who we fall for (as much as it would be nice to think that we do) or when it happens. To be honest, that is one of the reasons I love writing romance stories.

I hope you enjoy Pippa and Diego's story.

Happy reading!

Katherine Garbera

This book is dedicated to all believers in happy endings and the power of true love.

One

Diego Velasquez felt foolish as he stood in the wings waiting to be announced in the Five Families Country Club bachelor auction. He'd give anything to be with his horses on his ranch, Arbol Verde. He had tried to get out of participating in the annual charity event by making a huge donation, but his mom, a formidable morning newscaster on a Houston station, was on the committee and wanted to see her sons—all four of them—married. So there was no getting out of it, even though every year he and his brothers tried.

"What do you think, Diego? Got it in you to land a huge bid?" his youngest brother, Inigo, asked.

Diego was pretty sure Inigo had toyed with the idea of making one of the women who followed him on the F1 racing circuit his temporary bride to avoid the auction. But since their beloved mama was a devout Catholic, a temporary marriage was a no-no, so he'd flown in on his G6 this morning from Japan. Luckily for Inigo the F1 was racing in Austin in two weeks' time. Or maybe unluckily, because it meant there was no excuse not to be here, he thought as he watched Inigo messing with his bow tie.

Diego turned to his other two brothers, the twins. Alejandro did some sort of social media management that had made him a millionaire and he wasn't even thirty. And Mauricio had the golden eye when it came to spotting property in neighborhoods on the cusp of becoming "it" places to live and work.

Diego was proud of them. They were all the kind of bachelors that the charity auction should be promoting. Sure, it was annoying that Mama was competitive and wanted to see the Velasquez name at the top of the fund-raising leaderboard. But at the end of the day, it was a good cause, wasn't it?

"You look like you're thinking of bolting," Mo said.

"I am," Diego admitted. But before he could make good his escape, there was a commotion on stage.

"Ethan Caruthers is making a fool of himself over some woman. He just proposed to her," Inigo said, from his spot near the curtain leading to the stage.

"Crissanne Moss," Diego said, coming over to join his youngest brother. "While you were touring the world, this has been the big news in town. Ethan and Crissanne were living together and the Carutherses thought it was leading toward marriage. But then Crissanne's ex came back from the dead. Literally. People thought he'd died in a plane crash until he showed up in town, very much alive, wanting to know what was going on between his best friend and his ex-girlfriend."

"*Dios mio*, Diego, you sound like the town gossip," Alejandro said, coming up behind him and slinging his arm over Diego's shoulders.

"Don't remind me. I had dinner with Bi and Derek last night and Ma Caruthers was there spilling the dirt," Diego said.

"Ah, well, it looks like they might be getting back together," Inigo said.

"Yeah, it does," Diego said. He'd never met a woman he'd make a fool of himself over. Not like Ethan was doing right now. But as he watched Ethan go to Crissanne and embrace her...well, it made him wonder what it would be like to find one special person to settle down with.

"You're next, Diego," the stage manager said.

"Damn," he said. His chance to run was gone.

He heard Mo chuckling evilly behind him and turned to punch him in the shoulder, only softening it at the last moment because if he started a brawl with his brothers his mom would never forgive them.

"What are you afraid of?" Mo asked. "It's just harmless fun."

Yeah, it was. But as he got older, it felt like he should be retiring from this auction, not settling in as a permanent fixture. "Nothing. You're right. It's fun."

All four brothers watched the crowd as Diego's name was announced. Alejandro elbowed him, pointing to Kinley Caruthers's nanny, Pippa. She was close to the front of the crowd, a look of anticipation lighting up her heart-shaped face.

She'd caught his eye before. The cute blonde had come to Cole's Hill two years ago when Kinley moved here. Her hair was a honey blond and she usually wore it in a ponytail, but tonight it fell to her shoulders in soft waves. Her eyes were gray, but not icy at all. It was sort of a soft gray color that made him want to tell her things that he didn't even want to admit he thought about. Which made her dangerous. Her lips were full, and normally she wore only lip gloss—yeah, he'd spent a lot of time thinking about that mouth of hers. Tonight she'd used a red lipstick that made it impossible for him to look at anything but her mouth. Which was the last thing he needed because he already thought too much about what it would be like to kiss her.

She wore a figure-hugging dress in a deep blue jewel tone that made her creamy skin look even smoother than normal. He'd known her legs were long and slim because she tended to wear leggings around town, but tonight with a pair of fancy heels on they seemed longer, endless.

He groaned.

"Stop being a baby. I swear, Diego, you are the worst at this.

I know they are women and not your beloved horses, but it's not that bad," Mo said.

He glanced at his brother. "I know that. I'm not exactly afraid of women."

"Your reputation proves that," Mo said. "So what's the deal?"

Mo leaned toward the curtain with him and followed Diego's gaze.

"Oh, it's like that."

"Yeah. But she's not interested and I'm—"

"Out of time," Mo said.

"Mr. Diego Velasquez," the emcee repeated.

And Diego, with a shove from Mo, walked out onto the stage.

Pippa Hamilton-Hoff rarely went out and certainly didn't get dressed up all that often. But here she was, seated at the Caruthers table for the Five Families bachelor auction. Among the descendants of the original five families who'd founded Cole's Hill, there was a friendly competition to see which one could raise the most money.

Given that all of the Caruthers brothers were married except for Ethan—and he now seemed engaged—that family's chances were slim this year. But Pippa had already had other ideas. It certainly helped that she was twenty-five today and would soon have access to her fortune. She knew exactly who she wanted to spend this birthday with.

Diego Velasquez—a long, tall Texan who looked as comfortable in his tuxedo as he did on the back of a horse. Though if she were being totally honest, she preferred to see him riding his stallion Iago. She'd been out to visit him twice with Penny, the little girl she nannied. Penny was a horse-crazy four-year-old, the daughter of Nathan Caruthers, and Diego was her de facto uncle now that his sister, Bianca, had married Dr. Derek Caruthers.

The long road that she'd been on for the last four years was almost up. She no longer had to hide who she was—an English heiress who'd run away from her controlling father and had become a nanny while on the run, trying to figure out what to do next. Now that she was twenty-five her inheritance was hers to claim and do what she wanted with. For this one night she still wanted to be young and free. To be with a man who didn't know about her fortune, who would be happy enough with Pippa the nanny.

She'd run into him enough times in town to know that it wasn't coincidence. The owner of a large ranch on the outskirts of town with an internationally acclaimed breeding program didn't have to drive into Cole's Hill at 10:00 a.m. every Monday, Wednesday and Friday to get coffee, but he did. They always chatted, and she'd been careful to not let it be more than talk, but in her heart...she wanted more. He had the kind of chocolatey-brown eyes that reminded her of drinking hot chocolate, so rich and comforting. Yet at the same time he made her feel alive...feel things that she hadn't allowed herself to even think about since she'd walked out of that party in New York City four years ago and gotten on a bus.

Since then, her life had been a lie. One big deceit where she had to keep moving, keep thinking and never let her guard down.

Until now.

Tonight.

Ethan Caruthers had done the romantic thing and now he and Crissanne were in the corner snogging. Meanwhile, Pippa was sitting here with access to her fortune and looking up at Diego Velasquez. He wore his tuxedo with an easy grace that spoke of manners and class, but when their eyes met, she felt that zing. That sexual awareness that reminded her she was more than an heiress on the run. She was a woman with a plan tonight.

Not the one who'd hidden away for four years or the one who was afraid to claim things for herself.

No, she wanted Diego and was determined to have him.

The bidding started, and she raised her hand, increasing the bid. She just kept on until she and one of the women who worked with Diego at his ranch were the only ones left. Chantelle, Pippa thought her name was. Did Chantelle wish for a relationship that was more than boss/employee?

Pippa knew she was leaving. That as soon as the board of her family's company, House of Hamilton, read her email and accepted she was who she said she was, Cole's Hill, Texas, would be a distant memory. But she'd put aside so many things for the past four years. She'd denied herself for too long and she wasn't going to anymore. She raised her paddle and doubled the current bid, which made the emcee squeal with excitement and Diego raise his eyebrows as he looked right at her.

"I think someone definitely wants you, Diego, and unless there is another bidder who wants to top that bid…" The emcee glanced around the room, but she'd pushed the bid so high no one else raised a paddle.

For the first time since Diego walked onto the stage she was truly aware of the room and that everyone's eyes were on her. She started to sit back down, but Kinley put her hand on Pippa's butt. "Get your man, girl."

She had to smile at the way Kinley said it. Despite the fact that they had grown up in two very different worlds, Kin was a soul sister. Pippa had always believed that something stronger than coincidence had led them to meet on that Vegas bus the day Kinley went into labor. Pippa had been riding the bus trying to figure out her next move, since she was out of cash, and Kinley had been on her way to work when her water broke.

"I guess I will," Pippa said, carefully placing her paddle on the table and going up to claim him.

It was only for tonight, but then again, she felt tonight was all she'd had. She'd had four birthdays on her own in Texas, each of them fraught with tension and confusion. Only her determination had brought her to this moment, and as she climbed up the stairs at the side of the stage and went to him, she didn't worry about any of that. As she got closer, she noticed his smile, how tonight it wasn't as bold as it usually was. But it was still sexy and charming, and she admitted to herself she was smitten.

What an old-fashioned word, but it suited her and her emotions.

She hadn't really been paying attention to the other winners, so she had no idea what to do, but Diego caught her hand and pulled her close to him. "With a bid like that, I think you deserve my everything."

Up close she realized that his brown eyes had flecks of gold in them. His lips were full, and he winked at her as he dipped her low in his arms and then brought his mouth down on hers. She stopped thinking and just let go.

Diego stood in the line at the bar watching Pippa talking to Kinley and Bianca. His sister was a former supermodel, but Pippa outshone her in his eyes. He wasn't sure what they were saying, but he noticed that Pippa smiled and laughed easily. He ordered two margaritas and then made his way back over to her.

"So I guess we shouldn't wait up for you," Kinley said as he approached.

Pippa's gaze met his and she blushed, the pink tint moving up from her décolletage to her neck.

"You'll see me when you see me," Pippa said in her very proper British accent.

She reached around Kinley and took one of the margaritas from him. He lifted his glass toward hers and took a sip before he moved to stand next to her. Kinley hugged her and went to join her husband across the room.

"Mama is very proud of the Velasquez family tonight," Bianca said.

"She should be. She did a good job raising us," Diego said. "And we are all home tonight, which you know always makes her happy."

"She's not the only one who's over the moon," Bianca said.

"Benito can't wait until tomorrow morning for our family brunch. He loves his *tios*."

His nephew was four years old and had seen a lot in his short life. His father had died while racing, something that had made Diego's own mother more determined to try to find another career for Inigo. But his youngest brother had the legendary Velasquez hardheadedness.

"We adore him," Diego said.

"Of course you do. Now, I am going to try to claim a dance with my husband. He's got early surgery tomorrow, so we can't stay late," Bianca said, leaning over to kiss his cheek. Then she gave Pippa a hug before she walked away.

He glanced over at the woman who'd been shutting him down in town but tonight had made the highest bid to spend the evening with him. "You could have saved yourself some money if you'd said yes when I asked you out a few weeks ago."

"Oh, well, then the charity wouldn't have made as much tonight. Somehow, I think that makes it all worth it," she said.

There was something different about her tonight. She was more confident. She'd always seemed to be a little bit on edge, her eyes frequently going to the door of the café where they'd met. It used to bother him when he'd first started running into her in town, but now he'd gotten used to it.

"Was that what brought out your wallet? The charity?"

She flushed again. "It is a very good cause. Children are so vulnerable and really at the mercy of the adults in their lives."

"Were you?" he asked. He couldn't help but be curious about her past. And how could a nanny afford the generous bid she'd placed? Maybe it was because she didn't really have any expenses living in her own house on the Rockin' C ranch. And she'd told him at the coffee shop that her daily lattes were her only indulgence. But still. No one knew much about her. She never mentioned her last name, and he knew from Nathan—Kinley's husband—that Pippa had met Kinley on a bus in Las Vegas, of all places.

But she was a British woman with no apparent connection to her homeland. And Diego, who was proud of being American, didn't understand that.

"I had everything a child could wish for," Pippa said. "The best toys, a first-class education and a stable with horses that even the legendary Diego Velasquez would envy."

"Legendary?" he asked, ignoring the sadness that underpinned her words. So she had been born with money, but when she'd come to the United States, she'd left that behind. He'd seen the way she lived. *Frugal* was one word for it. But it was deliberate.

"Don't let it go to your head, but you are sort of a superstar with horses. I mean, when I've brought Pippa out to your stables to ride, I've seen the way the rowdiest stallion settles down for you."

"I get horses," Diego said.

"But not people?"

"Some people," he admitted. Mo had warned him to not talk about his horses or breeding program around women and bore them when he was in his early twenties. Diego had seen his success with the ladies increase after his brother's advice and still followed it now.

The DJ had gotten set up, and as the drinks from the open bar flowed, more people were moving toward the dance floor. Pippa finished her margarita.

"Do you want another drink?" he asked.

She shrugged. "I'm not a huge fan of tequila."

"What would you prefer?" he asked.

"Something sparkling. I want to celebrate."

He raised one eyebrow and took the margarita glass from her. "I'll be right back."

He went to get them both some prosecco and then returned. "How's that?"

"Much better," she said, lifting her glass toward his.

"What are we celebrating?" he asked.

"My birthday," she said. "I'm twenty-five today."

"Happy birthday, Pippa."

Twenty-five. She was five years younger than him, but the way she said it made him realize there was a lot more to the story. She took a sip of her drink and he did the same, making small talk until they had finished. The band was playing "Despacito" and Pippa was swaying to the music.

"So, Pippa, what are we going to do?"

She tipped her head to the side. "I'm not sure what you mean. What are we going to do about what?"

"This night," he said. He put his hand on her waist and drew her closer to him.

"I'm not sure," she said softly.

Her breath smelled sweet like the prosecco, and her face was so close that his lips tingled. He remembered how soft and succulent they had been beneath his earlier.

"Well, I'm yours…for tonight," he said out loud to remind himself that it was only for this night. "Tell me what it is you want me to do."

She tipped her head back and their eyes met. Her lips parted and he felt her hand come to rest on his shoulder. "Show me a good time, cowboy."

Two

Once the auction was over and the winners collected their bachelors, it was as if all the tension left the room. Pippa felt freer than she'd felt since…well, ever. Her whole life she'd felt the burden of her inheritance and knew that she'd have to make the right choices when she became an adult. Her mother had coached her and told her to take her time. Not to marry young, as she had, because even though she loved her family she felt she'd missed out on so much of life.

Her father was a different story. Having married into the House of Hamilton fortune, he had wanted to do everything to make his own mark on the legacy jewelry company. But instead he'd always come up short. She knew this from a frank discussion two of her cousins had had with her when she'd turned twenty-one. She had been at that odd age where she was both an adult and also not yet allowed to take over her inheritance, which she couldn't do until she was twenty-five. Her father had full power over many things including voting her shares and her position on the board.

"Another prosecco?" Diego asked, interrupting her thoughts.

"Uh, that, or champagne will do. I'm a sucker for anything sparkling," she said. Now that she'd won the man she'd been eyeing around town for the past two years she had to admit that she didn't know what to do with him.

Her life with Kinley and Penny had been quiet and sheltered. She knew all of Dora the Explorer's little friends but really felt awkward with a man. That was sad. She aimed to fix that tonight.

He snagged two champagne glasses from a passing waiter and handed one to her. "To a glittering night."

She clinked her glass to his and then took a sip. She loved the bubbles in champagne and how they felt on her tongue. She closed her eyes and let the sip stay in her mouth awhile before she swallowed. When she opened her eyes, Diego was watching her and the look in his eyes made her feel…well, not awkward anymore.

The DJ was playing a good mix of dance tunes and slower ballads, along with some standards that got the older generations up on the dance floor, but all Pippa could think about was that she was free. After staying hidden so long, and that being the focus of her every day. Hoping she wouldn't be found before she could claim her inheritance…and now that fear was gone. She'd known her father had private detectives searching for her. And she'd been careful to keep the Hamilton-Hoff name hidden. Not that she couldn't trust Kinley, but if she had to lie, that was her responsibility. Lying was her choice and not one she wanted to force her friends into. All she had to do was wait for her claim to be validated and then…her new life would begin.

"So do you dance?" he asked. Diego's voice was low and smooth. She'd spent way too much time thinking about the way he said her name. He lingered on the last vowel as if he liked the way her name sounded on his lips.

"I do, but mostly with Penny, and that little imp pretty much just jumps around and strikes crazy poses. I'm sure you're not going to want to see me do that," she said.

"I wouldn't rule it out, but maybe not in this venue," he said with a wink. "My nephew is a big fan of lying on the floor and spinning around when the music is on."

"Penny does that, too. I'm pretty sure that's a classic toddler move," she said.

"Can't recall it from my own past, but I hope I had a little more style," he said as the music changed and Justin Timberlake's "Can't Stop the Feeling!" came on. "Want to give it a try? See if you can control the urge to jump around and pose?"

She smiled and nodded. "This song is from the *Trolls* movie."

She groaned internally. She didn't even have a kid and yet kid stuff was all she could talk about. She'd turned into an old lady without even realizing it was happening.

"Please pretend you didn't hear that," she said. "Starting right now I'm going to be young and wild Pippa."

"No arguments here," he said, taking her hand and leading her onto the dance floor.

She'd expected him to let go of her hand, but he didn't. Just held her as they swayed to the music. She didn't have a hard time getting into it and remembered the last time she'd danced like this had been years ago when she'd gone to the winter formal at her boarding school before her mom had died and everything had changed.

After a period of grief, the board of the House of Hamilton had informed her father that he was no longer an official partner and would only be voting Pippa's shares until she came of age at twenty-five. Her relationship with her father changed after that. And when she turned eighteen, he had become obsessed with who she would marry and determined that she should choose a distant cousin of his who was his protégé.

Unexpectedly she felt the sting of tears and she shook her head until she could shove the emotion back down. She twirled away from Diego, who looked as if he were going to ask a question, and continued dancing with her back to him until her emotions were under control.

So much of her journey had been fed by her mom's death, but she was cool now. She was in control and she knew exactly what she was going to do.

The song ended.

"We've had a lot of requests for this song and I think it's about time I played it. 'Save a Horse' by Big & Rich, so, ladies, grab your cowboy and enjoy," he said.

She knew the song well as it was one of her favorites, but until tonight she hadn't had a cowboy of her own. She did now. She took his hand. All around them on the dance floor, there was laughter that soon turned into close embraces and kisses. But Diego just smiled and kept his eyes on hers as she sang and danced with him.

The crazy surge of emotion she'd had earlier changed into something else as she realized just how long it had been since she'd let her hair down and just danced.

At the end of the song, Diego pulled her close and their eyes met moments before he lowered his head and kissed her. Unlike the embrace on stage earlier, this one didn't feel like it was for show.

Diego and Pippa stayed on the dance floor for the next three hours. Some couples disappeared, then came back looking… well, like they'd enjoyed themselves. But Diego remained where he was. He drank champagne, which hadn't escaped Mo's notice. His brother gave him a look and Diego knew he was going to hear about it later. Alejandro was dancing with someone Diego didn't know, but he was pretty damned sure she wasn't his longtime girlfriend. According to the gossips at the coffeehouse, they'd had a fight about Alejandro's inability to commit and she'd dumped him about six weeks ago.

Pippa stuck close to his side and hadn't mentioned the kiss he'd been unable to stop himself from giving her. He knew that it was a bachelor auction, and all in good fun, yet as he'd held her hand and danced her around the floor, he'd wanted to be hers. He'd wanted her to have really claimed him.

"I don't want this night to end," she said as the DJ announced that there was time for only one more song.

"It doesn't have to," he said. "Wait here."

He went to the bar for a bottle of champagne and two plastic flutes before leading Pippa away from the party to one of the patios that overlooked part of the golf course. It was quiet as they moved away from the party.

"One of the things I really love about Texas is how big the sky is," she said, putting her hands on the railing and looking up. There wasn't that much light pollution out here, so the stars were visible.

"Me, too," he admitted. "Where are you from? I mean, you're obviously British."

"Caught that, did ya?" she asked as she turned and leaned back on the railing.

"Yeah, I'm smart that way," he retorted, pouring her a glass of champagne and handing it to her.

He poured another one for himself as she took a sip.

"I was born in Hampshire, but we mainly lived in London except when I was at boarding school," she said.

"I have to admit I have no idea where Hampshire is," he said.

"That's okay. I had no idea where Cole's Hill was until Kinley moved here," Pippa admitted.

"Why did you come with her? Las Vegas is way more exciting than this," he said.

"I had nothing holding me there. My job as Penny's nanny is important to me," she said, taking a sip of her drink. "I made Kinley a promise when Penny was born that I would stay as long as she needed me."

"You were there when Penny was born?" he asked. This was the most she'd told him about herself since they met, and he was curious.

"Yeah. We were on a city bus when Kinley went into labor.

I just stayed with her when she was taken to the hospital because she was scared and alone and we'd been chatting before her water broke… I think we both needed a friend in that moment," Pippa said. There was a note in her voice that hinted there might be more to the story, but she shook her head and looked over at him. "We've been friends ever since. What about you? Who's your oldest friend?"

He took a sip of his champagne. It was never going to replace Jack Daniels as his favorite drink, but the taste was growing on him. "If I'm honest, my brothers. Maybe Mauricio, since he's younger than his twin, Alejandro, by several minutes. Inigo is five years younger than me and closer to my sister, Bianca. He's a Formula One driver like Bianca's first husband was."

Why was he telling her all of this? But he knew. He didn't want to make any moves that would send her running away from him again. Even though she'd bid on him tonight, every other time he'd tried to connect with her she'd shut him down. And he didn't want to let this end.

Not now.

Not until… Well, not until he figured out the secrets behind those gray eyes. She always seemed so calm and controlled, but tonight there was a fire and passion in her gaze that he wasn't going to walk away from until he uncovered its source.

"You have such a big family…like the Carutherses. Is that a Texas thing?" she asked.

He had to laugh. "Well, they do say everything is bigger here. The families in Cole's Hill certainly are."

"I guess that's true," she said. "I do like this area of Texas. So lush and pretty with the green rolling hills. I mean, it's a bit of a stretch, but it does remind me of our country houses in England."

"Country houses?" he asked.

She shrugged. "You know, big old Georgian mansions that have been in one family forever."

"Then why are you here in Texas and not with your family?" he asked. "Sounds like legacy is important to you."

"It is and it isn't," she said. "This champagne is really good."

He knew she was changing the subject and he was tempted to let her do it. But the moon was full, and she'd claimed him for her own, at least for this night, and that meant he had nothing to lose.

"It is good, but what did you mean about your family legacy?" he asked. "You don't have to tell me, but I want to know everything there is about you, Pippa... I don't even know your last name."

"Do you need to?" she asked.

"If I'm going to kiss you again, I think I might want to know it," he said. "It's only fair. You know mine."

She was nervous to let him know her last name. It was silly. She'd reached out to her cousins and the board of directors to let them know she was very much alive and ready to claim her seat on the board. Yet here in the moonlight standing so close to Diego, she knew that she didn't want to tell him, because if he knew she was the House of Hamilton jewelry heiress it would change the dynamic.

He thought she was a nanny—

"Is it really that hard to trust me?" he asked.

"Yes. I've been keeping my identity secret for so long that I... Sorry, it's not you. It really is me," she said.

"Why are you hiding it?" he asked.

His voice was silky smooth, wrapping around her senses and making it hard to concentrate. "My father has a plan for my future and I want to choose my own path."

"Fair enough," he said. "So you are on the run?"

"Yes."

He came to stand next to her, leaning against the railing so they were facing the river rock exterior of the Five Families

Country Club. "Then just be Pippa for tonight. I promise you have nothing to fear from me."

She reached out without really thinking about it, put her hand on his thigh and squeezed. "I know."

But the electric tingle that ran up her arm made her wonder if she was close to getting in over her head. She wanted Diego. That wasn't a surprise. She'd been dodging him in town and trying to limit their contact for that very reason. It was one thing to hook up for a night but something else entirely to start anything with him knowing she was leaving.

And she was going to have to work really hard to prove herself once she was back in England. She wouldn't have time for anything else.

She groaned.

He turned his head to face her and in those deep brown eyes she saw desire. He quirked one eyebrow at her and she felt the brush of his exhalation against her cheek. He smelled faintly of expensive cologne and the outdoors. She closed her eyes and took a deeper breath. He smelled like everything she wanted. And tonight he was hers.

She had made a few missteps. Talking about herself and her past. She needed to keep those things quiet.

She opened her eyes and he was still staring at her.

Without saying a word she lifted her hand and ran it over the light stubble on his jaw. It abraded the skin of her fingers, but in a pleasant way. She ran her finger back and forth, and he caught his breath as his pupils dilated.

He reached out and touched her face in return, sending chills spreading down her neck and arms. Her breasts felt fuller and she felt the hot pulse of desire between her legs.

She wanted him.

Her lips parted, and he slowly cupped the side of her face with his fingers, rubbing his thumb over her bottom lip. The sensations intensified, spreading through her body in sync with her heartbeat.

She mirrored his gesture. He had a strong-looking mouth, but it was soft to the touch. And his breath when he exhaled was soft and warm. He'd kissed her twice, but both times had been restrained because there'd been so many people around. This time they were wrapped in a cocoon of intimacy with only the moon and stars to witness their closeness.

And that made this feel more real.

It wasn't just that he'd asked her for honesty and she'd changed the subject. It was that he wasn't deterred by her half-truths and evasions. He wanted her, she thought again. Just her. Pippa.

She didn't need the Hamilton fortune or her family connections for him to see the woman she was and be attracted to her, and that felt…well, like something she'd never expected to find.

He leaned forward and she removed her fingers from his lips, putting her hands on either side of his face. She needed to do this. He'd kissed her before, but she wanted to be the one kissing him.

She needed this for herself and the self-doubt that had driven her from the only world she'd ever known. In a way, kissing Diego was her way of reclaiming the parts of herself she hadn't meant to discard along the way.

Reclaiming her womanhood.

She wasn't the nanny or a runaway or even the key to the Hamilton-Hoff future. She was just Pippa.

"Diego." She whispered just his name as their lips brushed.

He caressed her, his fingers lightly wrapping around the back of her neck, one of them brushing the sensitive spot behind her ear. Her eyes were half-closed as her lips met his, and she felt his power. But it was tempered. He was letting her take what she wanted from him.

She parted her own lips and felt the heat of his mouth against hers as her tongue darted out and she tasted him. Just one little taste of this cowboy on this big Texas night would be enough to satisfy her.

Not.

Oh, my God, definitely not.

She thrust her tongue deeper into his mouth for a better taste of him. He tipped his head to give her greater access and she leaned in closer, felt her breasts brush against his chest. His hand on her neck was still light, but the pattern with his finger was driving her forward. Increasing that need to have more of him. To taste more of him.

His tongue tangled with hers and she heard him groan. The vibration filled her mouth and she shivered again as another pulse of liquid desire went through her.

She shifted closer, losing her balance against the railing, breaking the kiss. The air felt cold against her lips and she straightened. Her fingers went to her own mouth as she shifted away from him.

Their eyes met.

"I want to take you home with me."

Three

Diego took her hand in his. His voice was rough and husky, but he couldn't control that. He'd been turned on by her kiss. Just her kiss had gotten him hotter and harder than he'd anticipated. But she'd said she was on the run…something that he'd suspected, along with most of Cole's Hill. And he didn't want her to feel pressured to go home with him.

"I'd like that, too," she said. There was a look in her eyes that made him even harder and he stood, putting the champagne glasses on one of the tables that lined the patio.

He turned back to her and held out his hand.

She licked her lips and closed her eyes for a second. "You taste really good, you know?"

"I think it was you."

She walked toward him, her hips swaying with each step she took, and he groaned deep in his throat. Damn. She was hot, and she knew it. She kept eye contact with him, but he broke it, letting his gaze skim down her body. He didn't care if she saw how much she affected him.

He wasn't going to pretend she didn't have him hotter than a tin roof in July.

"We'll have to do it again and again until we figure it out," she said. Her voice was husky with a note of teasing in it.

"Sounds like my kind of plan," he said. "I have a town house I keep here in the Five Families neighborhood. Will that be okay?"

"Sounds good. I live out at the Caruthers Ranch and I'm pretty sure we don't want to drive all the way out there. I don't really want to wait that long to touch you again, Diego," she said. Her words adding kindling to the fire that was already burning out of control in his body.

"Good," he said, lacing their fingers together and leading her down the patio walkway toward the path around the golf course. "I hope you don't mind walking, but I've had too much to drink to feel safe driving even just through this neighborhood. It's only a ten-minute walk."

"I don't mind walking at all," she said.

He held her hand in his and tried to concentrate on getting back to his place. But her perfume smelled slightly of spring and she kept humming "Save a Horse," distracting him. Filling his mind with images of her naked, on top of him, riding him. He groaned again.

"Are you okay?"

"Sí," he said, falling back on Spanish. His family had been in the United States for generations—their original homestead had been a land grant from the Spanish King back in the 1700s—but their family had always been multilingual.

"I know a little bit of Spanish, but it's not the Mexican dialect that a lot of people speak here," she said. "I had a very funny conversation with Isabella about that the other day. She's one of the new hires that Kinley brought in to work in her wedding and event planning office in town."

Diego didn't really care about all that. But he liked the sound of her voice, so he just made a hmming sound and she kept on talking. Finally, he saw the cluster of townhomes and his own front door.

"This way," he said, leading her off the path and across the street to his place. These townhomes were only about five years old and had been built from the same river rock that had been used in the country club. The path leading up to the front door was made of smaller stones but smoothed out so that it was comfortable to walk on.

He reached into his pocket for his keys, which drew his trousers tighter against his groin, and he realized that even walking and talking about nothing for ten minutes had done nothing to cool him down. But that wasn't surprising. Pippa had had him tied in knots for the last few weeks.

"This is it," he said. "Still want to come in? If not, I can arrange for someone to take you home."

"Diego, I want you. I want this. I'm not going to change my mind," she said.

"You've kept me at arm's length for a while now and I know that there has to be a reason. I don't want you to regret this," he said. He never wanted that. This night felt like…well, a dream, and he didn't want anything to ruin it.

She threw her arms around him and hugged him close. "Oh, Diego, I don't deserve you, but I certainly want you."

"Of course you deserve me," he said, lifting her off her feet and lowering his mouth to hers. Her lips tempted him; the entire time she'd been talking, all he'd thought about was kissing her again.

He set her on her feet and led the way to his front door. He unlocked it, pushed it open and beckoned for her to enter first. They stepped into the foyer. He was a pretty traditional guy, so it was decorated with solid dark wood furniture, and the floor tile was a terra-cotta color that reminded him of the mane of his favorite stallion. He tossed his keys in the bowl on the large chest to the left of the entrance and then undid his tie, tossing it on the table, as well. In the round tile-framed mirror he caught Pippa's gaze.

She watched him with the stark, raw need that he recognized in himself. She moved closer, putting her hand on his shoulder and walking her fingers up toward his neck to slowly pull his tuxedo jacket down his arms and off.

Pippa was glad she'd left her heels on because Diego was taller than she'd realized—at least six-one. She reached around him from behind and slowly removed the studs that held his dress shirt together. It had been a long time since she'd been with a man and she wanted to make every moment of this evening last.

"Hold out your hand," she said, her voice huskier than she meant for it to be.

He did as she asked, and she dropped each of the studs into his upturned palm. She watched him in the mirror as her fingers moved down his chest. It was sexier than she thought to see her manicured nails so close to Diego's tanned chest as each tiny strip of his skin was revealed. Finally, she had the shirt undone to his waistband. She deliberately rubbed her fingers over his erection. His hips jerked back for a moment and then canted forward into her touch. She undid the button that fastened his pants before tugging the tails of his shirt out. It hung open, giving her a few tantalizing glimpses of his rock-hard stomach and the muscles of his chest in the mirror.

"How are you so muscly?" she asked.

He gave a half laugh, half groan sound. "I spend all my day working with horses that I charge a lot of money for other breeders to use as studs."

"So?" she asked.

"I want the entire operation to project strength and prosperity and success. That means I can't look like a schlub when they show up," he said.

"I like it."

She bit her lip to keep from just shoving her hands underneath his clothes and touching him.

Patience.

She could do this. She'd spent years waiting to claim her inheritance. By now she should be very good at waiting.

She reached for his free hand and undid the cuff link, dropping it in his palm with the shirt studs. Then he poured them into his other hand, the small studs and cuff link making an almost musical sound as he did so. She smiled.

Then she undid the other cuff link and dropped it with the other shirt studs. He closed his hand around them and shoved them into his pants pocket. She focused all her attention on Diego's body.

She pulled the sides of his shirt open and he rotated his shoulders, making it easier for her to take it off. His shoulder blade rubbed against her right breast, sending a hot pulse of desire through her.

He tossed his shirt on top of his jacket and she put her hands on his chest. Diego worked outdoors but didn't have a farmer's tan. It was clear to her that he had spent a good amount of time in the Texas sun without his shirt on. She ran her hands down his chest. There was a tattoo in roman-type lettering that curved around a scar right below his ribs. She suspected that the scar was old as she ran her fingers over the ridge of it. She put one hand on his waist and the other on the small of his back as she leaned around to read the tattoo he had on his chest.

Courage is being scared to death and saddling up anyway.

"What does this mean to you?" she asked.

"Just a reminder that getting knocked down doesn't mean I need to stay down forever," he said, putting his hand over hers and rubbing it up and down his torso.

There was a thin line of hair that disappeared into the open waistband of his pants. She traced the line with her finger as she straightened back up, but he stopped her. He took her wrist in his hand and drew her fingers back to his chest.

"I like the way you touch me, Pippa," he said, his voice that low growly sound that sent shivers through her body. Shivers that seemed to pool between her legs.

She wanted him.

It had been a long dry spell for her and she'd done her share of masturbating and fantasizing about men. Diego had figured prominently in those fantasies since she'd moved to Cole's Hill. She figured there was no way he could live up to them. She'd never had a sexual encounter that had. But there was a heat in Diego's eyes that turned her on. Way more than in her day-dreams.

"I like touching you," she admitted, pushing her hand into the open fly of his pants and stroking the hard ridge of his erection through the cotton fabric of his boxer briefs.

He groaned and reached for the zipper in the left side of her dress.

He'd done this before. She knew from the talk she'd over-heard in the coffee shop after he'd left that he was a player. There were a lot of women who had either dated him or wanted him in their bed.

"I'm lucky I got you tonight," he said.

"I got you," she pointed out.

"Yes, you did," he said, raising both eyebrows at her as he ran his finger down her side, touching her skin as the zipper opened and the fabric parted.

He slipped his hand in and around to her back and drew her toward him, swaying along as he sang a popular Blake Shelton song under his breath. She closed her eyes, wrapping her free arm around his shoulders while keeping her hand on his erection.

He leaned down, his lips brushing the shell of her ear as he whispered, "This is what I was thinking about each time I held you close to me tonight."

"Really?" she asked, opening her eyes and tipping her head

back. Their eyes met and that dark chocolate gaze of his held secrets and passion. She wanted it all.

"Yes, ma'am."

She fumbled around the elastic at the top of his boxers and reached inside to touch his naked flesh. "I was thinking about this."

He didn't say anything. His pupils dilated, and he brought his mouth down hard on hers. His tongue thrust deep into her mouth as he lightly drew his fingernail down her back, stopping at the small of her back. He dipped his finger lower, pushing aside the fabric of her thong panties.

An electric pulse of heat went through her as he cupped her butt and lifted her off her feet. She knew he was moving, but hardly paid any attention to it until he put her back down on the floor and lifted his head. They were in the master bedroom. She could tell by the deep, masculine colors and the large king-size bed behind her.

He disappeared for a minute and then was back with a box of condoms that he put on the nightstand. She was glad she hadn't had to bring up protection, that he'd just taken care of it.

"Now, where were we?" he asked, putting his hands gently on either side of her head and tipping it back. Their eyes met again and he brought his mouth down on hers.

And she forgot about everything.

She let her hand fall from his face to his chest. He was warm. She rubbed her fingers over the scar under his tattoo and then down his abdomen. He shifted his hips and his trousers slid down his legs.

"Impressive," she said.

He wriggled his eyebrows at her. "Thanks. I save that move for special occasions."

She couldn't help smiling at the way he said it. Of course, Diego wasn't like any other man she'd had sex with. He was at ease with his body and with her. There was no pressure to get to it and get it over with. She had the feeling that he wanted her to enjoy this night and that he intended to take his time. There was something sexy in his confidence.

His trousers were pooled around his ankles, but his dress boots kept them in place. His erection was a hard ridge straining against his boxer briefs and his lips were slightly swollen from their kisses. She felt that pulsing between her legs again and knew that she'd never seen anything more erotic in her life. He wasn't posing or pretending. He wanted her and he didn't have to put on moves to impress her.

He lifted the hem of her dress up over her thighs and then all the way over her head, tossing it aside. She stood there in just her tiny panties and no bra.

He groaned, and when he reached out to touch her, she noticed his hand shook slightly. Then he was cupping her breasts with both hands, his palms rubbing over her nipples.

He caressed her from her neck down past her waist, lingering over each curve and making her aware of places on her body that she'd never thought about before, like the bottom of her ribs. His fingers dipped between her legs, pushing her panties down her legs until she stepped out of them, placing her hand on his shoulder to keep her balance. He dipped his hand between her legs, rubbing his finger over her clit until she felt her legs go week.

He put his arm around her waist and lowered her back on the bed, coming down over her. She drew her hand down the side of his body, wrapping her hand around him, stroking him from the root to the tip. On each stroke she ran her finger over the head and around to the back of his shaft. He shivered each time she touched him there.

He ran his hands all over her torso, cupping both of her breasts this time. She shifted, keeping her grip on him but moving so that he could touch her the way she liked it.

She pushed her shoulders back and watched as he leaned forward. She felt the warmth of his breath against her skin and then the brush of his tongue. He circled her nipple with it, then closed his mouth over her and suckled her deeply.

She stroked him until she felt his hips lift toward her, moving in counterpoint to her hand. She reached lower and cupped him, rolling the delicate weight of him in her fingers before squeezing slightly. He groaned and pulled his mouth from her breast. He gripped the back of her neck and brought her mouth to his.

As he drew her against him, she didn't move her hand except to guide the tip of his erection to enter her.

He slid a little more into her and she reveled in the feel of his thick cock at the entrance of her body. But then he lifted his head and took her nipple in his mouth again, biting down lightly on her nipple, and she shuddered.

She tried to impale herself on him, but he wasn't about to let her have him now. He held her where she was with just enough connection to drive both of them mad.

"Are you ready for me?"

"Yessss," she said with a sigh.

A second later he thrust into her, filling her completely.

She rocked her hips, forcing him deeper into her body. He hit her in the right place and she saw stars dancing behind her closed eyelids as he pulled out and thrust back inside her.

He held her with his big hands on her ass, lifting her into each thrust, and soon she was senseless. She could do nothing but feel the power of his body as he moved over her and in her.

She held on to his sides while he continued to drive her higher and harder, and then she felt everything inside clench as her orgasm surged through her. She cried out his name as he tangled one hand in her hair and drove into her even harder and faster, and then she felt him tense and groan as he climaxed. He thrust into her two or three more times before shifting to rest his forehead against hers.

She looked into those dark eyes of his and knew that everything had changed. She had thought this night would be just sex. Just some fun. But Diego wasn't just a fantasy—he was a real, flesh-and-blood man.

He rolled to his side and disposed of the condom before settling back into bed and pulling her into his arms. "Thank you for tonight."

She nodded against his chest, unable to find the words she needed to say. He drifted off to sleep, but she lay there thinking about her future, which was so much more complicated now.

Four

Pippa stretched and rolled over, slowly opening her eyes. It was Monday morning. Usually Penny had her up before this, but then she remembered she'd stayed over at Diego's. She sat up and looked around the empty room. The house was very quiet and, if she had to guess, empty.

"Crap."

She hadn't meant to stay out all night. She put her hand on her head, thinking of walking back to the country club in her dress from last night while parents were making the school run.

She wasn't embarrassed by what had happened. She had woken up exactly where she wanted to be, but at the same time she had to face those moms and dads when she picked Penny up from preschool this afternoon.

She glanced at the nightstand. It was only seven. So not that late, but still. She saw there was a piece of monogrammed stationery with bold masculine handwriting on it. She reached for the note and rubbed her eyes before she read it.

Good morning,
I had to leave early to do the morning chores on the ranch. We have a mare coming in to be covered later today and I need to get things ready. I'd love to see you for lunch or dinner. Text me when you wake up. I had your car brought to the house and I've laid out some sweats and a T-shirt in the bathroom. Sorry I wasn't here when you woke.
Diego

"What am I going to do?" she asked the empty room as she fell back on the pillows. Diego was her one-night hookup. Her bit of fun before she left Texas and went back to her real life. She could just say no and never see him again. There was nothing stopping her from doing just that.

But she didn't want to.

She grabbed her phone to text Kinley and saw she had two messages. The first was clearly from Penny. The four-year-old used the text-to-talk feature on Kinley's phone all the time. The message just said Pippy, where are you?

Kinley's message said:

Ignore the scamp's message. I told her you had the morning off. I assume you are with the hot rancher you outbid everyone for last night. I want deets.

Ugh.

Double ugh.

She tossed her phone on the nightstand without responding, made her way to the bathroom and took a quick shower, avoiding looking at herself in the mirror until she was clean and wearing Diego's sweats. They were huge on her but super comfy. She took a deep breath. If she had a cup of coffee, she'd start to feel human again.

She went downstairs to find her clutch and found a coffee mug next to the Keurig machine. She made herself a cup and then went back up to the master bedroom to gather her stuff. Diego had even laid out a duffel bag and a pair of flip-flops near the foot of the bed. She had to smile. He'd thought of everything.

Which shouldn't really influence her decision to see him again, but it did.

Heck, everything about Diego made her want to see him again. It would be easy to say that waiting four years to have sex would have made any partner seem…well, better than they might really be… What the hell was she thinking? She could have had sex a week earlier with someone else and Diego would have wiped that from her memory. Her body ached to have him again. She remembered the way he'd felt between her thighs and craved more of him.

But he wanted… Well, it seemed like he wanted to get to know her. And until she reclaimed her inheritance, she really needed to lie low and stay off her father's radar.

In Texas…

It had been the perfect spot for her to hide out until she came of age. But now that the time had come, starting something with Diego, all the while knowing she was leaving in a few weeks… Was that a dick move?

She felt like it might be.

She saw a message flash on her phone and went to pick it up. Kinley again.

At the office, stop by if you are still in town.

Pippa knew Kinley would be brutally honest with her about the situation with Diego. Her friend was just always that way with everyone.

She grabbed the duffel bag, her phone and Diego's note and went downstairs to collect the rest of her things.

She found the alarm code on a Post-it on the inside of the front door and entered it to let herself out. She walked to her car without glancing at the street and got in, sitting there for a moment before starting the engine.

She drove through town to the bridal shop that Kinley ran as a satellite to her boss Jacs Veerling's Vegas bridal operation. It was through her work that Kinley had first come to Cole's Hill. She'd been sent here to plan former NFL wide receiver Hunter Caruthers's wedding. Of course, she hadn't wanted to come, given that Hunter was her baby-daddy's brother and said baby-daddy had no clue he had a kid. There had been a bit of a rough patch where Nate hadn't realized that Penny was his child, and when he found out, he blew up at Kinley. But after the family drama had died down they realized how much they loved each other and got married.

Pippa groaned as she noticed that all of the pull-in parking spaces were taken and she'd have to parallel park. When she was done about five minutes later, she walked into the bridal showroom. It was an elegant space that had been designed to suggest understated opulence. Classical music played in the background. Pippa knew that she'd take some of the design elements from this small bridal shop with her when she returned to London and claimed her place on the board of House of Hamilton. The royal jewelers needed to attract a younger crowd and Pippa was determined to do that.

She sighed, realizing she already knew the decision she would make regarding seeing Diego again.

It had to be a no.

She wanted the chance to prove herself to her family and the world more than she wanted a new lover.

Diego hadn't expected his younger brother to be waiting when he got home to Arbol Verde, but Mauricio was sitting in the breakfast room enjoying huevos rancheros that had been prepared by Diego's housekeeper, Mona. And he was drinking a Bloody Mary, unless Diego was mistaken.

"No need to ask how your night was," Mo said as Diego entered the room.

"Same. Struck out?"

Mauricio shook his head. "You don't even want to know. Breakfast or shower first?"

"Shower. I assume you're going to still be waiting when I get out," Diego said.

"Yes. It's business. I have a line on a piece of property on the outskirts of town that is exactly what you're looking for," Mauricio said. "Go shower. I'll wait here."

Diego started to turn away, but Mo had that look like he'd been rode hard and put away wet, which wasn't how Diego wanted to see any of his brothers.

He walked over and pulled out one of the ladder-back wooden chairs, spinning it around and straddling it. He reached out and snagged a piece of the maple and brown sugar bacon that Mona always had on the breakfast table.

"What happened last night?"

"Hadley was there," Mauricio said.

Of course she was. "I thought she moved to Houston."

"She did. But she came back for the auction," Mauricio said before he took a long swallow of his Bloody Mary.

"You broke up with her," Diego reminded his brother as gently as he could. Hadley and Mo had been a couple since high school. He'd followed her to the University of Texas, and when they'd come back to Cole's Hill, everyone expected them to marry, including Hadley. After waiting five years—longer than most women would, according to Bianca—Hadley had given Mo an ultimatum and he'd balked.

Hadley had packed up and moved out of the town house they'd shared and started dating again. Since then, if gossip was to be believed, Mauricio had had some wild hookups out at the Bull Pen.

The Bull Pen was a large bar and Texas dance hall on the edge of Cole's Hill. It had a mechanical bull in the back and live bands performed there nightly. It was respectable enough early in the evening, but after midnight things started to get rowdy.

"I know that, D. I didn't mind it when she was flirting with men. I knew she wasn't taking any of them seriously. But she was with Bo Williams. Sure, according to Mom he's one of the most eligible bachelors at last night's charity auction. But that guy isn't right for her. You know he's just using her to get back at me."

Diego knew the guy and understood his brother's anger. The two men had been fierce rivals all of their lives. They'd competed on opposing Pop Warner football teams during their youth, both bringing their teams to the Super Bowl more than once. And the rivalry had continued in middle and high school. But Diego had hoped now that both men were in their midtwenties, it was a thing of the past.

"Possibly."

"Whatever," Mo said. "I thought you'd be on my side."

"On your side? What did you do?"

Mauricio turned his head and mumbled something that Diego hoped he heard wrong.

"I couldn't hear that."

Mauricio stood up. "I told her that guy was just using her to get to me, and then he punched me, so I punched him back—"

"Where did this happen?"

"At the Grand Hotel bar. They walked in while I was there with Everly—just talking. You know, she's Mitch's gal. The evening didn't end well."

Everly was Hadley's sister and probably not a huge fan of Mo. "Ya think? Mo, do you want Hadley back?"

"I don't know," Mauricio said. "But I don't want anyone else to have her, either."

Diego stood up and put his hand on his brother's shoulder. "Dude, I know it's hard, but you can't have it both ways."

"I know that. I just need time," he said. "I told her that."

"Then she's the one with the reins," Diego pointed out as

delicately as possible. He knew his brother had to understand deep down; he was a smart, considerate man who really cared for Hadley.

"I'm screwed."

"Why? Move on."

"I can't. It's complicated. If I give in, she'll know she has me. That I care more for her than she does for me," Mauricio said.

"Love doesn't work that way," Diego told his brother.

"How the hell would you know? You've never been in love," Mauricio pointed out.

"True," Diego said as an image of Pippa spread out underneath him last night danced through his mind. "I just don't think couples should keep score. No one wins in that scenario."

"You're right," Mauricio said. "But I keep doing stupid things and she pushes my buttons, too. I mean, why did she bid on him?"

Diego had no idea. It would be so much better for Mauricio to have this conversation with their sister. Diego almost pulled out his phone to text her but knew that Bianca would want to know what had happened last night with Pippa, and he wasn't ready to talk about that yet. And Bianca wouldn't let it go the way Mo had.

"Women are a mystery. I mean, Pippa has been flat-out turning me down every time I've asked her out for the last three weeks, and then she bids on me last night. How does that make any sense?"

Mauricio shook his head and started laughing. "Damned if I know. I wish women were as easy to read as real estate."

"Never say that to a woman," Diego warned his brother. "I have some new horses coming this morning if you want to hang around and get your hands dirty."

Mauricio nodded and then went back to eating his breakfast. Diego got up, heading toward the hallway, ready for that shower.

"D?"

He glanced over his shoulder at his brother.

"Yeah?" he asked.

"Thanks. I know I'm being an ass where Hadley's concerned, but I can't help it."

"It's okay, Mo. You'll figure out how to let go and then things will be back to normal," Diego said with a confidence he wasn't sure was justified. Where his brother and Hadley were concerned, he doubted that anything would be that simple.

"So spill," Kinley said as she hung up the phone and turned her brown eyes on Pippa.

She flushed. "What exactly are you hoping to hear?"

"Something that will take my mind off Nate," Kinley said, shuffling papers on her desk.

"Uh, you bid on him and then pretended to lasso him on the dance floor before you led him out of the country club," Pippa pointed out with a smile. "Did you get to ride your cowboy? Maybe you should spill."

"Fair enough, but I need some more coffee. What about you? I assume you didn't stop at the coffee shop dressed like that," Kinley said, giving Pippa the once-over.

"No. I didn't want to get out of the car in Diego's sweats." She felt the heat creeping up her neck. She had no reason to be embarrassed that she'd slept with Diego last night. Yet somehow…she was. She knew it was because she liked him and she also knew she wasn't going to sleep with him again.

It was so complicated.

And she could even argue that she was the one who was making it so.

"Pip?" Kinley asked.

"Mmm-hmm?"

"I asked if you wanted an extra shot of vanilla in your latte this morning," Kinley said.

"Yes. Sorry. I'm trying to figure out Diego and everything and it's…complicated."

She had to come up with another way of describing this thing with him other than just saying it was "complicated." Kinley didn't even know that Pippa was leaving. She hadn't wanted to say anything to anyone—even Kinley—until she was in the clear. Old enough to inherit without any restrictions. She couldn't let a man throw her off course. True, it wasn't like this was the first time a man had thrown a wrench in her plans, but it definitely was different this time.

Diego made her want to stay and let him continue to interrupt her plans, while her father had made her chafe and eventually left her no choice but to run.

"Why? Also, two pumps of vanilla?"

"Yes. Two pumps," Pippa said. Normally she had only one because she liked to watch her sugar intake, but this morning she needed the boost of sugar and caffeine. "I have a lot to tell you."

"I've heard that Diego is a good lover," Kinley said.

"Not that, Kin. He is, but I'm not talking about that right now," she said.

"Why not?"

"I don't know. What do you want to know?" she asked.

Kinley waggled her eyebrows at Pippa as she handed her the coffee mug and then went back to make her own. "Everything. I told you about that hot night I had with Nate when we were on his balcony."

"You did. That was hot. Well, Diego was a very good lover. He likes to wait for my reactions and he made me feel like I was the only woman in the world that he wanted in his bed."

"Sounds perfect. How is that complicated?" Kinley asked, taking her own mug and coming to sit down on the love seat next to Pippa.

She took a deep breath and turned to face the woman who was closer to her than any blood relative. She hoped that Kinley wouldn't be upset when she told her the truth of her past.

"I— Well— I'm— That is to say—"

"For the love of God, what the heck are you trying to say?"

Kinley asked. "Whatever it is, I've got your back, girl. You know that, right?"

"I do know it," Pippa said, hugging Kinley with one arm. "That's what makes this harder to say. You know how I ran away from home and have been hiding since?"

"Yes," Kinley said, hugging her back. "Did they find you? Nate and I will protect you. And Ethan is a damned good lawyer, so he can get involved, too. Just tell us what you need."

"You are the best, Kinley," Pippa said. "I am so lucky I was on that city bus in Vegas when you went into labor."

"I feel the same way. So let me help you out. You've done so much for me," Kinley said. "What's going on?"

"Um, I ran away when I was twenty-one because I had no control over my inheritance or my life. My father was pressuring me to marry a man who he wanted to take my place on the board of our family company."

Kinley arched both eyebrows. "That's interesting. Who are you?"

"Um…well, Pippa is my name. I mean, everyone calls me that, but my given name is Philippa Georgina Hamilton-Hoff. My family owns the House of Hamilton jewelers by royal appointment of the Queen."

"Shit. Are you serious?"

"Yes."

"So what's changed?" Kinley asked.

"I turned twenty-five. That's when my shares in the company and my inheritance becomes mine to control. They are a legacy from my mother. My father had hoped by marrying me to one of his distant cousins that he would be able to bring his family into the business and take it over."

"That's a lot to take in," Kinley said. "You're leaving us, aren't you?"

She nodded. "I'm sorry. But you and Nate and Penny are a family now. You don't need me the way you used to."

"That's so not true. But I want you to have your inheritance and stop running, so I am not going to be mad about this," Kinley said. "How long do we have until you leave?"

"I'm not sure. I contacted my mother's solicitor in London yesterday—"

"Because of your birthday?"

"Yes. I mean, I could have waited, but I've been watching the company and they have a big board meeting at the end of November and I want to be able to vote my shares this time," she said.

"Okay. So has he gotten back to you?" Kinley asked.

"Yes. He has to verify I'm who I say I am," Pippa said. "So I'm still in limbo until I hear back from him."

Five

Diego resisted the urge to pull his cell out of his pocket and check his nonexistent text messages again. He had work to do to get the ranch ready for the sire that was being brought in later in the day. They had their own prize-winning sires and mares, but he liked to experiment with other lines to see if he could breed stronger horses. Diego, as the eldest son, had always been expected to take over the Velasquez stud farm. He'd worked closely with his father and later their foreman to develop his skills at spotting the signs when a broodmare would be ready for a sire. The signs seemed instinctive to Diego now; he found horses so much easier to read than people.

The fifteen hundred acres in Texas Hill Country had been in the Velasquez family since the late 1700s, and Diego and his father worked hard to maintain the ranch's clear roots in its history. The Arbol Verde operation of today encompassed the former Velasquez Stud and Luna Farm, legendary breeding operations whose decades of prominence ensured their bloodstock's continued influence on the modern thoroughbred.

Through Diego's careful stewardship of the land, Arbol Verde had grown in the last ten years.

He loved the ranch that spread out before him as he sat on the back of Esquire, a retired stud who'd sired three champions, including Uptown Girl. He patted the side of Esquire's neck and then tapped him lightly with his heels to send him running over the grass-covered hills toward the barn. Diego had always had a connection to this land and today it was serving to take the edge off while he waited to see if Pippa was going to text him.

He unsaddled Esquire and brushed him before putting him back in his stall. The ranch was busy and he heard the voices of his other grooms. One of them—Pete—asked for everyone to talk more softly when he noticed that Diego had returned.

His phone pinged and he used his teeth to pull his leather work gloves off before reaching into his pocket to retrieve it. He glanced at the locked screen. It was his sister.

Not Pippa.

Bianca wanted to bring his nephew out to ride later in the day. And given that he had no other plans—and wasn't about to contact Pippa first and seem to be more into her than she was into him—he texted back to come on out.

When he was finished working, he walked up to his house. He stopped for a minute to look around the land that had been in his family for generations. Originally his ancestors had been part of the royal horse guard of Spain. His father liked to say that they had been born with an innate horse sense. Diego didn't know about that, but he had no problems with his horses. They made sense. They behaved the way that nature intended for them to. Unlike women.

He rubbed the back of his neck. He wouldn't change his life for anything, but there were times when he wanted…well, things that shouldn't be important. The ranch was his life. His focus should be here.

He saw Bianca's BMW sitting in the circle drive and knew he had to push all thoughts of last night from his mind. His sister would jump on any perceived weakness, and while having a conversation with Mauricio had been one thing, talking to Bianca would lead to him admitting more than he wanted to about Pippa.

He entered through the mud room, taking time to shower off the dirt and put on the clothes that he'd left there. He entered his house and heard a song by Alejandro Fernández and Morat playing and smiled. Bianca had lived in Spain during her brief first marriage and brought back some new influences for their family. Alejandro Fernández was hugely popular there.

"Tio," Benito, his four-year-old nephew, called out as he came running down the tiled hallway toward him, his cowboy boot heels making a loud noise with each step.

Diego scooped him up and hugged him. "So, you want to ride this afternoon?"

"*Sí.* I have to practice every day because Penny lives on a ranch now and she rides more than me," Benito said.

"Why does that have anything to do with your riding?" he asked. But he knew his nephew and Penny were best friends.

"I like her," Benito said, as if that was the only explanation needed.

And since he seemed to be developing a crush on a girl who wasn't texting him, Diego got where his nephew was coming from way too well. "You are always welcome to come and ride. In fact, *Tio* Mauricio and I are looking into opening a riding center closer to town. Maybe you and your friend can ride there."

"Is that true?" Bianca asked, coming out into the hallway and joining them.

"Yes. He was here this morning discussing it," Diego said.

"Really? That's odd. I thought I saw your truck parked in front of your town house this morning," Bianca said.

"What were you doing up that early?" he asked. Bianca was five years younger than him, and as the only girl in a family dominated by boys, she'd learned to hold her own. In fact, Diego would rather get in a rowdy fight with all of his brothers than have a one-on-one conversation with Bianca.

"Derek was on call, so I went over to have breakfast with Mama and pick up *changuito*," Bianca said as she ruffled Benito's hair. She'd called him "little monkey."

"I had a bit to drink last night, so I figured I'd sleep in town," Diego said, hoping his sister would let it drop.

"We can talk about P-I-P-P-A later," Bianca said, spelling out the name so that Benito wouldn't know what she'd said.

"That's none of your business," Diego countered.

"As if that's going to stop me from asking," Bianca said.

Benito squirmed down from his arms. "What is P-I-P—"

"Nothing. Let's get you out to the barn and saddled up. Are you riding, too?" he asked his sister.

"Yes. I guess I can't keep spelling things around this little one," she said as they all donned straw cowboy hats and went to the barn.

"What else did he spell back?"

Bianca blushed. "You don't want to know. Derek thought it was funny, but it was embarrassing."

Diego didn't need any further explanation. He guessed it had something to do with sex and just shook his head.

He accompanied his sister and nephew to the stable, where he kept a mare she liked to ride. As Bianca started to groom her, Diego took his nephew out, distracted for the afternoon from his phone.

Kinley had a meeting with a bride who'd come up from Houston. Jacs Veerling was one of the top three bridal and event planners in the world and having Kinley running her operation in Cole's Hill was a coup. Many brides who didn't want to fly to Vegas to see the showroom or talk with Jacs were happy enough to come to Cole's Hill. With its close proximity to Houston it was very convenient.

Pippa was at loose ends while Penny was at her four-year-old prekindergarten program and Kinley was working. It gave her too much time to think and hit refresh on her email again and again waiting for a response from the House of Hamilton solicitor. Simon Rooney hadn't given her a timeline for when to expect his response, but because she'd kept close tabs on the company over the years, she knew that her twenty-fifth birthday coincided with a couple of crucial board changes. One of them was that her great-uncle Theo was retiring. He had no heirs, and though Pippa had some second and third cousins who were on the board, she was the only direct-line heir to the company.

And their charter expressed that a direct-line heir, male or female, had the first right to the chairmanship. And Pippa had been studying for the role. She knew that if House of Hamilton wanted to stay a top luxury brand they were going to have to be relevant in the modern world. She'd been researching the marketing strategies of brands like Tiffany and had focused on that topic in her online courses, earning a master's degree in business. She'd also taken classes in jewelry design in Vegas and Cole's Hill. She'd worked hard for this and was impatient to claim her rightful place at the company.

Though she hadn't used her real name in a long while, she'd prepared a prospectus that she'd sent to Mr. Rooney along with her birth certificate, passport and details of her identity.

"Okay, that's done," Kinley said from the doorway. She wore a slim-fitting skirt that had a slit on one side ending just above the knee. She also had on a pair of ankle boots and a thin sweater. Though it was September there had been a dip in temperatures that signaled fall was just around the corner. "Any news from jolly old England?"

Pippa had to smile at the way Kinley said it with her fake British accent.

"No. I'm jumpy, so I don't want to head back to the ranch. I hope you don't mind me just hanging out here," she said.

"Of course I don't mind. Tell me more about your family business," she said, then giggled. "I'm sorry, but when I hear family business, I think of the mob, and you are so far from that mafia princess image."

Pippa smiled back at her friend. "I'm not a princess, mafia or otherwise. The House of Hamilton—"

"My God. I still can't believe you're going to inherit that company! They're huge. Jacs is going to die when I tell her we have an in there. She's been trying to get them to allow her to use some of their designs for her wedding tiaras."

"I'm not even sure they are going to acknowledge me," Pippa said.

"They have to, right? I mean, you are the heiress," Kinley said. "I should call Ethan…he's the only lawyer I know. He could help you."

She shook her head. "Not yet. Let me see what I hear back from the family solicitor first. What kind of tiaras does Jacs want?"

Thinking about bringing in a new line of business was a nice distraction. It kept her mind from Diego. And she had to admit her thoughts drifted to him far too often. He'd told her to text him and she was ignoring that instruction. She didn't need another complication in her life, but at the same time, he was already distracting her.

She kept remembering how nice it had felt to sleep in his arms last night. To put her head over his heart as she cuddled at his side and listen to it beating. She'd been alone for a long time. Of course, she had Kinley and Penny, but that was different. Last night, for a few moments, she had almost felt like Diego was hers.

It was tantalizing, but at the same time she wanted to handle her situation with House of Hamilton on her own, and she had to wonder if it was a tiny bit of fear that was driving her to think of him as anything more than just a bachelor auction hookup. Fear of facing off with her father had her imagining what it would be like to stay here and pursue something with Diego.

He was a rancher. He was as much a part of Cole's Hill as

the Grand Hotel, the quaint shops on Main Street or the mercantile. He belonged here and he would never be able to leave. And after watching her father and mother, and the manipulation and struggle for power between the two of them, Pippa knew she was afraid to ever let herself commit to a man who would try to control her the way her father had.

And Diego was safe that way.

He was never going to leave Texas.

"What are you thinking about?" Kinley asked. "You have the oddest look on your face."

"Diego."

"Ah. Are you going to text him?" Kinley asked. "I think you should. Why not enjoy your time left in Cole's Hill until you hear back from the lawyer?"

"Because I like him."

"That stinks. I swear if I didn't love Nate, life would be so much easier," Kinley said, then shook her head. "I'm joking. Having Nate makes life so much richer."

She wanted that, yet at the same time it scared her. Then again, it wasn't as if she had a kid with Diego, so she and Kinley were looking at relationships through different lenses. But a part of her wondered what it would be like to have a man who she could be herself with. She quickly shut down those thoughts. Of course, that man couldn't be Diego, because his life was here and she'd told him only half-truths about herself.

Facing the prospect of dinner alone and plagued by the constant temptation to text Pippa, Diego told the housekeeper to take the night off and texted his brothers and Derek to see if anyone was available to head to the Bull Pen. He got two yeses. Mauricio couldn't make it; he was on his way to Dallas to meet with someone who had a portfolio that included some high-end property in the Cole's Hill area. He wanted a chance to be the agent on the listing. Inigo was due to head back to his team for the next stop on the Formula One tour, so tonight would be their last night together.

Diego needed to blow off steam. He pulled up in his Ferrari and got out just as Derek Caruthers pulled up. He waved at his brother-in-law. Derek looked tired—Bianca had mentioned that he'd had an early surgery this morning, which explained why.

"Thanks for the invite," Derek said. "I think Hunter and one of his former NFL buddies are going to join, too. The women are having a girls' night—did you know?"

Of course they were. He could even stretch his imagination and pretend that was why Pippa hadn't texted him back, but he knew when he was getting the brush-off. He'd done it enough times himself.

Yeah, karma was a bitch.

He'd known that forever, but he'd never expected to be on this end of it. Plus, he was nice to the women he slept with and for the most part always called when he said he would. Why would karma be coming for him?

To be fair, Pippa had never said she wanted more than last night. More than what she'd bid on.

"Nah, I didn't know. It's Inigo's last night in Cole's Hill for a while, and I thought we should give him a proper send-off. It's time for some payback for when he put me on a plane in Madrid with a massive hangover the last time I was there."

Derek clapped him on the back. "That's little brothers for you. I'm happy to do my part. It's been a long day for me."

"Bianca mentioned you had early surgery," Diego said. It seemed like Derek wanted to talk, but Diego didn't know the right questions to ask. And he knew a lot of things were private thanks to the HIPAA laws.

"Yeah, it was a tough one. Touch and go for a while. I just need to blow off some steam. And your sister is sweet as hell, so I can't let my temper out at home."

"Do you have a temper?" he asked. Derek had always struck

him as calm, maybe a little arrogant, but not someone with a temper.

"I just get short when I'm tired. It's better if I get that out of my system before I go home. I don't want to say anything to Bianca or Benito that would hurt them," he said.

They entered the bar, which had a mechanical bull in the back and was frequented by the astronauts and technicians from the nearby Mick Tanner Training Facility. The joint NASA and SpaceNow project was focused on training and preparing candidates for long-term missions to build a space station halfway between Earth and Mars. When they did come into town, they tended to get rowdy.

"I'm the same way, but it's just me, the horses and my housekeeper," Diego said.

"You need a woman, Diego," Derek said.

He had a woman. Or at least there was one specific one he wanted, and she hadn't texted him all day.

"I'm good. I like being a bachelor."

"Every guy says that when he's single, but the truth is we are all just waiting to be claimed," Derek said as they found a large high-top table in one of the corners.

"I can see I got here just in time," Inigo said, coming over to join them. "Don't let a Caruthers talk you into monogamy. They are all chained now and won't be happy until every guy in Cole's Hill is, too."

"I'm going to tell Bi you said I was chained to her," Derek said.

"Uh, I'm going to deny it, and I'm her baby brother, so she'll probably believe me," Inigo said with a grin. "Beer or whiskey, boys?"

"Beer for me," Derek said.

"Same," Diego said. It was always better to start slow when he was drinking with Inigo.

When Inigo turned and walked to the bar, Derek took a seat and said, "That one is trouble."

"He is. He's always been wild, and then something happened when Jose died," Diego said. "He's more out of control than he was before. Like he's trying to prove something to someone."

"Bi is worried about him, too. She wants him to stop driving, but there's no way that's going to happen," Derek said. "He's third in the point rankings, right behind his teammate and rival. He wants to beat Lewis. He's not going to stop until he does."

"One thing about the Velasquez boys is we are stubborn," Diego said.

"It didn't skip Bianca as much as she might want to think it did," Derek said. "And I'll deny I said that if you mention it to her."

Diego just shook his head. He felt something that could be a pang in his heart but wrote it off as heartburn from his late lunch. He didn't want to admit that he wanted what Bianca and Derek had. He was happy with his life. A woman wasn't a necessity for him.

But that didn't mean that he didn't wish that he was going home to Pippa tonight.

Six

Kinley was at her book club with Bianca and the other Caruthers wives. She'd kindly invited Pippa to join, but Pippa had declined. She wasn't sure she was ready to come face-to-face with Diego's sister. Not because Bianca was anything but kind; it had more to do with her own insecurities. She was trying damned hard to convince herself she wanted nothing to do with the long, tall Texan, but in reality she had done nothing but worry about her future, and a chunk of that worry had included him.

So she'd left the Jacs Veerling bridal showroom and driven toward Famous Manu's BBQ to get an early dinner. It had opened less than six months earlier and was a popular spot in town. The owner was retired NFL special teams coach Manu Barrett, who'd bought a second home in the Five Families neighborhood to be closer to his brother Hemi, who was part of the astronaut training program.

Pippa had found that the Southern pork sandwich, without the coleslaw, reminded her of the pork baps she could get back home. She'd placed her to-go order and now sat in the car waiting for her food to be ready, staring at her phone and the text message she'd written, deleted and rewritten a hundred times… Okay, that was a slight exaggeration, but it felt like she'd done it a hundred times.

Sitting in her car in a designer mother-of-the-bride dress made her feel silly. But not as silly as wearing Diego's sweats.

There was a rap on her window and she glanced up to see Diego standing there. *Speak of the devil.* What was he doing here?

"Saw your car and decided to come out and say hello." He was carrying a take-out bag.

"What are you doing here?" she asked.

"The food at the Bull Pen isn't as good as this place, so we walked over to eat, and then my brother noticed your car," he said. She could smell the hoppy scent of beer on him and she realized that Diego had already had more than a few drinks.

"I was going to text you," she said.

"Sure you were," he said.

Feeling defensive, she lifted up her phone so he could see the message she'd just retyped before he'd shown up.

He looked at it and then back to her. "So you weren't lying."

Not about this, she thought. Because now that she'd reached out to her family back in the UK, she probably should talk to Diego about who she really was.

"No. I just… I wasn't sure if you were being nice and I'm not sure if I'm staying in Texas and last night was perfect and I didn't want anything to ruin that," she said in a rush of words. *There.* She'd finally admitted out loud what had been dancing around in her brain for most of the day.

"Perfect?" he asked, leaning against her car. "I think I could do better."

She shook her head. "I doubt it."

"Challenge accepted."

"I'm not talking about sex," she said. "Well, not just the sex. The entire evening was like something out of a dream."

"I wasn't just talking about sex, either," he said, leaning into the window. His black Stetson bumped the top of the door and was pushed back on his head. He reached up, impatiently took it off and hit it against his thigh. "I like you, Pippa. I had a lot of time to think about it as I waited for you to get in touch today."

His words were heartfelt and so sincere she knew that she had to be careful with him. She liked him, too, of course, but most of that attraction was purely hormonal. He cut a fine figure of a man with his muscular shoulders and whipcord lean body. He was wearing faded jeans that clung to his thighs. She was intrigued by his strength. She remembered the way he'd lifted her onto the table in the hallway of his condo.

"Me, too," she admitted. "I know you are out with friends, but do you want to go someplace and talk?"

"Yes. Hell, yes. Let me go tell those yahoos I'm not coming back. Where do you want to go?"

"I don't know. I have my own cottage on the Rockin' C, but that's a little far out of town and you aren't in any condition to drive," she said.

"I'm not. I'll ask one of my ranch hands to come pick my Ferrari up in the morning. Dylan is always hot to drive it, so he'll be happy to do it," Diego said.

She nodded. This would be good. They could talk. She could put on her own clothes, and then maybe she could figure out what she wanted from Diego. She hadn't been lying to herself earlier when she acknowledged that she wanted more than sex. But she also knew she was in no position to ask for more than that.

She was leaving. It wasn't like she was going to fall in love with him and give up her heritage. She'd waited too long for this chance.

She got a text that her food was ready. "Let me go pick up my sandwich. Do you want me to order you anything else?"

"Nah, I'm good," he said. "Meet you back here in a few."

He opened her door for her, and when she stepped out of the

car, the slim-fitting dress fell around her thighs. She smoothed her hands down her sides, aware that she was way overdressed for barbecue.

"Damn. You keep getting better looking every time I see you," he said.

She shook her head. "I feel stupid in this."

"You shouldn't," he said. "Come on, I'll walk in there with you."

He held open the door to Famous Manu's and then put his hand at the small of her back as they entered the restaurant. People turned to see who was coming in and one woman muttered under her breath, but loud enough for Pippa to hear, "A bit overdressed."

Diego arched one eyebrow at her. "Mandy, be nice."

It was a small thing, but for the first time she felt like a man had her back. She was probably reading way more into it than she should, but it made her feel good deep inside.

They barely spoke on the drive to Pippa's cottage on the Rockin' C. She had the radio turned to Heart FM, which played soft rock music. The buzz he'd had going was starting to fade, but as usual just being in the same vicinity as Pippa was having a pronounced effect on him.

His skin felt too small for him and every breath he took smelled of her perfume and something that reminded him of sex. It was just her scent, but he couldn't smell it and not be turned on. He shifted his legs, making room for his growing erection as she drove. She was a careful driver, going just below the speed limit and signaling way before she got to the turn-in for the Rockin' C. They were about ten miles from the entrance to Arbol Verde, where he lived most of the time.

She pulled to a stop in front of a mason stone cottage that had a rough-hewn wood front porch. The motion-sensor lights came on as they got out of the car. On her front door hung a wreath that as he got closer he could tell had been made out of toy Breyer horses.

She noticed him looking at it as she shifted her bag of barbecue and fumbled for her keys. He took the food from her so she could unlock the door.

"Penny made it for me for my birthday," she said by way of explanation. "I'm sure you know that she's horse crazy."

"I do know that. Benito was out at my place earlier today getting riding lessons so he can keep up with her," Diego said, but a part of him suspected that his nephew was always going to be chasing after Penny.

"They are too cute together," Pippa admitted. "I missed seeing them today."

"I want to know more about how you came to be a nanny," he said. "Last night you mentioned you were on the run."

She led the way into the small entry hall. There was a tiled mirror and a table with a wooden bowl and a bud vase containing a single gardenia. She threw her keys into the bowl and flipped on a light as she continued into the great room. He saw a set of stairs to the left that led up to a loft. He guessed it was her bedroom.

Immediately an image of her lying naked in the middle of his bed sprang to mind and he shoved it aside. He'd been serious when he said it was more than sex he wanted from Pippa. Now if he could only get his body on board with that.

The far wall was made of river stone and had a fireplace and hearth dead center. There was a rough-hewn mantel that matched the wood on her front porch and a large clock above the fireplace with a swinging pendulum that ticked off the seconds. Two recliners with a side table between them faced the fireplace, and a large leather couch sat opposite an armoire that he suspected housed the television. The great room led to a breakfast nook with a round table and four chairs.

She led the way to the table. "Let me grab some dishes and cutlery and we can eat."

He set the food down next to a white bowl filled with oranges and continued to look around the house. He noticed there was a small office area in the kitchen with a laptop computer and a notepad. Yesterday's date had been circled several times in red on a calendar.

He saw that next to the calendar was an older-looking silver frame that had a distinctive patina. As he moved closer, he noticed it contained a black-and-white photo of a woman who bore a striking resemblance to Pippa, and was holding a little girl who looked just like Pippa, too. They both were smiling.

"That's my mum and me," she said as she moved past him. "My auntie took the photo."

"What happened to make you leave home?" he asked as they sat down. She'd set the table with place mats, cloth napkins and Fiestaware dishes in a turquoise blue. She had also poured them both glasses of water.

It was the fanciest setting he'd ever seen for pulled pork sandwiches, but at the same time it just sort of felt right considering he was with Pippa.

"Um…well, Mum died when I turned fourteen and my father took over the guardianship of me and my inheritance. He had a different idea for my future, including me marrying someone he'd chosen."

"Are you married?" he asked. He'd never thought she might belong to someone else. Then immediately he realized that he didn't think she was the kind of woman to sleep with one man when married to another. He knew it had been his own insecurity at realizing how much he didn't know about her that had prompted the question.

"No. Obviously not, given what you and I have been up to. I ran away the night he was going to propose," she said.

Diego leaned back in the chair, feeling like a fool as he watched her carefully. She hadn't been kidding when she'd mentioned that it was complicated. He couldn't imagine his father ever trying to control him. If he had, Diego would have done something similar to what Pippa had.

"I'm sorry for asking that. I knew you weren't married. It's just a shock to hear all of this… I mean, I knew you were more than a nanny, but this is bigger than just inheriting some jewelry, isn't it?"

"Yes, it is."

"So what's next? Can you return to England?"

"I have started the process," she admitted. "But they have to verify that I am who I say I am first."

"Is there some doubt?"

"Not really, but there will be questions, and my coming back will make things awkward for my father, who has been managing my assets while I've been missing," she admitted.

"I take it you two don't get along," Diego said. "Stating the obvious, right?"

Her relationship with her father was complicated. Over the last four years she'd spent a lot of time waking in the middle of the night and thinking about how much she hated him. Especially when Kinley was having a hard time making ends meet when she'd first started working for Jacs. If she weren't having difficulties with her father, Pippa knew if she'd walked into the bank and made a withdrawal she could take care of Kin's finances and let her give Penny the financial stake they needed to make a good life.

But at the same time, she'd be giving up her freedom.

Because her father had final say in practically everything she did with her money and her time until she turned twenty-five. And he got to vote her shares on the board as he saw fit. The only recourse she'd have had was to lodge an objection, which was virtually the same as having no power.

But she also remembered how broken he'd been after her mum had died. How the two of them had sat in their home mourning her. She knew that part of the reason why he had wanted to control so much of Pippa's life was due to losing her mum. But she hadn't been able to understand why his grief had taken this particular form: to control Pippa.

And time had brought her no closer to understanding him.

"I can't say if we got along or not. I had a typical loving child's view of my father before my mum died. But then when I turned twenty-one he gave me an ultimatum, which was the wrong thing to do. I mean, I know I look all sweet, but I'm really very stubborn," she said.

"*Sweet* isn't the first word I'd use to describe you," Diego said. "I've seen signs of that stubborn streak."

She arched one eyebrow at him. She wasn't going to ask what word he would use. Really, she wasn't. "When have you seen me stubborn?"

"When I paid for your coffee and you insisted on paying me back," he said. "You didn't want to owe me anything."

"Oh, that… Well, I didn't want to lead you on," she said at last.

"By letting me buy you coffee?" he asked. The amusement in his voice invited her to have a laugh at the situation, but she couldn't.

"Yes. I have been waiting to turn twenty-five since the moment I walked away from my old life and I didn't want to give you any encouragement that we could have anything other than—" She broke off, realizing she had admitted to him that she only wanted sex. That hooking up was fine, but anything deeper scared her.

Of course it did. But she hadn't meant to say it as bluntly as she had. "I didn't mean that."

"You did," he said. "Let's be honest with each other, okay? I'm not going to lie. I do want to do more than just burn up the sheets with you. So if we are going to have any chance of making this work, I think we have to both be honest with each other."

She nodded.

Honest.

She could do that.

She thought she could. She wasn't lying to him. She'd told him the truth.

"Fair enough."

"So where does that leave us?" he asked after a few long moments.

She stood up and started to clean the table. Diego helped her out. He rinsed the dishes and put them into the dishwasher without saying anything. She suspected he was giving her time to figure out what she wanted to say.

But like the text message she'd struggled to send earlier, she was still confused when it came to him.

"I'm waiting to hear back from my family attorney," she said, using the American term. "I can't do anything, make any real plans until then. Even my money is tied up until my identity is confirmed. So I'm planning to continue to help out with Penny and live here until that's sorted."

Diego wiped his hands on the dish towel and leaned against her kitchen counter. She tried to concentrate on what he was saying, but his voice was a deep rumble that reminded her of last night when she'd lain on his chest and he'd said good-night to her. The sound had rumbled under her ear.

She knew that she wanted Diego. Wanted to somehow figure out a way to have him and her inheritance. Like one of the fairy tales she read to Penny before bedtime, she wanted a happy ending of her own.

But she'd never been good at trusting others. If she had been, maybe she wouldn't have run away in the first place. Because she could admit that when she'd first come to the States, it was her temper and her stubbornness that had driven her from the upscale Manhattan hotel to the bus station with only a haute couture dress on her back and the cash in her wallet.

She could have tried to speak to her potential fiancé, but she hadn't known if she could trust him. She'd just felt like everything was out of control.

But in this kitchen with Diego watching her as if she were in charge, she realized she was exactly where she wanted to be.

"Pippa?"

"Hmm?"

"I asked how long you thought you had until they confirmed everything," he said.

"I would imagine a few weeks."

He uncrossed his arms and straightened to walk over to her, his boot heels clacking on the hardwood floor. He stopped when only an inch of space separated them, and she felt the brush of his breath as he exhaled on a sigh.

"As I see it we have two options," he said.

"They are?"

"I walk out of here and we continue the way we had been before last night, smiling politely when we see each other in town but otherwise pretending that there isn't a red-hot spark between us."

She nodded, nibbling on her bottom lip because it tingled when he stood this close.

"And option two?"

"We enjoy the time you have left in Texas together."

"I'd like that. However, tonight isn't good for me," she said. "I have to be over at the big house when Penny wakes up in the morning."

"I crashed your evening, and I'm glad that you allowed me to."

"I'm glad you did. I was feeling…unsure and I didn't like it. I've kind of stayed away from men for the last few years and I feel really awkward around you," she admitted. He seemed so confident, so sure, that she wished she was…well, stronger.

"You're perfect. Everyone says I'm better around horses than women."

"Who says that?"

"My brother, but he has been known to be an ass," Diego said, standing up and walking toward the door.

She followed him, not really wanting him to go but knowing she had responsibilities toward Penny and if he stayed she'd be distracted.

"Good night," he said, picking up his hat and settling it on his head.

"Good night." She reached out and touched his jaw before he turned and left.

Seven

"Mama said you're leaving," Penny said while she was taking her bath the next evening. Pippa had already washed the little girl's hair and was cleaning up the bathroom while Penny played in the water.

"I am, imp. You know my home isn't here in Texas."

"But I'm here," she said. "And Mama is, too."

She turned to look at Penny, whose red hair, so like Kinley's, clung to her heart-shaped face. There was sadness in her wide, blue-green eyes. The little girl was hurt that she was leaving.

"Nothing is going to change between us, Penny. I'm still going to be your Pippy and we'll talk every day on the video chat, like Benito does when his mommy is out of town," she said. "You have a daddy now and I think as you and your mama settle here in Cole's Hill, you are going to find you miss me less and less."

Water sluiced down Penny's little body as she leaned over to hug Pippa tight. Pippa wrapped her arms around her.

"I'll miss you."

"I'm going to miss you, too," Pippa said, feeling tears in her eyes. She'd been with this little girl since she'd been born. The bond they had was deep and important. "We'll always be the P girls."

"That's right," Penny said.

Pippa took the hooded towel from the heated rack and helped Penny dry off. Penny fastened the Velcro that made the towel into a sort of robe, put her hood on and ran into the bedroom to get dressed in the pajamas that Pippa had laid out earlier.

She pulled the plug on the bath water and finished cleaning up the bathroom, thinking of how much she'd liked the simple life. But a part of her knew that something had always been missing.

Kinley came in and they read Penny her bedtime story before tucking the little girl into bed.

"Glass of wine?" Kinley asked Pippa as she closed the door to Penny's room.

"Yes. I'm on edge waiting to hear back from London," Penny admitted when they were both sitting down in front of the gas fireplace.

"I'd be going nuts. You know how I am," Kinley said.

"I do. Penny asked me about leaving," Pippa said.

"Yeah, sorry I didn't give you a heads-up. It kind of came out and I decided I should probably tell her the truth," Kinley said. "But I should have had your back and told you first."

"It's okay. I hope that this doesn't change our relationship," Pippa said.

"I'm not going to let it. You know me better than just about anyone and you and Penny have a bond. You're like her best auntie," Kinley said. "You're not getting rid of us that easily."

"I'm glad to hear that," Pippa said. "I have really loved living with you both, but I think it's time for me to claim my life."

They talked about the different couples who had emerged from the charity auction Sunday night. And how sweet Ethan and Crissanne had been when he proposed. Pippa had had a good view of Mason, Crissanne's former boyfriend and Ethan's best friend, as it had happened. And he had seemed happy for the couple, despite the complicated circumstances that had brought them together.

"So what's going on with you and Diego?" Kinley asked in that blunt way of hers.

"Uh, we decided to date while I'm still here," she said. "I told him that I'm waiting to hear from the solicitor in England. I didn't want to lead him on."

"Good idea. So what does dating look like?"

"I'm not sure. He's busy with the ranch and I have Penny, so finding time to get together won't be easy," Pippa said, recalling how they'd been texting most of the day. But she didn't respond to texts while she was nannying, wanting to make sure Penny had her attention.

"Men are complicated," Kinley said.

"But worth the hassle," Nate said as he walked into the living room and gave Kinley a look so hot that even Pippa could feel the heat. She excused herself and walked the short distance to her cottage.

She let herself in and stood in the hallway with the lights off for a long minute. The house smelled of new wood flooring and lemon-scented cleaner, since Kinley had insisted that the housekeeping staff also clean her place. She'd decorated the rooms with some knickknacks she'd collected in town and while she'd been in Las Vegas. There was a small laundry/mud room off the kitchen and a den that Pippa would have made into a library if she were staying.

There were bookshelves on all the walls and a nice window seat that overlooked the Rockin' C pastures. The shelves weren't full, as Pippa's book collection was mainly digital, but she'd recently joined a book club, so one shelf had ten books on it.

She had obsessively checked her email all night long, so she limited herself to one last look at the smartphone that Kinley had given her but kept in Kinley's name, hoping the solicitor had gotten back to her even though she knew that with the six-hour time difference that wasn't going to happen.

Tomorrow was Wednesday. Realistically she knew it was going to take a few days to verify everything, but honestly it felt like this was taking way longer than the last four years had.

Her phone pinged as she was washing her face and she fumbled for her face towel before running into the other room to see who it was.

It was a text from Diego.

A little thrill went through her.

Instead of meeting for coffee in town tomorrow, would you like a tour of Arbol Verde and a late breakfast with me?

Pippa's reply was instant.

I'd love that. I have to take Penny to school so I could be there around nine.

Perfect. Are you afraid of heights?

No. Why?

Just asking. What are you doing now?

Getting ready for bed.

Wish I was there with you.

Me, too. She thought it but didn't text it. She wanted to keep it light and casual. Those were her key words for Diego.

What are you doing?

Fantasizing about being in your bedroom. What does it look like? I didn't get a chance to see it when I was there earlier.

Light and casual.

Yeah, right.

She hesitated for one more second and then tapped out the message she'd been wanting to send since she'd seen it was his name showing up on her phone.

Come over and see for yourself...

There was no response at first, then the three dancing dots that indicated he was typing.

On my way.

Diego had intended... Well, he didn't know what he'd intended. With Pippa he was like a horny guy who'd never been laid before. He thought about her whenever she wasn't with him, wanting her in his bed. Not living on Nate Caruthers's property. Which made him slow down for a second as he was driving his Bronco hell-bent-for-leather down the old country road that connected his property to the Rockin' C.

He drove past the big house and the bunkhouse to the smaller residences behind them. He knew from past visits that the largest of the three belonged to Marcus Quentin, Kinley's dad, the former ranch foreman who'd retired a few years back. The next one was dark and looked empty and the last one was Pippa's. As his headlights illuminated the house, he saw that she was sitting on the porch swing waiting for him.

He turned off the truck engine and sat there for a long minute in the cab of his truck parked in front of her cottage. If she'd changed her mind, he'd walk away.

And actually now that he saw her, that lust-driven rush that had made him hurry over to her was starting to calm. Once he was with her, he could take his time. It was only when they were apart that there was a problem.

Because he knew they didn't have much time before she'd be out of his life for good.

He put his head on the steering wheel.

What was he doing?

This was like Mauricio following Hadley when she was on a date with someone else, wasn't it? Of course, Diego wasn't going to start a fight with anyone, but the situation with Pippa was similarly an exercise in futility. He wanted more than Pippa was ever going to give…or at least that gnawing emptiness in the pit of his soul made him think he did.

He looked up and noticed how she kept rocking on the porch swing. Just sitting there waiting to see what he was going to do.

And he realized she was just as unsure about this as he was. The connection between the two of them shouldn't be this strong. They were supposed to be a bit of fun for each other, casually hooking up and then going back to their real lives.

Except that wasn't what was happening.

Not for either one of them, unless he missed his guess.

He got out of his truck and pocketed his keys as he walked up the stone path that led to her front porch.

"Hello, Pippa," he said.

"Diego," she said.

He couldn't help noticing she wore a cotton dress that ended at her knees and had a tie front that was undone, drawing his eyes to the hint of cleavage underneath it. She sat there on the swing as if she wasn't sure what to do now that he was here.

"So…still want me here?" he asked.

She nodded. "Yes."

He didn't say anything else, just climbed up the two steps that led to her porch and then went over to stand against the railing. She'd pulled her hair up into a ponytail and wasn't wearing any makeup, but he'd never seen her look more beautiful. It was as if each time he saw her he noticed once again how pretty she was.

"Tell me more about what is waiting for you when you go back to England," he said. It was the subject he was pretty sure was on both of their minds and he wanted to know the details… though he had no idea why. He wasn't going to leave Cole's Hill. His life and his soul were here. The land and his horses were so much a part of the man he was, he couldn't go with her. But he wanted to know what it was that she'd left behind.

She tipped her head back, looking away from him.

"The family business," she said. "My dad and I were never close, and when my mom died, the rift between us widened. He had control of my shares in the business and my other interests until I was twenty-five."

"Okay, so you're twenty-five and going back means you get to be in charge?" he asked, trying to figure out what was at stake.

"Yes," she said. "When I left, he was pressuring me to marry a man who sided with him when it came to the family business and that wasn't the vision I had for it. Obviously, he wasn't going to force me to marry, but I realized he was never going to listen to me. And if I disappeared, it would tie up my shares. He wouldn't be able to vote them until they ascertained what had happened to me. My shares haven't been in play while I was gone and the company has only been able to continue operating as it had been when my shares were last voted. So I was able to slow down his agenda and give myself some breathing room."

He moved over and sat down on the swing next to her, stretching his arm out on the back. She shifted until she was sitting in the curve of his body.

She put her head on his shoulder and then looked at him with those gray eyes of hers, so sincere and full of vulnerability that he wanted to wrap her in a big bear hug and promise she wasn't going to be hurt again. But he knew that wasn't a vow he could keep. The man who'd hurt her was probably going to fight tooth and nail to keep from relinquishing his control over her fortune.

"What can I do?" he asked.

"Just help me forget what is waiting for me," she said. "I like being with you, Diego, because you are so far removed from that world and…don't laugh…but you make me feel as though you like me for me. All the things that aren't perfect don't seem to matter when I'm with you."

"You are perfect, so I don't know what you're talking about," he said, slipping his arm under her thighs and lifting her onto his lap.

Pippa was talking too much. She'd meant to keep most of the past to herself, but there was something about Diego and the quiet confidence in his eyes that made her feel like everything was safe with him.

Her cottage faced the open pasture and the big Texas night sky. The bunkhouse, barn and main ranch building were in the other direction as was the home shared by Ma and Pa Caruthers. It almost seemed as if they were the only two people on the land tonight.

He settled her on his lap and she wrapped her arm around his shoulders. Their eyes met. His were so big and dark with only the porch lights illuminating them. She suddenly didn't know if her trust was misplaced. There was something in his eyes—a hunger—that made him almost…almost a different guy than the one who'd been sweetly listening to her.

There was something almost untamed about him. As much as her mind might warn her to step back from him, there was another more primal part that wanted to claim him. But she'd never be able to tame him because she wasn't going to have enough time to do that.

She shifted so that she was straddling him, and pressed her lips to his. He spread his thighs underneath her hips, forcing her legs farther apart. She rocked back and forth, feeling his erection against her as their kiss grew more intense.

His breath was warm and sweet and smelled of peppermint and whiskey. She pulled back, putting her hands on either side of his face. "Did you pop a mint in for me?"

He flushed, and that charmed her. "Yeah."

"Thank you," she said. "I didn't do anything to prepare for your visit."

"You don't have to," he said. She felt his hands on the backs of her thighs, rubbing up and down and coming closer to her butt with each stroke. He was moving his hands in a counter-rhythm to her hips.

With his big, hot hands on her thighs and his thick erection underneath her, she let her head fall back as she rode him. She felt the brush of his breath against her neck a moment before his mouth was on it. He kissed her softly at first, but then as his hands urged her to move faster against him, he suckled her neck and shivers spread down her body as she continued rocking against him.

Diego wore a Western shirt that had snap closures; she tugged lightly and they all came undone. She pushed the shirt open before shifting slightly back on his thighs. He eased his legs farther apart and she undid the snap that held his jeans closed and lowered the zipper to see the ridge of his erection hard against the cotton of his boxer briefs.

He shifted again, freeing himself.

He handed her a condom and she smiled as she held it in one hand while circling his nipple with her fingernail, scraping the line where it met the smooth skin of his chest. Then she scraped her nail down his rock-hard stomach, lingering to trace his tattoo before moving lower.

She took the condom out of the package and rolled it onto his length.

He sat up straighter, pulling her more fully into his arms until she felt the tip of his erection against her center. He groaned deep in his throat.

He undid the laces on the front of her dress even farther until her breasts were visible. She hadn't put a bra on tonight, so when he dipped his fingers under the dress fabric, he brushed over her nipple, which made her shiver and rotate her shoulders to thrust her chest forward.

She moved again on his lap, and his hard-on nudged at her center. She loved the feel of his big hands as he put them under her skirt, caressing her thighs and then cupping her butt. He kissed her neck, biting at her collarbone as she shifted so that the tips of her breasts rubbed over his chest.

She shuddered, clutching at his shoulders, grinding her body harder against him.

He moved his fingers lower on her body, until she felt the tip of one tracing her folds and pushing up into her. She was moist and ready for him and leaned forward to take his mouth with hers. He continued to trace the opening of her body with his finger.

She captured his face, tipped his head back and kissed him hard. Her tongue thrusting into his mouth as he shifted, she felt him inside her. She rocked down hard on him as he plunged into her.

He used his thumb to find her center and stroked her as she rocked against him. His free hand cupped her butt and urged her to a faster rhythm, guiding her motions against him. He bent his head. His tongue stroked her nipple, and then he suckled her.

Everything in her body clenched. She clutched at his shoulders, rubbing harder and tightening around his fingers as her climax shattered her. She collapsed against his chest and he held her close. She put her head on his shoulder and they stayed like that without saying a word.

Pippa wanted to pretend it was because there was nothing to say, but she knew it was because there was too much.

Eight

There were a lot of cute boutiques in the historic area of Cole's Hill, but Penny and Benito wanted to go to Jump!, an indoor soft play area out on FM145. Pippa had volunteered to pick them up after pre-K and take them to play and then pick out their Halloween costumes.

Bianca had flown to New York to do a one-off fashion shoot for a famous American designer. Rumor around town was that she had been asked to do his spring show but had declined. Kinley was working longer hours than normal and had gone to Vegas with several of her brides-to-be. So Pippa was having both of the four-year-olds for a sleepover that evening. Diego had suggested they go for a ride at sunset and then have dinner around a campfire on his property.

And after securing the permission of all the parents, she had accepted. They had fallen into a relationship that felt…well, like pretend, if Pippa was honest. They saw each other when their schedules allowed and had been sleeping over at each other's places at least three times a week.

She had a feeling in the pit of her stomach it wouldn't last…

probably because she knew it wouldn't. But it had more to do with the funky peace they shared. It was like they were both on their very best behavior. So what was developing between them felt fake; at least on her side, she was offering a fake version of herself. She wasn't as sweet and nice as Diego seemed to think she was.

Normally she would have given the barista a bit of attitude when she skipped her pump of vanilla in her coffee, but because Diego had been with her this morning she'd just smiled and said that was okay, she was watching her calories.

And she knew that there was no way a successful rancher like Diego would be in town every morning at the coffee shop. That was prime time on a ranch. She knew because that was when Nate and the rest of the population on the Rockin' C were the busiest.

So Diego was faking it, too.

Then there was the other night, when he'd said he'd rather watch a repeat of the *Real Housewives* than the Spurs basketball game, which she knew was a lie. She smiled at the memory of her teasing him and asking him which housewife was his favorite. When he'd gone into the kitchen to get popcorn, she'd switched it over to the Spurs game. She frankly didn't understand a thing that was going on during the basketball game, but seeing the surprise and relief on his face had been worth it.

She realized that some things weren't fake between them—their passion, for one. But in general, she suspected they were being so careful of each other's feelings because they had a nebulous expiration date on their relationship. They both knew that it would end but not exactly when. And neither wanted to spoil their last moments together.

Whenever they would come.

It had been almost ten days and she'd still heard nothing from the solicitor except that he'd received her information and confirmed her identity. As far as her claim to her entire fortune, and the chair on House of Hamilton's board, he was still working on it. He'd paid her a small stipend via wire transfer to the bank in Cole's Hill. So she had some of her own money, even though she didn't need her fortune to live in Cole's Hill.

Room and board were covered by Kinley and she had an Etsy shop where she sold art pieces she made to practice her skills at design. Some of them were pretty good to her mind, others just so-so.

"Pippy, that was so much fun. I hope that I can find the perfect costume," Penny said as she and Benito came out of the soft play area and she was helping them both to put their shoes back on.

"It looked like fun," Pippa said to her. "Did you like it, Benito?"

"Yes, I jumped the highest," he said.

"He did. I tried to beat him, but I couldn't."

"Not everything has to be a competition," she said to the two toddlers.

"We know," they said at the same time.

"What costumes are we looking for today?" she asked as they stepped out of the play area and she took their hands. The costume superstore was across the parking lot, and since it was a sunny, warm day there was no reason for them not to walk to it.

"Cowgirl," Penny said, skipping next to her.

"I'm not surprised, but you know that Halloween is a chance to be something different than who you normally are. And you're a cowgirl now," Pippa said.

"Really?" Benito asked her.

"Yes. What are you going to be?" the little girl said.

"I was going to be a doctor like Daddy." Benito's biological father had been killed when he was six months old. Since Bianca and Derek had married, he called Derek Daddy and referred to his biological father as Papa. "But I might be an astronaut."

"That's a good idea," Pippa said.

When they got inside the store, Penny went straight for the

cowgirl costumes, but she kept looking over at a pink princess one, as well. "What's the matter, imp?" Pippa asked.

"Could I be a cowgirl princess?"

"Yes. Or you could just be a princess," Pippa told her, finding the sizes in both costumes for Penny.

"Yay!" Penny said, turning to help Benito.

He decided on the astronaut and then they both wanted every piece of candy near the checkout, but Pippa got them to compromise on a lollipop and a jar of bubbles instead.

"What about you?" Penny asked. "What are you going to be?"

She didn't know if she'd still be in Texas at Halloween. Surely everything would be sorted before then.

"I haven't decided yet."

"I hope all the good ones aren't gone," Penny said.

"I'm sure they won't be," Pippa replied.

Diego was waiting in the barn when Pippa and the kids arrived. Every time they made plans he was aware of the fact that they might be canceled due to Pippa's situation, and it was setting him on edge. Plus, being perfect—or as perfect as he could be—around Pippa was making him short-tempered with his brothers. Mainly just Mauricio, which suited the other man just fine, since he was out of sorts over Hadley being seen around town with another man.

So the Velasquez brothers were spending way too much time in town at the kickboxing studio that a former army captain and his brother had set up. Diego had a few bruises on his ribs and his knuckles ached, since he and Mo preferred bare-knuckled fighting, but it had been worth it.

He smiled easily at Pippa. She wore a pair of faded jeans that made her legs look even longer than he knew they were and a pale pink button-down shirt that made her blond hair and gray eyes stand out. Penny was dressed in a pair of jeans and boots and had a pink cowgirl hat on her head and Benito had boots, jeans and his black cowboy hat on.

He had his ranch hands set up dinner on one of the ridges that was an easy thirty-minute ride from the barn. He had saddled the gentlest horses he had for Benito and Penny. Pippa had told him that she'd ridden as a child and Nate had said that she was a good horsewoman, so he'd given her a spirited mare who he hoped would match her skill.

"*Tio*, I'm going to be an astronaut for Halloween," Benito said as he came skipping over to him.

Diego scooped his nephew up and hugged him close. He had been happy when Bianca had moved back home after Jose's death, so he could watch his nephew growing up.

"Sounds like it should be fun. I met the brother of one of the astronauts at the training center. Maybe I can arrange for you to go and visit him," Diego said, thinking that Manu would probably be able to arrange that.

"Can I go, too?" Penny asked.

"I think Diego will need to make sure that kids are allowed to go out there for a visit first," Pippa said.

"Yes, I will. But one thing I know we can do is go for a ride on the horses right now. Who's ready?"

"Me!" the children both yelled. Benito squirmed to get down out of his uncle's arms. Diego placed the little boy on his feet and he and Penny joined hands and ran toward the barn.

"Sorry, I was promising something I couldn't deliver, wasn't I?"

"You were," Pippa said. "It's probably not that big of a deal, but Penny will go to school tomorrow and tell everyone you are taking them to the space station and it might start something."

"I guess you can tell I'm not around kids a lot," he said.

"I can and I like it. For once, I feel like I know more than you do," she said.

"That's not true," he responded. "You know tons more than I do about a lot of subjects."

"Not horses," she said.

"Nate said you were pretty good. Was he lying to me?"

She shook her head. “I can ride, but I feel weird sitting on a Western saddle. Kinley’s been giving me some lessons on weekends when the little imp insists we all go for a ride together.”

Diego pulled her to a stop just outside the barn. He could hear the kids talking to the grooms he’d had in waiting to help them with their tack.

“Won’t you miss her?” he asked.

She bit her lower lip. “Yes. I’ll miss her terribly, but this isn’t my life. I know it, and so do Kinley and Nate. They include me in their weekends, but I know they are looking forward to being a family on their own.”

Diego put his arm around her and squeezed her. “I can’t imagine what that must be like.”

But he could. He was dealing with that to a very small extent with Pippa right now. She was his for these few weeks. It had sounded like a great idea when he was horny as hell; when they were naked it always felt right. But now that he realized he could lose her at any minute, that when he planned an evening for the two of them he had to wait all day in suspense hoping she’d still show up, he knew it wasn’t.

If it had been only physical attraction between them, things would be easier. Or if Pippa were a snob to people. But she was sweet to everyone, even the barista who never got anyone’s order right. He’d lost it with her more than once, but not Pippa. She’d just smiled and put the other woman at ease.

It had made him realize how much he liked her. He was trying to be smart about this and not get in any deeper than he already was, but the only way that was going to happen was if he kept his distance from her and that wasn’t in the cards.

He didn’t want to waste a single second of the time they’d been given. So he was working longer hours around the times when she was available so he wouldn’t have as many regrets when she was gone.

“What are you thinking?” she asked.

"Just how much I'm going to miss you when you leave," he said, then turned and walked into the barn and went to his horse.

He saddled his horse Iago and heard Pippa talking to the kids as they donned their protective helmets and were assisted onto the horses by the grooms. He guessed he hadn't spent long enough in the ring with Mauricio today, because he was out of sorts and he needed to adjust his attitude.

Hopefully the ride would do that.

Pippa knew she'd upset Diego, and she got it. Really, she did. She probably should just leave Cole's Hill now and not prolong the inevitable. It was just that she had nowhere to really go until the solicitor got back to her. Even her passport was out-of-date. But hanging around here, starting something with Diego even though they'd both said it was just temporary, hadn't really been a smart idea.

"Texas is so different from Las Vegas," Pippa said as they rode. The kids were a little ways ahead of them and Diego never took his eyes off the pair.

"It's beautiful, isn't it? I can't imagine living anywhere but here," he said.

And that secret hope that she'd barely even realized she'd been holding on to died. Diego was never going to be a man she could bring with her to her new life. Not that she needed a man by her side, but it would have been nice not to return to England by herself. And Kinley obviously couldn't come with her.

"Stop your horse," Diego called out to the kids. "Do you remember how?"

"Pull back on the reins," Benito said.

"I knew that, too," Penny chimed in.

The two of them expertly stopped their horses and then held the reins loosely in their hands much the same way Diego did. He guided Iago next to the two children and Pippa watched them look over at him with rapt expressions on their faces. She fumbled for her cell phone and snapped a photo of them as Diego was giving them instructions.

She tucked her phone away before joining them, knowing the photo would be one of her most cherished because it would bring her back to the sun on her shoulders and this moment when she realized that Diego meant more to her than she had wanted him to.

After thirty minutes, they got to the spot where they were going to have the campfire dinner. She saw that Diego had gone out of his way for them. He had four chairs set up around the campfire and had torches lit. One of his ranch hands was cooking the meal and there were two others waiting to take the horses back to the barn. She noticed he had a four-wheel ATV parked to the side. There were jackets for the kids and blankets in case the evening turned cold, but so far the weather was perfect, with only a slight breeze.

"I made cowboy chili for dinner," Diego said. "This recipe has been in our family for almost two hundred years. In the old days they'd make a batch of this and it was all the hands would have to eat for a week."

Benito and Penny both went closer to him as he told them the history of the first Velasquez ancestor who'd come over to Texas by order of the King of Spain and started to carve out a life for himself and his family. Diego kept Pippa and the children entertained as they ate the chili, which he'd made mild enough for the kids to eat. When they were done, he brought out the makings of s'mores for dessert, which she'd never had growing up but had learned to love since being in Texas.

She realized as they ate dinner how much she would miss Diego and Texas. The stories here were big legends that fired her imagination, but more than that she was going to miss Diego. And it was clear to her that he wouldn't suddenly leave his ranch and come with her to England. He couldn't. His history was here. His horses and his equine breeding program, which had just received another award according to a couple grooms she'd overheard discussing it, were all here.

He belonged here. As much as she didn't.

"Cowboys and cowgirls used to use the stars to find their way back home," Diego was saying. The kids had their heads tipped up to the sky. They were far enough from town that there was no real light pollution except for the glow of the torches and the fire.

"I'll show you how when we're done eating," Diego said.

"This summer, Daddy is going to take me to a cattle drive," Penny said.

"Really?" Diego asked. "On the Rockin' C?"

"No. Fort something. Do you remember, Pippy?"

"Fort Worth," she said. "Apparently they still drive cattle down the street there twice a day."

"They do. It's one of the oldest traditions in the state. There used to be a cattle market there and everyone would drive their herds up for the sale," Diego said. As he continued talking to the kids about life on the cattle trail, Pippa just sat there and listened to him.

She wondered why he wasn't married. Diego was really good with the kids. They'd moved to sit closer to him, and he had them both cuddled on his lap as he talked. Their eyes met over the kids' heads and her heart beat a little faster. He winked at her and the earlier turmoil she'd felt between them disappeared at least for a few moments.

She closed her eyes and some of the resentment she had been carrying with her since she'd left her old life dissipated. She'd never have been here if not for those events that had driven her to run away.

"In fact, the Five Families of Cole's Hill used to pool their resources and they would journey up to the cattle markets together. Back then there were all kinds of dangers from snakes to outlaws to treacherous river crossings. That bond was what made Cole's Hill what it is today," Diego said.

They finished their food and Pippa cleaned up both kids' faces and hands. Then they piled into the ATV and Diego drove them halfway back to his ranch house, stopping in an especially dark area. "Close your eyes for a few minutes and then I'll show you the star that will point you to home."

Pippa glanced in the back seat of the open-air vehicle to where the kids were buckled into their car seats. When she turned back around, Diego was so close to her, their breaths mingled. And he kissed her. It was hard, passionate and deep but over before it began. "Couldn't resist your lips," he whispered.

"Open your eyes, kiddos, tip your head back and look toward the front of the vehicle. Do you see the star to the left of the moon?"

Both children weren't sure how to tell left from right, so Pippa moved to the back seat and sat between the two of them to help. She glanced up, pretty sure that Diego meant Venus when he talked about the star that would lead them home. A good Texas legend, she thought, just like the man himself.

She carefully pointed to the "star" so Penny and Benito could find it.

"Now you will always be able to find your way back home," she said.

"We all will," Diego added.

She clamored back over the seat and he drove them back to the ranch house.

"Want to come back to Pippa's for our sleepover?" Benito asked.

"Um..."

"Please," Benito pleaded.

"It would be nice if you joined us," Pippa said.

"Then I will," he said. "I have to be back at the ranch first thing in the morning."

"That's fine," she said.

Pippa got Penny into her car and Diego followed her with Benito. As she drove away, she couldn't help thinking that home wasn't what she'd once believed it would be. For one thing, she hadn't imagined she'd live anywhere but London, but now her idea of home was changing and morphing into something new. And that was dangerous.

Nine

Diego followed Pippa in his ranch truck with Benito buckled into his car seat beside him. His nephew talked excitedly all the way back to Pippa's cottage.

By the time they got there, the kids were exhausted from their outing. Diego helped Pippa get the kids bathed and into bed and then hung back waiting for her to check her email.

"Nothing firm yet. But I did just get a brief email. The solicitor said he should have news no later than Friday," she said.

It was Wednesday.

So that meant he had two more nights with her. His gut said he needed to take her as many times as he could. Imprint on her so that when she was back in the UK she wouldn't be able to forget him or their time together.

He took her hand. "Can you hear the kids if we're downstairs?"

"Yes. I have a monitor app on the smartphone that Kinley gave me," she said. "Why?"

"I want you," he said, under his breath.

She flushed. "Me, too."

He led her down the stairs after she made sure both kids were sleeping in her big bed, then into the kitchen, where he lifted her up onto the counter and tunneled his fingers into her hair and kissed her deeply.

He had told himself this was so she wouldn't forget him, but he knew this was for him. He wanted her as many times as he could have her and in as many different ways. For himself. For those long winter nights he knew were coming. Long nights when he'd be all alone and hungry and hard for a woman who had never thought of him as anything other than her temporary man.

She pushed her hands up under his shirt and then reached into the back of his jeans, cupping his ass and drawing him farther in between her legs. He shifted around, rubbing the tip of his erection against her. Running his hands up and down her back, he pulled her forward toward him, but there was too much clothing in the way.

His jeans, her jeans. He lifted her off the counter and knelt to help her take off her boots. She put one foot on his thigh. He grabbed the toe with one hand and the heel with the other and helped her take off the first boot. Then he made quick work of the other.

She was wearing socks with hearts and flowers on them. He pulled them off and tossed them toward her boots. Her feet were small and delicate in his big hands. Her pedicure was a racy red color that matched the lipstick he recalled her wearing to the bachelor auction.

His cock jumped as he remembered the way she'd looked that night, and he groaned at the pain. He straightened and reached for the button at his waistband and undid it, lowering the zipper so that his erection had room. She reached down and touched the tip of it, stroking with her fingers in the opening of his jeans.

He took her hand in his and placed it on the counter next to her. He was so close to the edge that if she touched him again, he'd spill himself right there and this would be the shortest encounter in history. And he needed more than that.

He undid her pants, pushing them down her legs along with her panties. As she scissored her legs and the jeans and underwear fell to the floor, he reached into his back pocket where he'd put a condom earlier this evening.

She smiled and took it from him.

"I like a guy who's prepared," she said.

"Just call me a Boy Scout," he said. He was always prepared for sex. But he was also trying to be prepared for when she left. He shook his head, tore open the packet and shoved his underwear down to put the condom on.

She placed her hand on his hip and he realized he was going too fast. The control he'd always taken for granted had deserted him. That email from her lawyer had just served to remind him of how little time he actually had left with her. And that was doing things to his emotions that he didn't want to deal with.

But she was his for now. That was about as much as he wanted to think about tonight. He pulled her toward him.

"Wrap your legs around me," he said. She did as he asked, and he shifted his hips, feeling the tip of his erection nudging at her entrance.

But she wasn't ready, and he cursed. He brought his mouth down on hers and his hands to her shirt, undoing the buttons while his tongue teased and played with hers. She sucked his deeper into her mouth as her hands cupped his backside and she drew him closer. She arched against him as his fingers found the cami bra she had on, and he fumbled around, trying to find a fastening before realizing there wasn't one. He pushed the bottom of the bra up until her breasts were free and then he rubbed his finger around her nipple, feeling it bead under his finger.

She parted her legs farther and he plucked at the nipple as he once again thrust against her. This time he slid easily inside. She arched her back and he looked down at her breasts angled toward him, lowering his head to catch the nipple of one in his mouth and sucking on it hard and deep.

She funneled her fingers through his hair and rocked harder and harder against him until he heard that tiny gasp and knew she was close to her climax. He lifted his head from her breast and took her mouth in an urgent kiss, swallowing her cries as he drove into her again and again until he came long and hard. She tightened around him, her body squeezing him so perfectly, and he kept thrusting until he felt her shiver in the throes of orgasm.

He held her against his chest as their breathing slowed and his heartbeat started to calm. She wrapped her arms and legs around his body and held him tightly to her.

And he hoped he wasn't the only one who was going to have a hard time saying goodbye.

Diego knew he couldn't spend the night, but he didn't want to leave. So instead he convinced Pippa to take the baby monitor with her to her back porch, where there was a fire pit. He lit a fire and then sat down on one of the big Adirondack chairs, pulling her onto his lap.

"Did you always know that you were going to take over the stud farm?" she asked, leaning her head against his shoulder.

He knew his arms were going to feel empty when she was gone and hugged her tightly to him without saying a word.

"Yes," he said at last. Sparks from the fire danced up into the night sky as a log shifted. He stared at it and pondered their situation.

If he were a different man, he'd just give up everything and follow her, but he wasn't. He'd always just known that he was meant to stay at Arbol Verde. He'd never had a moment of doubt. He'd gone to Texas A&M and studied animal husbandry, coming home on the weekends because he'd missed the land and his horses.

He was trying to find a way to keep seeing Pippa when she returned to the UK, not that she'd even suggested the possibility.

But Diego knew that he wasn't going to transition well to living without her. A part of him wondered how he could have such strong feelings for a woman he'd known for such a short time.

But she wasn't just a woman. She was Pippa.

She was classy and funny, feisty and sexy. But she was still a mystery to him no matter how much they talked and he knew that letting her go was going to be hard.

"Tell me about it," she said, a note of humor in her voice.

What was there to say? "You know how some people grow up and can't break free from their hometown?"

She nodded. "Yes, but I wasn't one of them. I wanted out from under my father's thumb something fierce."

"I didn't have that. My dad and I have always been on the same page when it comes to the stud operation. My earliest memories are of following him around the barn. I think I learned to ride as soon as I could sit in the saddle. There was never a moment when I felt like I didn't belong to the land," he said.

She nodded. "I wish I had that sense of belonging. I've felt lost over the last few years, but at least finding Kinley and helping her to raise Penny grounded me somewhat. I mean, I knew it was temporary, but at the same time I couldn't have wished to be anywhere else. It was the closest I'd come to having a home since my mom died."

"I'm sorry you lost your mother," he said. He didn't ever let himself think what life would be like without his mama. She was a force of nature. With her long career in television, she'd always been outspoken and encouraged her kids to be the same.

"Thanks. I didn't realize what a barrier she was between my father and me until she was gone. Most of the year I was at boarding school, but once she was gone, my father and I hardly saw each other. I had never realized how hollow that relationship was. I thought… Well, it doesn't matter because I was wrong," she said.

She turned to face the fire, leaning forward, and Diego realized that talking about her father made her put a barrier around herself. He doubted she was even aware of it, but she'd just changed. There was a coldness that hadn't been there a moment before.

He wanted to pull her back against him, but he was already holding on too hard and knew that he wouldn't do it. "Tell me about your family business."

"We design high-end jewelry," she said. "I have been taking business courses through an online university while I've been living with Kinley and I did a few extension classes in art."

"Have you made any designs to take back with you?" he asked.

"Yes. I've made a lot of them, but ours is a legacy brand. Part of the falling-out I had with my father was that I wanted us to move with the times, become more modern," she said.

"Will the rest of the board support you?" he asked. "You said he votes your shares, so I assume that all of the board members are family, is that right?"

She pushed herself off his lap, walked a few steps away and stared up at the night sky. He wondered what she was looking for.

She glanced back at him, her long blond hair sliding over her shoulder. "Yes. Most of them are family, but they are second and third cousins... I'm the main shareholder."

"So your father has been controlling the company because of that?" he asked, trying to understand what she was going to be up against when she returned to England.

"Yes. He and my mother were third cousins, so he has a small stake of his own in the company, but voting mother's shares, which are now mine, gives him a majority vote. I think he will fight against me being reinstated."

Diego hoped not. He could see the struggle in Pippa's face as she talked about the company and her father. It would be better if the old man just graciously accepted her return and stepped aside.

"Do you think there is a chance he's mellowed? Perhaps your

being missing for all this time has made him realize what he'd lost," Diego said.

"That's a nice thought," she said. "But I doubt very much that's the case."

He wanted to give her space. To be cool and pretend that she hadn't already made him care more than he wanted to. But he got up and went to her, pulled her back into his arms and held her until the fire died and they both went inside. He wanted to stay and claim every second he had with her before she had to leave. But the kids were upstairs. After saying goodbye, he drove home, away from her, wondering what the future held for her and how he was going to manage his part in it.

Penny and Benito were up early and Pippa, who hadn't really slept at all, struggled not to be cranky with them. She was very happy when Kinley, who'd come back from Vegas overnight, had volunteered to take them to school. She passed the children off to her friend, who looked like she wanted to ask questions, but Pippa just shook her head and waved them all off.

She went back to the computer. Still no email about her request to assume her position on the House of Hamilton board and be put in full control of her fortune. She was frustrated and more than a little angry with herself because she knew that a part of her wasn't upset about the lack of progress on that front. The longer it took to hear back from the solicitor, the more time she'd have with Diego.

And what did that say about her?

Hadn't she seen what happened when a man she cared about tried to take control of her life? Wasn't she right now in this mess because her father had taken more than he'd been given?

She showered and got dressed and then took her notebook and pencils out onto the porch. She remembered last night, sitting in Diego's arms. He made her feel…well, too much, she admitted. Safe, secure, lust, longing, a desire for something that she couldn't name.

She channeled all of that into her notebook. The dancing sparks from the fire were her guide and she created a sketch for a necklace that would have a series of rubies set in fine gold chain dancing up from a large stone.

She fiddled with it, realizing that the morning was gone by the time she finished. She felt better. After braiding her hair, she texted Kinley to see if her friend was available for lunch at the Five Families Country Club.

She wasn't, as she had a full-fledged bridezilla on her hands.

Pippa had never been the type of woman who was comfortable sitting in a restaurant by herself, so she thought about staying home. But there was no food in her fridge. So she got in the car but instead of turning toward town when she exited the Rockin' C property she turned toward Arbol Verde.

She shook her head as she realized this might have been her intent all along. When had she started lying to herself?

But she had.

She wanted to pretend that Diego meant nothing. That he was a friend with benefits, because it had been clear from the beginning that they had a bond that could almost be called friendship. But there was also something else.

Something she kept shoving further and further to the bottom of her emotional well and pretending didn't exist.

She turned under the sweeping wrought-iron banner that proclaimed the name of the ranch and drove slowly up to the main house. She saw Diego's truck and his sports car parked in the drive. Off to one side was a horse trailer.

She sat in her car with the engine on and realized that she probably should have called or texted instead of just showing up. As she started to back out of the circle drive, Diego walked around the side of the horse trailer and their eyes met.

He took his black Stetson off and lifted one hand and waved at her. She shut the engine off, got out of the car and began walking toward him as he put his hat back on and approached her.

"Hiya," she said. "I… I was on my way to lunch and wanted to see if you had time to go with me."

He leaned over and kissed her, in just the briefest touch of their lips, and stepped back. He smelled of sun, the fall air and his spicy cologne. She closed her eyes and realized she was exactly where she wanted to be. There hadn't been too many times that she'd been able to say that, but today she could.

"I'd need to shower and change if we're going into town and I have to finish giving some instructions to my staff. Or we could eat lunch here. I could have my housekeeper make us something."

"I don't mind waiting. I have to pick Penny up at two, so I need to leave by about one fifteen."

"Then let's eat here," he said. "Do you want to come to the barn with me? Or wait in the house?"

"The barn," she said. She hadn't come to his place to sit in his house with the housekeeper.

"Good. I have two new horses that I think we're going to be able to use at the riding center Mauricio and I are working on. We have secured the property and should have that finalized by the end of the week," he said. "I can't wait to get started on the building. A guy we went to high school with has a company that has been doing this sort of facility in North Texas, so we're hoping to get him to do the design."

"That sounds very exciting," she said.

"Are you okay?" he asked as they walked to the barn. He took out his phone and she noticed he was typing out a message to his housekeeper.

"Yeah. I'm waiting for the weekend, too. I should have some news by then."

"That will be a relief," he said. "It's not even my news, but I'm on edge. I hope I didn't push too hard last night, but I feel like I have to make the most of every moment we're together."

"You didn't," she said. "I feel the same way, which is why I'm here today."

"I'm glad you are," he said.

He led her into the barn, which smelled of hay and leather. The sounds of the horses were soothing. While he went to discuss something with one of his ranch hands, he left her in his office. She sat there taking in all the photos on the wall of a younger Diego with his father and admitted she was jealous of the life he had.

Of the family that had surrounded him with love and let him grow into the man he was today. Until her twenty-first birthday she'd just sort of coasted along following her father's script for her life, never realizing that she was invisible to him. That she only showed up on his radar to help him further his own agenda.

Ten

Lunch with Diego was nice, but she kept checking her phone the entire time hoping to hear from the solicitor. Sure, he'd said he'd get back to her by tomorrow, but she had run out of patience. Finally, Diego called her on it.

"What are you checking for?"

"Waiting for that email. I know it's getting later in London. I just don't want to miss hearing from the solicitor."

"I don't think there's any chance of that," he said.

"Sorry. I guess I shouldn't have come here," she said. But she'd thought they were friends and she needed someone who had her back right now. Because she felt too vulnerable and unsure of herself.

"Why did you?"

She shrugged. What was she going to say? The truth? That was complicated, and really, she wasn't even sure what was going to happen between them. She felt this bond. What could she say; when she felt nervous, her first thought was to find Diego. Just being with him calmed her down.

But that wasn't really fair to Diego. It made her feel like she was using him.

"I… You make me feel safe," she said at last. "So if I have bad news while I'm with you, I think I'll deal with it better."

He sighed and pushed his chair back before standing up and turning away from her. They were seated at a large table on his stone patio that overlooked the horse paddock and the rolling hills. He put his hands on his hips as he stared out at the land and she wondered what he saw when he did that. She knew when she stalked the House of Hamilton website she felt a sense of possession and expectation because she belonged as part of the company, not as an outsider.

Right now, she felt like an outsider.

Fair enough.

"I wish you wouldn't say things like that," he said.

"Why not? It's the truth," she said, carefully folding her napkin and getting up from the table. She went to stand next to him, looking out over the fields. "We said no lies."

"I thought that would be safer somehow, but it isn't."

"Safer how?"

"That maybe being brutally honest would make it easier to think of a time when you wouldn't be by my side, but that isn't the case at all. I hate that you are checking your email and waiting for the all clear to move so far from me. It's not like I have a claim on you, Pippa. I know that. Yet at the same time the thought of your leaving dominates my every waking moment and even some of my sleeping ones."

She put her hand in the middle of his back and then laid her head on his shoulder blade. Closing her eyes, she felt his heat and breathed in that scent that was so distinctive to Diego. She wrapped her other arm around his waist and held him.

She wished… She didn't know what she wished. That maybe he was just that bit of fun she'd found on her birthday night at the bachelor auction. But he had become so much more.

He put his hand over hers. "What do you expect the lawyer to say?"

"I don't know," she answered, because she didn't want to admit that she was hoping her father loved her enough to just step aside. But she had a feeling she was going to have to fight to get the right to vote her shares and she knew and expected that she'd have to prove herself. "I think it's going to be hard, but until I hear something it's so much worse. You know how when you're a kid and you hear a noise outside and you're sure it's a monster? That's how I feel right now. Everything seems like there is a monster under the bed. And I know I can fight it, but I'm not sure what kind of fight it's going to be," she said, pulling her arm from Diego and moving to stand next to him.

As much as she took comfort from being near him, she couldn't let herself start to rely on him. She needed to stand on her own. She'd known that all along, but she was still drawn here.

She was a mess. She hadn't felt like this before—never—and it was freaking her out.

"I'm used to having a plan. Every day for the last four years I've been waiting for this moment, but I had no idea what would happen when it came…and waiting even longer like this is just so much worse than you can imagine."

He turned to face her, hands on his lean hips, his hat back on his head so that his eyes were in shadow. "I get it. My brother-in-law Jose was in an airplane crash and for three days we waited to hear about survivors. We knew he'd been cheating—um, that's not for anyone else's ears—but as a family we weren't sure how to feel. I wanted Bianca to have a chance to confront him. But she never got it. So I understand how time can feel like it's moving so slowly and the wait is lasting too long."

She'd had no idea that Bianca's first husband had been unfaithful. The former supermodel was drop-dead gorgeous and one of the sweetest people Pippa had ever met.

"I won't say anything," she reassured him. "I guess you're right that you do understand where I'm coming from."

"I'm here for you, honey," he said, his voice sweet and gentle. And when he used that term of endearment, she felt things that she didn't want to admit to.

"Thank you. That means more than you can know," she said. Her phone pinged, and she looked at it and then back at him.

"Go on. See if it's the email you've been waiting for," he said.

There was a note in his voice that she didn't recognize, but she turned to her phone, picking it up and unlocking it. She'd set an alert for the solicitor's email, so she knew it was from him.

Diego stood there looking out at the pasture and paddock where his prized mares all roamed together. The breeding stock of Arbol Verde were his true assets. He sold some of the mares overseas, especially to clients in the United Arab Emirates. But today, for the first time in his life, the land didn't give him the pleasure it always had and he didn't want to try to process why.

"Okay. I need to talk to him on a secure video phone," she said. She had that edge in her voice that made Diego want to scoop her up and carry her far away so she didn't have to deal with this, but this was exactly where she needed to be.

"You can use my den," he said.

"Thank you."

He led the way into the house, which was cooler than outside but not cold. Given that it was early October, some fallish weather had arrived. This morning when he'd taken his stallion out for a morning run it had been almost cold.

His boot heels echoed on the Spanish tile and he heard the sound of Mona, his housekeeper, working in the kitchen. She was making enchiladas for the ranch hands for dinner and then she had her book club in town this evening.

So he'd be alone.

Unless he could convince Pippa that they should spend the evening together. But that felt like the worst kind of mirage.

Pretending that she was his regular, steady girl instead of acknowledging that she was leaving.

"Here it is. Do you want to use my computer for the video chat?" he asked. "You'll probably have a better signal, since it's hardwired to the LAN instead of a Wi-Fi connection."

"Okay," she said. "Thank you."

She tucked a strand of hair behind her ear. Maybe it was his imagination, but her demeanor seemed to have changed since she'd received the email. She stood taller. Her motions were more controlled and the passion and…joie de vivre he always associated with her were tamped down.

He walked over to his desk, which was made of Spanish oak and had been one of the treasures his ancestors had brought with them from Cádiz when they'd come over to this new land. He rubbed his hand along the edge, feeling the past in the wood grain as he always did. Then he pushed his Swedish-designed ergonomic chair back and reached down to log on to his computer. The screen background was one of the photos that they used on the stud farm website, featuring him riding on their prizewinning stallion King Of The Night.

"There you go. I'll be back in the barn if you need me," he said.

He tried to ignore how close she was as he turned to leave. The scent of her flowery perfume wrapped around him and he felt a pang realizing this was her first step toward goodbye. He moved past her and she put her hand on his arm. Her fingers were light against his bicep.

He looked down at her.

"Thank you, Diego," she said again.

"You're welcome, honey."

He walked away before he did something stupid like pull her into his arms and make love to her on his desk, trying to reinforce the bond that had been growing between them since the bachelor auction. He'd never been one of those people who believed in love at first sight and he still wasn't sure he did, but that was what he felt for Pippa, he thought as he stalked out of the house toward the barn.

When he entered the barn, he heard his brother Mauricio talking to Brenda, one of his best trainers.

"Just let him know I stopped by. I didn't want to disturb him, so I left some paperwork on his desk back there," Mauricio said.

"I got it, Mo. I promise I'll tell him that it's there," Brenda said.

"I'm here," Diego said.

"Thank God. This one is acting like I've never been given a message before," Brenda said, full of sass the way she always was. Probably because she had known him and his brothers since they were boys. She'd hired on to the ranch when she'd been eighteen and had watched them all grow up.

"It's not that I don't trust you, Brenda," Mo said with a smile.

"Of course not," she said, turning to walk away. "I have lessons this afternoon, so I need to go and get the horses prepared."

"See you later," Diego said as she walked by him and out of the barn.

"I didn't want to bother you, but the contract came through for the training center property and I know we want to get moving on that project," Mauricio said.

"You're not," Diego said, heading toward his office at the back of the barn.

"Wasn't that Pippa's car in the drive?"

"It was."

He sat down at his desk and drew the folder that Mauricio had left there toward him. He opened it and just stared at the writing on the contract like he'd never read a word before. His mind was swirling with the fact that Pippa was in his den and probably being given the keys to her old life. Paving the very path she needed to leave Texas and return to her old life.

"D?"

"Yeah?"

"Pippa."

Mauricio wasn't going to let this be. And Diego wasn't sure what he was going to say. How was he going to make it seem like it was no big deal that she was leaving when a part of him felt like he would die without her? Dammit, he was acting like a sap. He was stronger than this. He was going to be cool with Mo. And when Pippa left, he was going to get drunk and get over her.

"So?"

"So what? She came by for lunch. I think she's leaving tomorrow."

"Damn. That's—"

"Reality."

"I was going to say that sucks. I'll be back later," Mauricio said after Diego had signed all of the papers and handed them back. "I just have to get this over to the broker."

"You don't have to."

"We're brothers, D. Of course I do."

Pippa had never felt more nervous than when Diego walked out of the den and she took a seat in front of his computer. She double-checked the number in the email from the solicitor and then typed it in. He was expecting her video call.

As soon as the camera pop-up window opened on the screen, she took a good look at herself. She used to wear a bit more makeup and look more polished, but objectively she thought she looked okay. She smoothed her hair and then made sure that the necklace her mother had given her when she turned ten was visible in the opening at the front of her shirt.

She took a deep breath before hitting the connect button.

The solicitor Simon Rooney answered the call on the first ring.

"Philippa, we are so happy you were able to call this afternoon. I have your father in the other room along with Giles Montgomery," Simon said. Giles was House of Hamilton's COO, she knew from her reading up on the company.

"I'm just happy that you were able to verify my identity so quickly," she said.

"I am, too. Before I bring the others in, I wanted to let you know that your father will not sign off on the transfer of shares until he's seen you in person. Unfortunately, he's willing to take legal action to support his position, which would tie things up in the courts whether he has a case or not. You had mentioned in your first email that you were hopeful of voting your shares at the board meeting in November. We need you back in the UK as soon as possible for that to happen."

"I'm ready to leave," she said, not quite sure that was the absolute truth because she had so many friends here. She would miss them all…especially Diego. But this was what she wanted. "Also, I have a private jet from my friends the Carutherses at my disposal, so as soon as my renewed passport arrives I'm ready."

"Good. I've sent all of your documentation to the address you gave. It should arrive before six p.m. your time."

"Thank you, Mr. Rooney," she said.

"You're very welcome. Now, I'm going to bring your father in first. I'm not sure how much you have been following the House of Hamilton."

"Very closely," she admitted. "Or as closely as I can, being a world away. I've read about the rumored infighting between Father and the board."

"It's more than a rumor, I'm afraid. So Giles won't speak to you while your father is in the room. I'm afraid your reappearance comes at a very crucial time for the company. But I'll let your father and Giles explain their positions to you," Simon said.

"Thank you. Mr. Rooney—"

"Call me Simon," he said.

"Very well. Do you work for me or the company or my father?" she asked.

"I work for you," he said. "I hope once you've seen everything I've done for your trust over the last four years you will be happy with my work. Why do you ask?"

"I just wanted to know who was on my side," she said.

"I am."

"Okay, I'm ready to see my father first."

Simon nodded and disappeared from the screen. She heard the sound of a door opening and the rumble of voices.

Her palms started sweating and she realized she was breathing too shallowly. She closed her eyes and remembered the way that Diego had held her in his arms last night when they'd sat in front of the fire. Remembered how safe and confident she'd felt in that moment. Then she opened her eyes to see her father sitting where Simon had been.

He looked older, she thought. Of course, he was four years older, but he seemed to have aged a lot more than that. His face, which had always been thin, now seemed gaunt, and his blue eyes were duller than she remembered. His previously salt-and-pepper hair was now all gray.

When he saw her on his screen, he stared at her face. Probably processing everything, she thought, the same way she was.

"Father."

"Pippa," he said, his voice just as low and rumbly as it always had been. For a moment she was torn between the memories of the man who'd tried to force her to marry and the man who'd read her bedtime stories when she'd been very young.

"It's good to see you again," she said, her old manners coming to the fore.

"I find that very hard to believe given that you've been hiding from me for four years," he said.

"You gave me no choice," she said. "I didn't feel like I had any options."

He inclined his head. "I've only ever had the best interests of you and your mother at heart. I thought she would have wanted you married to a good man who would give you the life you'd always known."

Pippa felt the sting of tears at the mention of her mother. "I don't think Mum would have wanted me to marry a man who didn't love me and who was a stranger."

"We can agree to disagree on that. So you're coming back. What does that mean?"

"I will be voting my shares and taking my place on the board of directors at House of Hamilton. I think we are just waiting for your signature on the paperwork," she said.

"We are. I wanted to make sure it was you. I've had men looking for you for all these years. A few times we've had some false leads."

"Now you know it's really me."

"I do know. I will sign the papers once you return to London," he said, standing up, and she hugged herself around her chest, rubbing the goose bumps on her arms.

"Father?"

"Yes?" he asked.

"Nothing," she said. What was she going to say? Admit that she was glad to see him? Ask him if he was happy she was alive? There was no answer that would satisfy her.

He walked away from the screen and Giles Montgomery got on the call next. The COO said he was excited for her to take a temporary role in the company, and once she proved herself, to take a more permanent one.

"Pippa, I'm so glad that you're coming back. I am interested in starting discussions with you to catch you up on where we are today."

"Thank you," she said. "I'm interested in taking an active role and not just being a figurehead."

"We'd like that, too. We've been at a standstill while you were missing and we are all eager to start moving the company forward again."

"I am, too, and have a few ideas that I'd like to bring forward," Pippa said.

"When you land in London, we can start our discussions, but for now I thought you might want to know more about the directors and where we stand as a company. I've asked Simon to forward you a packet with all of this information."

"Thank you," she said. "I was planning to return to the UK at the end of October."

"We need you back before that," Giles said. "There's a labor dispute with our service staff, and now that you're back, if we had an emergency board meeting, we could resolve the issue regarding pensions."

The call ended almost two hours after it had started. Her back aching, she stood up and stretched. She walked out of the den and down the hall to the family room, where she found Diego sitting in a large leather armchair watching the doorway.

"Is it settled?"

She nodded. "I'm going to leave tomorrow."

Eleven

Diego sat there watching her as she stood on the threshold. Her arms were wrapped around her waist and she was looking…shaken.

"My father…he was all business," she said. "I guess I should have expected it. I think I've spent too much time in Cole's Hill around the Carutherses. I sort of expected the bond of family to be stronger than it ever was."

Diego stood up and walked over to her, pulling her into his arms. She stood there stiffly for a few moments and then hugged him back, burying her nose in the center of his chest. He rubbed his hands up and down her back and tried to tell himself he wasn't turned on by her, but the fact was any time he held her or thought about her he reacted this way. But that wasn't what this moment was about, so he shifted his hips so that she wouldn't notice.

"So you're leaving tomorrow, then?"

"Yes," she said, pushing away from him. He let her go. "If I can use the Caruthers jet like Nate has offered. I just have to double-check that. My passport documents are being delivered to the Rockin' C today." She rubbed her hands up and down her arms. "I have so much to do."

She really did, and not a lot of time to get it done. Diego mentally went over his schedule for the next week and assigned most of the tasks to different people who worked for him. If he did some careful maneuvering, he might be able to take a week off.

"I know this is spur-of-the-moment," he said, "but do you want me to come with you to London?"

She tipped her head to the side. Her gray eyes met his and her lips parted. "Can you do that?"

"It will take a little bit of juggling in my schedule, but yes, I can do that."

"Oh, Diego, yes, please. I'd love to have you come with me."

"Then I will. I need to make some calls and go and talk to my hands," he said. "Do you need me to do anything else?"

"Not right now," she said. "Are you sure you want to do this?"

No, he wasn't, but he didn't want to say goodbye to her now and like this. She had other things on her mind and he cared about her. More than he wanted to think he could. But the truth was, no woman had ever dominated his thoughts and feelings the way she was...well, aside from his sister or his mom.

He might not be the smartest of men when it came to the opposite sex. But something his father had said to him when he was a teenager and dealing with his first breakup had stuck with him. His dad had told him to never let a good woman slip away until he was sure they weren't meant to be together.

"I'm positive. Do you need to head back to the Rockin' C right now?"

"I... Why?"

"I have to talk to my staff and then pack. Frankly, I have no idea what to bring to London," he said.

"How about you go and talk to your staff and I'll lay out some clothes for you before you go? It will be cold and rainy and it's not unheard of for it to snow in October."

"Snow? What have I gotten myself into?"

"It's not too late to change your mind," she said.

He walked over to her and caressed her cheek because being this close to her and not touching her was nearly impossible. He ran his finger down around the back of her neck, bringing his mouth to hers and kissing her.

"Yes, it is," he said when he broke the kiss. "I gave you my word. And to a Velasquez a promise is a promise."

She nodded.

"That means a lot to me. I mean, I can do this on my own. I'm a total 'hashtag girlboss,'" she said, making air quotes, "but it's nice to know I don't have to."

"I know where you're coming from even though I'm not a 'hashtag' anything," he said with a wink. "Just make a list of things I should pack, and then if you don't mind I'll come over to your place tonight. That way I'll be ready to go when you are."

"That sounds great," she said.

She turned and walked down the hall to his bedroom, and he watched her go for a minute thinking of the things he should be doing but knowing there was only one thing he wanted.

Pippa.

In his bed for the last time.

The depth of the need he felt for her surprised him and that was the last thing he wanted to dwell on. He wanted this to be physical. He was running out of moments like this.

Moments when she was his.

"I thought you had things to do," she said.

"I do," he replied. "At the top of that list is you."

"Me?"

"Unless you don't want me."

She shook her head as she leaned against the door that lead to his walk-in closet. "Don't be foolish. I will always want you."

He hoped that was true, but he knew she was leaving and going back to her real life. Soon the rancher from Cole's Hill would be a memory. He had no idea what her future held, but he was pretty damned sure it didn't involve a long-distance affair with him.

And that made him angry and sad at the same time. He had no idea how to ask her to stay. He knew he had no right to. She had to focus on returning to her old life and claiming what she'd walked away from, but it was what he wanted.

"Diego?"

He shook his head. He couldn't talk. Not right now. At this moment he needed his woman in his arms.

He pulled her into an embrace, and her breath caught as he lifted her off her feet and carried her into his bedroom, setting her down at the edge of the bed. The fabric of her dress was gauzy and soft under his fingers but not as supple as her skin.

The navy color of her dress made for a striking contrast with her blond hair and creamy skin. He found the zipper at the side of the dress and slowly drew it down the side of her body, watching as it parted and each inch of her skin was revealed.

She lifted her arms up, twining them around his neck as he pushed one of his hands into the opening, caressing her and then skimming his fingers along her back until he could reach the clasp of her bra. He undid it with one hand.

He felt her fingers on his chest, slowly pulling apart the buttons of his shirt. He heard the pop of each one as she freed him and then pushed the shirt open and down his arms. The buttons at the wrists held the fabric in place and she carefully undid each of them. He let his shirt fall to the floor.

Leaning forward, he felt the brush of her hair against his torso and the warmth of her lips as she nibbled at his pecs and then found the scar and tattoo, tracing it with her tongue. He couldn't help the growl that escaped him as he felt the sharpness of her teeth against his muscles as she nipped at him.

He could only watch her as she slowly moved down his body. His jeans were getting tighter and tighter by the moment. He watched her tongue his nipple and his hips jerked forward as her hand moved over the button fly of his jeans.

He shifted against her, lifting and holding her with one arm under her hips. She put her hands on either side of his face and their eyes met. He wanted to think he saw the same affection and desperation in her gaze as he felt deep in his soul.

Her mouth came down on his hard, their tongues tangled and he realized he was desperately hungry for her. That there was no way he was going to be able to fill that hunger in just a week.

He pulled his mouth from hers, letting her slide down the front of his body. Once she was standing in front of him again, he pulled her arms out of her dress and pushed it down her torso. It caught at her hips, which were pressed to his. He ran his finger along the edge of her matching navy-colored bra where it met the creamy globe of her breast.

She trembled against him as her hips came into contact with the tip of his erection. He pulled her bra away from her skin and down her arms, tossing it toward his shirt on the floor.

Then he pulled her to him, letting their naked chests rub against each other. He loved the pebbly hardness of her nipples against his chest. He rubbed his hands up and down her back and lowered his head to the crook of her neck, where the scent of her perfume was stronger.

He felt her hands rubbing down his shoulders, her nails scraping down his back, and then she forced her hand between their bodies, tracing each of the muscles that ribbed his chest as she let her fingers move lower toward the fastening of his jeans.

His heart was beating so fast that he felt his pulse in his erection. He was seconds away from losing control and coming in his jeans, but he had to hold back. He wanted this time to last.

She stroked his shaft, running her hands over the ridge of it through his jeans. Everything inside him quieted and all he could think about was her naked on his bed. He needed to be inside her.

Now.

He pushed her backward and she fell onto the bed. He undid the top buttons of his jeans as he put one thigh between her parted legs. He patted her through the fabric of her underwear. She moaned his name and her legs parted even farther as he brushed the backs of his knuckles over her mound.

The lace fabric was warm and wet. He slipped one finger under the material and didn't pause for even a second as their eyes met.

She watched him through half-closed lids and sucked her lower lip into her mouth as her hips arched and thrust against him. It was only the fact that he wanted her to come at least once before he entered her that made it possible for him to keep himself in check. That and the tightness of his jeans.

She shifted against him and he pushed his finger into her, teasing her with feathering touches.

"Diego..." she said, her voice breathless and airy.

"Hmm?"

"This is nice, but I want..."

"This?" he asked, pushing his finger deep inside her.

"Oh...oh, yessssss," she said. Her hips rocked against his finger for a few strokes. He wanted to get her to the place where she was once again caught on the edge and needing more.

"Diego, please."

He used his thumb to trace around her clit. She rocked harder against his hand, her hips bucking frantically against him. She arched her back, which drew his eyes to her full breasts and hard nipples. He shifted over her on the bed and caught one in his lips, suckling her deeply as he continued to finger her. He kept his thumb on her clit as he worked his fingers deep inside her body until she threw her head back and called his name.

He felt the tightening of her body against his fingers. She kept rocking against him for a few more minutes and then collapsed into his arms.

He kept his fingers inside her body and slowly started building her toward the pinnacle again. He tipped her head toward his so he could taste her mouth. Her lips opened over his. He told himself to take it slow, to make this last. He didn't want this to end, needing to prolong their ecstasy as long as possible. Because once they left the bedroom, she would begin the final process of moving away from him, even if he was going to accompany her to London for a week.

But Pippa didn't want slow. Her nails dug into his shoulders and she shifted so that when she arched her back the hard points of her nipples brushed against his chest.

He held her with his forearm along her spine and bit lightly at the column of her neck as he used his other hand to cup her backside.

Her eyes closed and she exhaled hard as he fondled her. She moaned a sweet sound that he leaned up to capture in his mouth. She tipped her head, allowing him access. She held his shoulders and moved on him, rubbing her center over his erection.

He unbuttoned his pants, freeing himself. He then reached for the box of condoms he kept in the nightstand drawer. He fumbled for the box, finally getting one out, and shifted back to remove it from the foil wrapper and put it on. When he was done, he came back to her and put his hands on either side of her hips as he shifted his erection so that he was poised at the entrance of her body.

He scraped his fingernail over her nipple and she shuddered. He pushed her back a little bit so he could see her. Her breasts were bare, nipples distended and begging for his mouth. He lowered his head and suckled.

He kept trying to make this last, taking it slow as he slid his body up over her so that they were pressed together. He lowered his forehead to hers and their eyes met, their breaths mingling, and he shifted his hips and plunged into her. He stopped once he was buried hilt-deep inside her and held his breath.

He wanted to remember the feel of her underneath him and wrapped around him forever.

He wanted her to remember him, as well. Long after he'd returned to Cole's Hill and his lonely bedroom and she was back at the helm of her family business.

He needed to know that she wouldn't be able to forget him.

So he claimed her, claimed Pippa as his, even if it was only in his soul that he could acknowledge it.

He thrust into her sweet, tight body. Her eyes were closed, her hips moving subtly against him, and when he blew on her nipple, he saw gooseflesh spread down her body.

He loved the way she reacted to his mouth on her. He sucked on the skin at the base of her neck as he thrust all the way home, sheathing his entire length in her body. He knew he was leaving a mark with his mouth and that pleased him. He wanted her to remember this moment and what they had done when she was alone later.

He kept kissing and rubbing, pinching her nipples until her hands clenched in his hair and she rocked her hips harder against his length. He lifted his hips, thrusting up against her.

"Come with me," he said.

She nodded. Her eyes widened with each inch he gave her. She clutched at his hips as he continued thrusting. Her eyes were half-closed, her head tipped back.

He leaned down and caught one of her nipples in his teeth, scraping very gently. She started to tighten around him. Her hips moved faster, demanding more, but he kept the pace slow, steady, building the pleasure between them.

He suckled her nipple and rotated his hips to catch her pleasure point with each thrust. He felt her hands clenching in his hair as she threw her head back, hair brushing over his arm where he held her.

He varied his thrusts, finding a rhythm that would draw out the tension at the base of his spine. Something that would make his time in her body, wrapped in her silky limbs, last forever.

"Hold on to me tightly."

She did as he asked, and he rolled them over so that she was on top of him. He pushed her legs up against her body so that he could thrust deeper. So that she was open and vulnerable to him.

"Come now, Pippa," he said.

She nodded, and he felt her body tighten. Then she scraped her nails down his back and clutched his buttocks, drawing him in. Blood roared in his ears as he felt everything in his world center to this one woman.

He called her name as he came. She tightened around him and he looked into her eyes as he kept thrusting. He saw her eyes widen and felt the minute contractions of her body around his as she was consumed by her orgasm.

He rotated his hips against her until she stopped rocking. Then he rolled to his side holding her in his arms until the sweat dried on both of their bodies. Neither of them said a word and after a short time had passed he got up and carried her to the shower.

He made love to her again in the shower and then forced himself to leave the house to talk to his staff. Otherwise he knew he would beg her to stay.

Twelve

"I wish I could go with you," Kinley said as she stood next to Pippa's closet.

"Me, too," she said. "I had no idea I'd accumulated all this stuff."

"Don't worry about that. Just pack what you need. I will get this all boxed up and sent to you."

Kinley came over and hugged her tightly. "I thought I was prepared to let you go, but I'm not. I mean, I still haven't decided what to do about Nate and having another baby. And you're the only one I can bitch about him to because you know I love him and am just being a spaz because I'm scared."

Pippa hugged her friend back. "I feel the same way. I haven't even had a chance to tell you about Diego or how cold my dad was on the call… We should have a standing date on video chat."

Kinley stepped back and sat down on the edge of Pippa's bed. "I love that. Let's do it on Saturday. That way Penny can chat with you, too. She's mad at you, by the way. Told me that I could tell you bye-bye from her."

Pippa's heart broke a little hearing that. "I wish there was some other way, but I can't stay."

"I know. We both know it. Even Penny. She made you this," Kinley said, going over to her big Louis Vuitton Neverfull bag and retrieving a small stack of papers that was bound with yarn. She handed it to Pippa.

"It's a book about the P girls," she said, looking down at the cover, which had a hand-drawn picture of two stick-figure girls, one with red hair and one with blond hair. She hugged the book to her and blinked to keep from crying.

"Look at it later," Kinley said. "We've been working on it since you told me you were leaving."

"Thank you, Kin. You're closer to me than a sister and I can't help wondering what a mess my life would have been if it wasn't for you," Pippa said.

"It was no big thing," Kinley said. "We found each other."

"We did," Pippa said, going to her dresser and picking up the box she'd placed there earlier. "This is for you."

"You didn't have to get me anything, but thank you."

Kinley opened the box. It contained two matching wire necklaces with pendant charms that Pippa had made over the summer during her class at the Cole's Hill Art Center. She'd known that she would be leaving in the fall and had wanted to create mementos for Kinley and Penny. "The smaller one is for the imp."

"We are going to miss you so much. These are so perfect," Kinley said.

There was a knock on the door before she could say anything else. "I'll go get it. You finish packing."

Pippa sat down on the bed after Kinley left and wrapped her arms around her waist. Who would have thought leaving her pretend life would be this hard? But then again it wasn't pretend. Everything about her time with Kinley and Penny had been real. They'd been so young and scared when they'd found each other.

She was proud of how far they'd each come. But she knew that as hard as it was to say goodbye she couldn't stay here.

Someone knocked on the wall near the entrance to her bedroom and she looked up to see Diego standing there. He held a small bag in one hand and his Stetson in the other.

"Is that all you packed?"

"Nah," he said. "I left my suitcase downstairs. Kinley said to remind you that the jet would be ready whenever you are. I suggested that you might want to leave tonight."

She hadn't thought about that. She'd been sort of pushing off the moment when she'd have to get on the plane and head to England. "Yeah, that makes more sense. I guess I'm dreading seeing my father and not really sure what's waiting for me."

"Well, I'm just along for the ride, so whatever you decide is fine with me."

He might have been along for the ride, but only temporarily. She knew he was a crutch she was going to have to let go of. But she was glad she'd have a week with him. Diego couldn't stay longer than that. He'd told her earlier that he had a sire coming in two weeks and it was too important to trust to any of his staff.

"Let me finish this up and then I'll be ready to go. Will you let Kinley and Nate know that we'll leave tonight? I should be ready to go in an hour."

"Sounds good to me. I'll drive us and leave my truck at the airport so when I come back… I'll be able to get home."

The weight of that lay between them as their eyes met. Then he turned and walked down the stairs. She realized how much she was giving up to reclaim her heritage. It made her mad that she'd ever had to leave it, because she realized that a part of her wanted this life she could call her own here in Cole's Hill. But another part of her wasn't willing to let her father win. The man who couldn't tell her he missed her and had looked at her like she'd irritated him.

She knew Diego understood, which made it that much harder as she walked out of the house next to him to say goodbye to everyone. The entire Caruthers clan had shown up. Little Benito gave her a sweet hug and at the last moment Penny came running outside and threw herself in Pippa's arms.

"Take care, imp."

"You, too, Pippy."

She put Penny down and got into Diego's truck, turning her head toward the rolling pastures so she could pretend she wasn't crying and that a part of her soul wasn't suddenly barren and sad.

She was nervous. He could tell by the way she kept looking out the window, but he had no words to comfort her. He knew her father had been as cold as ice on the call. But Diego had no idea what to expect when they landed in London. The private plane that the Caruthers family owned had been a boon. A chance for them to be alone as they returned to her uncertain future.

Even though he was accompanying her they both knew his stay in the UK could only be temporary. He had Arbol Verde, which he couldn't walk away from. And even if he was willing to contemplate that, he wasn't a citizen, for one thing, and he wasn't sure he wanted to live in a cold, foggy city. Though knowing that he'd have Pippa by his side was almost enough to tempt him to try.

He swirled around the mint he'd popped into his mouth at takeoff and looked over at her. She sighed again. She wore a faux-fur jacket around her shoulders. They were the only passengers on the plane. The pilot and copilot were up front, but it was only the two of them in the back.

"Are you wearing panties?" he asked.

She shifted in her seat and looked over at him. "I am. Why?"

"Go take them and your blouse off. Come back with just your fur coat on."

"Diego—"

"Do it, baby. It will take your mind off whatever is waiting for you when we land," he said.

She licked her lips. "I… Okay."

She got up slowly. He'd expected her to go to the bathroom at the back of the plane, but instead she lifted one of her legs encased in a knee-high stiletto boot. "Can you get that zipper?"

He nodded, stretching his legs out as he started to get hard. He lowered the zipper and then drew her foot out of the boot, setting it on the empty chair next to his. Then he helped her with the other one. When she pulled her slim-fitting skirt slowly up her legs, he saw that she was wearing garterless thigh-high stockings. She held her skirt up at her waist.

"Will you give me a hand, Diego?" she asked coyly.

He put his hands on either side of the waistband of her small bikini-style underpants, letting the backs of his fingers brush over her pubic area before slowly drawing the cloth down her thighs, making sure to spread his fingers out so he could caress each inch of her skin. He pushed the tiny ivory-colored panties down to her feet and she stepped out of them. He picked them up and put them in his pocket.

She arched one eyebrow at him and he just smiled at her.

She slipped the coat off her arms and set it on the padded chair she'd been sitting on and then slowly pulled the tails of her fitted shirt out of the waistband of her skirt. She undid the buttons one by one. The curves of her breasts pushed up by her demi bra became visible. When she had the buttons of her shirt undone, she slipped it off and turned around, bending over to put her blouse in her carry-on bag.

But honestly all he could see was the heart-shaped curve of her ass. He reached out, tracing the seam running down the center of her skirt. She pushed her hips back toward him and he groaned again. She stood up and turned, still wearing the bra, which shoved her breasts up and brought his gaze to them. He saw the tiniest hint of her nipple peeking out of the top of one cup as she reached between her breasts and undid the clasp.

She took the bra off and held it out to him. "Do you want this, too? It'd be a shame to break up the set."

He took it and shoved it in his laptop bag and she stood there, her shoulders back, breasts bare, proud and confident. This was the Pippa he wanted to see. Not the one who'd been so worried a few moments earlier.

"Are you sure about the fur coat?" she asked.

"I am. I think you'll like the feel of it against your nipples," he said.

He took it from her chair and stood up, holding it out for her. She turned away from him and reached back to slip her arms into the sleeves. Once she had it on, he pulled her back against him, wrapping his arms around her and cupping each of her breasts in his hands. He kissed her neck as he plucked at her nipples, feeling them harden under his touch.

Then he drew the satin-lined coat closed and rubbed the fabric over her engorged nipples. She gasped, shifting her hips back and rubbing her butt against his erection.

He bit lightly at the spot where her neck met her shoulder and then slipped one hand inside the opening of her coat to tease her nipple while he continued to suckle her neck.

She moaned and shifted in his arms as he rubbed the ridge of his erection against her backside, fitting himself nicely against her. He reached lower, drawing up the fabric of her skirt with his free hand until he felt the tops of her thighs where the elastic at the top of her hose met her smooth skin. He traced one finger around the edge of the fabric and then drew his hand higher, rubbing the seam where her thigh and hip met.

Then he brushed over her mound with his fingers. She moaned, putting her hand over his, and he quickly changed their positions, putting her hand under his and using her fingers to part her slick folds.

"Open up for me," he whispered into her ear, and she shivered against him as she nodded.

He touched her exposed clit lightly with his finger, just

tapped it as gently as he could. With each touch she let out a soft moan. He continued to increase the pressure of his touch, rubbing his finger around her sensitive bud and then tapping it again and again until she was writhing in his arms. She clawed at his wrist with her free hand, arching her back and turning her head to find his mouth. Their tongues mingled and she sucked hard on his as he plunged one finger deep inside her. He felt her tighten around it as she rocked her hips against his hand and cried out with the force of her orgasm.

He lifted her off her feet and sat down in his large chair, holding her on his lap. She curled her head into his chest as he kept his finger between her legs, thrusting in and out until she calmed in his arms.

Curled in Diego's arms wearing only her skirt and a fur coat, she never would have guessed she'd feel so safe. And dare she say it, so accepted.

He made her feel so warm and whole. No one else who'd known her given name, known of her life and fortune in London, had made her feel like none of it mattered, that she was enough. No one before Diego.

She reached between their bodies and pushed his zipper farther down until she could fit her hand into his pants. He was still rock hard, and as she awkwardly maneuvered herself until she could straddle him, she felt a drop of moisture on the tip of his erection. She captured it with her finger and brought it to her lips, licking it off. He groaned and shifted around. "Can you reach my wallet?"

He lifted his hips off the seat.

She felt her way around to his back pocket and found his wallet, struggling to pull it out and almost falling off his lap, which made her yelp and him laugh.

She handed it to him. He opened it and took out the condom she'd seen him put in there earlier. "What if you can't find any in England?" she joked.

"I think we'll manage," he said with a wink.

She thought they would, too. At least while it lasted between them.

At least for one more week.

As he put the condom on with one hand, she looked down at him, totally clothed except for his naked erection. She loved the idea of how respectable they might look to anyone who saw them when they were out together in public, but that secretly she was on the edge.

She could lie to herself and pretend that this thing with Diego was an affair, but she knew it was much more. He brought out parts of her that she'd never explored or thought about exploring.

Putting her hands on his shoulders, she shifted around until she could feel him at the entrance of her body and she shifted forward. "My favorite kind of ride," she said, putting her hands on either side of his face. She reached between them and took his erection in her hand, bringing him closer to her. Spreading her legs wider so that she was totally open to him.

Their eyes met as she slid all the way down on him, embedding him deep within her body. She let her head fall back and felt his breath on her breast a moment before his mouth closed over her nipple. She shivered and wrapped her arms around his shoulders, drawing him closer to her as she started to move on him.

He bent down to capture the tip of her breast between his lips. He sucked her deep in his mouth, his teeth lightly scraping against her sensitive flesh. His hand played at her other breast, arousing her, making her arch against him in need.

He lifted his head; the tips of her breasts were damp from his mouth and very tight. He rubbed his chest over them before sliding even deeper into her body.

She eased her hands down his back, rubbing his spine as he pushed himself up into her. She stared deep into his eyes, making her feel like their souls were meeting.

She was hoping he'd forgive her because she hadn't wanted to go back to London on her own.

"Pippa. Now."

His voice set off a chain reaction and she arched against him again, head falling back as her climax ripped through her body. He kept driving up into her and his hands tangled in her hair, bringing their mouths together as she came harder than before. She felt him thrusting into her and rode him hard until he grunted and she felt him jerk as he came.

She collapsed on top of him and he held her with his arms inside her fur coat, his hand rubbing up and down her back. She drifted off to sleep in his arms.

He held her closely knowing this was the last moment that they had before she would have to be Philippa Hamilton-Hoff, billionaire heiress and head of a legacy company that had been floundering in the last four years. He wondered if he'd made a big mistake by saying he'd come with her to London, but he knew that there had been no other choice for him.

He wasn't ready to let her go.

Not yet.

Thirteen

Diego put on his shearling coat as they exited the immigration area at the private airport where the Caruthers jet had landed. It was overcast and a light rain fell. The pilot and copilot were going to stay in the UK for a week and fly him back on Saturday. Diego was grateful for that, though he could have flown commercial and wouldn't have minded.

"I'm so nervous. Simon said he was sending a car for us and I'm not sure if my dad will be at the town house that I inherited in Belgravia," Pippa said.

He put his hand on the small of her back and walked beside her until she came to an abrupt halt. A severe-looking man stood before her, blocking her path.

"Father."

"Philippa."

Diego looked at the older man dressed in a suit with an overcoat. There was someone next to him who held an umbrella over his head to keep him from getting wet.

"Hello, sir. I'm Diego Velasquez."

"Mr. Velasquez, are you my daughter's… What are you to my daughter?" he asked.

"Her friend," Diego said.

"I wasn't expecting to see you today," Pippa said to her father.

"I asked Simon to keep me posted. I needed to catch you up on where our family stands as far as the decisions that Giles Montgomery has been making," her father said. "Perhaps we can discuss it over breakfast?"

Diego noticed that her face went very still and hard. "I can't, Father. I have a meeting with Giles this afternoon and Diego and I were hoping to get settled at the town house before then."

He nodded. "So you've already made up your mind? Giles has turned you against me."

"Father, that's not what happened. I've had four years to think about what you would do when I saw you again and—" she broke off, realizing she was getting very emotional. Had she lost her British stiff upper lip after years of living in the United States?

Diego rubbed her back and her father reached over and squeezed her hand.

"Me, too."

Just those two words. Clipped and not very emotional. But there was a look in his eyes that told her she might be missing something.

She looked at Diego and he subtly nodded. She turned back to her father.

"Okay. Let's have breakfast and you can tell me what you've been doing."

Her father looked relieved and nodded. "I'll give you both time to settle in and perhaps we can meet at the Costa near your town house in two hours. Will that do?"

"Yes."

Pippa's father turned and walked to the waiting Bentley and Pippa looked over at him. The misty rain had coated her hair and she looked cold. But for the first time he saw a sign of stubbornness in her expression.

"I can't tell if he was trying to manipulate me or if he feels something for me. But if he thinks he can manipulate me, it's not going to be easy."

"I believe that," Diego said as they were approached by a man in a black suit.

"Ms. Hamilton-Hoff?"

"Yes."

"I'm your driver, Dylan. And I'm here to take you to your town house, and of course wherever you want to go," he said. "Is that your luggage?"

He pointed to the three suitcases stacked near the curb.

"Yes, it is."

"Let's get you both in the car and then I'll see to it," he said.

Diego followed Pippa to the car and got in the back seat next to her. She didn't say anything and for once he had no idea what to do. She was giving off don't-touch-me vibes and he was smart enough to just sit next to her quietly.

"Sorry about that. I think my dad is going to be difficult about everything," she said.

"It's okay," he said. He felt bad that her father hadn't tried to hug her or anything like that. But maybe that was just some sort of British stiff upper lip that he wasn't used to. He only knew that both his father and mother had driven out to Arbol Verde to hug him and tell him to be safe before he'd left for this trip. And it was only a week. If he'd been gone for four years, he knew that his parents would start off with a lot more than conversation about the family business when they were reunited.

"He looked like he couldn't care less that I was back. I mean, I thought maybe it was because of the video chat and him being restrained because he was in Simon's office the last time…but no, he really doesn't like me," Pippa said.

Diego reached his arm along the back seat and pulled her

into the curve of his body. "Everyone shows emotion in a different way."

She pulled back and glared at him. "Really? Do you think there was a shred of emotion in him?"

"No," he said. "But I don't know him. You do. You said that after your mother died he kept you in boarding schools. Maybe his way of dealing with emotion is to lock it away… I don't know."

"I don't, either," she said. "I know that was bitchy. Sorry. I'm tired and everything here is harder than I thought it would be."

And they hadn't even left the airport yet. He wondered if he'd made a mistake in coming with her now. He knew that his purpose was to help her, but it felt like the next few days were going to be hard and he didn't have anything to bring to the table. It wasn't like her family owned a horse ranch or were breeders. They were jewelers to the queen. That was a completely different world than the one he lived in.

And as the driver got behind the wheel and started to take them to her house, he realized how different this world was. He had to mentally adjust to driving on the opposite side of the road; for the first few minutes, he kept feeling like the driver wasn't paying attention. But as they got on the M25, it really struck him that he definitely wasn't in Cole's Hill anymore. There were no trucks, just luxury sedans and hatchbacks. When they exited the highway and headed toward Pippa's town house, he couldn't help but notice how pristine the Georgian rowhouses were. And there wasn't a lot of space like he was used to. He was out of his element and he knew that caring for Pippa wasn't going to be enough.

When they entered her town house, he began to get a real sense of how wealthy Pippa was. It was filled with antiques, the kind of place his mom would love. She had decorated her condo in Houston very similarly.

Pippa immediately showed him to their room and told him he could sleep.

"Where are you going?"

"I have to meet my father, and then I have the thing with Giles, but I should be back for dinner."

"Okay. I'll go with you," he said.

"I think you'd find that boring," she said.

And she didn't want him there.

"Okay. What time for dinner?"

"Seven," she said.

It was just 10:00 a.m. now.

"Thanks," she said, giving him a kiss that brushed his cheek before she left to meet her father and her attorney.

Diego watched her go, sitting in a house that wasn't his. It was about 4:00 a.m. back in Cole's Hill, so Diego texted his brother to call him when he was awake. While he was here, he needed to stay busy because otherwise he would feel like he'd followed Pippa for reasons he didn't want to admit.

He wanted her in his life. He cared about her. But she wasn't in any position for that kind of relationship, he realized. She was focused on claiming her heritage and he had to hope he was strong enough to support her while she did it.

Mauricio called him when he woke up. Talking to his brother made him feel better.

"D, I heard that there's a riding stable not too far from where you're staying. In Surrey, I think. It's the kind of operation we've been talking about setting up here."

"I'll go and check it out. Send me the details."

"I will. So how's jolly old England?"

"Cold," he said. And lonely. But he wasn't about to say that to his brother.

"Good thing you have Pippa with you to warm you up."

"Good thing," he said, ending the call after that. He had a plan. He called the riding stable in Surrey and set up an appointment for the next day. Then he got a text from Bartolome Figueras, a friend of his who was a jet-setting polo player, who wanted his opinion on a horse he was going to buy. When he texted the photo, Diego realized they were both in the UK and made plans to meet with him later in the week. Now he had something to do for the rest of the week other than sit around and wait for his heiress.

Six days of being in London and she was still trying to catch up to everything. She'd gotten home late every night and spent a few minutes trying to listen to Diego tell her about his day before she'd fallen asleep. Sometimes he made love to her in the middle of the night, but mostly she was too tired. When her alarm went off every morning, they both groaned, and she dashed out of bed and to the House of Hamilton's offices on Bond Street, where a uniformed doorman with a top hat always greeted her by name when she arrived at their showroom before going up to the office housed on the fifth floor.

She wasn't even close to getting to design jewelry or talk about new revenue streams. The power struggle between her father and the board had taken its toll on the company and she was caught in the middle. Now that she was back she had to make some hard decisions and she was ready to make them. From a standpoint of emotional revenge it would be easy, but from a business standpoint it was harder.

Some of her father's ideas were actually quite good, but all of the infighting had made the board dismiss them out of hand. On top of that, her father's arrogant ways made it harder for her to side with him.

She needed someone to talk to, but when she tried to get Diego to come meet her for lunch, he'd told her he was on his way to meet some breeders in Hampshire. She felt a little annoyed but then reminded herself he'd come with her because he'd wanted to and, really, she couldn't expect him to just sit around while she wasn't there. But a part of her—the tired and unsure part—was annoyed that he hadn't.

"My meeting is at ten and according to the GPS I should be able to get back to London by two. Do you want to meet then?" Diego asked her on the phone.

"I can't. I have a meeting that starts at two fifteen," she said.

"We could talk while I'm driving. Except that this thing keeps trying to take me down narrow single-lane roads. I think there is something wrong with the mapping app on my phone. I'm going to have Alejandro look at my phone. He's a genius with apps."

Pippa didn't really have time to chat like this. "I think that's just the way the roads are out that way. I'll talk to you later. Don't forget we have dinner tonight with the board. It's black tie. If you don't have—"

"I'm not a country bumpkin, Pippa. I can figure out black tie. Are you coming home first or should I meet you at the venue?" he asked.

There was a tone in his voice that made him sound like a stranger. It wasn't something that she'd ever felt with Diego before. Even when they'd been meeting at the coffee shop and exchanging small talk, he'd never seemed so aloof. "I'm going to try to make it home."

"Okay. I'll be ready when you get there," he said.

"Diego?"

"Yes?"

"Thank you for coming with me," she said. She knew this week wasn't turning out the way either of them had anticipated and he was due to head back to Cole's Hill on Saturday. Two days from now.

"You're welcome. I'm sorry that everything that comes along with your inheritance is harder than you anticipated."

She was, too. She had expected this to be hard, but not this hard. In fact, she was surprised that her father wasn't even the biggest obstacle she had to surmount in taking control of the company. But she also realized that for years now, she'd had a fantasy about her return: that she'd just waltz back in, present her jewelry designs and make her suggestion for a wedding line, and they'd all applaud her. Things would be smooth, as though she'd never run away or had a power struggle with her father.

But coming back to the House of Hamilton wasn't like that at all. Not even close.

"I guess that's reality, isn't it?" she asked.

"It is," he said, then she heard a horn honk and Diego curse savagely.

"I should let you go," she said. "Be careful."

"You, too," he said.

The call ended, and she put the phone back in the cradle on her desk and glanced up to see Giles standing in the doorway.

"Do you have time for a quick coffee?" he asked.

"Sure," she said. But Giles was part of the problem. As she had coffee with him, she realized that he and her father were playing her. They both assumed that she was going to back one of them to keep control of the company.

"I know you mentioned partnering with Jacs Veerling for a limited-edition wedding collection and I wanted to let you know that once we have everything sorted at the board meeting we'd like you to start discussions with her."

"I'm glad you like the idea. I've already started discussions, Giles. I know that we're going to want to move quickly to bring some new products onto the market in the second quarter next year. My father and you both have strong ideas for the company."

"We're both men who know what we want."

"You are," she said, realizing that she needed to figure out what she wanted. She'd been sincere when she'd told him she wanted to take an active role in the company, but as far as she could tell, Giles thought she'd side with him and let him move the company in the direction he wanted. She needed to find out where the rest of the board stood because every day when she walked into the House of Hamilton showroom she was reminded of her heritage and felt a responsibility to keep that luxury and quality going for another generation.

She finished her meeting with him and knew she had to go talk to the other board members because the only solution she could come up with was one where neither man retained any control over the day-to-day running of the business.

She made a few calls and then left the office, going to the meetings she'd set up. She'd been surprised to learn that many members of the board hadn't realized she was back to take her place at the helm. She spent the rest of the afternoon and early evening convincing them that she was ready to do just that.

She reflected on how she had her work cut out for her as she took a taxi back to the Belgravia home she'd been sharing with Diego. She let herself into the house and could hear voices down the hall.

She walked toward the sound and saw that Diego was entertaining two very beautiful women and a man. He stood up when he saw her.

"Pippa, I'm so glad you're here," he said. "Please come and meet my friends."

But she didn't want to meet his friends. She needed to talk to him about what she'd learned today and they had to be across town in less than forty minutes.

"I have to get changed," she said, turning on her heel and walking out of the room.

What had she expected? But she knew she'd anticipated more from Diego. She entered their bedroom and knew she'd behaved horribly to his guests and she wasn't being a very good...what? She wasn't his girlfriend. He was leaving on Saturday and she was going to be here working hard to save her heritage.

There was an ache deep inside her that she pushed aside. It was about to be over between her and Diego. She knew she would mourn, but she was going to be very busy making sure that House of Hamilton had the future she knew it deserved.

Diego had been surprised when he'd run into Bartolome Figueras at the stables of the breeder he'd visited earlier that day. The Argentinian polo player turned model now spent his days working closely with breeders for his award-winning ponies. They'd met last year when Bart had come to Arbol Verde to look at Diego's mares for breeding. So earlier in the week, when Bart had texted him about the horse, Diego had invited him to stop by for drinks before dinner, hoping that he could talk shop but also introduce him to Pippa.

For the first evening since he'd been here, he hadn't just felt like her boy toy—he'd felt like he had a purpose of his own in London. But then she'd stormed in and been so rude to his guests.

Bart arched his eyebrow as Pippa left the room. The two women with him, his sister Zaira and her friend Luisana, looked at each other. "I'd say she's not too happy we are here," Luisana ventured.

"She's under a lot of stress," Diego said.

"I read a bit about it in *Hello!*" Zaira said. "I have often thought of running away and hiding from my overbearing brother, but alas, he holds the purse strings, so I have to stay."

Luisana laughed and Bart just shook his head. "We will go and leave you with your lady. But I would like to bring my sire to Arbol Verde, Diego."

"I'm looking forward to it," Diego said. He showed his guests out and then went upstairs to find Pippa.

She had changed into a lovely navy velvet gown that was fitted on the top and then flared out from the waist to her knee. She'd twisted her hair up into a chignon and had a string of pearls around her neck.

"I'm sorry I was rude. I've had a really long day," she said.

"It's all right. Bart was in the UK and I have an opportunity to do business with him, so I thought it might be nice for you to see that I'm more than just…what is it you think I am?" he asked.

He could excuse her tiredness, but this felt like more than fatigue. He had felt a distance growing between them from the moment she'd had her first meeting the day they landed.

"What do you mean?"

"I mean that you ignore me most of the time, and then when you need me, you expect me to drop everything—"

"Don't do that. I was just surprised that you had guests. I acted like a toddler and I'm sorry. Just leave it at that."

He would, except he was leaving in two days and he knew that this was something that had to be discussed in person.

"I can't."

"I know," she said, sitting down on the bed. And he could tell that she had already made her decision. "Coming back into this world has been harder than I thought it would be. Even though I'm not good at showing my appreciation, having you with me has given me the strength to stand up for myself and to try to see more clearly what it is that I can bring to the table."

He wasn't convinced. He sat down next to her, but he felt like they were oceans away from each other. Felt the gulf between her world and his very clearly. It wasn't a monetary one but more about lifestyle. And he'd never thought about that before this evening.

"I'm glad to hear that. I have felt very out of place here, but today going to meet with the breeder helped. I'm sorry that you've had a bad day."

She sighed and stood up, and he looked up at her. She had her back to him and he noticed the deep vee of her dress and how creamy her skin was. He wanted her as he always did, but he sensed she was trying to say something.

Possibly goodbye.

"It's more than a bad day. I had no idea of the amount of work that I am going to be required to do. I think I thought I could have you and the company and everything would sort itself out. But that's not fair to you. You have a life and a business of your own," she said.

"I do. But I'm… I think we both knew this was never going to be more than this week," he said at last. He'd hoped for more, but the truth had always been staring them both in the face. He couldn't live here, and her place was in London.

He needed to be back in Cole's Hill, despite how great it had been to meet Bart today and talk about future business. His core breeding program was for the US market, and as much as he thought it would be nice to expand to Europe and maybe the polo market, he knew that he was fooling himself. He had been trying to come up with a reason to stay. A reason to come back to London so he could see her more often.

And she obviously had no time for a man or a relationship.

"I think you're trying to figure out how to tell me this is it," he said. "That the good time you wanted from the bachelor you bid on and won back in Cole's Hill is over."

"Oh, Diego, I don't know if that's true," she said.

But he heard it in her tone. She did know.

"I do. It's been fun, Pippa, and I wish…well, I wish we were different so that this could have worked, but I think it's time for me to go."

She nodded, standing there awkwardly, her arms wrapped around her waist. She waited for him. He hoped to see some sign that she wanted him to stay, but he didn't find one.

He walked to the armoire and took out his suitcase. Chewing on her lower lip, she watched him for a minute.

"Goodbye, then."

She walked out the door and he watched her leave. Just stood there, way calmer than he felt on the inside, and let her go.

He packed his bags while she was gone and left a note and

the bracelet he'd picked up for her earlier in the week when he'd still had hope that he could figure out a way to make this last. And then he left.

Fourteen

That night in October, Pippa had known that Diego would be gone when she got back from her dinner, but it had still hurt when she'd walked into the empty house and found him gone. She hadn't opened the note he'd left her on the nightstand but had worn the bracelet he'd left. It was a tiny House of Hamilton hinged bangle in rose gold with two diamonds on either side. But that wasn't what made it valuable to her. He'd had it engraved.

Courage is being scared to death and saddling up anyway.

Just a little bit of Diego's courage on her wrist. She'd taken back her company from Giles and her father and it had been too late to get any new product ready for the Christmas season this year, but they had a solid plan in place for the coming seasons.

December was lonely, and Pippa admitted she missed Kinley and Penny, who had been so much a part of her holidays until this year. Despite talking with Kinley on video chat once a week like she was currently doing, she still felt lonely and missed Texas.

"Are you even paying attention?" Kinley asked.

"No. I'm not," she admitted. She'd been looking at her bangle and wondering when the ache of losing Diego would go away.

"Well, at least you're honest about it," Kinley said. "I have news."

"Is it that you're pregnant?"

"No. Don't even say that too loud. Nate said he would give me some space and he's been so sweet," Kinley said, looking over her shoulder. "I stopped taking the pill."

"Good. You know I'm your friend and I support you, but you and Nate need more kids. The imp is turning into a diva. She needs a sibling to bring her in line," Pippa said.

"She does. Plus, Bianca is expecting, so Nate and Penny are both in a tizzy."

"I'm sure Nate appreciates you saying he's in a tizzy," Pippa said. It was nice hearing about everyone in Cole's Hill, but she wanted to know about Diego and wasn't sure she should ask.

"He's out riding with Penny, so it's safe," Kinley said. "In fact, I asked him to take her because I have to give you some tough love today."

"What about?"

"Diego."

"There's nothing to be tough about, Kin. I told you we both decided it wouldn't work out," Pippa said. "I have been very busy getting the board in order over here and renewing contacts and working with Jacs. We're both happy with this decision."

Kinley leaned forward on her elbows. "You are a rotten liar. I know you miss him, and unless you're going to be stubborn about this, you'll admit it."

Pippa sank back against the cushions of the armchair she was sitting in and looked out at the street. There was a light snow falling and she could see her neighbor's kids outside playing in the snow. Of course she missed him. She had never expected him to be so important to her. Never guessed that she could fall for a man that quickly or completely.

She had tried dating since he'd been gone, but no one could hold a candle to Diego. It was him she wanted.

She touched the bangle on her wrist.

"I miss him. But we both made the decision, Kin. I can't just show back up in his life. Besides I have to be here and he has to be in Cole's Hill."

Kinley shook her head. "Girl, those are details. I fly to Vegas for two weeks each month and Nate and I are making it work."

"You have a kid together," Pippa pointed out.

"That has nothing to do with it and you know it. If you love him, then the other stuff will be easy to sort out. You do love him, right?"

Yes. But she wasn't ready to say those words out loud. And she didn't want to say them to Kinley. "What if he doesn't want me anymore? What if he's moved on?"

"You must think I'm some kind of crappy friend," Kinley said. "Would I bring him up if he'd moved on?"

Pippa shook her head. "No, of course you wouldn't. How is he?"

"Well, he was drinking at the Bull Pen last night and Derek had to break up a fight between him and Mo. Those two are both brokenhearted…the entire town says so. Mo at least deserves it—everyone knows he wouldn't commit to Hadley. But no one can figure out what happened to you. They figured that being an heiress, you can live anywhere."

She sighed. "It's not that simple. Running House of Hamilton takes a lot of time and energy and I don't want to walk away from it."

"I think Diego would be willing to work something out with you. You know he's started a breeding program with Bart something-or-another. That hottie Argentinian. Even Nate had to admit he was good-looking."

"Exactly how did you get Nate to admit that?" she asked.

"We were both drinking with Diego," Kinley said. "That's not the point. If you love him, you need to come and claim him.

He is miserable and so are you. And I think he feels like he can't ask you to come back. Plus, I miss you. Even if you were only here once a month or every other month, it would be nice."

Pippa hung up with Kinley a few minutes later, but her mind was on Diego and how he'd come here and supported her. And when she'd told him she needed space, he'd given it her. If she wanted him back in her life, she was going to have to go to him. Support him and show him that she was there for him.

She knew that Kinley was right. She loved Diego and it was time to go back and claim her rancher.

She'd need some help to do it and she knew just whom she could turn to for it.

Diego woke up with a hangover, which wasn't surprising, since he and Mauricio had decided to shut down the Bull Pen again. And Manu had been there celebrating the high school football team winning the state playoffs. Things had gotten more than a little out of hand.

But it had distracted him from the fact that it was only three days until Christmas and the only thing he wanted was a certain British woman who had made it very clear she needed nothing more from him.

For the first few weeks he'd been back in Texas he'd expected her to contact him. The bangle had been a sentimental gift and he'd thought...well, that she'd—what? Suddenly realize she loved him and come running back to him?

Wake up, loser.

He knew she had a life in London. He'd kept up-to-date with her takeover of House of Hamilton by reading the *Financial Times* and watching the profiles cable business networks had done on her. She'd come back into her own and was setting the tone for the company, repositioning it for a new generation of high-end customers.

He'd been impressed and proud of her.

Because no matter how long he was away from her or how far apart they lived, he knew he was never going to get over her.

It hadn't taken him very long to realize that. He'd gotten on with his own business and he had Mauricio developing the riding center on the outskirts of town. Bart had come to visit and stayed for a few weeks in November and they were going to start a new breeding program, building on the stamina of his horses and the agility of Bart's. They were both excited about the prospect.

Honestly, his business had never been better. Every night during the week he fell into bed exhausted. Even so, he got only a good thirty minutes of sleep before he woke in a fever for Pippa. Taking her that last time in his bedroom had been one dumbass idea because every time he lay on his bed he remembered holding her in his arms there and it made him miss her more keenly than before.

He got out of bed and walked naked to the bathroom. He showered but didn't shave, and got dressed in a shirt and jeans. That was all he'd need. Technically it was winter, but December in Cole's Hill wasn't always that chilly. The highs were in the 70s this week.

His sister was waiting in the breakfast room when he came downstairs. Benito was sitting quietly next to her.

"Bianca, what are you doing here?"

"I'm worried about you," she said. "I sent Alejandro to check on Mo. You know they're twins and sometimes that bond helps. But you. What's going on?"

"Well, I'm planning to eat breakfast and then probably check on my mares. We have two that might foal early, which of course isn't good news."

He helped himself to the breakfast burrito that his housekeeper had left on the counter and a cup of coffee before sitting down next to Benito. He gave his nephew a kiss on the top of the head and Beni hugged him before hopping down from his chair.

"Can I watch TV now?" he asked.

"Yes. Let me get you set up," Bianca said, standing and taking him into the other room.

Diego took a huge bite of his burrito, wondering if he should just ghost while Bianca was in the other room. He stood up, pushed his chair back and was halfway to the back door.

"Don't even think about it. I'm pregnant, have already been sick once this morning, and if I have to chase you down, it's not going to be pretty," Bianca said.

"Uh, sorry, sis. I just don't want to have this conversation," he said.

"Me neither," she admitted. "You're my big brother and one of the best men I know, so I hate to see you like this."

"It's nothing," he said. "I'll get over it soon. I just need time."

She shook her head. "I don't think time will heal this."

"I do."

He wasn't going to talk about his broken heart and the way he kept waiting for something to happen between himself and Pippa. Something that wasn't going to happen.

"Fine. Are you sure you're okay?" she asked.

"Yes," he said, sitting back down. "Thank you for caring."

"Of course I care, you big dummy. Listen, I have a friend flying into Houston later this afternoon and Derek is on call, so he can't go get her. And like I said, I've been sick this morning... Would you mind picking her up?"

"Is this a setup?" he asked. Because there was something in his sister's tone that made him very suspicious. "I'm not ready for that, Bianca."

"I know," she said, putting her hand on his wrist. "Believe me, I know. It's not a setup. I just need someone to pick her up."

"Okay," he said. "I'll do it."

"Thanks. I'll text you the details of where to meet her. But I think bag claim would be a good spot."

"Will she know where to find me?" he asked. He still wasn't sure that his sister wasn't up to something, but he wasn't going to keep questioning her. He wondered if while he was there, he should book himself a ticket out of town for the holidays just to get away from everything that reminded him of Pippa.

"Yes, I told her to look for you," Bianca said. "Wear your black Stetson so she can spot you."

His sister stayed for a few hours. They talked about Christmas day and how odd it was now that she had to split her time with the Velasquez family and the Carutherses. He thought he did a good job of coming off as normal, but as soon as Bianca left he felt that gaping emptiness again and knew he wasn't adjusting as quickly as he should be.

He didn't want to keep missing Pippa for the rest of his days.

But the thought of spending Christmas without her made him sad. He promised himself that starting January 1 he was moving on. He had to. He didn't like the man he was becoming: drinking, fighting, wanting something that was beyond his reach. He wasn't that man.

It had taken her longer to get through immigration and border control at the Houston airport than she'd expected. She'd barely had enough time to dash into the ladies' room to fix her makeup and tidy up her braid. She still looked nervous and tired when she looked back at herself in the mirror.

She almost—*almost*—wanted to run back to the departure lounge and head back to London. But she wouldn't.

Not unless Diego told her he wanted nothing to do with her. And she was perfectly prepared for him to do just that.

She was just going to… She had no idea what. But Bianca had promised to pick her up, since Kinley was in Vegas with Nate and Penny today. Bad timing on her part, Pippa thought. She'd rehearse what she was going to say to Diego on the drive from Houston to Cole's Hill.

She texted Bianca and got back a text saying to meet in the baggage claim area. She towed her suitcase behind her in that direction and then froze as she saw a familiar long, tall Texan with that distinctive black Stetson on his head, standing off to the side of the luggage carousel.

Bianca had tricked her. But Pippa didn't blame her. She guessed that it would be better to do this here in Houston. But not in the baggage claim area with all these people around.

She was trying to think of a plan to use the priority lounge to change into something more presentable when he looked up and their eyes met. Suddenly it didn't matter where they were or what they were wearing.

He was surprised to see her. That was the first thing she noticed. And then she realized he'd let his beard grow in. She liked it.

He straightened from the wall and walked toward her, and she left her suitcase and ran to him. She threw herself into his arms and he caught her. She put her hands on his jaw, framing his face, and kissed him for all she was worth.

"I missed you so much."

"I missed you, too," he said.

He kissed her and then put her on her feet. "Let's get out of here and we can talk."

She nodded. But she didn't let go of his hand. Seeing him had reinforced what Kinley had said to her. There had to be a way to make this work.

He got her suitcase and they walked out into the afternoon Houston sun. The sun felt good on her skin.

She had missed more than Diego, she realized.

He led the way to his truck and put the tailgate down, lifting her up onto it after he'd tossed her suitcase in the back. He leaned on it next to her.

"So...you're back for Christmas?"

"Yes and no," she said. "I'm really back for you, Diego. I realized I should never have let you leave. I love you. I want to figure out a way to make our lives work for us."

He didn't say anything, and she realized he might not love her. Why hadn't she thought of that before?

But it didn't change anything. She still loved him.

He rolled his hip along the edge of the tailgate and stepped between her legs, putting his hands on her hips.

"I love you, too, Pippa," he said. "God, I've missed you."

She pulled him close, wrapping her arms and legs around him and kissing him hard and deep.

"So how's this going to work?" he asked.

She shook her head. "I have a few ideas, but really I wasn't sure what to expect when I got here."

"Fair enough. Let's go home so I can make love to you and welcome you properly back to Texas. And then we can figure out how to make this work."

"I can't wait."

He drove her home and they made love as soon as they were on his property. He pulled the truck off the road and took her hard and deep. They stared into each other's eyes and professed their love.

When they got to his house, they made love again in the bathtub and then sat in his big bed and talked about the future.

"How long can you stay this time?" he asked.

"I'm off until January 7," she said.

"Good. I can fly back with you, if you'd like me to," he said. "Do you remember Bart—the polo player?"

She groaned. "How could I forget. I was a grade-A bitch to him."

"You weren't, and everyone understood what you were going through. He and I have been working together here in Texas, but he has purchased a large country house with a stable that he wants to use to develop polo ponies in the UK. I am one of his investors now."

"That's great. So you would be staying with him?"

"During the week I would," Diego said. "Then we can spend the weekends together. I can't be away from Arbol Verde for more than three weeks at a time."

"That will work for me. I can come here and work from Texas

for a few weeks. We can sort of play it by ear until we figure out what works for us."

"I like that. Together I feel like we can do anything," Diego said.

They knew it would be hard to make their relationship work, and at first Pippa was going to have to spend more time in the UK than in Texas, but they came up with a plan that they thought would work for them.

"The important thing is that we are both in each other's lives," she said.

"Amen to that."

* * * * *

Her Sexy Texas Cowboy

Ali Olson

Ali Olson is a longtime resident of Las Vegas, Nevada, where she has been teaching English at the high school and college level for the past seven years. Ali has found a passion for writing sexy romance novels, both contemporary and historical, and is enthusiastic about her newly discovered career. She loves reading, writing and traveling with her husband and constant companion, Joe. She appreciates hearing from readers. Write to her at authoraliolson.com.

Books by Ali Olson

Harlequin Blaze

Her Sexy Vegas Cowboy

To get the inside scoop on Harlequin Blaze and its talented writers, be sure to check out BlazeAuthors.com.

All backlist available in ebook format.

Visit the Author Profile page at millsandboon.com.au for more titles.

Dear Reader,

So much has changed since my first book, *Her Sexy Vegas Cowboy*, was published: my husband and I started traveling full-time; we welcomed our sweet baby, Annabelle, into the world; and I completed my second Harlequin novel, which you hold in your hands. Quite a bit of it was typed one-handed on a phone while caring for a newborn. Lucky for me, she was a pretty good sport about the whole thing and let me bounce ideas off her.

Once I finished *Her Sexy Vegas Cowboy*, it was clear that Jeremiah would need his own story; with his humor and constant optimism, he's my kind of hero, and I wanted to hear more from him and whether or not he would ever find his own happily-ever-after. In addition, the first "fan" email I received from a reader (shout-out to Caitlin!) asked if I was planning on writing a book about him.

I struggled with this book at first, though. I wasn't sure who the heroine was or where the story would be set. After going through a lot of (bad) ideas, I realized the story had to happen right before Jessica and Aaron's Texas wedding, and then it became obvious who Jeremiah would fall for—the sister of the bride. After that, everything fell into place.

The antics of Renee and Jeremiah made me smile, giggle and sigh. I hope it is the same for you and that you enjoy reading about these two as much as I enjoyed writing about them.

Cheers,

Ali Olson

For my baby girl, Annabelle. You're going to read this one day. That's going to be a very weird day.

One

"Jessica, it'll all be fine. You just need to stop worrying," Renee said in her most soothing voice, trying to calm her sister's newest anxiety issue. She couldn't help but roll her eyes, though, and was glad her sister couldn't see her through the phone.

"I know you're rolling your eyes at me over there," her sister chirped back, "but this is *important*. What if the whole thing is a disaster? I've been planning for months for every possible problem, but I never expected this."

Renee sighed. "Stew is a nice guy. You're just freaking out because you haven't met him yet and it's a little weird to think of Mom having a boyfriend. What do you think he'll do, scream obscenities during the ceremony? Take off all his clothes and bathe in the potato salad at the reception?"

She snorted, picturing her mother's slightly stuffy boyfriend doing anything of the sort. "Besides," she continued, "I thought your wedding was going to be super low-key. You're having it at your house. How much could there possibly be to plan, or to screw up? You said you were keeping it casual."

She looked at the bridesmaid's dress hanging on the back of

her door. It was all clean lines and conservative cuts. Pretty, but definitely not something she would wear to a gala or anything. The only thing that kept it from being something Renee might wear to a dinner with friends—besides the fact that she was always too busy to go to dinner with friends—was the color: a gorgeous violet, the color of a summer evening right after the sun set.

It was a beautiful color, but Renee knew it was all wrong for her. She pushed her shoulder-length, strawberry blond hair behind her right ear, wishing she'd been gifted with Jessica's lustrous auburn locks. Her sister could pull off that color just fine, but Renee was certain it just made her look even more washed-out and freckly than normal. Not that she'd say anything like that to her worrier of a sister.

"It's casual," Jessica replied, "just a very *planned* casual. I don't want to have to worry about anything that day, and the only way that'll happen is if I have everything planned. That way, I won't need to feel anxious about anything."

"That's why I'm flying in tomorrow, Jess. I'm tying up the last few things at work tomorrow morning, and then I'll have the whole week completely free to help with everything. We'll make sure it's all ready and you can enjoy the weekend without needing to triple-check anything, because we'll have already taken care of it."

Renee waited for her sister to see the logic in what she said, though she seriously doubted Jessica's ability to go an entire day, *especially* her wedding day, without feeling anxious. Still, it was her job to keep her sister from freaking out, and she was prepared to do her damnedest. No matter how difficult it was for her to go an entire week away from her job.

She heard Jessica let out a deep breath and smiled to herself. After twenty-six years as sisters, she'd gotten pretty good at figuring out how Jessica was feeling, and she knew she'd said the right thing.

"You're right, Renee. It'll be great, I'm sure. Thanks again for coming down early and helping. I owe you."

"It's nothing," she answered, even though her fingers itched when she thought of all the work she'd be missing over the next week. "I have the vacation time just sitting there, and we can spend some time doing sisterly things. It's been a long while since just the two of us hung out." Renee picked up another pair of jeans and tossed them into her half-filled suitcase.

"Definitely. Oh! I almost forgot. Is it okay if Aaron's friend Jeremiah picks you up from the airport? He's going to be in town anyway. You remember him from Vegas, right?"

Renee felt her ears burn, so glad her sister couldn't see her blush. She remembered Jeremiah, all right. Her heart thumped harder in her chest just thinking about Aaron's drop-dead-gorgeous friend. She had flown to Las Vegas in early December to surprise her sister with her perfect "bachelorette party," which meant dinner and drinks with family and Jessica's best friend, Cindy.

Renee hadn't expected to be introduced to the sexiest man she'd ever met, but when Jeremiah walked in with Jessica's fiancé, she nearly fell out of her chair. Even over a month later, she could still picture his sparkling brown eyes, easy smile and thick dark hair, which she had spent more time than she'd like to admit imagining running her fingers through. The blood rushed away from her face and to a much more intimate location just thinking about it.

"Renee?"

She was brought abruptly out of her reverie by her sister's voice. "Sure, that's fine," she responded, hoping her sister didn't notice her sudden breathlessness.

"Great. He said he'd meet you at baggage claim. See you tomorrow, little sis. Thanks again."

"Love ya, big sis. See you tomorrow."

She hung up and sat at her table, letting her mind wander right back to Jeremiah. She hadn't really talked to him that night in Vegas, and that was on purpose. Throwing herself at the best friend of her sister's soon-to-be husband was definitely a no-no, and trying to have a normal conversation with someone that sexy seemed impossible. Avoiding the situation altogether had been her only plan of action.

Still, she couldn't help but notice how friendly and easygoing he was with the whole group. She also couldn't help but notice the way his muscles moved under his shirt and the way his lips begged to be kissed. He had been playing the starring role in her fantasies since then, and those lips had played a *very* important part.

And now she was going to be spending a significant amount of time with him in close quarters. She gave herself about a fifty percent chance of getting through the car ride without saying or doing something incredibly stupid.

Renee shook her head, trying to get herself together. This week was about Jessica and Aaron, not her desire to jump into bed with Jeremiah. Maybe if she told herself that enough times, she'd remember it when she actually saw him.

Jeremiah's eyes, the color of coffee, captured her and sent jolts of excitement along her spine. He stepped so close she could feel the heat from his body all the way down hers, and he placed his hand on her neck, his thumb rubbing along her jawline, making her purr in response.

His other arm slid around her waist, pulling her even closer, until her body was pressed against his and she could feel his hardness and strength. Renee let her hands graze over the muscles of his arms as they moved up and around his neck.

When he spoke, his voice was a low growl, his usual carefree tones darkened with primal urgency. "You have no idea how long I've wanted to do this."

Her breath came in short gasps as she waited while he leaned toward her with agonizing slowness, his lips drawing ever closer. Her mouth opened for him, inviting him in.

Renee sighed and opened her eyes. Her dark bedroom greeted her, feeling much colder and emptier than it usually did. She glanced at her phone for the time and groaned. Her alarm would be going off in five minutes. Not nearly enough time to slip back into her dream and enjoy the image as completely as she would like.

She told herself to get up, but stayed under the covers with her eyes closed, allowing the picture to last just another moment.

Finally, after another sigh, she pulled herself out of bed and turned on the light, running her fingers over her face and through the tangles of her hair. She hadn't seen Jeremiah in weeks, yet she could still picture exactly how sexy he was. And if she couldn't keep her hands off him in her dreams, how was she possibly going to get through the next week around him?

Maybe he wasn't as fantastic in real life, she told herself. Maybe she'd let her imagination run away with her since Vegas, and he'd end up being a complete disappointment when she saw him again.

Yeah, right.

She shook her head to quiet her thoughts and tried to refocus her mind on the tasks she wanted to tackle this morning, but even her job couldn't completely erase the image of Jeremiah with his arm encircling her. She shook her head again and went to make some coffee. It was going to be a long day.

Forty minutes later, Renee walked through the snowy streets to work. It was only a couple of blocks from her apartment, but her toes felt frozen by the time she stepped into the building, and she gratefully breathed in the blast of hot air that greeted her. New York City was bitterly cold in February, and her dress slacks and heels didn't exactly keep her toasty. At least Texas would be warmer, she reminded herself, trying to create some excitement about her trip to replace her nerves over seeing Jeremiah again and the guilt of being away from her job for so long.

In the elevator, she took off her thick coat and brushed

her hair back off her shoulders, watching the numbers climb until it stopped on the twentieth floor. As the doors slid open, the two-foot-high letters loomed above her, as they did every day, and just like every other day, they made her smile. The *Empire Magazine* head office had been her home for almost four years, since she became an intern fresh out of college, and she felt her heart jump with excitement in the same way it had since her first day.

Renee's friends constantly told her she was a workaholic and needed to take a break, but the truth was, she loved her job. She had meant to take today off as well as next week, but in the end she hadn't been able to do it—there were a few last things she wanted to tweak before going, and Renee couldn't bring herself to leave the work for the others on her team. Or worse, just submit everything as it was.

Striding quickly through the hallways, Renee made her way to her office, smiling at coworkers as she went.

As her computer booted to life, she settled into her chair. She just needed two hours to finish perfecting one of her spreads for the next issue, and then she would leave, she promised herself.

A head covered in black curls popped into her doorway as Jeff, a man on Renee's design team, leaned in. "You're not supposed to be here, remember? That's how vacations work."

Renee smiled. "I know. I'm just not quite finished with the layout of one of my articles. Then I'll go, I promise. I've got a flight to catch."

"Well, Patty heard you were in the office. She wants to see you, whenever you have a second."

She thanked him, wondering what her boss could possibly want to see her about. She was probably just going to lecture her about overworking again. Patty did that every few weeks, and had been overjoyed when Renee told her she needed to use some of her vacation time.

Renee glanced at her computer once more before leaving her office. The spreads would need to wait a few more minutes.

Four hours later, Renee rushed out of the building into the icy air, praying she would make her flight. Her mind was such a jumble with what Patty had told her that there was hardly any room for anxiety to creep in.

After forty years in the business, Patty was retiring. And she wanted Renee to take over her position. Renee still couldn't believe it. She had thought it would be years before she'd get this opportunity, and here it was, so close she could taste it.

As she hopped out of the cab and dashed into the airport, thoughts of her new job stuck with her, sending flurries of excitement through her stomach.

Or maybe that was from the thoughts of Jeremiah, who would be waiting for her when she landed Texas. He hadn't been far from her thoughts the whole morning, either.

Two

Jeremiah parked his truck in the concrete structure outside of the airport. He was glad Renee's plane wouldn't be landing for another fifteen minutes, because he needed some time to pull himself together and calm down. Not that he'd been able to do that all day, or really since he'd met her in Vegas weeks ago.

For the thousandth time, he reminded himself that this was Jessica's little sister and he'd have to be an idiot to even try to make something happen with her, no matter how fast his blood surged through him when he pictured her. He'd spent enough time around Jessica since she moved down to Texas from New York to know exactly how badly it would go if he made a move on Renee.

Not that he and Jessica didn't get along, but dating someone in her family was a whole different story. He knew just how protective Jessica was about her little sister, and he was pretty sure Jessica thought of him as some kind of pickup artist. Not the kind of guy you'd want your sister with.

He could only imagine what Jessica had told Renee about him. Even if she wasn't off-limits, the chance that she'd be interested was slim enough. She probably thought he was a playboy who spent the majority of his time flirting with random strangers. Which, he had to admit, wasn't far from the truth for the majority of his adult life. But he was almost thirty now, and for the past year or so the excitement of that life had dwindled and died.

And then he met Renee, who put the final nails in that coffin without even knowing it. She had passed into and out of his life like a breath of fresh air, making the prospects of other women seem dull and stale in comparison.

He didn't even know what it was about her that had struck him so forcefully, but he'd been knocked backward when he first saw her. Their first night in Vegas, he and Aaron and Jessica had gone to dinner with her bachelorette party, which consisted of Jessica's best friend, sister and mother. The moment they entered the restaurant and he saw Renee laughing about something her mother had said, he'd been awestruck.

She was beautiful, certainly, but no beautiful woman had ever made his jaw drop like that. It was also the first time he'd actually felt nervous when meeting someone. He never felt anxious, even that one time he'd asked out and been summarily dismissed by that supermodel. Aaron had laughed about that one for weeks. Somehow, Renee cut right through what Jessica called his "devil-may-care attitude" and left him feeling awkward and uncertain.

There was something about the way she laughed, the sparkle in her eyes, the way her light red hair fell over her shoulders, the freckles across her nose that made her look wonderfully fresh and happy, the sexy tilt of her chin that seemed to exude self-confidence. Whatever it was, something about her made it hard to think straight.

And even though they'd hardly talked, he had a suspicion that she might just be interested in him, too. When they'd been introduced, a light flush had spread up her neck, and she had let go of his hand just as quickly when they shook for the first time. Like she had felt the same jolt of electricity as he had.

Just the memory of her was enough to make his body jump to attention, and he felt an uncomfortable swelling in his jeans.

Jeremiah took another deep breath, trying to relax his body, and climbed out of the truck. If he could just get through the next hour without doing anything stupid, he would be able to keep his distance from her for the rest of the week and avoid the almost-overwhelming temptation to kiss her.

Renee stepped into the airport restroom and went straight to the mirror, looking at the damage done by her flight and trying to put herself back together. She glanced at her skirt and blouse, trying to straighten out the wrinkles, ignoring the tiny voice reminding her that Jeremiah was off-limits.

Of course he was off-limits. She knew that, and he certainly wasn't the reason she'd opted to ditch her comfy travel clothes and instead wear makeup, heels and her black skirt that hugged in the right places—not to mention the silky black underthings. She just thought it would be nice to look her best when she showed up at her sister's house.

The voice laughed at her unconvincing lies.

After taking one last look in the mirror and trying to wish away the dusting of freckles across her nose that made her look like a Girl Scout, she gave herself one more silent pep talk. *Remember, nothing can happen with Jeremiah, and he probably just thinks of you as Jessica's little sister, so seeing him for the first time since Vegas is no big deal. There's definitely no reason for your stomach to feel like this. So stop staring into a mirror like a crazy person and leave this bathroom.*

She didn't budge. Renee swore under her breath at her idiocy and steeled herself for what would assuredly be a very not-sexy week full of helping Jessica and staring at a guy who hardly knew she existed. Then she finally managed to walk out of the bathroom and through the terminal exit doors to baggage claim.

She found herself standing in a cavernous room studded with numbered carousels slowly circling luggage.

Her first thought was that she'd never find Jeremiah in this huge area, but that lasted less than four seconds before she spied him standing about twenty yards away, looking at her. Their eyes met, and she froze for a moment like a deer in headlights.

He wasn't as gorgeous as she remembered. He was even more so. Her daydreams hadn't done justice to the way his slightly shaggy, dark hair fell across his forehead or how his shirt clung to his chest. Not to mention his low-slung jeans and what was sure to be underneath. The quivering in her stomach turned into melting, an ache that made her knees feel weak.

Then someone bumped her elbow as they tried to walk around her, and she realized she was blocking the doorway and staring like Meg Ryan in one of her romantic comedies Renee loved to watch. She could feel a blush start low on her cheeks as she imagined how ridiculous she must look to him. How was she ever going to get through an entire drive alone in the car with him without making a complete fool of herself?

Another person knocked against her. She adjusted the bag on her shoulder and started moving toward the sexy cowboy who was waiting for her. As she got closer, Renee smiled and gave a tiny wave, vividly remembering the first time they shook hands. If she was going to get through this, there had to be no touching, that was for sure. If she could keep things casual, everything would be fine and Jessica wouldn't need to kill her for groping someone she hardly knew instead of helping with the wedding.

"Hi, Jeremiah. Thanks for picking me up," she said, hoping she sounded normal.

He smiled back, a little stiffly, making her wonder exactly how inconvenient this errand had been. But then he shrugged and his lips softened. "No problem. I was coming into town anyway. Do you have a bag to pick up?"

She looked up and noticed that the carousel closest to them displayed her flight information and luggage was starting to slide down the chute. She nodded, and after an awkward pause that seemed to stretch between them, she was grateful to see her bag coming her way. Before she could do more than place her hand on it, though, he had it by the handle and was picking it up as if it weighed nothing. She briefly imagined him picking her up with the same strength before stopping herself.

No sexy thoughts, she reminded herself yet again. Jessica freaking out. Jeremiah not interested.

Except something in the way he looked at her made her think that maybe that second one wasn't true.

She tried to shake off the thought as she followed him out of the airport and into the parking structure, where he stopped at a large silver truck that screamed cowboy. It was huge. *Everything's bigger in Texas,* she thought to herself, sneaking a peek at Jeremiah, her mind drifting off into forbidden, jean-clad areas. She couldn't stop herself from smiling.

"What's so funny?" he asked, a good-natured grin on his face as he broke the silence between them.

She blushed for the second time in as many minutes, a bad omen for their drive together. There was definitely no way she would admit where her thoughts had gone, so she thought up something else as quickly as she could. "Nothing. Just the sheer number of trucks. It's all so very… Texas."

He smirked, and her heart skipped a beat. He said, "Most people in the city drive them for that reason. They don't actually get used to haul stuff around."

He settled her suitcase into the truck bed, among a variety of boxes, some plants, a bunch of metal rods and a number of other things Renee couldn't identify. Before she could reach for the door, he had it open for her and helped her climb in, making her fingers tingle where they touched. She tried to keep her mind on acceptable topics. "You clearly use yours to haul around plenty. What is all that stuff?"

He gave her a crooked grin. "Most of it's for your sister, actually. She had a whole list of things she needed to pick up, and

I volunteered since I was coming into town to replace a broken generator."

She looked out the back window and tried to identify the wedding items. "Those metal rods are some kind of arch thing, I'm guessing?" He nodded. "And the plants, of course. And me. She's really putting you to work," Renee finished, laughing.

Jeremiah chuckled and raised an eyebrow. "I'm positive it's nothing compared to what she has in store for you."

Renee laughed again. A little of the awkward tension was gone and she felt lighter than she had since seeing him, but that ache didn't go anywhere. He was even sexier when he was being funny, God help her.

Jeremiah swung the truck out of the parking structure. Renee racked her brain for any safe topics that could keep the silence from settling between them again. When they were quiet, her mind wandered, and she didn't want to spend the entire drive wondering whether or not the bench seat of his vehicle was long enough for them to act out a few of her spicier fantasies.

"So, how far away do you guys live from the airport?"

"You guys?" he repeated with a thick Brooklyn accent. "You're never going to fit in around here with talk like that. We say *y'all* around here."

Renee tried again, this time putting the thickest drawl she could muster into her voice. "Well lookee here, Jeremiah, just how long of a ride do we have in this here fancy horse buggy till we mosey into y'all's neck of the woods?"

He let out a peal of laughter that reverberated through her chest, so loud and genuine that it made her laugh in response. He had an amazing, infectious laugh, and she was swept away in the silliness of the moment. When was the last time she'd joked with a guy? It seemed far too long.

"We all live about sixty miles away," he said, finally getting himself enough under control to answer her question, adding an adorable Texas accent to his words.

An hour alone with him. God help her. Renee looked out

the window. The city—if you could call it that—was already shrinking in the distance, leaving them surrounded by a few homes and a lot of open land. "And that's the closest town to you? To get a generator, you need to drive all the way to, um—" she panicked for a moment as she realized she didn't remember the name of the city she had just flown into "—Tyson?" she finished, hoping it was right.

He raised his eyebrow and smiled at her again in the way that made her insides twist. "You mean Tyler?"

She flushed, embarrassed. "Yeah. That."

"There are a couple of small towns that are closer, but Tyler's the biggest nearby. We'll be at Jessica and Aaron's before you know it."

Although that was what she told herself she wanted, the idea was not a pleasant one. She was enjoying talking to Jeremiah, and didn't want it to end *too* quickly. "Was it weird to start calling it 'Jessica and Aaron's' instead of just 'Aaron's place'?"

He thought for a moment, tilting his head. "Not really. They just fit together so well that the moment she moved in, it became their place, you know?"

Renee nodded, but didn't really understand. She looked at the window as they flew past large homes and swaying trees, already well out of the city. The fields in the distance were a wintry brown, showing off a wide expanse of countryside. How did Jessica transplant her whole life to this strange place and settle in so smoothly? Renee felt like a fish out of water looking at the vast nothingness around her.

Jeremiah tried to keep his eyes on the road, but his gaze was continuously drawn to the woman only a few feet away. He'd been failing miserably at self-control since the moment she walked into baggage claim in that sexy, curve-loving skirt and heels that made him want to drop to his knees and worship her legs. There were a lot of things he'd like to drop to his knees and do to her, in fact.

He focused back on the present, trying to stop those thoughts. They were exactly what he couldn't let himself get caught up in this week if he wanted to survive.

He glanced at her again. Instead of thinking about the way her shirt moved against her breasts as she shifted in her seat, he tried to think of something to say to her. Her mood had switched from silly to thoughtful in a matter of seconds, and he wasn't sure what he should do. For a guy who'd always felt so confident around women, this was a new one on him.

He grabbed at some new topic of conversation. Anything to keep her talking. "It's nice of you to fly in a week early to help your sister. According to Aaron, she's been fighting off a state of panic for the past week or so, worrying that things won't be ready in time."

Renee nodded, as if this wasn't new information. "She's always been the anxious one. She wouldn't be Jessica if she wasn't worried. Really, though, it should be Cindy here. She's always been the enthusiastic, creative one. I'm not sure how I'm going to be able to help much, but with the pregnancy and all, Cindy couldn't take that much time off from work."

"If Jessica's the anxious one and Cindy's the enthusiastic one, what are you?" He wasn't sure if he was prying, but he just had to know more about her.

She paused, thinking. "I guess I'm the focused, driven one."

Jeremiah tried to read between the lines. "Is that code for 'workaholic?'"

Renee gave him a small smile. "Pretty much."

"And what else are you?"

She shrugged. "I don't know. I think that's about it."

He could think of some other adjectives that described her, but didn't say them out loud. He wasn't sure if she even realized she was the funny one, the sexy one, the dear-God-I-wish-she-was-in-my-arms-right-now one.

He tried to think of something else to talk about. Normally he'd be fine with silence, but silence around her made him want to say and do things that were all on the "terrible ideas" list. At least when they were talking, he could focus on their conversation instead of on the way her hair fell across her shoulders and that one darker freckle just below her left ear.

Lucky for him, she seemed just as willing to keep up continuous chatter as he was, and the rest of the drive passed quickly while she described her favorite things about New York, asked questions about her sister's life in Texas and told him about her job.

"It's not a sure thing yet, but the lead designer spot would be amazing. I've been working toward that exact position since high school. It's my dream job."

He glanced at her out of the side of his eye, even though her face was already indelibly printed in his mind. She couldn't possibly be older than twenty-eight. "You've managed to land your dream job before turning thirty? Is that some kind of a record?"

Renee smiled and her eyes lit up, changing her face from beautiful to stunning. "I'm younger than a lot of people on my team, but I have just as much experience as pretty much anyone there if you look at the work I've done. I usually pick up a few extra pages each issue, and my work hardly ever needs to be retouched. I don't think my age will matter."

"I guess you were right about being the workaholic one."

"That was your word," she pointed out. "I said I was the focused one."

Jeremiah was impressed, but something about her dedication to her job sent up an alarm. "How do you manage to do all that and still have fun? Doesn't it make it hard to relax, take vacations, date?"

Jessica had mentioned at one point that Renee was single—Jeremiah was sure she had no idea how that offhand comment had affected him—and he'd been perplexed as to why. Now he was beginning to suspect the reason.

"I don't really have the time for that kind of stuff. My job is too important to me and I wouldn't want to screw that up because of those types of distractions."

Renee's shrug seemed casual, but her voice sounded very serious to him. Jeremiah wondered if she was sending him a message between the lines. If she was, he got it loud and clear.

Even though he'd known from the start that there would be no dating this woman, here was yet another example of why he needed to let go of all the little fantasies and quit mooning over her.

For a guy who was normally so great at looking on the bright side of things, he couldn't seem to find the silver lining for this one.

Relief swept through him as he drove up to Jessica and Aaron's house. He'd made it through the entire drive without saying or doing anything inappropriate, and now he could try to keep his distance and avoid being alone with her for the rest of her visit. Once she went back to New York, it would probably be years before he saw her again.

He didn't enjoy that thought.

He parked on the side of the large yellow ranch house, angling the truck so it would be easy to empty the wedding contents from the back. After turning off the engine, he shifted to look at Renee, who had turned her body toward him, as if she wanted to say something.

"Thanks for the ride, Jeremiah," she said, and he looked into her eyes deeply for the first time since they had left the airport.

It was no problem.

Anything for Jessica's sister.

That's what you do for friends.

All of the correct responses died in his throat. There was only one way he wanted to answer her, and before he knew what he was doing, he leaned across the small distance between them and pressed his lips to hers, his hand grazing across the soft skin of her cheek.

It took him less than a second to realize how awful that decision was, but then she pressed back into him, parting her lips and tilting her head, her urgency matching his. Any self-control he could have used to pull away dissipated when her tongue slid against his, sending tendrils of heat through his entire body.

His hand slid from her cheek down her neck, slowly inching lower. Before he could fall deeper into the kiss or his hand could move past her collarbone, though, she leaned back, separating from him. Her breathing was heavy and her eyes wide, and he realized what had just happened. He rubbed his hand across his face and tore his eyes away from her, checking to be sure Jessica was nowhere in sight. Dear God, he'd kissed her. How could he have been so stupid?

Still, he couldn't help but feel excitement course through him. She had kissed him, too. He looked at her again. She was shaking her head, her eyes closed, her hands covering her face.

"I'm so sorry—" he began.

"That was so bad," she moaned, cutting him off.

He grimaced. "The kiss was bad?" he asked, unable to help himself.

She shook her head even more furiously. "The kiss was too good. That's what makes it so bad."

Jeremiah knew he should feel awful, but he was happier than he'd been in a very long time. Just to be sure, he asked, "So you liked the kiss?"

She looked at him through her fingers. "That's not helping. There's no way we can do that again. Jessica will flip if she finds out. She doesn't take unexpected new information well, and this is her *wedding* week. A curveball like that might send her into seizures."

Jeremiah wasn't sure if Renee was talking to him or herself, but her arguments seemed much less convincing than they might have been a few minutes before. There seemed to be one pretty glaring way around the issue, after all. "I'm not going to tell her about it. Are you?"

"No way," Renee responded immediately.

"So..." he said slowly, picking his words with care, "if neither of us tells her, and she doesn't see us, is there any reason why we can't do it again?"

Three

Renee was about to roll her eyes at Jeremiah and explain exactly why they could never do anything like that again, but something stopped her before she could. Her libido spoke up with full force, demanding why exactly that was such a terrible idea.

She'd been thinking about this guy for weeks, and here he was offering her a chance to live out a few of those fantasies that had been running through her mind. It wasn't like she'd have another chance this good again.

And the look on his face wasn't helping her make any prudent decisions, either. The hope in his eyes combined with a smile that promised so much more. How could she let this opportunity go by?

Renee took a deep breath and looked out the front windshield in order to keep herself from leaning toward Jeremiah again. She tried to focus some of her attention on the view, but the trees and mountains spread before her were overshadowed by the sexy cowboy sitting inches away. "Okay," she answered, and out of the corner of her eye she saw his smile widen into a full grin. She had to force herself not to smile back. “But,” she continued, “there have to be ground rules. Number one—Jessica and Aaron absolutely can*not* find out about this. Jessica would turn it into such a big deal, and even though Aaron’s your best friend, he might tell Jessica. And number two—once I go home, we’re done. This is just a casual thing. Just sex.”

She continued looking out the windshield, waiting for a response, but was met with silence. It was only then that she realized he’d never said anything about them having sex. They’d had one two-second kiss and she had already good as told him that she was ready to jump into bed with him at a moment’s notice. What kind of woman did that make her?

The kind of woman that hadn’t gotten laid in a long time and had spent way too much time thinking about getting laid by this particular guy. But had she gone too far too quickly?

She looked over at him, hoping for some kind of positive response. Jeremiah was looking at her, that half smile still on his face.

Jeremiah stared at Renee, surprised. She couldn’t get much more straightforward than that. Just sex? He had given up the casual-sex thing months ago, and was serious about finding something more than that. Did he really want a secret one-week fling? To risk hurting his best friend’s fiancée for something that would be over in just a few days?

Then she looked at him, her green eyes silently questioning, and reminded himself that Jessica wouldn’t find out, and therefore couldn’t be hurt. He knew it was a weak argument, but really, there was only one answer he could possibly give this beautiful woman beside him.

He leaned forward again, pulling her into another kiss, this one slow and deep, full of the promise of more to come.

She responded immediately, falling into the kiss, but he pulled away after just a few moments. The indignant expression on her face made him want to laugh. The way her erect nipples showed through her shirt made him want to tear her clothes off. He took a breath. "Rule number one, remember? It'll probably be pretty hard to keep this thing a secret if Jessica finds us making out in front of her house."

Renee's eyes grew wide and she turned to look out the back window, searching for her sister, worry evident on her face. This time he couldn't stop the laughter.

Once she had carefully scanned for any sign of Jessica, she looked back at him and smiled. "Right, so maybe this isn't the most discreet location."

He knew they only had a few more seconds of privacy together, and he didn't want to separate without planning something. He needed to have another opportunity to kiss her in the near future, or it would drive him crazy. "When can we meet?"

She shrugged. "I don't know what Jessica has planned for me. I might be able to get away at some point tonight, but won't you need to go home?"

Jeremiah smiled. "I think I can manage to stick around here for the evening."

She looked like she was about to say something else, but before she could, a door somewhere nearby closed loudly and two voices started moving toward them. Jeremiah tried not to look too disappointed. "That'll be Jessica and Aaron," he said, opening his door and tearing his eyes away from the beauty next to him.

He climbed out of the truck cab just as Aaron and his tall, leggy fiancée walked around the corner of the house. Before Jeremiah could walk around the truck to help Renee down, she was clambering out herself and moving with quick footsteps to hug her sister.

Jeremiah watched, comparing the two women. At first glance, they looked very different: Jessica was tall, with long auburn hair and lightly tanned skin. Renee looked almost petite next to her, though she couldn't be under five foot six, with strawberry blonde locks barely grazing her shoulders and freckles dotting her pale cheeks and nose.

There were plenty of similarities when looked at more closely, though. They had the same shape of face, and something about the way they stood made it clear they were related.

He watched them embrace, their wide smiles nearly identical. He kept looking at Renee, studying the way she held herself, the tilt of her head, and thinking about what he might expect when they managed to find themselves alone together. Would she be as straightforward as her talk and her kisses implied? If so, he was in for one hell of a week.

He relived the kiss in his mind, feeling the sensations again as her tongue slid across his teeth. His heart revved back up to sprinting speed just thinking about it.

"Hey man, thanks for grabbing all that stuff and picking up Renee and everything," Aaron said, startling Jeremiah out of his reverie. While he'd been absorbed in every movement Renee made, he had completely failed to notice that his friend had come up beside him.

Jeremiah looked at Aaron and tried to sound casual, as if he hadn't been mentally undressing his buddy's sister-in-law. "No problem."

"Everything okay?" Aaron asked, his forehead creasing as he lifted an eyebrow. "You seem a little distracted or something."

Jeremiah wanted to smack himself. It hadn't even been two minutes and Aaron could already tell something was up. How was he going to manage to keep this thing quiet? It didn't help that he was a horrible liar. He just had to act normal, that's all. Jeremiah shrugged and replied, "I'm fine," then waited to see if he had pulled it off.

Aaron looked at his friend for another moment, then moved toward the bed of Jeremiah's truck. "Let's get this stuff unloaded," he said.

Glad to be out of the spotlight, Jeremiah immediately went to work.

* * *

Jessica hugged her again. "It's great to see you! How was your flight? And the drive in? I hope it was okay that Jeremiah picked you up."

More than okay, thought Renee as she glanced at Jeremiah, who was standing with Aaron. Just the sight of him made her heart beat loud in her chest, and she hoped she hadn't started blushing. She suddenly felt warm despite the cool February weather.

"Everything's been great. I'm ready to be put to work. Should we start unloading the truck?"

Before she could even turn to make good on the offer, though, Aaron and Jeremiah were tackling the job. Jeremiah climbed into his silver monolith of a vehicle, and Aaron shook his head at the two women. "We'll take care of this. You ladies go catch up."

Jessica ran over to her fiancé and gave him a kiss, which seemed to Renee as if it was going to turn into much more when Aaron looped his arm around Jessica's waist and lifted her up, pressing her body against his. Renee looked at Jeremiah again, and found him looking back at her and smiling. She wasn't sure if it was because of his friend's antics or because he was thinking of what he would do to her when he got the chance to get an arm around her. The latter was probably wishful thinking and she was definitely projecting some of her own thoughts on him.

But a girl could hope.

Then Jessica was back, a little breathless. She grabbed Renee's hand and started steering her toward the front of the house.

"Are you sure we shouldn't help?" Renee asked, partly because her New York sensibilities rankled a bit at the idea of letting the guys do all the work and partly because she wanted to watch Jeremiah using those very sexy muscles she could see straining beneath his shirt.

She didn't let herself think about how much weight each reason held in her mind.

Jessica shrugged. "Nah. It's a bit of a battle trying to get these

Texas boys to stop doing stuff for us. They're very gentlemanly. There are definitely worse problems to have. Anyway, I want to show you around and hear how things are going, so we can let them win this one."

If Texas is a state where "letting the guys win" means sitting back while they unload a full truck, maybe it isn't such a bad place after all.

She had without doubt warmed up to Texas over the past ten minutes. And if she kept thinking about Jeremiah's lips against hers, it would soon become one of her favorite places.

Before Jessica could pull her around the corner, Renee took one look at Jeremiah. He stood in the back of his truck, his body all muscle and hard lines, which made the perpetual smile crinkling his lips and eyes that much more breathtaking.

Jeremiah watched Renee disappear around the corner of the house. Just before she was out of sight, she turned and gave him a smile. Not the sweet smile he'd seen her use on her sister, or the tentative one he'd seen when he first picked her up from the airport. This smile held a promise that made his pulse pound in his ears. It was only for a moment, but it was enough.

He had to figure out how to get her alone as soon as possible, or he might internally combust from all the heat flowing through his veins.

He would have kept staring at the place where he'd last seen her, picturing all the things that smile hinted at, but Aaron interrupted his train of thought.

"You're staying for dinner, right?"

You couldn't drag me away. Aloud, though, all he said was, "Yeah, if that's okay."

Aaron nodded distractedly as he started pulling at the assorted bars and wires which would eventually become a wedding arch. Jeremiah moved to help him. As they pulled out each wedding-related item, Jeremiah said, "It looks like there's still quite a bit to do before the ceremony next weekend. Will everything be done in time?"

He really wanted to ask if Renee would have any free time at all or if Jessica would keep her so busy that he would almost never see her, but he couldn't think of a way to say it that didn't sound too much like he was asking when he'd be able to bang Aaron's sister-in-law.

"It should be pretty simple, actually, but Jessica wants to double-check everything, so that'll take some time."

"She's really putting in the effort to make sure nothing unexpected happens, huh?"

Jeremiah didn't know why he would ask that. Maybe he was trying to remind himself exactly why he had to keep his hands off Renee. In public, at least.

Aaron smiled what Jeremiah called his "Jessica smile." It was full of love, pure and simple. "Jessica wants everything to be as planned as possible, and she's willing to do everything she can to make that happen."

Jeremiah had no idea why that made Aaron smile, but he was glad his friend was so happy. Ever since Aaron had met Jessica in Las Vegas two years ago, he'd been happier than Jeremiah had ever seen him.

Being in love definitely didn't seem that bad.

Renee sat at the small circular kitchen table, trying not to fidget with her cup of tea. What was taking Jeremiah and Aaron so long?

After Jessica had taken Renee on a quick tour of the large, beautiful home she shared with Aaron, complete with white lace curtains like something out of a movie, they had settled into the kitchen so Jessica could keep an eye on dinner while they went over her notebook of wedding details to complete that week.

If Renee hadn't been so focused on finding some time to get Jeremiah to herself, she would've probably had trouble not rolling her eyes at her sister's binder full of lists, receipts and diagrams. It was detailed to the point of seeming neurotic.

Finally, after Jessica was nearly through all the pages regarding flowers, the back door opened and Aaron walked in, followed by Jeremiah. Aaron went over to the stove to check on something bubbling in a pot, while Jeremiah leaned against the counter near the back door they had just entered.

Jessica stopped her monologue and joined Aaron in the inspection of the meal, and Renee took advantage of the moment free from her sister's view to take in all the glory of the man from her fantasies as he moved toward her. She stared at his jean-clad legs and slowly moved her eyes up his body, lingering on a few choice places. God, he was gorgeous. It made her breath catch in her throat.

When she finally reached his face, he was looking right at her, a sexy smile on his lips, as if he knew exactly what she'd been doing. His eyebrows were raised in question, and she gave him her final assessment with a smile of her own and the tiniest of nods. She very much approved of what she saw.

At the end of their silent conversation, Jeremiah turned to the two talking at the stove. He said, "I'll take Renee's suitcase upstairs and get her set up in a guest room."

Renee jumped up from the table, nearly knocking over her tea, in her eagerness to follow him out of the room. After he'd gotten the nod from the couple and started to make his way toward the stairs with her suitcase, though, she hesitated for a moment. Was this really such a good idea? Flirting and some quick kisses in his truck were one thing, but was she really going to go through with this idea? The whole clandestine affair thing was so not like her.

But then Jeremiah turned and crooked a half smile and her insides melted, and she knew she wouldn't give up this opportunity for anything. She scurried after him up the stairs, nearly bowling into him on the landing, where he'd stopped to wait for her.

As soon as she was near enough, he wrapped an arm around her waist and pulled her in close, pressing her body against his. She gasped at the heat and strength she could feel where her breasts and stomach touched him. Her nipples budded at the contact.

The force of her reaction to him made her nervous for a moment, but then he was kissing her and her ability to think evaporated.

As soon as his mouth was against hers, every notion of stopping fell away at once, and she leaned even closer into his heat. In the truck, the first kiss had been quick and impulsive; the second short, slow and full of promise. This one, however, could only be described as passionate. Very very passionate.

So passionate she was vaguely surprised her clothes didn't disintegrate on contact.

Jeremiah's tongue plunged into her mouth, taking everything he could, but giving so much in the process. Time slowed as every ounce of her focused on the physical sensations: the feel of his mouth against hers, the tingling of her fingers, the warm heat that had pooled low in her belly, making her push against his body even harder.

And what she felt there, hot and hard against her, only turned her on more.

Jeremiah hated to pull away from Renee's kiss yet again, but he managed to force himself to break away, though he kept his arm around her waist. When she tried to lean back in, he chuckled. She was deliciously disheveled, and he wanted both to tuck her hair behind her ear and to mess it up even more. He was able to keep himself in check, though. "We should probably move to someplace a little more…private…than here."

Renee looked down the stairs, as if she expected to see Jessica looking up and glaring at them. "Right," she said once she seemed sure that they were still alone. Her voice was low and she sounded out of breath, which sent even more blood pumping straight to his already-painful erection. “Which room is mine?” she asked, looking at the doors on both sides of the hallway.

Jeremiah gestured with his chin to the door on the left, keeping his eyes on her lips, only just able to keep himself from kissing her again. She broke away and turned to open the door. He reluctantly let her withdraw from his embrace. It surprised him how much he hated to have her leave his side, even if it was only for the moment it took to get inside the room.

He lifted her suitcase and followed her into the room, hoping he hadn’t ruined the moment enough that he’d just be setting down the luggage and walking back downstairs, but he didn’t have to wait long to be satisfied on that count.

He walked into the room and only had enough time to notice that Renee hadn’t turned on the overhead light, leaving the room in only the dim sunlight filtering through the window, before the door was closing behind him. He turned around just as the door clicked shut and Renee rushed back into his arms, picking up right where they’d left off.

Every curve of her was touching him, driving him wild. He pressed against her until she was backed up against the door, slipping one hand under her shirt. She moaned deep in the back of her throat as his hand slid up from her waist to her breast, and he echoed the sound as his fingers found her nipple, hard and erect.

He teased the peaked tip as he moved his mouth to her earlobe, eliciting another moan from her, and his unoccupied hand moved down to her thigh. Jeremiah knew they didn’t have much time, but he planned to take full advantage of this moment. The skirt she was wearing had ridden up dangerously high, leaving so much of her shapely legs exposed for his viewing pleasure. He drank in the sight as he pulled the skirt even higher, wishing the room was brighter so he could see Renee in all her glory.

When his fingers slid past her lacy panties to her folds, she gasped, and his entire body tensed as he felt her wet heat. He put his mouth to the place on her neck where her heartbeat throbbed as he stroked her with his fingers, dipping first one inside her, then two, and continuing to rub at her mound until she was holding on to him tightly, her head pressed back against the door, her eyes closed.

Renee could barely stand as Jeremiah continued stroking her core, kissing along her throat and teasing her breast. He was playing her like a violin and damn if he wasn't good at it. The growing tension low in her belly built until she couldn't resist the wave as it crashed over her. She came hard, her entire body shivering with it as it ran through her.

She opened her eyes and saw Jeremiah smiling at her, his eyes smoldering with barely controlled need. And how she wanted to fill that need.

Renee reached down to the button of his jeans, anticipation boiling inside her. Just as she pulled down the zipper and moved to expose what, from the feel of it against the fabric, was a huge erection however, Jessica's voice floated in from downstairs.

"Dinner's ready! Time to eat!"

Damn. Renee stopped what she was doing and looked at Jeremiah. His expression was so pained that it made her laugh.

"Really? This is funny?" he asked, a smile crossing his own lips.

Renee leaned her head forward, letting it rest against Jeremiah's chest as she tried to take a few breaths to calm herself down. But when she breathed in his scent, a mixture of some cologne that made her think of the outdoors and his own masculine smell, she had to lean back again. She wasn't ready to go be around her sister and talk wedding so soon after that spectacular orgasm.

As if Jeremiah knew what she was thinking, he took a deep breath of his own. "I'll head down first," he said. "I can tell them you're getting settled in your room and washing up."

He sent one last smile her way as she moved away from the door, and then he was gone.

One thing she could say for him: Jeremiah was a good sport.

Four

Renee took a shuddering breath and moved away from the door Jeremiah had just closed behind him, flicking the light on as she went. The house was large and had several guest rooms, each a different color. She suspected this was Jessica's doing—it seemed very much like her sister to tell someone that they were staying in "the blue room," and then give them a set of towels that matched.

Renee was in the green room, the mint-colored walls bright and friendly in the light thrown from the bedside lamp. Green vines crisscrossed the white background of the bedspread, and even the white chest of drawers had green accents. It was all so sweet and pretty that she had to smile.

She opened her suitcase on the floor and grabbed out a pair of pants and some fresh underwear, sliding out of the clothes that were suggestively mussed from her interaction with Jeremiah and putting on the new outfit, trying to flatten her hair as she did so. After a glance in the mirror and a swipe at her smeared makeup, she readied herself to go back downstairs.

She took one last calming breath, opened the door and made

her way to where the rest of the group sat. When she stepped into the kitchen, she found quite the happy scene: Aaron's arm around the back of Jessica's chair, her body leaning into his and both of them laughing at something Jeremiah must have just said. He looked a little embarrassed, but was laughing, too. Everyone seemed comfortable and content, almost like a little family. How did she fit in here?

Her good mood sank a little as she realized that she didn't. They were all Texas, and she was New York.

But then Jeremiah looked in her direction and his eyes lit up at the sight of her, and she was able to push those thoughts aside. She didn't need to belong here. She would have a great week, fulfill a few fantasies, and then go back to New York to her dream job.

That was better than belonging in this little group, she told herself.

By the time she'd gone through these thoughts and felt reassured that her life was already everything she could want, really, Jessica had spotted her. She gestured at the full plate and empty seat clearly meant for her. "Come and get some food. I'm sure you haven't had a decent home-cooked meal since… when was the last time you ate at Mom's?"

Renee thought for a second as she sat down. "Almost two weeks ago."

"What have you been living on since then?"

Renee didn't want to answer, especially with Jeremiah watching her, that perpetual grin on his face, as if he was enjoying the interaction. "This and that," she answered vaguely.

Jessica raised her eyebrows. "Sandwiches from the deli down the street and leftover pizza?"

"Veggie pizza," Renee added, knowing that it didn't make it sound any better. "I'm busy. And I don't know how to cook. This looks amazing," she said in an attempt to change the subject from her terrible eating habits.

Jessica smiled, clearly proud of herself. "It's just an easy chicken recipe. Now get to eating," she said, pointing at the plate.

Renee took a bite, reveling in the taste of fresh vegetables and roasted chicken. She really needed to eat real food more often, but after working all day, she was too exhausted to do more than grab something on the way to her apartment or toss old pizza in the microwave. Another thing to push from her mind. This was not the week to examine her faults.

"What were you laughing about when I came in?" she asked, trying to get the conversation going on another topic.

Aaron smiled at her. "Jeremiah was telling Jessica about the time he was hitting on our waitress at a diner in Tyler."

Renee forced herself to smile, trying to tell herself that it was good to remember that Jeremiah wasn't a settle-down kind of guy. According to the stories Jessica had told her, in fact, he was more of a hit-on-any-female-with-a-pulse kind of guy.

And that was very good, because there was no way she'd be falling for him. Fantasy sex only.

"Tell her what happened," Aaron prompted, hitting Jeremiah lightly on the shoulder.

Jeremiah looked down at his plate, his blood pumping hard. Aaron had brought it up in the first place, and now he had to tell Renee about hitting on other women. Great.

He wanted to punch Aaron "playfully" on the arm, at least hard enough to leave a bruise, but he didn't want to raise any eyebrows. There was no way he'd forget Renee's number one rule and ruin the possibility of an amazing week.

"It was *years* ago," he clarified, hoping Renee understood that he wasn't that guy anymore.

Aaron leaned in toward Renee, clearly missing Jeremiah's discomfort. "We sat down to get some lunch, and Jeremiah just *has* to hit on the really hot waitress. Because he's Jeremiah and isn't afraid to get turned down by anyone."

Jeremiah forced himself not to glare at his friend. He had to keep it casual, no matter how much he wanted to kill the guy. *If he tries to tell the story about the supermodel,* he thought, *I'll tackle him right here at the table.*

Aaron continued the story, completely oblivious. "He must have asked her out or made sexual innuendos one too many times, because, you know those 'We reserve the right to refuse service' signs? Yeah, I had to drive home hungry all because Jeremiah thought he might be able to get laid in the walk-in freezer or something."

Aaron laughed again at the story. Jeremiah looked over to Renee to see her reaction. She was smiling and nodding, but he didn't like the look in her eyes. Stupid Aaron.

After a silence that felt way too long to Jeremiah, Aaron started talking again. "Hey Jeremiah, tell Renee what happened with the—"

If he says supermodel I'm going to destroy him, Jeremiah thought, holding his fork in a death grip.

"—generator," Aaron finished, to Jeremiah's immense relief. That was another embarrassing story, but at least it didn't make him look like an asshole.

Jeremiah launched into the story before Aaron could say anything else. "Okay, so my generator was out of gas, right? Luckily, I have a few gas cans sitting around and poured some gas into it. Or at least what I thought was gas…"

Renee watched Jeremiah go through the whole story, laughing aloud as he gestured wildly to show exactly how thick the smoke was as it billowed from the ruined piece of machinery.

For the most part, though, her attention wasn't on his epic tale. It was on the width of his shoulders, the way his hair fell across his forehead, the mischievous glint in his eyes, the strength of his arms.

God, she wanted him. Just looking at him from across the table made her squirm in her seat. And judging by the performance upstairs, it was going to be amazing once they managed to get more than five minutes alone together.

She'd never felt so impatient in her life.

After dinner, Jessica turned to Renee and said, "Well, tomorrow we'll start with the wedding stuff, but tonight I want to catch up, if you aren't completely exhausted."

Renee looked at her sister's smile and tried to smile back, but it wasn't easy. She realized that none of the scenarios running through her mind, most of which involved Jeremiah tearing pieces of clothing from her body, was going to happen tonight. There was just no way to get Jeremiah alone without letting Jessica in on the situation, which absolutely wasn't going to happen. Stupid rule number one.

Renee could see that Jeremiah realized it, too, and he didn't look too happy about it.

Dinner flew by. Renee tried not to look at Jeremiah, but constantly caught herself glancing over to where he sat. He seemed all casual confidence, and the ease he exuded amazed her. How could he be so relaxed after that little episode upstairs?

After dinner was done and the talk had lulled, though, his demeanor changed. Almost as if he should leave, but he didn't want to. She didn't want him to leave, either, but there was nothing to be done.

Finally, Jessica pulled the notebook out again and Jeremiah said his goodbyes. His eyes lingered on Renee for an extra second before he turned away. She watched as he walked out the door.

She cursed to herself. That was one opportunity gone.

Jessica had started talking to her, but she'd missed it. All Renee could think about was how she couldn't wait until some unknown time to kiss him again. And what if she never got the chance?

She could hardly bear the thought. She was too close to let this lie.

"I think I left my phone in Jeremiah's truck," she blurted

out, then rushed to the door without waiting for her sister to comment.

She imagined getting to his truck just before he pulled away and giving him one hell of a sensuous kiss that would leave him thinking of her all night.

Renee was off the porch and rounding the corner of the house in a blink, only to see Jeremiah just a couple feet away, walking toward her and directly in her path. She couldn't stop herself in time and ran into him at full speed with a very unsexy "Oof."

Slamming into his chest was like hitting a brick wall, and she bounced off and fell to the ground, the wind knocked out of her. As she sat in the dirt, a little cloud of dust settling around her, she was glad it was dim enough that he couldn't see how red her cheeks were.

Jeremiah knelt close. "Are you all right?" he asked, trying to look her over for damage.

Even through her embarrassment, she couldn't help but feel aroused. His hand, which was resting casually on her thigh, took her attention away from how silly she must look sprawled on the ground.

She stood, brushing dirt off herself. "I don't know which is bruised more—my butt or my ego," she murmured, half to herself.

He stopped his ministrations and cocked his head to one side. "That sounds familiar. Is that a quote from a movie?"

She was stunned he recognized it. "It's from *It Takes Two*. Why do you know an obscure quote from a decades-old movie made for little girls?"

Jeremiah laughed. "I have a little sister. She loved those movies. Haven't thought about them in years."

There was a quiet moment. Then, "What were you doing running around the house?" he asked, the smile on his face indicating that he had a pretty good guess as to the answer.

Renee suddenly felt shy. It was one thing to run up and kiss someone, and another thing entirely to explain that plan while brushing dirt off your ass.

His smile widened as the silence grew, and before she could figure out a way to explain without making herself sound like a dork, he leaned in close and kissed her. His lips and tongue drove any thoughts of embarrassment from her mind. In fact, they drove out pretty much everything that wasn't X-rated.

And then, yet again, the kiss was ended far too soon. Renee briefly considered hopping into Jeremiah's truck and going with him to his place before coming to her senses. She cursed Jessica under her breath.

Jeremiah stepped back, creating enough distance between them that she was able to get herself under control. Mostly.

"I better get going," he said, but he made no move to turn around and walk to his truck.

"Are you going to be around tomorrow?"

She had to ask. It would kill her to spend the next twenty-four hours wondering when they could continue where they had left off upstairs. It made her knees wobbly just thinking about it.

He grinned. "Can't get enough of me, huh?"

She leaned in, pressing her body against every inch of his. "From that bulge in your pants, I don't think you've had enough, either."

She backed up, watching the pain of separation cross his face and feeling exactly the same. Her little tease was just as bad for her, and she almost regretted having made the move in the first place.

He let out a deep breath. "I haven't had anywhere near enough. I'll find a reason to be here tomorrow."

The thought sent a thrill through her.

Reluctantly, they went their separate ways. Renee heard the door of his truck close behind her as she entered the house, wishing she was spread out on the bench seat of that truck.

"Did you find it?"

Renee almost asked what Jessica was talking about before her brain caught up, remembering her excuse for running out there in the first place. "Oh. No. It must be in my bag somewhere," she replied, hoping she wasn't blushing.

Jessica didn't seem to see anything off about her behavior, which was a relief. Before Renee knew it, she was settled on the couch, tea in hand, her sister relaxing next to her. "We'll be talking wedding all week, I'm sure, but for right now I really want to hear what's happening back in New York."

Renee raised an eyebrow. "We talk every week. How much do you think you're missing?"

"Lots!" Jessica exclaimed. "I want face-to-face communication. So start talking."

"Actually, I do have some news."

Jessica leaned forward. "Guy news?"

Renee had to laugh. "No, work news."

Jessica deflated a little. "All you ever have is work news. You work too much. When was the last time you went out with a guy?"

Renee thought for a moment. Not counting those kisses with Jeremiah, it had been… Well, longer than she'd like to admit.

Before she could formulate an answer, Jessica shook her head and said, "I thought so. What's your work news?"

Renee told her sister about the meeting with Patty. By the time she finished, Jessica's eyes were wide. "That's a lot of responsibility. I'm so happy for you, but does this mean you'll be working more than you already do?"

Jessica, always the worrier. Renee shrugged. "Patty always managed to keep things in balance. I'm sure I'll be fine."

She didn't want to admit to her sister that she was prepared to throw herself into this job with everything she had. If it meant a few more hours at the office, what did it matter? What else did she have to do?

The evening passed quickly, the two sisters swapping stories from their lives. Renee tried to stay focused on the moment, but her mind kept wandering to its two favorite subjects: work and Jeremiah.

If she wasn't designing the perfect layout for the magazine's next issue, she was imagining Jeremiah's hands running all over her.

After the third time she caught herself with no idea what Jessica had been saying, Renee smiled apologetically at her sister. "I'm sorry, but I'm exhausted."

Jessica jumped up, shaking her head. "Of course you are. I don't know what I was thinking. We can talk more tomorrow."

With that, she disappeared down a hallway and came back with fluffy yellow towels in her arms. "Here are some towels in case you want to rinse off before going to bed."

Renee was amused. "And I was betting the towels would be green to match my room. I guess I was wrong on that one."

Jessica looked appalled. "You put your things in the green room? You're supposed to be in the yellow room across the hall."

Renee tried not to laugh. The towels were color-coordinated with each room. The woman was insane. Aloud, she just said, "It's fine, I can move. I'm sure you went to a lot of trouble to get towels that matched the rooms exactly. I can't go ruining that."

Jessica seemed relieved. "Thanks. I didn't buy towels that matched each room, though. Aaron's mom did that."

Before Renee could comment on how neurotic that was, Jessica sighed and looked down at the towels. "Such a good organizer. I wish I could have met her. We would have gotten along so well."

Renee shut her mouth and said nothing. Jessica turned and began leading her to the stairs. Over her shoulder, she said, "I don't know why I didn't think to tell Jeremiah to put you in the yellow room. Since that's usually his room, he would never have known that you needed to take it over for this week, but we just don't have space to spare with everyone coming in for the wedding."

Renee stumbled, but managed to get her feet back under her. She was going to be staying in the guest room Jeremiah had slept in. With the sheets he slept in and the towels he used if he ever took a shower here.

She pictured him, slick with water, wearing only one of the canary yellow towels, somehow managing to make the color incredibly sensual.

Oh Lordy. She needed help.

Be casual, she reminded herself. "Jeremiah has his own room here?"

Jessica nodded without turning around. "We have more room than we need, and it means he can spend the evening over here drinking and hanging out without worrying about how to get home. We like having him around. He's a great guy."

Renee didn't need to be told that. He was a lot of adjectives. *Sexy, fun, incredibly attractive. Great* was certainly on the list.

After Jessica helped Renee move her luggage into the correct room, Jessica turned to her sister and threw her arms around her in a tight hug. "I'm really glad you're here, Renee. I know that you don't like to take time off work. I just want my wedding to go smoothly, with no surprises, and I don't think I could do it without your help."

Renee thought of Jeremiah and felt guilty. If she was going to keep Jessica from finding out, they would need to be more discreet than they had been so far. She didn't want to be the reason Jessica was unhappy so close to the wedding.

Really, it would be better if she just broke off the thing with him entirely. It's not like she had time in her life for a guy anyway, and a one-week fling wasn't like her. Maybe it would be best to stop now before things became even more complicated than they already were.

Even as she considered backing out, she dismissed it. There was something there with Jeremiah that she couldn't let pass by. Even if it was only for a week.

She hugged her sister back, keeping all her thoughts to herself, and silently promised to be a good sister and help her have exactly the wedding she wanted.

No surprises.

Five

Jeremiah tossed and turned all night, thinking of Renee. The way her hair fell in her face when she leaned forward, the way the corner of her lips turned up when she said something clever, the way she squeezed her eyes shut as she came.

Especially that last one.

Why couldn't she be a girl he'd just met at random? Why did it have to be Jessica's little sister? If she'd been anybody else, he would have asked her out to dinner. And breakfast. Lots of them.

Not that he was entirely sure she would even agree to dinner. From the little she'd told him about her life, it seemed likely she would have told him she was too busy with work to date.

And that bothered him even more than needing to keep the whole thing a secret. After all, it was only a secret because she wanted nothing but a week of sex. If this was more, wouldn't she be okay with telling Jessica?

She didn't want more, though.

But what did he want? He wasn't sure, but it didn't seem like eight days of Renee would be enough.

He stretched out in his very empty bed, reminding himself

that he would just need to go with it. Anything to get to see her eyes squeezed shut like that again.

The next morning, Jeremiah watched the clock, forcing himself to wait. After what seemed like an eternity, it was past nine and he could text without making Aaron suspicious.

He double-checked the message he'd written to be sure it gave nothing away before sending it. His phone made a *woosh* sound as the text rushed off to Aaron's phone.

He responded two long minutes later: We could definitely use some help. Jessica wants to organize the stuff for the ceremony today. Come over whenever.

Jeremiah grinned at his phone. He was sure he could find a way to pull Renee aside for a few minutes without anyone noticing, and he was going to take advantage of any possible chance they had.

Renee dug into her plate of eggs, bacon and hash browns, savoring the taste of another meal not purchased from a stand or heated up in the microwave. She hadn't felt this good in a long time. Fresh food and a great night's sleep did wonders. Even though she was still feeling antsy, wondering when she would see Jeremiah next, the orgasm he'd given her the evening before was still working its magic, and she had slept hard and deep almost as soon as her head had hit the pillow.

Not before she had inhaled the faint scent of Jeremiah, though. It seemed to be embedded in the pillows in her room. The smell had engulfed her as she drifted off, and greeted her this morning when she awoke. If only she could get his scent wrapped around her while still attached to his body.

She wanted to ask Aaron when his friend would be around, but there was no way she could think of to say it casually, so she forced herself to push that to the back of her mind and give her attention to the delicious meal in front of her.

"Aaron, this is amazing," she called over to her almost-brother-in-law, who waved off her compliment with a smile and went back to his cooking.

He was standing next to the stove in a ridiculous apron. It was a sickly pink with frills and pictures of baking utensils and hundreds of cats, of all things. Renee turned to her sister, who was sitting next to her inhaling her own plate. "Why does Aaron have an apron like that?" she asked, needing to know the story behind the awful accessory.

Jessica laughed and shook her head. "Jeremiah got it for him when I first moved in. He thought it was hilarious. I don't think he ever expected Aaron to actually use it, though."

Aaron shrugged and turned to the women, showing off the apron in all its glory. "It's useful. And I kind of like the cats."

Jessica looked at her fiancé with the overly dreamy expression she seemed to wear every time she glanced his direction.

Then Aaron's phone buzzed, and Renee felt anticipation build in her stomach as he fished the device out of his back pocket. It could be anyone, but…

"It's Jeremiah," Aaron said, confirming Renee's hope. "He wants to know if we need help today."

Please say yes, Renee thought at her sister.

Jessica nodded. "Yeah, that'd be great. I want us to work on getting that arch together and setting up things in the barn for the ceremony."

Renee was so excited, she almost missed everything Jessica said after "yeah." Once she soaked in her sister's words, though, she couldn't help but comment. "You're getting married in the barn?"

Jessica smiled at her. "Don't make fun of me. It'll be warm and dry in case it rains, and it's going to be really pretty. Plus, this is Texas. If we *didn't* get married in the barn, people would talk."

Renee turned to Aaron. "Let me guess. You're going to wear cowboy boots, right?"

Aaron nodded proudly. "Oh yeah. It's going to be great."

Renee put a hand to her forehead. She felt like she was living in an alternate dimension. One full of giant silver belt buckles and saloons and horses. She missed the cold streets of New York City.

"I told Jeremiah to come by whenever," Aaron said to Jessica as he sat down with his own plate of food.

Renee's homesickness disappeared in a blink. She imagined them sneaking away together to continue where they'd left off the night before. There were some advantages to living in this alternate dimension, for a little while, at least.

Jeremiah showed up less than a half hour later, while Jessica and Aaron were washing the dishes. Aaron looked over his shoulder at his friend. "That was quick," he commented.

Jeremiah shrugged, but shot Renee a look that sent tendrils of fire snaking through her. "Might as well get the day started. It's not like I have anything else I want to do today."

Renee smiled at him, reading his message loud and clear. Jeremiah sat down beside her, making her pulse race. "Hi," he said, in an almost-conspiratorial whisper.

"Hey," she responded, feeling that they were saying so much more than perfunctory greetings. The space between them felt charged, like the air right before a lightning storm.

"Well," Aaron said, oblivious to the interactions going on behind him, "you missed breakfast, but I could fry a couple of eggs for you real quick."

"No thanks," he responded before turning back to Renee with a grin. "Did he wear his apron?"

She chuckled. "I have no idea how you managed to find an apron that god-awful."

His eyes lit up at the approval in her voice, and she almost melted into those dark pools of coffee. She was so close to him, she could see tiny flakes of lighter colors mixed in with the dark.

Renee was on her way to getting lost in them when Jessica came over to the table, wedding binder once more in hand. Renee forced herself to drag her attention away from the man beside her, trying to remember rule number one for the week. She hated to think about how obvious it seemed like they were being, and could only hope that either it wasn't as noticeable as she thought or Jessica was too wrapped up in wedding details to pay attention.

Her sister didn't seem to think anything was amiss, though, and Renee breathed a quiet sigh of relief. Jessica opened the binder to a diagram, and began explaining her vision for the ceremony. "We don't have the chairs yet, so that'll need to wait, but I want to get the arch put together and in place here—" she pointed to one end of the diagram "—and get the plants and strings of lights taken care of so I can be sure this layout will work."

Renee listened to her sister, but a large part of her brain—and all of her body—was focused on the man sitting so close to her. She could hear his breathing, and a shiver slid along her spine each time he breathed out, as her body remembered that hot breath in her ear while he touched her.

By the time Jessica closed the binder and the three of them stood, Renee felt hot and flushed, and the ache in her belly was clamoring for attention.

Aaron joined the group, and together the four of them trooped out to the barn. As they rounded the side of the house and the barn came into view, Renee stopped walking and took in the scene before her. She had to admit, it was a stunning location for a wedding.

The barn was a crisp clean white with wood trim, not the bright red she had expected. It sat long and regal, contrasting beautifully with the tall trees behind it. The clear blue sky only added to the picturesque view.

To make it even more enticing, Aaron and Jeremiah had reached the large barn door and were sliding it open. At this distance, she could see the muscles rippling under Jeremiah's shirt, and when he turned to look at her, brushing his hair out of his face, her knees nearly gave out.

Her design-trained eye reveled in the lines and colors of the scene before her, and her libido roared at the impossibly handsome man that dominated it. She wasn't sure which urge was stronger: the one telling her to throw herself at him or the one telling her to grab her computer and create the perfect spread for the image to adorn.

She wished she had a camera and her computer in her hands so she could give life to the image in her mind. And she wished she had nothing but Jeremiah, up close and completely to herself.

But now wasn't a time for any of that. She needed to help her sister and put aside all the distractions warring inside her.

As if to remind her of that, Jessica put her arm around Renee, pulling her close to her side. "See? It's better than you thought."

Renee nodded, leaned her weight on her sister and answered, "You win. It's beautiful. I won't make fun of you for getting married in this barn. Just don't wear a cowboy hat, okay? It won't match your dress."

Jessica kissed her on the cheek and started pulling her toward the building. "I'm not making any promises," she answered.

Renee rolled her eyes and laughed, following her sister into the barn.

Jeremiah watched Renee laughing with her sister. His muscles tensed just looking at her and he ached to touch her. He didn't know how, but he was going to find some way to get her alone.

Jessica's voice broke through the fog in his brain that Renee was so good at creating, and he wrenched his attention to her. "The arch goes over there," she explained, pointing to the far end of the building. "That's where the officiant will stand. We'll need to hang lights through the rafters and clean up the ground today. I may be getting married in a barn, but that doesn't mean I want hay stuck to me as I say my vows."

Aaron leaned in to his fiancée, speaking in a low voice that

Jeremiah could nonetheless hear. "Having hay stuck to you isn't so bad. I like finding it in your hair after."

The way Jessica's cheeks flushed, Jeremiah was sure she was picturing a very specific incident. He hadn't thought of it, but of course they'd had sex in the barn. The way they couldn't keep their hands off each other, he imagined it would be difficult to find a place where they hadn't done it.

Their relationship had been one of the key causes of his change of heart regarding casual sex in the first place. If it was possible to find someone irresistible who you also loved being around outside of the bedroom day after day, shouldn't you try to find it?

He sneaked a glance at Renee. *Not her*, he told himself.

She was irresistible, sure. And they did seem to have a spark between them that went beyond just the physical, but there were some necessary ingredients missing to make this a forever thing.

The biggest one, of course, was that she clearly didn't want anything serious.

He pushed the thoughts aside, not liking where they were going.

Better to think about other things, like how to get Jessica and Aaron working on something somewhere else. Preferably not within hearing distance of the barn, because once he had Renee alone, he wanted to be able to hear her, and if she screamed out like he pictured, they were sure to break the first rule.

He smiled to himself at that.

Renee kept her eyes off Jeremiah despite the fire inside her and started moving one of the potted plants the two men had taken out of Jeremiah's truck the night before. She dragged it along the ground as Jessica directed her where to go and moved her own identical plant.

Renee had no idea what kind of plants they were, but the bright green leaves and little white flowers gave off an intoxicating scent that seemed almost erotic to her, in her current state.

She had to find a way to get him alone.

For two hours, though, she couldn't think of any way to get Jessica and Aaron out of the barn. She moved plants, shifting them a couple of inches here and there until Jessica declared them perfect. Meanwhile, Jeremiah and Aaron were putting together the arch and bringing stacks of chairs into the building, leaning them against one side.

With each surreptitious glance at Jeremiah, more often than not catching him looking back at her, her body ached for him more. The air around her seemed too warm, and she began to feel desperate. She tied gauzy white fabric to each plant and silently begged Jessica to give her just a few minutes alone with him.

As if Renee had telepathically sent a message to her sister, Jessica stretched and said, "It's about time for a break, I think. Aaron and I will get some lunch together."

Renee didn't know if her sister expected her to follow them, but there was absolutely no way she was going to be leaving that barn.

She forced herself to nod as casually as she could and didn't look at Jeremiah. She wanted to know if he was as close to the breaking point as she was, but either it would be written all over his face, which would be bad, or it wouldn't. And she didn't want to see that. Better to wait.

Aaron walked over to Jessica and wrapped his arm around her waist. They were so easy and confident in their love for one another that it made something in Renee twinge. Not with jealousy, of course.

She didn't have time for a relationship like that, and besides, who could be as perfect for her as Aaron was for Jessica? Her eyes flitted over to Jeremiah. The only man she'd been at all attracted to in years couldn't possibly be anything other than a one-week romance, no matter how hard he made her heart pound.

No, that was definitely not something she wanted right now. She was happy for Jessica, but that was it.

Her inner monologue came to an abrupt end when two muscular arms slid around her the second Jessica and Aaron had walked out the door. His breath was hot against her ear, his voice low and deep, vibrating through her as he pressed his chest against her back. "I've been trying for two hours to come up with some way to get you alone. Are we still on?"

She answered by spinning around in his grasp and kissing him for all she was worth. There wasn't any time to spare. He kissed back just as enthusiastically, his tongue diving into her mouth in a way that made her fingers tingle. His teeth scraped against her lower lip as his hands moved under her shirt, and she felt like she was going to orgasm right there in the middle of the barn.

That thought brought her somewhat back to sanity, and she had enough of her mental faculties together to remember that they couldn't let Jessica and Aaron walk in on them like this.

Jeremiah was clearly thinking the same thing, because he pulled back slightly, breathing heavily, and nodded toward a nearby ladder. "How about we go up to the loft?"

She didn't need to be asked twice.

Renee climbed the ladder and found herself on a platform twenty feet above the ground, the rafters of the barn low enough that she needed to duck when she walked under them. A large pile of Christmas lights sat in one corner, waiting to be strung around the room for the wedding.

While the rest of the barn was lit by the open door and windows, the loft was steeped in shadow, an oasis of evening even in the middle of the day. Renee stood and placed one hand on the rafter in front of her, looking out across the expanse below.

It was quiet and peaceful. The arch graced one end of the barn, tall and white and covered in greenery. The potted plants formed a walkway from the door to the arch, like escorts waiting to usher Jessica down the aisle.

She pictured her sister, beautiful and happy, walking down that aisle to the man she loved, and she felt that twinge again. As sure as she was that she didn't have time for any of that in her life, she had to admit that it would be nice to feel so loved.

And then Jeremiah was behind her again, his hands slipping across her stomach, and the scene dissolved. She leaned backward into him, and his hands roved higher. By the time they slid beneath her bra and found her breasts, her nipples were tight and aching for his touch.

His tongue and lips caressed her neck, sending jolts of electricity down her spine, and his fingers teased at her already-sensitive nipples, making her gasp with the intensity. She pressed her entire body back against him, feeling the bulge in his jeans. He growled deep in his throat at the contact, and she reveled in the powerful feeling that came with knowing that she drove him wild.

Then he rolled one nipple between his fingers and any sense of power disappeared. There was only need.

She turned to face him, her fingers dancing down across the muscles of his arms, all the way to the hem of his shirt. In a flash, she had his shirt over his head and soaked in the view of his naked torso. Even in the dim light, she could see that her fantasies hadn't done full justice to him. She moved one hand over his abs, marveling at the flesh below her fingers. He sucked in his breath at her touch. "You need to be careful doing that," he said, "because after being interrupted last night, I can't promise I have much control left."

She smiled wickedly and stroked his stomach again, making him groan. He said, "Remember on the ride from the airport, when I asked which one you were? You are most definitely the sexy one."

Renee laughed. In a lineup with her tall leggy sister and her perky blond best friend, Cindy, she highly doubted she would ever get labeled "the sexy one." But Jeremiah said it with such sincerity that a different kind of warmth flowed through her, this time headed straight for her heart.

That wasn't a good sign. Not if this was only going to be a one-week thing. She needed to bring it back to just physical. "You're even hotter than in my fantasies. I didn't even realize a guy could *have* an eight-pack."

With that, she ran her fingers along the waistline of his jeans, stopping at the button and working it open as quickly as she could. His stomach muscles shuddered again at her touch, and her stomach clenched in anticipation. "What exactly occurred during these fantasies of yours?" he asked, his voice deep and full of the same desperate need she felt.

Renee felt a blush coming to her cheeks, but she answered honestly. "There have been a lot of fantasies since Vegas, and we've done so many things in them, it would take too long to go into detail."

He growled deep in his throat and leaned down to kiss her neck again. "Well, which one would you like to do now, in real life?"

That question had been running around her head for hours. Instead of answering with words, she lowered the zipper on his pants and reached in, her hand gliding across the smooth skin of his penis, rock-hard, as if it had been eagerly waiting for her touch.

Which it had been, she thought with a smile. He moaned, and his caresses suddenly turned urgent, his teeth grazing the skin of her neck and his hands kneading the tender flesh of her breasts until the clenching in her stomach had nearly reached a crescendo. One of his hands moved from her chest down toward her pants, and anticipation ran through her.

That was when they heard voices. Jessica and Aaron, getting louder as they approached the barn.

With another groan, this one of frustration, Jeremiah pulled himself away from her. The areas where his warm hands had been were suddenly exposed to the cold air. Jeremiah rubbed one hand across his face and gave her an exasperated look. "I'm going to kill Aaron, and he's not even going to know why."

Renee had to laugh, but she felt the same way about Jessica. Her stomach still felt tight and dissatisfied with the rude separation, and it didn't help that Jeremiah grabbed his shirt and tugged it back on.

"Renee? Jeremiah? Where are you two? Food's ready!" her sister called from somewhere below.

Jeremiah took a deep breath, gave Renee a grin and a wink, and leaned over the edge of the loft. "We're up here! Just working on untangling the lights so we can hang them up," he said, his voice much more lighthearted than Renee felt.

"That's such a good idea. Thanks, Jeremiah."

She couldn't see Jessica, but the genuine relief in her voice filled Renee with guilt. Her sister desperately wanted help getting everything ready for the wedding, and they had been seeing to their own desires instead.

Jeremiah gave her a look that said he was thinking the same thing, and they each rearranged their disheveled clothing without a word. Before they could start down the ladder, though, Renee said quietly, "I think we need to cool it, at least for today. I have to be here for Jessica, you know?"

Part of her prayed he would come up with an argument that would convince her otherwise, but he just sighed and nodded and she knew it was the right thing to do, no matter how delicious he looked.

He gave her a lopsided grin and shrugged one shoulder. "You just let me know when you can take time off from being a good sister and I'll be there."

His smile was so endearing she wanted to tackle him right there. But then he disappeared down the ladder and she took a deep breath of Jeremiah-free air and was able to strengthen her resolve before following him.

Jessica was waiting for them near the door, and they walked

together to the house. Over sandwiches—ones that blew Renee's corner deli out of the water—Jessica discussed next steps.

"Since you two started on the lights," she said, pointing at Renee and Jeremiah, "you can finish untangling the lights, checking that all the bulbs work, and stringing them up through the rafters while Aaron and I meet with our reverend in town. Does that sound okay?"

Renee wanted to slap her forehead. Or Jessica's forehead. She wanted to be a helpful sister, but it was as if Jessica was *trying* to put her into situations that made it impossible. Now she was supposed to spend a bunch of unchaperoned time up in the loft with Jeremiah, and Jessica expected them to get anything done?

If she wasn't careful, only one thing would get done up there, and she was positive it wasn't on her sister's list.

Jeremiah gave her a brief glance that told her exactly where his mind had gone, and she pressed her hands against her legs under the table to stop them from jittering.

No, she told herself. They would have to get the lights taken care of first. If they finished and had time to spare, though…

Jeremiah couldn't wait for lunch to be over. All he'd wanted was more time up in the loft with Renee, and here was Jessica, handing him just that. Once they were back in the barn alone and climbing the ladder again, however, Renee went straight to the pile of lights and began tugging at them.

He wanted to make her forget all about the damn lights, but he thought of the conversation they had had before lunch. She was just trying to be a good sister, and he didn't begrudge her that, no matter how much the pressure in his jeans protested. He sat down beside her and grabbed a knotted section of lights and set to work.

"We need to get this done for Jessica," she told him.

He hoped she meant they needed to do this *first*, because their last two encounters had left him desperate for more, and if he had to go home without getting to touch her again, he thought he might go crazy. Still, he nodded and set to work.

After just a few seconds of silence, the tension in the air became too much for him. The quiet gave him too much time to think about the delights they could be having, and it made him feel precariously close to throwing down the lights and pressing her against the rough boards they were sitting on.

"So," he began, not really sure what he was going to say, "we've established that you're the workaholic one and the sexy one. What else are you?"

If he wasn't allowed to kiss and touch her, he could at least learn more about her. She smiled and shook her head, but didn't glance up from her task. "*A*, I'm not the sexy one by any stretch of the imagination. And *B*," she continued before he could argue, "*workaholic* sounds way too negative. I prefer the term *driven*."

He laughed. "I'll let the workaholic thing go, but you're definitely the sexy one. It's cute that you don't see it."

She shook her head again, but he could tell she was flattered. He hoped she understood that he wasn't just saying that; her captivating eyes and the curve of her smile set his blood on fire. Not to mention the perfect size of her breasts and an ass that made him hard just thinking about it.

He ripped his thoughts back to more appropriate aspects of her. If he had to sit next to her without groping her or going insane with lust, he'd need to control those thoughts. "I bet you're the funny, clever one," he said, hoping she didn't notice how he shifted position so his erection wouldn't be too painful.

She shrugged. "Very few people would consider me to be the funny one. My sense of humor is, let's say, more unique than Jessica's."

As the guy who was always considered the entertainment of the group, he had to hear more. She continued, "Jessica is better at being sarcastic. I'm more…punny."

"Punny? I don't think that's a word. Give me an example."

She sighed, and he could tell even in the dim light that

she was blushing. “You really don’t want to hear my jokes, I promise.”

“Tell me just one. Please?” he begged.

He tried to pay attention to the lights, but he was so interested to hear her response that it was hard to do much more than fumble around with them.

“Fine,” she answered, sounding both amused and exasperated. “But you asked for it.”

She paused for a second, then, “Did you hear the one about the three holes in the ground? No? Well, well, well…”

He groaned and laughed simultaneously, delighted. “That was so corny.”

She smiled and shrugged again in that way she had. “I told you. Please don’t ask me for any more, because that was my best one.”

He thought about the terrible joke again, chuckling while he tried to come up with a new topic of conversation.

He wanted to know more about her, everything about her, but he didn’t know what to ask. He looked down at the lights and thought about how she’d taken a break from her beloved work to come decorate for her sister’s wedding. “Have you and Jessica always been close?”

Renee smiled, but she kept her eyes down on the lights. “We’ve never had any big fights or anything, but we weren’t very close until our dad got sick.”

Jeremiah nodded. He knew the story about their father and his long illness. He’d died two years ago, the same weekend that Jessica and Aaron had met. Jeremiah wished he hadn’t reminded Renee of it—the way her voice grew quieter as she said it made him ache inside.

She continued, “We both pitched in to take care of him, so it helped us connect a bit more than we had as kids.”

He tried to turn the conversation away from her dad. “Why weren’t you two better friends when you were kids? Was she a mean older sister?”

Renee brushed her hair behind her ear as she thought. It was a simple unconscious move, but something about it struck him as particularly endearing. "No, she was fine. We're just different people. Always have been."

Before he could ask another question, she shot one back at him, asking how long he'd been friends with Aaron.

The time passed quickly as they chatted. After two and a half hours, they had untangled the lights, checked for missing or blown bulbs, and begun stringing them up. They'd also told each other about their childhoods, first crushes (his, a girl in his third grade class named Claire Isaacs, hers, Jonathon Taylor Thomas from *Home Improvement*), favorite movies (*The Truman Show* and *When Harry Met Sally*, though Renee confessed she secretly loved *High School Musical*), and she'd gotten him to admit that yes, the songs from *Frozen* were actually pretty catchy and he knew more of the words than a man his age should. "My niece loves that movie," he tried to explain, "and we had to watch it at least twenty times the last time I visited."

Renee nodded and said, "Sure, I believe you. Your *niece* likes it," but her smile was more like a Cheshire cat grin than anything else, and he loved it.

In fact, he loved almost everything about her. Her laugh, her terrible puns, the way she raised one eyebrow when he said something she thought was strange.

He'd been pretty sure before, but now he was positive: this thing wasn't going to end easily for him at all. He was getting further and further from casual sex, and there wasn't any way out that he was willing to take. He was already hooked on her, and without some sort of drastic change over the coming week, he would be left alone and worse off than before once she went back to New York.

Renee stood on the edge of the loft, holding a rope of lights bunched up in one hand. When she tossed it, it unraveled as it flew through the air. Jeremiah, standing on a ladder several feet away, deftly caught the end of the string and began circling it through a rafter above him. They had been working for hours, and she thought it would be torture to be so close to him for so long without finishing what they'd started.

In a way it was, but talking to him had been pretty amazing, actually. He was as pleasant and amusing as Jessica and Aaron made him out to be, but more than that, too. He was sweet and confident, and there was an air of honesty about him that was incredibly refreshing. It wasn't something she saw a lot in New York.

She plugged in the final strings of bulbs and climbed down from the loft. She and Jeremiah stood just to the side of the door in order to survey their work. The barn was still romantically dim, but the bright dots of light threaded through the rafters added a fairy-tale quality to the whole place. She hoped Jessica would like it.

"We're done," she said, not sure how to transition from lighthearted conversation to making out. She suddenly felt awkward around him.

"It was an en-*light*-ening experience," he said, grinning and lifting his eyebrows. "Get it? Because of the lights," he added. "That's your kind of joke, right?"

She laughed and leaned into him, meaning to bump him playfully with her shoulder, but he wrapped his arm around her and pulled her tight before she could do so, and in an instant they were kissing.

Renee fell into the kiss, letting her mind blank as he enfolded her.

Then she froze as she heard Jessica gasp. *Oh shit*, she thought, pushing away from Jeremiah.

Her sister stood in the doorway, not ten feet from them, looking up at the ceiling. Relief flooded through Renee as she realized Jessica hadn't noticed them. She took a deep breath and looked at Jeremiah, whose facial expression had gone from panic to amusement in the two seconds it took for him to comprehend what had just happened.

They smiled at each other and Jeremiah shook his head in exasperation. She felt the same way. Would they ever get enough time alone together to actually make something happen?

Renee shrugged back and turned her attention to her sister. "You like it?"

Jessica nodded, still gazing at the room before her. "You two did an amazing job. Thank you so much!"

As frustrated as she was at yet another interruption, Renee was happy she'd done something for her sister instead of being completely selfish and using all that time to indulge in fantasies.

Well, somewhat happy.

Anyway, she was sure they'd find time.

Jessica looped her arm around Renee and squeezed. "I owe you big-time." Renee thought about the interrupted kiss. *You sure do,* she thought.

"I think that's enough work on the barn for today," Jessica said, to Renee's chagrin. "Let's head back to the house. We can spend the rest of the day double-checking the menu and going over seating arrangements."

Renee knew her sister was meticulous, but this seemed a touch overboard. "I thought there were only thirty guests or something. Do you really need seating arrangements? Can't people just sit wherever?"

Jessica looked at her like she was crazy, and Renee knew this wasn't a battle she could possibly win. "Seating arrangements it is," she said before Jessica could explain to her exactly why they were so important.

It was her sister's wedding, after all. Whatever made her happy.

Jessica smiled. "I know you think I'm neurotic," she began, and Renee didn't disagree, "but it'll all be worth it, I'm sure."

With that, Jessica gestured toward the door. "Come on. You

two have spent all day in this barn. Let's go back to the house and relax a bit."

She led the way out. The moment Jessica was past the door, Jeremiah leaned in close to Renee and murmured, "That woman must have a spidey sense or something. If that's going to happen all week, I don't think I'll survive."

Renee nodded and followed her sister, trying not to feel too disappointed.

Six

Jeremiah watched Renee walking ahead of him, captivated by the way her jeans hugged her butt. He didn't think his body could take much more of this.

In the house, Jessica pulled Renee into the living room, binder in hand. Renee gave him one last glance before disappearing from view, and then she was gone. He didn't think Jessica expected him to follow, but he was going to do it anyway, when Aaron walked out of the hallway and came toward his friend. "Thanks for all the help today. I think getting all that done eased Jessica's mind some. You must've been really bored to want to come by today and work on wedding stuff."

Jeremiah didn't trust himself to respond. Aaron knew him too well, and he was worried that anything he said might sound suspicious.

Aaron didn't notice. He said, "Well, tomorrow the girls are going into town so Renee can do a dress fitting and cake tasting, so you're off the hook for wedding stuff."

Jeremiah tried not to let his frustration show. The week was just getting started and he was already down a day, and for no good reason. Really, the only good reason would be something along the lines of saving puppies or getting a limb amputated, and even then he was pretty sure he could work around it. But there was nothing he could do. It wasn't like he could say anything.

He hated secrets.

"I thought you and Jessica had decided your cake flavors already," he responded, for lack of anything else to say.

"We did, a month ago, but Jessica wants to be sure that we made the right choice. And she wants Renee to try them so she can get input from someone who would tell her honestly if the flavors we picked are good."

"And that's not you?"

"With cake, I'm completely honest, but I guess my bar is set too low or something because I thought we should order every flavor they make. Seriously, we should buy wedding cakes from this shop as a weekly thing."

Jeremiah couldn't do anything about that day, then, but he wasn't about to lose any more of them. "Well, think of something for me to do on Monday. The wedding will be here before you know it."

"Actually, I have to go pick up the rings on Monday. Want to go with me? You'll be holding on to them anyway."

"Sure. How about I come over for breakfast and then we can go."

Aaron smiled at his friend. "You want free food out of this deal?"

"Hey, a man's got to eat," Jeremiah replied, but he wasn't thinking about the food.

The more time he spent in their house, the more time he got around Renee and the more chances he had to be alone with her. If he could come up with a plausible reason, he'd live there for the next seven days. With Renee right across the hall…well, they would definitely be able to come up with a few fun ways to spend their nights.

Since that didn't seem feasible, he would take what he could get.

Renee was sitting with her sister on the couch reviewing the menu when Jeremiah and Aaron walked in. Aaron sat beside Jessica in a space so small that she was nearly sitting on his lap—which he didn't seem to mind in the least—and Jeremiah grabbed a chair nearby.

She wished she could be sitting in his lap at the moment, but instead had to fight to hide the way her body reacted the moment he walked into the room. This fun idea of secretly indulging in her fantasies was rapidly becoming torture, but she didn't see any way around that if she wanted to have her cake and eat it, too. And Jeremiah was the most addictive cake she'd ever seen.

"Does everyone think corn bread is the right choice over sweet rolls?" Jessica asked, looking around at the small group.

"Corn bread matches the whole Texas country theme you've got going on," Renee answered, trying not to sound amused.

Jessica seemed relieved by Renee's answer, which just made it harder for Renee to keep a straight face. Jessica had only been in Texas for two years, but she seemed to have jumped on the country bandwagon wholeheartedly as soon as she and Aaron started living together.

"I love corn bread," Jeremiah answered. "In fact, if it's really great corn bread, I might end up eating way too much of it, leaving your other guests to starve and making myself sick in the process, effectively ruining the entire—Ow!"

Jeremiah rubbed the spot on his bicep where Aaron had just punched him. He and Renee shared a grin as Aaron settled back into his spot on the couch.

Aaron wrapped his arm around Jessica, pulling her tight against him. "The corn bread will be great," he said, kissing her temple.

Jessica gave her fiancé that dreamy smile again, then turned to Jeremiah. "No joking allowed about anything wedding-related," she told him pointedly.

"I never agreed to that," Jeremiah responded, flashing Renee another grin that made her weak in the knees.

Jessica saw the smile and wheeled on her sister. "And don't you start conspiring with him, Renee."

"I didn't do anything," Renee answered, holding up her hands in innocence.

"Let's keep it that way," Jessica retorted, crossing her arms and snuggling back into Aaron's chest, trying to look as serious as she could. "I can still un-bridesmaid you, you know."

Jeremiah grinned. "She's stuck with me because I'm the only groomsman, but she's still got Cindy if she kicks you out. You're expendable."

Jessica nodded in agreement and Renee laughed.

"No conspiring," Renee promised.

It wasn't precisely true, Renee thought, but not in the way Jessica was thinking, so there was no reason to say anything about that.

The rest of the afternoon passed in much the same way, with Jessica trying to get serious answers and Jeremiah and Renee alternating teasing her. Finally, Renee set a hand on the binder. "It all sounds perfect, Jessica. You did a great job."

Jessica took a deep breath and closed the binder, to Renee's relief. She had come up with a way to get Jeremiah alone again, and been waiting nearly an hour to implement it. She stood and stretched, glancing sideways at Jeremiah. "I think I need to take a walk."

Right on cue, Jeremiah jumped up. "Me, too. I can show you around the property."

Excitement welled inside Renee as she imagined them out under the trees together. It was a little cool out, but she was sure they could think of ways to stay warm.

"That's a great idea," Jessica said. "We have some time before we need to start getting dinner ready. Let's all go for a walk."

Renee bit her lip in frustration. Her sister was going to be the death of her. Either that or she would be the death of her sister.

Jessica and Aaron led the way out of the room. Renee looked over at Jeremiah, who was shaking his head in disbelief. Without a word, they followed the other two out of the house and across a wide expanse of lawn. Jessica started talking about the acreage and features of the property like a motivated real estate agent, but Renee only half listened. Most of her mind was focused on Jeremiah walking beside her. She could almost feel him, like an electric charge that was building up, about to explode.

She wondered if it was possible to burst into flames from sexual frustration.

When they were nearly at a paddock full of horses, Jeremiah grabbed her hand and pulled her behind a tree. The moment they were out of sight, she leaned in for a kiss. It was hardly any privacy, but at this point beggars couldn't be choosers.

Jeremiah leaned away, though. In answer to the look she gave him, he said, "Sorry, but if I get any closer to you I won't be able to control myself, and I'm pretty sure Jessica would notice if we started having sex up against this tree."

Renee's attention shifted to the tree. Maybe if they were really quiet…

She couldn't believe she was even considering that. She needed to get laid. Bad.

Jeremiah continued, his voice husky with pent-up desire, "It doesn't look like we'll be able to see each other tomorrow—" the tree was looking better and better—"but I'll be here Monday, and I will come up with a way for us to get alone that afternoon. Several ways, just in case your sister pulls something like this again. Because I don't know if I can take much more of this."

Renee nodded, and Jeremiah pushed a strand of hair behind her ear, leaving a trail of fire where his fingers touched her skin.

Monday. She could probably survive until then.

After one last long look at each other, they broke apart and came out from behind the tree, walking casually up to where Jessica and Aaron stood fifty feet away.

"Where'd you disappear to?" Jessica asked when they approached.

"I was telling Renee about the trees on the property," Jeremiah answered.

Jessica nodded and turned back to the horses. She began telling Renee about them, giving each one's name and breed. Renee tried to pay attention, but her mind was too distracted for her to care much about horses.

When they got back to the house, it was time to start dinner. Renee didn't even dare to hope that she and Jeremiah would have some time to themselves, and she was right. "Jeremiah, can you make your sauce for the pork chops?" Jessica asked the moment they stepped in the door.

"What should I do?" Renee asked when she realized she'd be sitting alone in the other room if she didn't volunteer to help.

Since Renee didn't have any actual cooking skills, she was given salad duty. In no time, the four of them were sitting around the table, one or the other occasionally going to check on something as dinner cooked.

Once everything was nearly ready, Renee set the table, making sure that she and Jeremiah would be sitting beside each other. If that was the only way she was going to get close to him, by God, she was going to take advantage of it.

After washing his hands, Jeremiah walked back to the table that was now prepared for dinner. He paused for only a moment when he realized that Renee had placed them next to one another, then went to his spot with what he hoped was nonchalance. They would be under the gaze of Jessica and Aaron the whole time, but at least he could hope for some opportunities to brush against Renee's arm, even touch her hand under the table. At least it would be something.

And then Renee slipped her hand into his lap, rubbing against his upper thigh, obliterating any chance Jeremiah had of staying under control.

"Are you okay, Jeremiah?" Jessica asked, looking concerned.

No surprise there. He probably looked like he'd choked on his own tongue, which had very nearly happened when he realized what Renee was doing. Her hand inched higher ever-so-slightly, and it took everything he had not to react.

"Yeah, I'm fine," he said, hoping his voice didn't sound as weird to them as it did in his ears. "I just swallowed wrong." He coughed to give his story credibility and prayed the couple didn't notice he hadn't eaten anything yet.

Jessica went back to her food and Jeremiah relaxed a little bit, giving Renee a quick glance out of the corner of his eye. She had her water glass up to her mouth, but he could tell by the tilt of her lips that she was having difficulty suppressing a laugh.

Two could play at that game.

Luckily, the table was big and solid, large enough to fit twice as many people, and high enough to hide any activity going on below. He intended to take complete advantage of it. As he leaned forward to grab the butter for his roll with one hand, the other rubbed suggestively against the denim of Renee's jeans—first on her thigh, then moving quickly to her center. He knew the pressure had hit home when a tiny gasp burst from her. It was his turn to hide a smile behind a water glass.

Jessica and Aaron were fortunately so absorbed in conversation—he had no idea what they were talking about, but whatever it was clearly interested them—that they didn't notice anything odd about what was happening on the other side of the table. And it was a good thing for him, too, because Renee answered back with a foot riding so far up his leg she had to be double-jointed or something.

That thought made the room feel much too warm. He needed air, but there was no way he'd be getting up from that table.

Not while Renee was still doing things that might make him implode.

By the end of dinner, he was so hot and bothered that it took several minutes before he was able to stand.

Long past dark, Jeremiah left, his body aching for release. He didn't know if that woman was sent from heaven or hell, but either way, all he could think about was the next time he'd be able to get her alone. All the things he wanted to do to her, should the opportunity come up, raced through his mind as he eased himself into his truck for the long, lonely ride home.

The next morning, Renee stood under the spray from the showerhead, splashing the hot water on her face. She knew she had to pull herself together—she and Jessica would be tasting cake in two hours—but she felt terrible. Her night had been restless, her brain conjuring fantasy after steamy fantasy of Jeremiah. If she wasn't able to fulfill some of them soon, she was pretty sure her body would seize up and send her to the hospital out of spite.

She still couldn't believe she'd been so brazen during dinner the night before. What had she been thinking, playing footsie like that, with Jessica right there?

She hadn't been thinking at all, plain and simple. Jeremiah was so damn sexy that being near him made her brain shut off.

And the worst part was, she couldn't regret one moment of it. Just thinking of his hand sliding up her thigh sent her blood pressure skyrocketing, and she couldn't wait for him to touch her again. Whenever that would be.

Rinsing her hair, she pictured what it would be like to have Jeremiah in the shower with her. Soapy. Wet. Naked. So very naked.

She bit her lip in frustration. How much more of this could she take?

One day, she told herself. If she survived today, Jeremiah had promised that the next one would make up for it. In the meantime, though, she would need to do *something* to get her through the day.

Her hand slid down her body, edging through the dark thatch of curls covering her sex, her finger sliding over her clitoris as she allowed her mind's eye to return to the picture of Jeremiah in the shower with her.

Her body was so ready after all the sexual torment of the past few days that it only took a couple of minutes for her to shudder as an orgasm shot through her. The tension in her body eased, but didn't disappear entirely. She had a feeling she would need Jeremiah in the flesh, and *only* the flesh, in order to completely satisfy her.

By the time she got downstairs, she had cooled down enough to face her sister and the day before her. The sexless, Jeremiah-less day.

At least there would be cake.

Renee stood in front of the mirror, taking one last look at her dress. She had gotten it tailored weeks before, but Jessica had asked her to try it on one last time at her bridal boutique, so here she was. The seamstress, a plump, grandmotherly, silver-haired woman, studied the satin dress carefully. "It's a perfect fit," she declared at last, "and quite lovely on you, dear."

Renee glanced at her reflection. To her surprise, the color didn't seem to contrast quite as terribly with her hair as she had first thought. And all the cake they'd eaten that morning hadn't attached itself to her hips quite yet. She didn't look bad at all.

"I told you it was fine," Renee called to her sister, who was hidden from view by a large curtain.

"It never hurts to check," Jessica called back, her voice muffled.

The seamstress smiled at her. She was clearly familiar with Jessica. The curtain slid back and her sister stepped out of the dressing room, and their attention shifted to the woman in the beautiful white wedding dress.

The lace halter of the dress showed off Jessica's tan skin, the bodice hugged her curves and the skirt flowed to the floor in waves of fabric. Renee felt a pang of jealousy for her sister's height and perfect proportions. She was certain no wedding dress would ever look that good on her.

Not that she was anywhere near needing or wanting one, she reminded herself. There was too much to do before that even became an issue.

Jeremiah's easy smile flashed through her mind, but she pushed it away. Thinking about sexy flings while in a wedding shop was a definite no-no.

Jessica stood in front of the mirror. "What do you think?" she asked her sister.

Renee wanted to hug her, but was afraid of wrinkling the dress, so she made do with a squeeze of her hand. "You look so beautiful."

Jessica sighed and ran her hands across the silky skirt, that dreamy look back in her eyes. The one she had whenever she looked at Aaron. Renee had that feeling in her gut again, the not-jealousy one.

"It looks like it's ready to take home," Jessica said, turning her back to the mirror and eyeing the train.

Renee nodded. Jessica did one last thorough check, then started moving back toward her dressing room. "I better get this off before something happens to it," she said.

Renee looked around at the sterile environment. "What could possibly happen to it here?"

"I don't know. Somebody could walk in with tomato sauce and trip and spill it all over me or something."

Renee didn't say a word. There was no point commenting every single time her sister worried about something ridiculous.

As Renee moved toward her own dressing room, her sister turned back to look at her with a smile. "Remember when we were kids and would play dress-up wedding with that old white dress of Mom's?"

Renee chuckled at the memory. "Yeah. That was fun."

Jessica's smile widened. "We'd take turns being the bride and the bridesmaid."

"You were really bad at taking turns. You always wanted to be the bride."

"Well, I've grown up and gotten much better at taking turns."

Renee wasn't sure exactly what Jessica was talking about, but she had a bad feeling as to where this was going. "What do you mean?"

"It's your turn," Jessica said, pointing to the dressing room.

Renee moved the curtain that served as the door to her dressing room, and there was a giant mass of white fabric that hadn't been there before. "Oh no," she muttered.

"Oh yes," Jessica responded, triumphant.

"I'm not putting that on." What was Jessica thinking?

"Come on. I saw it here months ago and thought of you. Please? For me?" Jessica begged.

Renee cautiously moved closer to the dress, as if she was afraid it would bite. The strapless bodice sparkled, and the full skirt looked light and airy. "Rhinestones make you think of me?"

"Just try it on," Jessica demanded.

Renee pressed her lips together. She'd do it, but only because it was her sister's wedding week and she was trying to be nice. Not because the fabric was beautiful or she was at all curious how it would look on her.

One of the saleswomen followed her into the dressing room and helped her into what looked like miles of fabric. "When are you getting married?" the woman asked.

"I'm not," Renee answered as she wriggled herself into place. "My sister is making me do this."

The woman began lacing up the back and adjusting the dress until it sat comfortably on Renee's hips. "Well, I think she picked the perfect dress for you. Now you know which one to get whenever you and Mr. Right decide to settle down."

Renee had to force herself not to shake her head. Clearly the woman was trying to make a sale, because there was no way she could pull off a dress like this. On some tall curvy woman it might be beautiful, but she was sure that she'd look like a little kid playing dress-up, just like she and Jessica used to do.

She stepped out of the dressing room, hoping Jessica would let her change back into her regular clothing as soon as she saw how ridiculous this dress looked on her.

Jessica was standing there in jeans and a T-shirt. When she saw Renee, her eyes widened.

"You really thought I could pull this off?" Renee asked, gesturing at the full skirt that poufed out from her hips.

Jessica just pointed at the mirrors. Renee sighed and walked over to them. Then her breath caught in her throat as she took in her reflection. She didn't look silly at all. The rhinestones on the corset top and the wide tulle skirt should have looked like too much, but somehow it just looked elegant and...well...

Beautiful, she admitted to herself. She looked beautiful.

Renee couldn't stop staring at her image in the mirror. Jessica beamed at her. "I knew you'd love it."

Renee couldn't deny it.

Finally, reality set in. What was she doing goggling at herself in a wedding dress? She wasn't getting married. Not even close.

She looked at her sister. "I'm not getting married anytime soon, Jessica. So why did you want me to try on this dress?"

"For one, I was sure it'd be perfect on you," Jessica answered. Then her expression became more serious. "And for another, I think you're hiding from any opportunity to find a relationship that makes you happy. I thought maybe this would help."

Renee didn't know what to say, so she just continued to look at her reflection. Was her overly blunt sister right? "I'm too busy for a relationship, Jess."

Jessica rolled her eyes. "You choose to be too busy. Don't think I haven't noticed, even from Texas. You never go out on dates, and you work every chance you get. You've been doing this to yourself for years now. Have you thought about why?"

Renee tried to push away her sister's words, but it was hard. She reminded herself why she worked so hard, and how it was finally paying off with her dream job so close she could smell it.

Those thoughts didn't stop the roiling in her stomach, though. Maybe she'd eaten too many cake samples that morning, she told herself.

She wasn't sure she believed it.

With difficulty, she tore her eyes away from her reflection. "Can I put on my regular clothes now?"

She tried to sound exasperated, but by the look on Jessica's face as she nodded, Renee doubted it worked.

After changing back into her jeans and T-shirt, Renee left the store with Jessica, wedding dress in tow. Renee said nothing about the other dress, but her sister's triumphant expression didn't leave her face the entire way back to the ranch.

Renee felt unsettled about the whole thing. Even the perfect dress and Jessica's words shouldn't change her feelings about marriage and all that, but for some reason, she didn't feel nearly as terrified by the prospect as she used to. She was going to be too busy with her new job to even consider a serious relationship, but the usual relief that came with that idea was no longer there. It felt more like resignation.

Maybe her sister was right. That thought left a bad taste in her mouth and she pushed it away.

She seemed to be doing that a lot lately.

When they walked inside Jessica and Aaron's home, Renee flopped on the couch, exhausted. She felt like she'd had more cake and self-reflection than anyone should on one day.

Jessica sat beside her, and Renee could feel her stare. She opened her eyes and waited for whatever her sister was going to say.

"I know it's been a long, wedding-focused day, but do you

mind going through the receipts with me to make sure I haven't missed anything?" Jessica asked, a pleading look in her eyes.

Renee was absolutely positive her sister hadn't missed anything, but nodded anyway. At least Jessica didn't seem inclined to discuss the dress or Renee's relationships or anything like that. She wasn't sure she would've been able to take much more of that in one day.

"Great!" Jessica exclaimed, bouncing up to grab her binder, a large manila envelope and her laptop. She passed the computer over to Renee. "I'll read off an item, and you can go through the folder on my desktop. I have a few paper copies," she said, pointing to the envelope, "but almost everything is digital."

Renee placed the laptop on her legs and began to open the folder labeled Wedding when something else caught her eye—a document titled "City Girl, Country Life." While Jessica flipped through her binder in search of the right page, Renee opened the document and began reading.

Her eyes skimmed down through the pages. It was an article all about transitioning to life on a ranch. And it was good. Renee could easily imagine it as one of the articles she'd design spreads for back in New York.

"Did you write this?" she asked, turning the screen toward her sister. Jessica looked up, confused, but she blushed the moment she saw what Renee had opened.

"Oh, that's nothing. Just something I wrote when I first moved here," Jessica said, trying to lean over Renee to close it.

Renee pulled the laptop back, out of her sister's reach, relieved to find something new to focus on that had nothing to do with weddings or sexy cowboys. She was finally in an area where she felt confident. "This is great, Jess. You should submit it for publishing. I bet *Empire* would run it. We're always looking for pieces with interesting perspectives."

Jessica waved her fingers in front of her face, as if trying to clear the air around her. "I don't think so. It was just for fun. I'm an editor, not a writer, remember?"

Renee pointed at the screen. "Looks to me like you're both."

Jessica grabbed the computer from Renee and closed the document before opening the wedding folder. "*Anyway*, back to the receipts."

Renee didn't say anything else about the piece, but she decided that she would get her sister to submit it to the magazine before the end of the week.

They spent an hour going through every item, and as expected, everything was in order. "I don't know what you're so worried about," Renee told her sister as they stood and stretched. "You've planned it all in excruciating detail. At this point, it doesn't seem like there's anything you could have missed."

Jessica nodded and held her beloved binder tight to her chest. "I know, but I just have this feeling that something's going to go wrong, and I'm trying to catch it before the big day."

Renee put her hand on her sister's shoulder. "You've got it all taken care of. Just enjoy this time, okay?"

Jessica nodded, but she still didn't seem reassured. Renee shrugged and began climbing the stairs to her room. She'd tried for years to stop her neurotic sister from worrying, but it never worked. Meanwhile, she had enough on her plate, between helping with the wedding, preparing for her new job and trying to simultaneously have a sexy tryst with Jeremiah and keep it totally under wraps.

As she dropped onto the bed and smelled his already-familiar scent, she finally allowed herself to think about him and their few short stolen kisses. He had been on her mind all day, but it was only now that she let herself truly delve into it.

Renee knew they would never be in a serious relationship, but she couldn't stop her heart from fluttering when she thought of him. Something was different now, though. Ignoring her sister's earlier words and trying to forget that dress was harder than she liked.

She grimaced and sat up, rubbing her face with her hands.

Was that going to ruin her one chance to have a spectacular time with the sexiest man she'd ever met?

Renee hoped not, but it was all getting tied up in her head, and she didn't like that. She grabbed her laptop and opened a page she'd been designing for a future issue. At least work could keep her mind off things. Life was always a little clearer when she was working on a project.

For the rest of the evening, Renee worked on the page, tweaking it until it was close to perfect. When she went down to eat, Jessica said nothing about their earlier conversation, to Renee's relief.

By the time she finished the page, it was late enough to go to bed, and Renee pulled up the covers, ready to be done with this day.

Jeremiah had promised that tomorrow would be their chance, but suddenly she felt more nervous than excited. The whole thing suddenly seemed like a train wreck waiting to happen, and she didn't know if she had the power to prevent it.

Seven

Jeremiah looked out the window of his house, watching as the color of the sky slowly shifted from pink and gold to blue. Yesterday had been frustrating, to say the least, but it was finally over. Today was going to be different, he was sure. After he and Aaron went to pick up the rings, he would finally get some real time alone with Renee.

He thought of her smile, the way her hands felt pressed against his chest, and his body reacted immediately. He leaned his forehead against the cool glass and closed his eyes. The same thing had been happening over and over since he'd first seen her. He just hoped that he would be able to work whatever this was out of his system by the end of the week.

Aaron's text from yesterday popped unbidden into his head. Aaron had thought it was hilarious that Jessica managed to get Renee to try on a poufy princess wedding dress, but it wasn't that funny to Jeremiah.

He didn't really know how he felt about it, but amused definitely wasn't one of the competing emotions.

* * *

Renee was just finishing yet another delicious breakfast when Jeremiah walked in. She'd been anxious all morning, waiting for him to arrive so he and Aaron could go pick up the wedding rings, but his sudden appearance still made her almost choke on her bacon. She felt her face go warm. Why was it that every time she saw him, a jolt went through her entire body?

He smiled at her with one eyebrow raised, and she knew he was enjoying her inability to control her reactions. Impulsively, she dabbed her finger into the syrup on her plate and sucked it off, not taking her eyes away from him. The grin fell away from his face and his mouth opened slightly as he watched. A feeling of power coursed through her. She wasn't the only one who could be thrown off balance.

Any hesitations that might have resulted from her conversations with Jessica the day before disappeared as she felt her blood surge. Whatever her issues were, she wasn't going to let them—or her sister's opinion of them—stop her from taking advantage of this once-in-a-lifetime opportunity.

Aaron jumped up from the table. "Great. I'm glad you came over early. Let's get going."

Renee saw disappointment flash across Jeremiah's face. "Will the store even be open this early?"

"No, but there are a few other things we need to take care of. That's okay, right?"

Renee knew there was nothing he could say that wouldn't give away that something was going on, so he shrugged one shoulder and turned to leave back through the door he'd just entered from, but not without sending a look of regret her way.

Renee was simultaneously disappointed that he had to leave so quickly and secretly pleased that he had tried to come over early so he could spend time with her.

And then he was gone, and the warmth that had flowed into the kitchen when he arrived disappeared, too.

She remembered his promise about the afternoon, and a thrill ran through her. She would just need to occupy herself for a few hours.

Renee turned to her sister. "What's on the docket today?"

Jessica looked excited, like she'd hoped Renee would ask her that. "We need to create the centerpieces and wedding favors," she said, holding up a bag of what looked like art supplies.

Renee waited for more of an explanation. She didn't have to wait long. "We need to spray paint wine bottles," Jessica continued, "and decorate some flower pots. Once they're dry, we'll be able to start adding the plants and arranging them on a test table."

Renee smiled at her sister. It sounded more fun than going over receipts or seating charts again, at least.

Three hours later, Renee brushed the hair out of her face with the back of one paint-speckled hand. She looked over the sea of flower pots spread out before her in varying stages of completion. Some were still their original terra-cotta color, others were bright white and still others had painted stenciled flowers drying along the top. Jessica sat beside her, cheerfully dabbing paint onto yet another pot.

"What do you think?" Aaron asked, turning the tiny box so the diamonds on the wedding band nestled inside glittered in the light.

"I think I'm the luckiest girl in the world!" Jeremiah exclaimed.

Aaron rolled his eyes as Jeremiah laughed at his own joke. "Is it too late to get a new best man?"

Jeremiah waved off the question. "You know Jessica will love it."

"I hope so."

"Stop worrying. At this rate, you're both going to have breakdowns, and I don't want to be the one picking up the pieces."

Jeremiah took one last look at the ring as Aaron handed the

box back to the jeweler. It was a strange thought, his best friend getting married. They had gone through childhood and wild young adult years together, and now Aaron was officially moving into the next stage. The wife-and-kids stage.

And Jeremiah was happy for him, even as he wondered when he'd be moving into that stage, too.

The sexy redhead, never too far from his mind, resurfaced again. She wasn't looking for anything serious. He knew that.

But he was an optimist. Maybe by the end of the week it could turn into something more.

Renee looked in the mirror, checking to make sure she'd gotten all the paint off her face. Her stomach roiled in anticipation. Jeremiah could be back at any time, and then they'd enact whatever plan he had. And she could finally play out a few of her fantasies.

She suppressed the urge to dance around her room.

As Renee straightened up, her cell phone began to ring from the bedside table. She could only think of one person who might call her today, and a surge of either excitement or fear shot through her. Renee picked up her phone and looked at the screen. It was Patty, just like she thought. Nervous tension knotted inside her. What if it was bad news? What if they'd found someone else to take the position?

She took a deep breath and answered. "Hello?"

"Hi, Renee, it's Patty. I just got out of the meeting. I told them you were perfect for my position and recommended that they have you step in when I leave."

She paused, and Renee thought she might have a heart attack before Patty told her what happened.

"They trust my opinion, Renee. We'll iron out the details when you get back."

Breath whooshed out of Renee's lungs. Relief flooded her. This was actually going to happen.

"They just want to see some of your work, pages that haven't been edited by anyone else, to make sure they're happy with what you do. You'll need to pick a few of your pieces and get them to me. It's just a formality, so don't worry about it at all this week. Whatever you pick when you get back into town will be great, I'm sure. I know they'll be impressed."

Renee began planning immediately. Patty's voice cut through her thoughts. "Next week, Renee. You don't need to work on it right now. I just knew you would want to know."

She thanked Patty and hung up. She was still standing in the same spot she'd been when she had picked up the phone, but now she dropped onto the bed.

It was actually happening. She couldn't believe it.

Despite Patty's parting words, Renee knew it would be impossible for her to wait the entire week to get started. She would need to go through each of her best pieces and check them for any problems, then choose which ones to submit.

An idea popped into her head, making her fingers itch for her laptop. She could take Jessica's article and design an amazing page around it, with the picture of the barn front and center.

She knew it would be impressive and show off her skills, but it would take time. She would need to get started on it immediately.

It was midafternoon when Jeremiah and Aaron pulled up to Aaron's house. It had been a long day, and Jeremiah could barely contain his excitement as he walked into the house. This was it. He and Renee would finally get some time alone.

"I've got an idea," he said to his friend, as if the thought had just sprung to mind. "How about I take Renee out to town for dinner and some sightseeing? That way you and Jessica can have some time alone together. It must be weird having someone else around all the time."

Aaron smiled and narrowed his eyes at Jeremiah, giving him a sly look. "Are you trying to get together with Renee?"

Jeremiah laughed like the idea was crazy. He'd been prepared for this. "I just know how depraved you two are. It must be killing you not to grope each other every ten minutes."

Aaron nodded. "You have no idea."

"So I'm a great friend. Remember that." If things went the way Jeremiah hoped, he'd need all the brownie points he could muster.

With that, Jeremiah waltzed out of the room, ready to find Renee and get out of that house. A few hours alone, then a nice dinner together—maybe he could convince her that they had a future after all.

She was sitting on the living room couch, hunched over her laptop. He paused for a moment and just stared at her. His heart sped up as he imagined what her face would look like when he did all the things he wanted to do to her.

He walked up behind her and placed a hand on her shoulder. Even that much contact made his body react. She looked up, and the flush on her cheeks made it clear that she felt it, too. He couldn't wait another minute to kiss her. "We've been paroled. Let's go," he said in a whisper, gesturing toward the door.

She hesitated, looking back at her computer, and he knew something was wrong. "I'm kind of in the middle of something important. Give me a few minutes."

His good mood dampened. She hadn't seemed very happy about the idea of being alone with him, and the thought stabbed at him. He tried to put that thought out of his mind. It must be something else that was making her act like that. "Work?" he asked.

She nodded, staring at the screen. "My boss called this morning. They're going to offer me the job, but I need to send them a few of my page designs."

"And they're making you work on it while you're on vacation?" He felt annoyance on her behalf.

She looked at him. "Well, no, but I had an idea and wanted to get started on it."

"So, there's no good reason for you to be working on this right now? You're joking, right?"

He knew it came out harsher than he'd wanted, but he couldn't believe that she was putting off what they'd both been looking forward to for this. The thought that she wasn't as excited as he was only made his mood darker.

He could see her jaw working and knew she was frustrated. Hell, so was he. She shut her laptop with a snap and stood, but it was clear this wasn't over. Instead of walking over to him, she turned to leave the room, heading toward the stairs. "This is important to me," she threw back at him as she disappeared.

And I'm not, he thought, filling in the implied meaning.

Jeremiah wasn't sure if he wanted to storm out or race after her. Instead, he stood there, still looking at the door she'd disappeared through, until he heard a door upstairs close. Without another word, he left.

Renee stood in her room, trying to figure out what the hell had just happened. Why had Jeremiah acted like that?

She asked herself the question, but she knew the answer. The real question was, why had she hesitated? She'd been looking forward to this opportunity, and when it finally came, she'd stalled. What was she so afraid of?

Renee sat down on the bed and put her head in her hands. When he touched her on the shoulder, it was warm and sweet, and looking up at him made her heart light on fire and melt at the same time. It was the melting that had scared her enough to put off her chance to go with him.

But there was no reason to worry about falling for this guy. He certainly wouldn't be falling for her, and anyway, it was only one week. Then she'd be heading back to New York. Did she really want to go back without having any of the fun she'd promised herself?

God, she was an idiot. She stood and raced out of the room

and down the stairs, not letting herself think too much about what she would do or say.

But it wouldn't have mattered anyway. She got to the door just in time to see his truck disappear.

She trudged back upstairs, to her laptop and pages. They suddenly didn't seem quite so interesting or important.

Jeremiah made a circuit of the outside of his house, thinking. He felt like an idiot, and a meandering drive after leaving Jessica and Aaron's hadn't helped at all. He should never have imagined that he and Renee could be more than a short-term thing. He'd known from the beginning that she didn't want anything more than a casual fun week. She was a workaholic who refused to let anything more serious happen; she'd made that clear right off the bat.

So why had he let that fact get him so frustrated?

He sat on the stairs of the porch and looked up at the darkening sky. He'd let himself believe that maybe he could change that about her, but that was ridiculous. You can't change someone after just a few days of kisses and conversation.

No, he needed to accept that if he was going to have any type of relationship with Renee, it wasn't going to be anything more than her indulging a few fantasies. She wouldn't let her heart get involved.

That was what he'd agreed to, and if that was all he could get from her, so be it. Without ever entering the house, he got back into his truck. He needed to go apologize and see if he could salvage this thing.

By the time he got to Jessica and Aaron's, stars were dotting the sky above him. He walked in and found the two of them sitting at the kitchen table, the remnants of dinner still in front of them. Aaron looked up at him. "Hey, what happened?"

Jeremiah wasn't sure how to answer. In addition to making a mess of things with Renee, he hadn't exactly given his friend the privacy he'd promised. "Renee was working on something for her job," he answered with a shrug.

Jessica said, "She just came down for a second when I called her for dinner. Didn't even eat. She just said she was working. She didn't look good. Do you think she's sick?"

Jeremiah shrugged again, feeling guilty. Had he made her feel that bad? He was such an ass.

Aaron stood and grabbed a bottle of Johnnie Walker from the cupboard. "You don't look so good yourself. Here, have a drink."

Jeremiah couldn't really say no, and a drink sounded like a great idea. If Renee was that upset, giving her a little space was probably a good thing.

Renee sat on her bed, staring at her computer screen. For over three hours, she'd been trying to work on her design, hoping she could lose herself in the clean lines of the page, but it wasn't working. Her mind wouldn't blank. It kept filling itself with Jeremiah, blocking out everything else, even work.

She looked at the clock. It wasn't even nine yet, but she was done with this day. She turned out the lights and lay down. The previous sleepless night caught up to her, and she was quickly asleep.

"Slow down, man. Is everything okay?"

Jeremiah looked at his empty glass. He hadn't meant to drink it all, but he'd been thinking about how he and Renee had left things and before he realized it, the whiskey was gone. He tried to decide what he could tell Aaron.

"I don't really want to get into details, but I'm trying to make things happen with a woman, and it's not quite working out the way I'd like."

Aaron leaned forward, interested. "What woman? Why is this the first I'm hearing about it?"

Jeremiah shook his head. "Not ready to talk about that, Aaron."

"Is she related to you or something?"

Jeremiah punched Aaron in the arm.

"Ow! What? It happens more than you think."

Jeremiah shook his head. "Anyway, she doesn't want anything serious."

Aaron raised his eyebrows. "And you do? Whoa. I didn't expect you to be ready to settle down."

Jeremiah didn't say anything else. He'd probably already said too much, but Aaron had been his best friend since kindergarten. It seemed weird to go through all this and leave him completely in the dark.

Aaron refilled their glasses. "Without knowing more, I can't really give you advice. But I say, if you think she's worth it, don't give up hope."

Jeremiah took another swallow of the brown liquid and thought about what Aaron had said. He'd never been the type to give up hope, so why would he start now? He wasn't sure if it was that thought or the alcohol, but he felt better.

Now he just needed to mend things with Renee.

"Is it okay if I stay the night?" he asked Aaron. "I don't want to drive home," he explained, gesturing at the empty glass and glad for the excuse.

Aaron nodded, and Jeremiah walked resolutely up the stairs, ready to patch things up with Renee. Thinking about spending time alone in her room made his body react immediately, but he tried to calm it back down.

Once he got to the top of the stairs, he paused and took a breath before knocking on the door to the left.

No answer.

He eased the door open. The room was dark and quiet, so he shut it again, disappointed. She was already asleep.

Jeremiah stood there for a long time, looking at Renee's door. He wanted to apologize, wanted more than anything to kiss her and finally do what they'd been edging toward since she arrived. But she had made it clear only a few hours ago that she was mad at him, so barging in, even to apologize, while she was sleeping when he was a little beyond tipsy, seemed like a terrible idea in so many ways.

He wanted to see her so badly, but even through the alcohol he was able to convince himself that it wasn't the best time. He finally turned to the door on the right, his usual room. He promised himself that he would talk to her in the morning, when she was awake and he was sober.

He went into his room, leaving the light off. Jeremiah pulled off his shoes and pants and dropped into bed before he could make any stupid decisions.

Renee woke slowly, not wanting to let go of the delicious feeling of Jeremiah's hard body spread out next to her like a yummy treat. She pressed her lips against his, opening in invitation. It was only as his tongue slid enticingly over her teeth that she realized she was no longer asleep.

This couldn't be real, could it?

She opened her eyes. The room was dark, but there was just enough light coming in through the window for her to see Jeremiah's outline beside her. "You're real," she said aloud before realizing how stupid it sounded.

"Real," he affirmed, before leaning in to kiss her again.

She wasn't sure when he'd sneaked into her room, or even what he was doing at Jessica and Aaron's house in the first place, but those questions fled from her mind as he kissed her even more deeply, groaning with the sensation of it.

She pressed herself against him, sinking into the kiss. Any worries or hesitation she had had before were gone. All that was left was her need to touch him everywhere. Her hands slid down his bare stomach until they reached his boxers and his erection.

He was definitely real. No question about it. She wrapped her fingers around him and squeezed.

He groaned again. "You're killing me, Renee."

She gave him a devilish grin he couldn't see. She hadn't even begun.

He leaned in to kiss her again, this time his breathing ragged and quick. His fingers clenched in her hair for a moment before starting a slow crawl down her body.

When his hand reached her breast, her already-speeding pulse increased, making her feel light-headed. Her nipples tightened into hard nubs at his touch, and the sensation was so intense she thought she might orgasm right then and there.

She pushed him flat on his back, and leaned over him, kissing his chest, tasting and teasing his skin as she moved downward, inching closer to his iron-hard erection. "Whoa, what are you doing?" Jeremiah asked, in a voice that said he knew exactly what she was doing.

He just wanted to hear her say it.

She smiled in the dark, pressing a small bite to his abs. "What I've been wanting to do since I saw you in Vegas."

With that, she slid down his boxers and took him into her mouth, relishing the taste of him.

He moaned again and throbbed against her lips. A feeling of power surged through her—this incredibly sexy man was totally under her control, and she reveled in it. After only a few moments, though, Jeremiah sat up, and before she was sure what happened, she was flat on her back. "I wasn't finished," she told him.

He chuckled. "If I let you keep going, I would be, and I don't want this to be over yet."

With that, his hands and lips went to work on her body, moving over every inch of her until she was so alive with sensation that she couldn't think.

He moved between her legs, his mouth and hand converging at her center. As his fingers curled inside her, he applied his tongue to her mound, sending her over the edge so sharply that she had to bite her hand to keep from screaming out. She shuddered as the spasms of sensation hurtled through her body.

She clenched and unclenched her hands, trying to bring herself back under control, but Jeremiah seemed to have no intention of allowing that. He bit her thigh, then soothed the spot with his tongue, continuing the pattern down one leg, then back up the other. His caresses only gave her a moment of respite before bringing her back to the cliff's edge. She couldn't wait any longer. "I want you in me," she said, hardly able to create a coherent sentence. "Now."

Jeremiah didn't need to be told twice, which was good because Renee had used the last of her ability to speak on that sentence. He leaned away from her, leaving only cool air in his wake. For a moment, she wanted to call him back to her, but then she heard the ripping of a condom wrapper. In a moment he was back with her, his hard, hot body against her, then on top of her. Finally he slid inside her, filling her. The sensation making her gasp.

She wrapped her legs around him, pulling him even deeper, and he groaned out her name, his voice deep and primal. They rocked together, breaths mingling as they kissed. As much as Renee had imagined and fantasized about it, she still couldn't believe what was happening. The incredibly sexy Jeremiah was ravishing her mouth with his tongue, while the rest of him moved in a slow rhythm building toward what she knew was the inevitable conclusion.

Slow curls of ecstasy wrapped through her as he began to move faster, and she lost herself in the sensations. He nipped at her earlobe and whispered her name, and she fell over the edge once more. He squeezed her hand in his as he followed.

Eight

Jeremiah opened his eyes. The early-morning light streamed through the window, making Renee's hair blaze like a reddish-blond halo framing her face. She was so beautiful he wanted to run his hand over her cheek to be sure she was real, but resisted the urge. He didn't want to wake her up.

His mind replayed everything that had happened. He had thought sex with her would be great, but it was so much more. Incredible, that's what it was. Everything about her was amazing. The way her lips felt against his, the way she tasted, the little squeals she made as she came for him.

He wanted it all, over and over again.

As if she could read his thoughts, Renee snuggled closer to him, kissing his shoulder as she opened her eyes. "Good morning," she said with a nibble that shot through his heart and straight down to his groin.

"If you keep doing that," he said through his teeth as he struggled to maintain control, "I'm going to have to do things to you."

"Oh yeah?" she responded with a mischievous smirk. "What kind of things?"

"The kind that would probably come to Jessica and Aaron's attention."

Her groan of annoyance was so adorable that he chuckled, which turned quickly to a sharp intake of air as her fingers slid along his already-hard shaft. He pulled her hand away, cupping it in his own. "You should probably head back to your room before they wake up," he told her, wishing he was saying something very different.

Confusion swept across her features before being replaced by understanding. She sat up. "This is your room," she said.

Jeremiah was nonplussed. "Whose room did you think it was when you sneaked in here last night?"

Renee shook her head. "You don't understand. Jessica switched me into this room. *You* sneaked into *my* room. On accident, apparently."

She sounded deflated, and it took him a moment to figure out why. Then he realized and squeezed the hand he still held. "I tried to go to your room last night to apologize, but the light was off and I didn't want to wake you up." He laughed. "Apparently I was being polite to an empty room."

Her mood brightened immediately, and his heart thumped harder in his chest. "So, I guess I should go back to my room, which isn't my room?" he asked, a little confused.

She nodded, but the regret on her face was too much for him. He wished he didn't have to go, but then he had an idea. He sat up beside her and kissed her and in seconds they were both breathless. "Throw on some clothes," he told her.

She looked so disappointed he didn't know if he should laugh or hug her close. "I have a plan. It's a good one, trust me."

The disappointment was replaced with curiosity, but he shook his head before she had the chance to ask. "Just put on some clothes. I'm going to the other room for a minute. I'll meet you at the bottom of the stairs, okay?"

He tossed on his clothes and opened the door carefully, trying to keep it from squeaking. As soon as he was sure the coast was clear, he hastened across the hall to what he had believed to be Renee's room. After a few seconds making the bed look slept-in, he was back in the hallway and bounding down the stairs as quietly as he could. He was filled with a nervous excitement as he assured himself that the house was still quiet, its owners still asleep.

Renee came down the stairs only a minute after him. He raised a finger to his lips to let her know to be quiet, then grabbed her hand and pulled her after him out the door. He didn't need to hold her hand for this part, but it just felt so good. They began walking down the property, the barn ahead and slightly to the right of them.

Once they were outside, she asked, "Where are we going?"

"To see the river that runs along through the trees."

"Maybe I should have grabbed a coat," she said, rubbing the goose bumps on her arms.

The cool morning breeze swept over them and she shivered. He wrapped his arm around her and pulled her close. They began to pass the barn. "The river is silvery with tiny waterfalls. It babbles and everything."

"It sounds nice," she responded, clearly still wondering what he had in mind.

"What does the river look like?" he asked her as they passed behind the barn.

Her forehead wrinkled. He waited, and after a beat she answered, "Silver with little waterfalls?"

"Perfect," he said, then stopped walking. "Now you know how to answer if Jessica or Aaron asks you about it."

With that, he opened a small door in the back of the barn and gestured for her to follow. Renee's confusion changed to delight as his plan became clear, and she walked quickly to catch up to him.

In no time, they had made their way through the building and up to the loft. The excitement in Jeremiah's stomach was reaching a fever pitch. The moment they were hidden away in the hay-scented loft—either as an added protection against discovery, or because it seemed really sexy—Jeremiah pulled Renee toward him and gave her the long kiss he'd been waiting for all morning.

In moments, Jeremiah's blood was pounding in his veins, and his erection was straining the zipper of his jeans. His hands roved over Renee's body, enjoying every piece of her they could find. He leaned back for a second to get a full view of her face. Her lips were swollen from the kiss, her hair disheveled, and she wasn't wearing any makeup. She was the most beautiful woman he'd ever seen.

He moved back toward her and kissed her again. This was the best morning of his life, hands down.

Renee put her hand on Jeremiah's chest and grabbed a fistful of his shirt, as if hanging on for dear life. Which, in a way, she was. Last night had proven that her fantasies hadn't even come close to the real deal. Her knees were still weak from those bone-shattering orgasms, and here she was moving quickly toward another one. With Jeremiah's arm wrapped around her, holding her up, who needed knees?

Jeremiah's lips and tongue and teeth moved down her neck, leaving a wet trail that sizzled with heat. As he moved lower, he said, "You told me you fantasized about us getting together. What exactly did you imagine us doing?"

With another guy, Renee would feel embarrassed about describing her fantasies, but with Jeremiah there was just the thrill of knowing that whatever she said, he would be an incredibly willing participant. "I pictured myself on top of you, riding you until I came."

Jeremiah stilled for a second and the breath whooshed out of him. "Good fantasy," he murmured against her ear.

And then he got to work undressing them both. Renee's hand was no longer holding a fistful of his shirt, but instead lay flat against his chest, feeling the warm, taut skin stretched over muscles that would make any woman melt.

She pressed her hand against him, directing him to lie down on the floor of the loft. His eyes were dark with arousal, and his cock stood straight at attention as she unrolled the condom along his length.

She kissed his chest as she positioned herself on top of him, straddling him. He groaned. "Really, *really* good fantasy."

When she took him inside her, a small scream escaped her at the pleasure of it. Every glorious inch of him filled her. She began to move, the friction where their bodies joined making her entire being feel tight and sensitive. Then his thumb moved between her legs, sliding against her nub until she cried out again.

He touched and teased her as she rode him, his head thrown back and every muscle taut. She moved faster, rushing toward release. It exploded through her, making every part of her quiver, and he came with her, gasping her name.

She leaned forward, her body on top of his, feeling deliciously spent. His skin smelled of sweat and sex, and she breathed it deep into her lungs, enjoying it. His arms slid around her, holding her close.

Renee opened her eyes, suddenly uncomfortable. It felt more like a love scene than she liked. It was just sex. Really good sex, but that was it. She couldn't let it turn into anything more than that or she'd be nursing a broken heart when she went back to New York. There was no other way for that path to end.

Jeremiah shifted slightly to look at her face. "Hey, you okay?" he asked, concern in his voice.

She sat up and slid off him, hating how empty she felt when he was no longer inside her. She forced herself to be perky and pleasant. "Yep, I'm fine. Do you think Jessica and Aaron will be up?"

He looked like he wanted to ask something else, but to her relief he just shrugged. "Probably."

She stood and started getting into her clothes. "Good, because I'm starving and the only breakfast food I'm capable of making is toast." She cringed at her own fake tones.

"Don't knock toast. It's the key to a great breakfast," he answered, giving her his lighthearted smile.

She tried to ignore the fact that only his mouth smiled. His eyes still held concern.

Renee turned to the ladder, trying to get away from those eyes. "I only burn it like sixty percent of the time."

Once she was at the bottom of the ladder, she brushed herself off one last time, feeling anxious in Jeremiah's presence, though she wasn't completely sure why. When he was standing beside her, she turned for inspection, more to mask her discomfort than anything else. "Is there any hay or anything on me? I don't want to leave any clues for Jessica to pick up on."

Jeremiah took a step closer, halting her nervous movements. The deep brown of his eyes sucked her in, calming her jitters. "Would it really be the worst thing in the world if Jessica found out?" he asked her.

She knew he wasn't asking just that question. He was asking another one, a question that sent the panic monster running through her brain. She turned her eyes away from his, breaking away from that intoxicating stare. It was time to make this completely clear for both of them. "Yes. If Jessica knew what was going on, she would either be horrified that her little sister was having a fling instead of helping her with the wedding, or she would get excited and think that this is going to turn into something more, which it won't."

She paused for a second, letting her words sink in. She still couldn't look at him. "Since it can't go beyond this week, Jessica absolutely can't find out."

For what felt like a very long time, neither of them spoke. Then he began walking toward the barn door. "Rules one and two—Jessica can't know, and this is just for the week. Got it."

She followed him as he walked in silence back to the house.

Renee wanted to bring back the fun, easygoing banter she so enjoyed with him, but couldn't think of anything else to say.

When she was lying there with him, it didn't feel like a simple fling—it felt more serious than that. And that was exactly what she *didn't* want. She just needed to get back to fun and flirty, and nothing else. Once she figured out how to break through this awkwardness.

As soon as they were inside the house, the sounds and smells of breakfast bombarded her senses. Aaron was at the stove again in his garish apron.

"That thing looks ridiculous on you. You know that, right?" Jeremiah said as he sat down.

"Well, good morning to you, too. I like this apron. Best present you ever gave me."

"What about that football I got you that was signed by the entire 1995 Dallas Cowboys team?"

Aaron's eyes shifted. "That...kind of exploded."

"What!"

"I hooked it up to the electric pump to inflate it a little bit, but you look away for one second—apparently there's a limit to how much air it'll hold."

Jeremiah seemed suspicious. "One second, huh? Was Jessica in the room?"

Aaron answered with a grin. Jeremiah shook his head. "You win. From now on, I'm not getting you anything but girlie kitchen items."

"Great! I need pot holders."

Jeremiah glanced at Renee and smiled. A real, genuine smile that she couldn't help but return.

She sat down next to him, stifling a laugh, either of amusement at the boys' conversation or relief that the unease between her and Jeremiah was gone. This was the Jeremiah she wanted, not the sweet, caring one who made her heart ache in a way that bothered her.

Jessica walked into the kitchen. "Good morning. What have you two been up to?"

Renee tried to keep her face from betraying her. "We went for a walk to the river."

Jessica's eyes lit up. "Isn't it beautiful?"

"I love the little waterfalls," Renee responded, seeing Jeremiah's grin out of the corner of her eye and almost breaking character.

Jessica seemed satisfied and shifted her attention to Jeremiah. "Sorry I gave away your room without telling you. Aaron and I didn't realize how weird that must have been for you until this morning. I hope it didn't cause any problems last night."

Renee purposely avoided looking at Jeremiah, but she knew exactly what he was thinking. *It caused a lot of very good things.* He just said, "No problem," and they moved on without getting any closer to that land mine.

Aaron served up another amazing breakfast and Jessica began discussing the tasks for the day, including setting up the chairs in the barn.

"If you need to work," Jeremiah said, turning to her, "I can help out setting stuff up."

It was such a sweet gesture, and he was so clearly apologizing for the day before that she was halfway to a puddle of goo before she managed to get a hold of herself.

She certainly had a lot to do if she wanted to get that spread perfect before the end of the week, but she'd come all this way to help her sister. Thoughts warred inside her.

Finally, she decided on a compromise. "How about we both set up the chairs? Everything will get done faster, and *then* I can do some work before…"

Before what? Before they spent another night together? God, she hoped so.

His lips twitched at the corners and he nodded.

"It's settled," Jessica said, her voice slicing the moment to shreds. "Let's eat, clean up, and then we can all get to work."

They ate and made conversation, but Renee missed pretty much all of it. She was far too intent upon Jeremiah's hand, which pressed lightly against her thigh under the table. It wasn't much, definitely not something that would catch the attention of the other two, but oh man, it caught hers.

By the time breakfast was over, she could feel her eyes glazing over, and she was little more than a puddle. How could he do so much to her with just the backs of his fingers under the table?

Unfortunately, there was no time to explore the question in more detail. Jessica was already divvying up tasks. "I need a quick shower," Renee said before Jessica could give her another job. After the night before and then the romp in the loft, she felt like she was exuding sex out of her pores, and any moment, Jessica was going to catch on.

Jessica nodded. "You do that while we wash the dishes."

Renee stood, a little shaky on legs made of jelly. Jeremiah shifted uncomfortably before standing, and Renee laughed quietly under her breath. Apparently his little bit of below-the-table teasing had tortured him as much as her.

Renee didn't realize her sister was standing next to her until she spoke, startling her. "What's funny?" Jessica asked.

Renee couldn't think of a thing to say. Her mind was blank.

Jeremiah saw Renee's panic and thought of something as fast as he could. "You were thinking about that terrible joke I told you on the walk back, weren't you?" he said.

Both women turned to him.

"What's the joke?" Aaron asked, picking up the dishes.

"Okay, but prepare yourself. It's pretty bad," Jeremiah said, turning on his "joker" setting to full blast to get the attention off Renee. "Did you hear about the circus fire? It was intense."

There was a silent pause.

"Get it? *In. Tents.* A circus fire."

Jessica nodded. "You're right. That's a horrible joke."

The moment was over, and Jessica and Aaron started to turn

back to cleaning off the table. Renee, however, was still staring at him. As he watched, her silent giggles turned into loud guffaws. She was laughing so hard she looked like she could barely breathe. His heart seemed to leap in his chest as he watched her, blown away by how adorable she was.

When she finally got control of herself and moved to leave the room, she sent him one last look, and it sizzled across the space between them. They were both thinking the same thing, he was sure, but Jessica and Aaron would *definitely* notice something was up if he went with her into the shower.

So instead he would stay downstairs and wait until she appeared again, driving himself crazy with the image of her soapy and wet with water running down her silky skin. It seemed like the only thing to do.

Renee leaned forward until her head was fully under the hot streaming water and she let it run over her. She hated to admit to herself how much she wanted Jeremiah there with her, and not just for his sexy body.

That was one reason, certainly, but not the only one. She wanted to talk to him more, just to hear what he would say. And that was a problem she would need to get over.

In a week-long one-night stand, it seemed better not to love the guy's personality. That just made things harder when the week ended.

She finished rinsing and turned off the water. Once she was dry and dressed, she went downstairs, where the rest of the group sat at the table. The look in Jeremiah's eyes as she stepped into the kitchen made a zing of electricity shoot through her. Instead of being satiated by that recent sexcapade and rocking orgasm, she was ready to curl her legs around his body and take him for another ride.

That just wasn't in the cards for the moment, though. Jessica was already up and ushering them out of the house, and there was no choice but to follow.

As they all trouped out to the barn, Jeremiah sidled up beside her and slowed down, allowing Aaron and Jessica to get ahead of them. The air crackled between them, shooting sparks of desire through her. There was so much Renee wanted to say, but the only words that formulated in her brain were: *I want you so badly right now.* And that wouldn't help either of them get through these next few hours.

"Thanks for saving my ass back there. And nice joke," Renee told him under her breath instead.

She clasped one hand in the other to keep from reaching out and touching him. Jessica might not be the most observant person, but she'd probably notice if Renee started groping the best man.

"Glad you liked it," he answered quietly. "I've been saving it to tell you. That seemed like a good time."

His fingers brushed hers for just a second, sending another jolt through her, and then he sped up to help Aaron push aside the heavy barn door. She took in a deep breath, trying to keep the bones in her body where they were instead of turning to mush and melting into a pool of desire.

Just as she had the time before, Renee stopped to watch as the two men rolled open the large door to the picturesque barn. Her mind managed to focus on the scene in front of her, and immediately the gears in her head began to turn.

"Jessica, you have a decent camera, right?" she called to her sister.

Jessica looked confused about the seemingly random question, but nodded. Renee ran up and grabbed her hand, pulling her back toward the house. "I need it."

"Now?"

"Now." Renee turned to the men, who had just gotten the door fully open. "Shut the door again, guys. I need to get a picture of you opening it."

She didn't wait for a response. Her mind was buzzing too fast to slow down as she hustled Jessica back inside. The sunlight, the barn, the men. It was all perfect, and she needed that photo to grace Jessica's story and her page design. But she had to move quickly if she wanted to capture that magic.

In no time, she had the camera around her neck and was running back down toward the barn. "Open the door slowly," she commanded to Aaron and Jeremiah, raising the camera to her face.

The shutter clicked again and again as the barn door opened, and once it was in place, the two men turned to Renee. "What was that all about?" Aaron asked.

"Something for work," Renee mumbled, not looking at him, her thoughts occupied.

She stared intently at the screen on the back of the camera, reviewing the photos she'd captured. There. Renee couldn't help the grin that spread across her face. She had found the perfect one for her page.

Giddy, she turned to Jessica. "This photo will look perfect with your article."

Jessica narrowed her eyes at her sister, but then she looked down at the screen and her expression changed. "Wow. That's an amazing picture."

Renee noted that Jessica hadn't said anything about *not* using the article. Could this day get any better?

She took the camera back to the house, holding it carefully, as if it was a priceless treasure.

Renee set the camera on her bed. She was itching to sit down and work on the spread, but everyone was expecting her to return to the barn and the business of wedding preparations.

At least in the barn she'd be able to watch Jeremiah. Her lips curled into a smile as she thought about the muscles in his arms rippling as he moved heavy objects. Maybe she'd even get lucky and he would need to bend over to work on something, giving her a great view of his ass.

That thought sent her bounding down the stairs and to

the door. Before she could open it, though, Jeremiah stepped through, and his lips were on hers.

Renee had no idea why he was there or if Jessica would be following right behind him, but she couldn't care too much when Jeremiah was kissing her like that.

Just as the kiss began to deepen and her fingers crept along the waistband of his jeans, he stepped away from her, leaving her kissing nothing but air.

"We'd better get back," he said. "Jessica forgot her wedding notebook and I volunteered to grab it for her, but if I take too long, she might get suspicious and come looking."

Renee nodded and started for the door, but before she could reach it, Jeremiah grabbed her arm and pulled her in for one last kiss. This time, she was the one who pulled away, though reluctantly. "The notebook, remember?"

He gave her his sexy sideways grin. "Couldn't help myself. I'll see you out there."

She left him to search for the notebook and headed back to the barn, heady from the kiss.

This day was definitely in the running for the best day of her life.

Nine

Jeremiah moved another chair into place as per Jessica's instructions, and went to grab a few more. Renee was a couple of rows ahead of him with Jessica, adjusting the angle so the seated guests would all be facing the altar area at the far end of the barn. Her strawberry blond hair fell in her face in a way that sent a delightful pang through his heart.

He had it bad, there was no denying it. What kind of trouble was he getting himself into?

Once they were all working as per Jessica's instructions, she disappeared inside to double-check something while the rest of them continued with the barn. Jeremiah hoped Aaron would leave as well and give him some time with Renee, but no such luck.

When they were finished, Aaron said, "I'm heading back to the house. You two coming?"

Finally, Jeremiah thought.

"I want to adjust a few of these rows first," Renee said immediately.

"I'll help. We'll meet you up there in a few minutes," Jeremiah added.

The moment Aaron was gone they headed for each other. A couple of minutes was all they had, but they took advantage of it.

Renee was in Jeremiah's arms immediately, and the carnal passion of her kiss sent fire through his veins and straight to his groin. When her tongue slipped past his teeth, it was all he could do not to pull her to the ground and take her right there.

"We'd better go in," Renee said when they broke apart, much too soon for Jeremiah's taste.

"I'm right behind you," he said, trying to bring himself back under control.

He watched her walk toward the house, a now-familiar pain in his heart.

Renee walked into the house and almost tripped over a suitcase. Her suitcase. Before she could formulate any thoughts beyond the oddity of her suitcase being in front of the door, Jessica was walking into the room with her phone to her ear. She didn't look happy.

"We'll see you tomorrow then. And you're sure it'll be dry by Thursday?"

She nodded to herself, thanked whoever she was talking to, and hung up with a sigh. Renee was still standing in the doorway, utterly confused.

Jessica looked at her sister with an exasperated smile. "You know how something always manages to go wrong?" she asked.

Renee walked over to her sister, preparing herself to deal with a Jessica freak-out. *Wrong* was one of her sister's least favorite words. "What happened?"

"A pipe burst upstairs while we were out in the barn. The carpet in the guest rooms is completely soaked."

Renee's eyes grew wide. Jessica just shrugged, and Renee wondered if she'd actually heard her sister correctly. How could she be so calm? "You're handling this really well," she said.

"I panicked at first, but a plumber's on his way, and I just got off the phone with a carpet cleaning company. They'll be coming by tomorrow, and they promised everything will be dry and ready by the time people start arriving on Thursday. It's all under control."

Renee's suitcase suddenly made sense. "My room—"

"Flooded," Jessica finished.

Renee nodded. "I'll just get a hotel room for a few days. No big deal."

Jessica shook her head. "You don't need to do that. I'm sure Jeremiah will help us out and take you in for a couple days. If that's okay with you."

Renee's heart started to pound so hard it hurt, and she felt like jumping in the air. A couple of days—and nights—at Jeremiah's? Yes, please.

She forced herself to nod calmly. "That's fine."

Her inner self was dancing a jig, and it seemed like every inch of her was revving up for what surely lay ahead. *Lay* being the operative word.

Was it too soon to leave?

Apparently not, as Jeremiah walked in the door and placed his hand on the top of her suitcase. He acted casual, but his eyes were gleaming with a fire that heated her entire body. "Did Jessica tell you about the pipe?" he asked.

She nodded.

"Are you okay staying with me for a couple of days?"

She wanted to laugh at the hesitation in his voice. She wanted to fist pump the air and have an impromptu dance scene like in a Bollywood film.

She nodded again.

He smiled. "Great. I'll get your suitcase in the truck. We can leave whenever you're ready."

Oh, she was ready.

Jessica gave her a quick hug. "Thanks for being so good about this. You two can come over tomorrow if you want, but we'll be able to get along fine without you if you want to explore the town or something. Thursday will be a busy day, though."

Renee's brain was only capturing words in fits and starts, but she understood the gist. Sex all day tomorrow.

After reassuring herself that her sister really wasn't freaking out over the carpets, Renee followed Jeremiah out to his truck and hopped in. Hell, she practically flew in. Jeremiah got behind the wheel, and then they were on their way to his house and complete freedom.

Neither spoke at first, but the grin on Jeremiah's face spoke volumes. Renee clasped her hands in her lap, trying to keep them off Jeremiah until they were at his house. It took only a mile for her to fail in that attempt, and she unbuckled her seat belt, slid over on the bench seat and buckled into the middle seat, tucking her body close to Jeremiah's.

She saw his jaw tighten, and a rush of desire enveloped her. He was attempting desperately to hold himself together, but he was going to break if she had anything to say about it. She ran her hand along his leg, from his knee up to his thigh, then up a little farther.

"We're never going to make it the five minutes to my house if you keep doing that," he told her through his clenched teeth.

"Maybe I don't want to wait that long."

Renee had spent enough time on their first ride imagining them having sex in his truck that she was pretty sure they could make it work just fine. And she was certainly willing to try it. Leaning over to nibble on his ear, she said, "Five minutes seems like a very long time."

He growled in agreement, and the truck bounced slightly as he pulled it off the road and behind a small copse of trees. Before she had time to react, the engine was off, as were their seat belts, and she was engulfed by his scent and warmth as his arms wrapped around her, pulling her onto his lap.

She found herself settled between him and the steering wheel, his lips and tongue drawing a line of fire along her collarbone as his hands danced around her breasts, turning her nipples into hard buttons of sensation. Feeling his hard hot erection pressed against her leg made her pulse jump, and her heart pounded so hard in her chest that she might have been worried if she'd had the ability to think.

She leaned back against the wheel, giving him more access, and he took advantage of it. Her bra was unhooked in seconds, and her shirt was lifted, exposing her chest to his ministrations. His tongue swirled around the areola of first one breast, then the other, and then he took each of her nipples into his mouth in turn.

She pressed herself back into the steering wheel harder. It took several seconds and Jeremiah's anguished movements away from her chest before she realized she was leaning on the horn.

Jeremiah groaned. What the hell was he doing? Had he really been planning on them having sex right here, in this very not-secluded spot fifteen feet from the highway? The loud insistent horn was just the icing on the cake to ensure that they would be caught.

As delicious as Renee was, he forced himself to stop. He wanted her naked, but he would need to wait the few minutes until they reached his house. It was definitely a view he wanted to keep all to himself.

Renee slid off his lap onto the seat beside him, then moved back to her original spot, leaving the middle seat open between them. Jeremiah knew he should be happy for the brain-clearing space, but all he wanted was to pull her back on his lap. Not touching her seemed like an impossible challenge.

He fumbled with the key, trying to get the engine to start, but all his attention was on her. With her hair and clothes disheveled, her skin tinged with pink, as if she was very warm, she looked so sexy that he couldn't pull his eyes away.

It was only when she looked at him with that fire in her eyes and in a husky whisper told him, "Your place. Now," that he managed to turn to the task at hand.

With herculean effort, he got the truck started and back on the road. Neither of them spoke, but their heavy breathing filled the cabin with barely controlled desire.

When they were almost at his ranch, he had himself under control enough to glance at Renee again out of the corner of his eye. She had put herself mostly to rights, but her parted lips and lowered eyelids gave away the fact that she hadn't managed to calm down completely.

Perfect.

He forced himself not to speed too much the last mile, and then they were parked beside his house. The moment the engine died, Renee was back on his lap, by his efforts or hers, he couldn't be sure.

He kissed her, plundering her mouth and sending his body into a frenzy. He managed somehow to get the truck door open, and without removing his lips from hers, he held her tight to his body and got them both out of the truck.

Once they were on solid ground, Renee straightened up and stood beside him. "You can show me your place later," she said, breathless, as she pulled him toward the door.

He fumbled with his keys in his haste to get the door open, but somehow he managed it, and then they were inside. The moment the door shut behind them, Renee was back in his arms, her body pressed against him, making him groan deep in his throat. God, she was sexy.

She pulled her shirt over her head, and he ran his hands over her creamy smooth skin. She shivered at his touch. Another shot of heat went straight through his heart and down to his cock, pushing the zipper of his pants to its limits.

Renee slipped off her bra, exposing her luscious breasts, her erect nipples. He leaned over to suck one into his mouth, satisfaction coursing through him as she gasped. He wanted to give her the time of her life. "Tell me another one of your fantasies."

She was silent for a minute, as if she was thinking. He moved to her other breast, swirling his tongue around the pert nipple before bringing it into his mouth, his teeth scraping lightly against her skin, earning him another gasp, this time turning into a moan that he felt through to his core. "Cowboy hat," she managed.

He had to smile. "The New York City girl has a thing for cowboys, huh?"

"Not until I saw you," she said.

He liked this woman. Every second that he passed in her presence made him more and more sure that he wanted to be with her beyond just this week.

He pushed that thought away. For now, he was just going to enjoy the present, and he was going to make sure she enjoyed it, too. He pushed her gently onto the couch and opened the coat closet near the door, grabbing his cowboy hat from the shelf.

"No shirt!" she called out from her spot on the couch, making him chuckle.

"Yes ma'am," he said in his most twangy cowboy accent.

As per instructions, he took off his shirt and placed the hat on his head. When he turned around, he gave her his most smoldering smile, tilted his hat to her, and said, "Howdy."

He'd never actually said "howdy" to anyone before in his life, and the moment he said it he realized how stupid it sounded. She laughed, and so did he. He took off the hat. "Didn't really pull that off, did I?"

She shook her head. "Nope. How can you be so bad at acting like a cowboy? You *are* a cowboy."

"I've been so busy taking care of horses and other actual cowboy things that I forgot to take lessons on how to say 'howdy' just like they do in the movies. I never learned how to spit tobacco juice, either."

Renee grimaced at the idea of airborne tobacco liquid. His heart thumped. How did she manage to make a grimace cute? Man, he had it bad for this woman. "Okay, no fake cowboy talk.

I can still pull off the hat, though. After all, this is my actual hat, so I should be able to make it seem real."

He put the hat on his head again, tipped forward, and then pushed it up with one index finger so it slid backward. Fire danced in Renee's eyes, and she exhaled slowly, nodding. She didn't say anything, but she didn't have to.

Walking over to her, he noted how her eyes roved over his entire body. He wanted to move faster, so it could be her hands instead of just her eyes that were doing the touching, but if this was one of her fantasies, he wanted to do it right.

When he reached where she was sitting on the couch, he dropped to his knees in front of her. She spread her jean-clad legs farther apart to allow room for him, and he put one hand on each of her legs. As his hands slid along the fabric toward her thighs, he could feel her body tensing with excitement.

His hands kept going until they reached where the material joined, and one hand rubbed over the area, creating pressure on the sensitive skin beneath. When she leaned back at his touch, spreading her legs wider for him, the pressure in his own jeans reached a new capacity he would've imagined to be impossible.

He kept rubbing, reveling in her pleasure, and his gaze slid from the damp spot on her jeans that showed exactly how excited she was up along her smooth stomach, lingering on the luscious peaks of her breasts, and finally landing on her entrancing face. Her head was tilted back against the couch cushions, her lips slightly parted. Her eyes were open and looking down at him, watching what he was doing.

His whole body tightened as he looked at her. He took the hat off his head and placed it on hers, then leaned forward and began kissing, biting and licking the silky skin of her stomach that he'd admired moments before. He pressed in closer, spreading her legs even wider and giving his mouth access to her pert breasts, teasing the already-hard nipples with his tongue until Renee's breathing turned ragged.

He kept going, touching and licking until her body shook as

an orgasm washed through her. She cried out with the force of it, and his dick jumped so hard at the sound that he would have worried about the zipper of his pants if he'd been able to think of anything but Renee.

As she came back to Earth, he leaned back slightly to get a better view of her face beneath the cowboy hat. Her eyes were closed, all the muscles of her face relaxed. "Was that what you had in mind?" he asked her.

She began to nod, then opened her eyes and smirked at him from beneath the brim of his hat. "Well, it was a good start, but the fantasy isn't over yet."

With that, she pushed lightly on his chest until he was resting on his haunches. Then she undid her jeans and slipped them off, revealing lacy black panties and shapely legs. When she took the panties off, too, he could hardly control himself, but he stayed still, watching to see what she would do next.

She planted her legs on either side of him once again, opening herself fully to his view and making his heart pump so forcefully that one part of his mind wondered vaguely if he might have a heart attack. If he did, it definitely wasn't the worst way to go.

Renee leaned forward and hooked a finger into one of the belt loops of his pants and tugged him back onto his knees in the space between her legs. She stopped tugging, but he kept moving forward, placing one of those smooth bare limbs over his shoulder as he leaned in to taste her.

As his mouth slid over her sex, she moaned his name. Fire shot through his veins. "Dammit, Jeremiah," she said in a husky voice, "I was trying to be the one in charge, and now I can barely move."

"Do you want me to stop?" he asked, moving back slightly.

"God, no."

He chuckled and leaned forward again. His tongue flicked her clitoris until he knew she was almost at the edge of another orgasm, and then he slipped a finger inside her. She gasped out, "You. Inside."

He couldn't have made a coherent sentence at that moment, either. He unzipped his jeans and finally let his throbbing erection free. As he slipped on a condom, she took the hat off her head and put it back on his.

Before he could change positions, she looped her hands around his neck and pulled him toward her, and then her lips were on his, kissing him as if her life depended on it. She wrapped her legs around him, and still crouching in front of the couch, he entered her. She groaned deep in her throat, but didn't break off the kiss.

He sank into her warmth, then pulled almost entirely out, then back in. As he started a rhythmic motion, she copied it with her tongue inside his mouth. It drove him wild, and he moved faster and faster until they were hanging on to each other, gasping with the intensity of the moment. And then she was gone, crying out his name as she climaxed, and he followed.

Once Jeremiah had slightly regained the ability to think, he tightened an arm around Renee's waist and shifted until he was on the couch with her on top of him, her weight settled on his chest. He wasn't quite ready to slide out of her yet. It felt so good to be with her like this. So *right.*

She lifted her head and gave him a contented smile. He wondered if she felt it too, but he wasn't ready to ask. Not yet.

Instead, he said, "I need a shower. How about you?"

"A shower sounds fantastic," she replied.

They left their clothes in a disorderly heap on the living room floor, forgotten.

Renee woke up slowly, enjoying the pleasant ache in her body from so much physical activity. The night before replayed in her mind and she smiled with her eyes still closed. Then her stomach grumbled and she realized she was starving.

She was more than glad to be out from under Jessica's watchful eye, but dammit if she couldn't use one of Aaron's epic breakfasts.

She finally opened her eyes and saw that she was alone in bed. Where was Jeremiah?

As Renee got out of bed to search for him—and hopefully find food along the way—she remembered that all her clothes except what she had worn yesterday were in her suitcase, which was still in the back of Jeremiah's truck. And the clothes she was wearing had never made it off the living room floor.

In her relaxed state, jeans seemed way too much hassle even if they were easy to find.

A quick glance around, though, and she discovered that her jeans actually were very easy to find. All her clothes, in fact. They'd been folded and placed on an overstuffed chair in the corner of the room, beside a clean pair of men's pajamas.

Her heart started to melt before she reminded it that this was a fun fling and there was to be no heart melting involved. It was a nice gesture, sure, but not something to get all gooey about.

Just to prove that this was all supposed to be sexy and not real life, she left the pajama pants on the chair and only put on the shirt. It was long enough to cover her, but not by much.

Then she went off in search of Jeremiah.

The moment she opened the bedroom door, she could hear music playing somewhere in the house. She saw that her suitcase was beside the door, where Jeremiah must have put it while she slept, then continued to follow the music down the stairs.

She hadn't noticed the decor the night before, but Jeremiah's sprawling home was painted in warm Southern tones, with wooden furniture throughout the place. It was elegant, but so very country. She half expected to find a painting of a desert on one of the walls.

By the time she had made her way through the living room to the kitchen, she recognized the song and couldn't stop the smile that spread across her face. He was listening to *Sexy and I know it* by LMFAO.

She stepped into the kitchen doorway just as it reached the chorus, and was greeted with Jeremiah dancing at the stove, a spatula in his hand, singing along. His back was to her, so she stood and took in the scene without interrupting.

"I'm sexy and wiggle wiggle wiggle wiggle, yeah! Wiggle wiggle wiggle wiggle, yeah!" he sang, slightly offbeat.

He shook his jean-clad ass with every "wiggle," and she had no idea why it was sexy when it should have been absolutely ridiculous, but man, he had a nice ass.

Then he noticed her and turned down the music. "Was it too loud? Did I wake you?" he asked.

She shook her head. He didn't seem self-conscious at all about being caught wiggling with a spatula in his hand, which just made him even more adorable.

Sexy, not adorable, she reminded herself. And it was sexy, though how that was possible, she had no idea.

"Nice dancing," she commented.

He gave her a smile that turned her legs to jelly. "Yeah, I considered becoming a professional, but you know how it goes."

His eyes lit up as they raked over her from head to foot, lingering at the hem of the shirt that only just covered her. Her pulse sped up and she could feel heat flood her body. There seemed to be more than just shallow attraction in his expression, though. Something akin to contentment was mixed in with the desire in his eyes, and that made her hesitate. She wanted to say something sultry, to keep things flirty and sexy between them.

That was when she noticed what he was wearing over his clothes. It was a neon-green apron—covered in cats. Her train of thought veered wildly.

"You bought *yourself* one of those ugly aprons? I thought that thing was a joke you played on Aaron."

He looked down at the hideous item in question. "There was a sale going on. Buy one, get one half off."

She tried to stifle her laughter, but wasn't very successful. "You still paid money for it, though? Real dollars?"

He smiled and nodded. "I thought it was pretty bad at first, but it's grown on me. And the green looks way better than Aaron's pink one. And everyone loves cats."

His self-confidence amazed her. She'd never met anyone so comfortable with themselves. How did he do that?

Jeremiah's voice broke into her thoughts. "Breakfast? I made waffles and sausage," he said, gesturing with his spatula.

Her stomach growled in response, and she sat at the table as he brought over a steaming plate that smelled absolutely delicious. She wasn't sure what made her mouth water more: the food, or the cook.

He caught her gaze as he set down the plate and gave her a look that liquefied her insides. The cook, definitely. Even in his silly apron.

A thought occurred to her as she doused her waffles in syrup. "Does Aaron know you have one of those aprons, too? He didn't talk like he did."

Jeremiah shook his head. "No, and you can't tell him. Otherwise I won't be able to tease him about it anymore, and what's the fun in that?"

She tried to come up with some reply, but her thoughts were distracted by the crispy, sweet creation she had just stuffed into her mouth. As soon as she swallowed, she shook her head. "What is it with you guys and amazing breakfast food? Is that a Texas thing?"

"No, it's a 'my mom' thing. She insisted I help with the cooking when I was a kid, and Aaron was over so often as we grew up that he learned, too. I can also make a mean chicken parm. And my snickerdoodles kick ass."

"Is there anything *not* awesome about you?" she asked. She said it jokingly, but in a way she was serious.

Why did this guy, the one who lived far away and she'd met at the worst possible time, have to be so absolutely perfect? Why couldn't he just be a sexy way to spend a week, no strings attached?

Because she hated to admit it, but strings were attaching all over the place, and it was going to hurt when all those strings broke.

"I can't roll my tongue, I always lose at Monopoly and you just saw my dancing. No more to say about that."

Dammit, none of those was bad enough. She took another bite, savoring the flavors and trying to push the worry out of her head. She would just need to enjoy the here and now, and prepare herself for the inevitable end of this whole thing.

As she looked around the kitchen, she noticed one strike against him. "Don't forget that you decorate with antlers."

Jeremiah looked at the antler chandelier hanging down from the ceiling. "Yeah, I guess it must seem pretty crazy to someone not from around here. It's just the way everything's always been and I never thought to change it when my parents moved out."

Jeremiah went back to the stove and got his own plate, then sat down beside her. He poured syrup on his waffle while he said, "So, did you want to go into town today and see some of the sights, or—"

"Or. Definitely or," she said, cutting him off.

He gave her a grin so full of promise that the temperature in the room went up by a few degrees. She resisted the urge to fan herself with her hand. This was what she'd wanted. No more of that gooey sweet stuff. "Good," he said, "because there isn't really anything to see in town. I don't know what we'd do there."

"We can just stay here, then. I'm sure we can come up with ways to pass the time," she responded with a flirtatious raising of an eyebrow.

Jeremiah took one of her hands and brought it to his mouth, biting lightly at her palm. The sensation shot through her body, settling low in her stomach. "I have a few ideas," he said.

She wanted to giggle like a schoolgirl. Yes, this was going to be a good day.

When they were finished eating, she picked up the plates and took them to the sink, aware that she was giving him a good view of her backside as she did so. By the way he cleared his throat and the flush on his skin when she turned around, she was sure he'd taken full advantage of the opportunity.

"Well, what should we do first? We have the entire day free," she said as she walked back toward him, aware of just how much of her legs was on display.

He held out his hand as if asking for help out of his chair, but when she took it, he pulled her into his lap instead of getting up himself. She could feel his body hard against her in more ways than one.

"Well," he began, sliding the collar of her shirt off one shoulder and nipping at her skin in a way that sent bolts of pleasure through her. "I can think of a few different options."

His bites and kisses traveled across her exposed shoulder and onto the base of her neck.

"Like what?" she asked in a hoarse whisper. She tilted her head back to give him more access, and he immediately took advantage of it.

"We could play hours of Monopoly, or we could have sex."

His hands slid under the hem of the shirt and began moving along her body, leaving trails of heat wherever they touched.

"Hmmm, let me think about that," she said, her eyes closed as she enjoyed his attentions. "I actually hate Monopoly," she told him.

"Good. Me, too."

Ten

Jeremiah sat up slightly, looking up and down Renee's beautiful body, his fingers trailing along her side. She squirmed slightly at his touch and moved even closer to him. His heart slammed in his chest. Opening her eyes and stretching, she said, "I haven't taken a nap in years."

"How was it?"

She sat up and gave him a sleepy grin. "Wonderful. The US should really get on board with this *siesta* thing."

While he was watching her sleep, he'd been considering something, and now he came to a decision. He got up and started dressing. "I want to show you something, Renee."

She leaned on her elbow and looked at him, as if she was trying to figure out what was going on. He knew that getting closer frightened her, but he needed her to know about this side of him, even if she wasn't totally ready for the next step. For a moment, he thought she might refuse.

She nodded and rose, putting on clothes without a word.

His heart started pounding again, but this time for a different reason. Very few things made him nervous, but he was anxious about this. Still, he was going to go through with it, come what may. He wanted her to know about him, just like he wanted to know everything about her.

Once they were both dressed, he walked with her down the stairs and out the back door to a large old wooden shed that used to hold gardening supplies and other equipment. When they got there, he leaned against the door and looked at her.

She smiled at him, a little nervously, he thought. At least he wasn't the only one. He took a deep breath before opening the door and ushering her inside. Dust motes floated in the sunlight filtering through the windows around the room he'd turned into a studio, and here and there the light bounced off his statues, making colors dance on the ceiling.

Renee walked among them silently, studying each one with a deep solemnity, as if she was wandering through a cemetery. When she reached out and ran her hand along the edge of the one he called *Mother and Daughter*—two leaf-shaped pieces of copper, the larger curled around the smaller—he couldn't wait any longer. "What do you think?"

"You made these?" she asked.

He bit back his nerves, which he thought might break if she didn't give him her opinion. "I started a couple of years ago. I wanted to learn how to solder and cut different types of metal, so I practiced by making different designs and it just sort of turned into this," he said, sweeping his hand around the studio. "I know they're not great—"

"Are you kidding?" she said, interrupting him. "These are amazing. You're an artist."

All the tension eased out of his body. She liked them. "I wouldn't call myself an artist. It's a hobby."

He tried not to let her know how much it meant to him, but she seemed to know anyway. And her earlier reticence seemed to have disappeared. She touched another one, her fingers dancing across the overlapping aluminum squares. "You could sell these, you know. I'm sure you could."

How many times had he thought about trying to sell them? Hundreds, probably. He'd even gone so far as to research different places that might want to purchase them. But something always made him decide against it. "You think so?" he asked, his self-consciousness draining away.

She touched another one, her palm resting against the spidery slivers of wire that had taken so long to shape, and she moved around to see it from every angle. "I can't believe Jessica and Aaron haven't forced you to share these with the world. They're so beautiful."

When he didn't answer, Renee glanced up at him. He didn't need to say anything. "Why haven't you told your best friend about this?"

Jeremiah shrugged. "It's really personal. I don't think he'd get that."

"But you showed me," she said. It wasn't a question.

He nodded. There was so much he wanted to tell her. How much she meant to him, despite how short their time together had been. How this sort of thing didn't come along every day and they needed to see where it led.

But he didn't say any of that. Not yet. He didn't want to scare her away. Still, she must have seen some of it in his eyes, because she suddenly seemed nervous again and turned back to the statues, away from him. Her voice took on a light, friendly tone, in stark contrast to the quiet seriousness of a few moments before. "Well, I'd buy one for sure if I didn't live in a shoe-box-sized apartment," she said, standing next to one piece that was taller than her.

Jeremiah wanted to tell her to pick her favorite and it would be waiting here for her, but he stopped himself. The idea had too much future in it. She wasn't ready for future. Luckily, he was a master at keeping things light and carefree. Wasn't that what he'd done most of his life?

"Yeah, I guess I haven't really scaled them for New York City living. Maybe I should work on paperweight-sized ones. There's good money in the paperweight business, right?"

She seemed to appreciate the change in mood. "Oh yeah, paperweights are booming right now. People can use them to hold down their flash drives full of documents."

"Maybe I can make digital statues to hold down documents flying around in the cloud."

She chuckled and wandered around the last few pieces with a lighter step. He leaned against the wall, not feeling very light-hearted at all. Why was she so scared to get close to him?

When she was finished studying each statue, they walked back to the house. He was glad he'd shown her, but couldn't help but feel like he was just setting himself up for heartbreak. Every time he tried to get closer to her, she pulled away. Did he need to be hit over the head to see that she wasn't interested in a long-term thing? Why couldn't he get that through his thick skull?

Still, he couldn't stop himself from hoping that over the next couple of days he could convince her to give this thing a shot. It was too good, too right, to be for just one week.

Once they were back in the house, Renee turned to him and gave him a devilish smile, and that was all he needed to put away those thoughts for another time. He would deal with all that later. For now, there was only one thing he wanted to think about.

He walked up close to her and placed one palm on the small of her back, pressing her against his body as his lips met hers. They had an entire day alone together, and he wasn't going to waste it.

"I have been waiting for this moment," Jeremiah said.

Renee gasped as his arm encircled her waist, pulling her tight against his body. She melted into his eyes as he leaned in, his soft kiss promising so much more.

Applause and cheers surrounded her, taking her attention away from the sinfully sexy man in front of her.

They were in the barn, standing under the decorated arch. Renee looked down. The white fabric of her dress glittered in the light.

Renee sat up in bed, groaning. This was very bad. Her mind replayed the dream, and the feeling it evoked wasn't fear. It had been a happy dream, and *that* was what made her nervous.

She looked over at Jeremiah, able to just see him in the early dawn light. He was sleeping peacefully, and the sight of him made her blood rush with that insatiable desire she had felt since meeting him, despite the sexual escapades of the day before. But there was something else, too.

Her heart twisted in a tender way that made her want to jump out of the bed and get away as quickly as she could. She had a pretty good guess what that feeling was, and it was the exact feeling she didn't want to have. Not here.

Panic rose in her throat as she pictured herself in Jessica's shoes, living in a big country home in Texas, miles away from everyone and everything. Her dream job no more than a memory.

She couldn't let that happen to her. She wasn't going to be some Texas wife, whatever her feelings might be.

Suddenly antsy, she got out of bed and went to her suitcase lying open on the floor. Grabbing some clothes and her computer from her suitcase, she left the room and eased the bedroom door shut behind her.

Downstairs, she dressed and sat on the couch with her laptop. The best thing to do when her thoughts were jumbled like this was to work. It had gotten her through confusing and difficult times before; it would get her through this.

Renee opened the page she had begun to design and started her tweaks. She wished she had gotten Jessica's article and the photo onto her computer before leaving so she could have them in place while working on the page, but she had noted the length of the article and had the picture imprinted in her mind, so she could create the mock-up without them.

If she wanted this to look good, it would take time. Luckily, time was what she had, and she desperately wanted to fill it with something other than thoughts about Jeremiah and a future with him that couldn't possibly work.

She settled in, her eyes glued to the screen, and got down to business.

Jeremiah began to wake, but he felt so content and comfortable that he was in no hurry to get out of bed. With his eyes closed, he reached out to Renee to pull her closer. His hand only met empty space where he expected warm skin, though, and he opened his eyes. She wasn't in bed, and based on the cool spot beside him, she had been gone for a while.

He rose and threw on some clothes, wondering where she had gone and what she could be doing. The thought of her cooking breakfast made him chuckle. If she was, he'd happily eat her toast, burned or not.

When he got downstairs, he found her in the living room, not the kitchen, and felt slightly relieved. If she was as bad at cooking as she claimed, it was better that way. He started running through his list of possible meal options, trying to decide which one she'd like the most. He loved the way she looked when she bit into something delicious.

As he walked up to her from behind the couch, he could see her laptop on her knees, a magazine page blossoming on the screen. She was absorbed in what she was doing and hadn't seen him yet, so he stood for a minute and watched her work, adding lines and tiny details to the page that elevated it from a regular magazine page to an eye-catching design akin to a piece of art. It was still in an infancy stage, but he could see the final product shining through, and he was impressed.

His eyes shifted from studying the screen to the woman in front of it. Her hair was falling forward into her face, but she didn't seem to notice. Her entire being seemed focused on what she was doing, absorbed in her work. He wondered if he'd be able to create a statue that would capture the drive and focus she exuded from every line of her form.

Finally, he walked up to her and knelt behind the couch, only inches from her. "You really have a talent," he said.

She jumped, startled, and looked over at him. He gave her a smile, but it took her a couple of beats before she returned it, and his stomach turned unpleasantly. Something had changed since the night before. He didn't know exactly why, but a feeling of foreboding washed over him.

"Are you hungry?" he asked, hoping to dispel the unpleasant thought.

She nodded and turned back to her screen, not looking at him. "Yeah, but I need to get a little more work done."

"I'll whip up some omelets," he said, rising from the back of the couch.

"You don't *have* to, but I can't say no to that offer."

Her words were pleasant, but she still wasn't looking at him and her voice had the quality of someone reading from a script. He went into the kitchen and began working on breakfast while his mind tried to work through what might have changed since last night.

As he chopped, whisked and flipped, he managed to come up with a few theories, but nothing seemed to make sense, except that for some reason she'd decided to put more distance between them. It made his heart sink to think that she might be done with him, satisfied with her fling and ready to walk away.

His suspicions only grew when she came into the kitchen for breakfast. After politely thanking him for the meal, she said, "I should move back to Jessica and Aaron's today. I need to help with the last few wedding items, and the rest of the guests will be starting to arrive."

He chewed a bite, then swallowed. "What's going on, Renee?" he asked.

He needed to know. She finally managed to look him in the eyes. "I just think this shouldn't go any further. We've had our fun, but now I need to get back to reality. Finish my project for work and help Jessica."

He considered arguing with her, but let it go for the moment. They ate in silence, and once she was done she pushed back from the table. "I'll wash the dishes. Then will you take me back to Jessica's?"

"Is that really what you want?"

She gave him a forced smile. "Well, I'm not the biggest fan of washing dishes, but it seems only fair," she said.

He knew that move too well. He'd done it plenty of times, and he wasn't about to let her off the hook.

"That's not what I meant, and you know it."

She turned her back to him, as if she didn't want him to see her face, and began running water over the dirty dishes. "I think it's best for both of us if I get back to helping Jessica prepare for the wedding. It's why I'm here, after all."

Jeremiah opened his mouth to say something, but after a moment he closed it again. What was there to say? What she said was true. If she didn't want anything more than a quick fling, it would be better for them to stop before he got in so deep he couldn't get out again.

Not that he was by any means certain that hadn't already happened.

He watched as she finished washing the dishes and left the kitchen to gather her things, avoiding his gaze the entire time. When she left the house with her suitcase in hand, he followed.

Renee hated every second of the drive back to Jessica and Aaron's, which was all the more reason to leave Jeremiah's. She couldn't risk losing the willpower needed to break things off with him, and the more time she spent around him, the worse it would be. Better to get it over with now.

She wasn't sure if the drive felt like an eternity or far too short, but once they pulled up to the house, everything in her shouted to stay in the car, go back with Jeremiah and forget about all that other stuff.

She had to get out of that truck as fast as she could. Renee took off her seat belt and was about to open the door, but Jeremiah turned to her, the determination in his eyes pinning her in place. Renee willed him to just let her leave. No discussion, no explanation.

He put his hand on hers. "I want more than just this week, Renee," he said.

Renee's insides twisted painfully. She wanted to run away, but couldn't.

"One week isn't enough for me. I think this has a shot."

He looked at her with such sincerity that her heart melted a little, but she forced it to freeze over. There was too much at stake. Her career, the city she loved, her life. She couldn't let herself fall in love with this guy and lose all those things that were so important to her.

He seemed to be waiting for an answer. When she didn't say anything, he asked, "Don't you think we have something here?"

She pulled her hand out from under his and turned to the door so he wouldn't see the hurt in her eyes, the lie on her lips. "No, I don't."

Before he could say anything else, she had the door open and was out in the brisk morning air. She made her way to the house as quickly as she could, praying he wouldn't come after her before she could make it to the door. She wasn't sure what she would say if he did.

Her resolve could only last so long against those coffee-colored eyes.

When she made it inside the house without his intervention, Renee told herself what she felt was relief, though she wasn't quite sure she believed it. She took a deep breath to calm her roiling emotions, and hoped her face belied the truth festering underneath when Jessica appeared.

Clearly it didn't, as her sister's expression changed immediately from welcoming to worry. "What happened, Renee? Are you okay?"

Renee didn't want to deceive her sister again. There had just been too many lies lately. But she couldn't bring herself to explain the situation with Jeremiah, either. "I fell and hurt myself," she said.

It wasn't really a lie at all. Jessica looked at her with concern. "Are you okay?"

Renee said, "I will be," hoping it was the truth.

Without another word, Jessica ushered Renee into the kitchen and got her a cup of tea. Renee sipped the hot liquid, trying to settle her feelings. Aaron walked in from outside, carrying her suitcase. "Jeremiah just left. He asked me to bring in your bag," he said to Renee.

"He left without coming in? That's weird," Jessica said.

Aaron shrugged. "I know. I expected him to offer to stick around and help with everything today, but he said he was busy."

Renee didn't say anything, just took another swallow of her drink and tried to convince herself that it was good he left. It was over now.

She took one more swallow and grabbed her bag. "I'm going to get some work done before we get started on wedding stuff, if that's okay," she told them.

Jessica said, "That's fine. The tent guys should be here in an hour or so. Once it's up, we can get everything ready for the reception. You'll have some time to work this afternoon, too, when Aaron and I head over to the airport. Cindy and Mom and Stew are flying in today."

Renee remembered Jessica's freak-out over the phone about Stew coming to the wedding. It was just a few days ago, but felt so much longer. At any rate, Jessica seemed to have accepted his presence at the wedding.

Renee gathered her suitcase, the camera and—with only a little reluctance on Jessica's part—the article she planned to use in her spread design, then went up to her room and settled herself at the desk in the corner of the room, determined to get down to work.

She got everything she needed loaded onto her computer, then stared at the screen. She usually felt a level of excitement when she was putting the pieces together and perfecting her design, but she didn't feel that at all. She felt…

Sad. That was the only word she could come up with to describe it.

Her work had always helped her get over any negative emotions, and she was sure it could now. She just needed to focus. She put her hands to the keyboard, telling herself to just get started already.

She began clicking through various icons, opening Jessica's article and the picture she had taken. Her hands fell from the keyboard as she stared at the picture. It wasn't the barn or the brilliant sky or any of a hundred other aspects of the photograph that caught her attention. It was Jeremiah.

The picture only showed him from the back as he helped Aaron slide open the large door, but it was enough to render her speechless. His mop of dark hair was messy in a shaggy-chic kind of look, and his shirt was slightly wrinkled, as if he'd been working all day doing manly things, but she knew the truth of those little details.

They were like that because Renee had been riding him up in the loft not long before the photo was taken.

God, he looked good.

She closed the laptop with a snap and stood. She just needed some air and a couple of minutes to get her head in order, and then she'd be fine.

Before she could examine the idea too closely, she was on her way out the door she had just entered minutes before.

She saw Jessica and Aaron sitting in the living room as she passed from the stairs to the front door, but she didn't say anything and they didn't try to follow her, which was a relief. She just needed to be alone.

Well, not alone. You need to be with Jeremiah.

She hushed the voice in her head, dismissing the thought. She did *not* need him. She didn't need anyone. As long as she got this dream job, she would have everything she needed to be happy.

Yeah, right.

She had really started to hate that voice.

Renee walked as quickly as she could, trying to outrun it. It was only when she found the sun blocked by leaves that she realized she had walked into the shade of the trees behind the barn. She kept walking, breathing in the cool, wet air, until she heard the burble of a stream. It had to be the river she and Jeremiah had pretended to visit.

After a few more steps, she could see it. Shafts of light broke through the leafy ceiling and landed on the water, creating shining reflections on the surface. The spots where the water broke over rocks made it sound happy, as if the water was giggling.

A small smile touched Renee's lips. She really *did* like the tiny waterfalls. At least that was one less lie she had on her conscience.

The sound of the water was soothing, and she walked along beside the stream until her fingers felt stiff from the cold morning air. When she finally broke through the trees once more, she saw a group of men setting up the tent where the wedding reception would be held. It was huge and pure white, with windows dotting the sides.

Jeremiah's voice rose up in her mind. *The circus fire was intense. Get it?*

She chuckled, but wasn't sure the emotion she was feeling could be called amusement. Before more thoughts of him could overwhelm her good sense, Renee blanked her mind and went to find Jessica. If anyone could keep her so busy that she didn't have time to think of those coffee-colored eyes, that delicious body and adorable smile, it was Jessica.

Her sister was standing near the tent, watching as it grew to full height. Renee guessed Jessica was going over every inch of it with her eyes, looking for some tiny tear that might get caught by a gust of wind and somehow cause the entire thing to fall apart.

She pasted on a smile as she approached her sister. No sense in making her worry. "It's a beautiful tent, Jessica. It looks like everything is going according to plan."

Jessica nodded, but didn't seem fully convinced, though Renee wasn't sure if her sister was concerned about the wedding or about Renee.

Either way, Jessica said nothing and Renee didn't press her to find out.

In short order, the tent was in place and the horde of workers had packed up and gone, leaving the large, empty structure behind. Renee turned to Jessica. "What's first? Tables? Where are they?"

Jessica eyed her, as if she was suspicious. "Yes, but we can wait for Aaron, and he can call Jeremiah to see if he can help—"

"No!" Renee interrupted before realizing how odd it must seem. "I mean, we can lift a few tables without the guys. Strong, independent women and all that."

The "few tables" ended up being ten huge round ones that had to weigh a hundred pounds each, along with a dozen rectangular ones that weren't much lighter. Within fifteen minutes, both women were out of breath and sweating, despite the chilly morning air. Jessica and Renee dragged and rolled the tables until each one was in place.

Renee wished there were even more of them. Nothing like a little heavy lifting to stop the mind from wandering into forbidden territory.

The moment they were done, Jessica sat down on the ground, her face red, and she took a big breath. "Well that was fun."

Renee dropped to the ground beside her. "It wasn't that bad."

Jessica didn't answer, and they rested for a minute, looking around the tent. The circular tables were spread out over most of the space, waiting to become seating for the guests. Rectangular tables were relegated to the perimeter, where they would hold the cake, food and gifts. There was still so much to do before it would be ready, but Renee could picture how it would look, and it was beautiful.

Her heart ached a little and she felt a burning behind her eyes that couldn't possibly be tears. She stood again and turned away from her sister. "What's next? Chairs?"

From behind her, Jessica said, "You're kidding, right? Don't you want to take a little break? We have time."

Renee absolutely did not want a break. Breaks were when thoughts and feelings could intrude. Better to keep working. "Where are the chairs?" she asked in response.

Jessica heaved herself up with a groan and led Renee to the barn. Her eyes immediately flew to the loft as images swam to the surface of her mind, but she shoved them back into the past where they belonged and brought her eyes back to ground level. The chairs were standing bunched in a corner, as out of the way as fifty or so large and starkly white chairs could get. They must have been delivered the day before, Renee realized. While she was at Jeremiah's.

Before more unwelcome images could come calling, she grabbed a chair and started moving. They were heavy, not cheap fold-away chairs by any stretch of the imagination. Renee could feel her muscles burning, but she ignored them.

After they had moved nearly half the chairs, Aaron showed up. "I didn't realize you two were going to start all the heavy lifting without me or I would've been quicker with the horses," he said.

Jessica went over to him, settling into his arms like they had been made for her. She said something Renee couldn't quite catch, but she assumed it was about her pushing them to get things done. And what was wrong with that?

With Aaron helping, the job sped up, and soon all the chairs were in the tent, encircling the tables. Renee was about to ask what the next job was, but before she could, Jessica was shaking her head. "Nope, I'm calling a lunch break. We've done enough for right now and I'm starving."

Renee didn't feel hungry at all, but what could she say? She shut her mouth and followed her sister back to the house.

Eleven

Jeremiah sat on his couch, the silence of the empty house heavy in his ears. Renee was gone. And she had made it perfectly clear that she was done with him and their whatever-it-was. He had tried to make her believe that they had a future, but it didn't work, and her "No" as she left the truck still sat on his chest like a heavy weight crushing everything beneath it.

Now that he was home, he knew there was plenty he could do to distract himself, to stop his mind from going back to its favorite topic, Renee, but instead he sat on the couch.

Maybe if he could talk to her, really explain how he felt and why she should give them a chance, she would see the truth in it. They were great together. In the bedroom and out. He couldn't just let that all go so easily, could he?

But he'd need some kind of gesture, something more than just words. An idea formed in his mind. It would take time, but if he started immediately, it should be ready by tomorrow evening, the rehearsal dinner.

He stood and rushed to his studio, a determined smile on his lips.

* * *

Renee heard the sound of tires on gravel through her window and shut her laptop. She had managed to paste in the article Jessica had written and adjust the layout design to match the length. She had also added the picture of the men opening the front door of the barn.

Those things would normally take less than a half hour, but it was over two hours since she had sat down to work. She hadn't been able to find her focus.

She was also missing the sense of accomplishment that usually came when she completed a task for a layout.

Renee ran her fingers through her hair. Work had always been there for her, and now, when she most needed it, she felt dissatisfied.

She pushed away from the desk and headed downstairs. The babble of overlapping voices coming from outside grew louder as Jessica, Aaron and the newcomers approached the house.

As Renee moved to the front door, it burst open, and Renee's mother entered, all smiles. She was followed by her boyfriend, Stew; Jessica's best friend, Cindy; and Cindy's husband. The bustle was a welcome relief. If she was busy talking and catching up, maybe she could forget about the way Jeremiah's eyes sparkled when he was happy, or the way they dug into her soul when he was earnest.

After chatting into the evening, however, Jeremiah was no closer to disappearing from her brain. The only thing her attempt at distraction did was give her a headache. Pretending to be happy and pleasant was more work than she'd thought.

Finally, she couldn't take it any longer. "I think I'm going to head up to bed," she said, hoping she would get out of the room without much argument.

"Are you okay, Renee? You look pale," her mother said, concerned.

Renee shrugged. "I just have a bit of a headache."

Boy, was that the understatement of the year.

Everyone sent her to bed with well wishes, making Renee feel even crappier. All these loving, sweet people were here for Jessica's wedding, and she couldn't even pull it together for them? Over a guy she had no future with?

She dropped into bed, her stomach roiling with unpleasant emotions.

Another sleepless night and it was the day of the rehearsal dinner. Renee spent the day staying as busy as possible, determined to stick out the entire day and not let herself pine over something so tiny that didn't feel tiny at all. Everyone helped to decorate the tables for the reception and get everything ready for the rehearsal dinner celebration that evening. With everyone working together, though, it was finished in a few hours, and Renee had run out of things to do.

She steeled herself to make small talk and be a perfectly pleasant helper to Jessica, even though her heart wasn't in it. Luckily, Jessica came up and put a hand on her shoulder the moment the last table setting was in place. "Renee, you still look a little ill. I think you should take a break before the rehearsal dinner."

Renee was about to protest, but Jessica shook her head before she could say a word. "Go take a nap or something. Please."

The concern on Jessica's face tugged at Renee's heartstrings, and she threw her arms around Jessica and squeezed her tight. "Thanks, sister. I love you."

She hoped Jessica wouldn't ask Renee to explain any of her odd behaviors, and felt relieved when Jessica hugged her back and only said, "Love you, too. Now go get some rest."

Renee didn't need to be asked twice; she was exhausted.

The moment she dropped onto the bed, however, she sat back up. There was just too much Jeremiah in this bed for her to be comfortable. Instead, she grabbed her laptop and decided to bury herself in her favorite distraction—work.

The rehearsal dinner would be starting in a couple of hours, and Renee was sure she wouldn't have an opportunity to get much done until after the wedding the next day, so this was the best time to get some work in.

When Renee sat down at the desk with her computer, though, she couldn't find the motivation to get started. Why was she even putting herself through this? She had plenty of great pages that showed off her skills. She didn't need to make a new one.

And even if she still wanted to submit the new page, did she really need to put in hours of work to make it just a tiny bit better? She opened what she had done so far. It wasn't perfect, but it was very good already. Certainly good enough.

Renee shook her head. When had she ever thought something was "good enough"? She wasn't sure what had happened to her, but she knew exactly who it was that had started it. Jeremiah.

She hadn't seen him since she'd climbed out of his truck two days ago, but that didn't mean his presence hadn't been felt for those two days. In fact, now that she let herself admit it, all that time she'd spent with her mind blank, when she was hauling heavy tables into place and chatting with her mother, Jeremiah had been front and center, whatever she tried to do.

This fun fling, this impractical relationship, was making it impossible for her to do her job. Renee's frustration came out as she slammed down the lid of her laptop and paced around the room.

Jeremiah would be at the rehearsal dinner, and this was the time to end things once and for all. She needed to burn that bridge so it would stop beckoning to her, inviting her to cross into Texas housewife territory.

If she did, there would be no going back. Her career, her life in New York, were all too important to risk. If she needed to lose a bit of her heart in the process, well, then that was a sacrifice she was willing to make.

Jeremiah could feel his heart in his throat as he climbed out of his truck. He touched the bulge of his chest pocket, gathering strength from it. He would give Renee the gift as a peace offering, and then perhaps she would reconsider their relationship. Even if it was just temporary.

Temporary was better than nothing, and maybe it would be able to turn into something more. He could imagine her reaction to his present, and the thought of it made his heart beat faster. He was sure she would love it, and if he gave it to her in private, maybe they could have their own little party before rejoining the rehearsal dinner.

He walked along the side of Jessica and Aaron's house, following the light and noise, excitement making his pace nearly a jog. Now that he was here, he couldn't get to Renee soon enough. Behind the house, two dozen or so people were gathered, talking in small clumps. Large heaters were spaced throughout the crowd to keep away the chill that had been in the air the entire day, and everyone seemed happy and comfortable. The smell of barbecue and music filled the air.

The rehearsal dinner looked just as Jessica had described it: long tables laden with classic Texas barbecue and sides, friends and family mingling. He saw Jessica and Aaron surrounded by people they cared about, smiling and laughing, and felt lighter for a moment. At least this whole thing with Renee hadn't ruined anything for them.

And if he was lucky and things worked out, he was sure they would be happy about him and Renee being together.

Now he just needed to convince Renee.

Jeremiah's eyes found her almost immediately, standing beside an older version of herself and a man who looked like an elderly professor. It had to be her mom and the boyfriend, whom he had heard about from Jessica.

Before he could walk up to her and ask her for a private word, Renee saw him and hurried over. His heart jumped at the sight. *Maybe she finally sees that we have something bigger than a fling*, he thought.

Once she got closer, though, her eyes and expression turned

his hope to worry. She didn't look happy to see him—she looked exhausted. And determined.

She left the circle of light and music and gaiety, striding ever closer, and suddenly he didn't want her to get any nearer. He could see from her face that whatever she planned to say or do, it wouldn't be good. The excitement that had been building in him died.

Renee stopped several feet away from him, out of arm's reach. Before he could say anything, she said, "I wanted to let you know before you entered the party that I still don't want anything more to happen between us, just in case you were considering trying to discuss it with me. I've sowed my wild oats, and now it's over. We're done. Please leave it at that."

She didn't look him in the eyes once, and she left without his saying a word.

Renee walked away, wondering what she would do if Jeremiah stopped her, if he saw the tears in her eyes. She hadn't wanted to be harsh, but it was the only way to cut things off for good. Why did she have to say that thing about wild oats, like he was nothing to her?

You had to. He'd keep pushing otherwise.

Still, she couldn't stop thinking about how much that must have hurt him, and she knew that this had to be the last time she let herself get close to him. She'd only allowed herself one glance at him before turning away, but the pain on his face in that second had hit her like a punch to the gut, and she couldn't let herself fall into his arms again, only to hurt him another time. It was clear that he wanted far more than she could give, which was all the more reason to stay away from him altogether.

If luck was on her side, she thought, he would keep his distance until the wedding was over, and then she could go home and retreat into her work, into her little New York life, and that would be that. He could find a sweet girl who would be happy to live on a ranch in Texas, living the content country life, and she would…

Well, she would have her dream job. That would need to be enough.

She rejoined her mother and Stew. "What was that about, Renee?" the older woman asked once Renee was with them once again.

Renee tried to give a convincing smile. "I just needed to talk to Jeremiah real quick about something. For the wedding."

She left it at that, hoping her mother would drop the subject, and her stomach felt knotted with tension. Once this weekend was over, Renee was done with lying, that was for sure.

For a moment it seemed like her mother would ask another question, but then she turned back to discussing the cruise she and Stew would be taking in a few weeks. Renee breathed out a secret sigh of relief and tried to focus her attention on the two people in front of her, not the one she had left on the edge of the party.

Jeremiah left the circle of light and walked around near the horse paddock, avoiding the merriment of the rehearsal dinner. Ever since her very clear dismissal, Renee refused to even look at him, and it was driving him nuts. He could feel the object he'd brought for her weighing down his breast pocket, and now he felt stupid working so hard to have it ready in time. He took it out and looked at it.

He had made her a miniature statue of copper and silver pieces intertwined in a tiny dance. He knew she would like it, but how could he give it to her now? She wasn't going to let him get close enough to talk to her, let alone willingly follow him to somewhere private so he could at least hand it to her.

She had made it incredibly clear that she wanted nothing more to do with him, and now he was stuck at this party, watching her ignore him and feeling the weight of his gift like an albatross around his neck.

The nearest horse snorted at him, and he reached out and patted her nose. It was chilly away from the heaters that protected the party from the cold, but he didn't care. At least if he stayed away from the whole thing, he wouldn't have to constantly be hit over the head by the fact that she was completely done with him.

And then a distraction came along in the form of a brunette wearing glasses. "Jeremiah!" she called out, rushing over to him and giving him a big hug.

He returned the embrace, trying to push Renee from his mind and give her a genuine smile. It was an impossible task. "Hi, Kiki. I didn't think you were going to be able to make it."

"I wasn't sure I would, but I managed to wrap everything up in time. I flew in last week, but you know how my mom is. This is the first time I've had a chance to see anybody since I got back."

"It'll be good to have you around for a bit," he said.

She stared at his face intently for a moment. "How are you?" she asked, concern edging her voice.

How could she already tell something was wrong?

Before he could respond, Kiki's infamous mother appeared as if from nowhere. "I was wondering where you disappeared off to, Kerstin. You really should go visit with Aaron and the bride for a bit. He is your cousin, after all, and it's rude not to chat with her some," the older woman said while pushing Kiki's hair out of her eyes.

Jeremiah watched Kiki's controlled expression and wondered how hard it was for her to keep from rolling her eyes. If he hadn't been feeling so crappy, he would have found this to be pretty amusing.

"I already talked to them, Mom, and set up a lunch date with Jessica for after their honeymoon. I thought it would be better to let them talk to their out-of-town guests right now," Kiki said.

"Oh pshaw," her mother returned. "You're their *family.* I'm sure they would love it if you sat down with them for a bit."

Jeremiah wondered if Kiki would point out that all those other guests were also family, but instead she gestured at Jeremiah. "I can't right now, Mom. Jeremiah just asked me to dance and I said I would. It would be rude to go back on my word."

Her mother seemed disappointed, but said nothing. The last thing Jeremiah wanted to do was dance, but he couldn't leave Kiki in the lurch. They had been friends since grade school, and he was sure she would do the same for him. He took her hand and moved closer to the music, away from her mother's stifling presence.

Once they were dancing, she said, "Thanks. I owe you one."

"Your mom hasn't changed one bit, has she?"

Kiki shook her head, her lips pursed with what had to be unpleasant reflections. He thought it best to change the subject. "How was Beijing?"

Her expression smoothed into a small smile. "It was great. But we can talk about that later. Let's talk about you first. For instance, we can talk about what has you so down in the dumps."

He had thought he'd been pulling it off pretty well. He wasn't ready to talk about the whole Renee thing quite yet, however. Not with her sitting twenty feet away. Maybe once she was back in New York. Though Beijing was probably not far enough away to get her out of his mind, let alone New York.

Kiki seemed to sense his reluctance because she said, "Okay, different question—are you still playing the field? Sowing wild oats?"

Jeremiah had to smile. The humor of the situation wasn't lost on him. "No, I'm ready to settle down, I think."

"With a strawberry blonde bridesmaid?" Kiki asked, though by her tone it was clear she already knew the answer.

Jeremiah stopped dancing. "How did you know?"

Kiki smiled and shook her head. "You're easy to read, Jeremiah."

He shouldn't be surprised. She'd always been observant. "Yeah, well, she was just having fun and now she's over it. I knew she wasn't looking for anything serious from the beginning, but I let myself get in a little too deep. I'm getting what I deserve, I guess."

Kiki looked at him like he had just said the dumbest thing she'd ever heard. "You're kidding, right?"

He tried to figure out what she was thinking, but gave up. "What, Kiki?"

"You think that the woman who keeps looking at me like I stole her Christmas present was just in it for a little fun? Are you serious?"

Jeremiah seemed to be having trouble processing her words. "Stole her Christmas present?" he repeated.

"And knocked down the tree. And then set the house on fire. Still not clear enough? She definitely doesn't like that I'm dancing with you, Jeremiah."

Hope bloomed in his chest. "You think she's not done with me?"

Kiki slapped her own forehead. "I thought you were a pretty smart guy. Stop proving me wrong. Either she wants more than a fling and has some serious feelings for you, or she's crazy and a little scary."

Renee wished she could magically transport herself away from this rehearsal dinner, but she was stuck forcing pleasant conversation with her mom and Stew when she felt anything but pleasant. She felt on edge and sleep deprived, and now she had to watch Jeremiah dance with a pretty brunette.

The worst thing about that was the knowledge that she had no right to dislike the way that woman smiled at Jeremiah. After all, Renee had told him they were finished, so what could she do but watch him move on to someone else?

Even though they were outside, she felt claustrophobic. She needed space to breathe. She turned her attention back to her mom, who was looking at her expectantly. She'd clearly missed something in the conversation and had no idea what kind of a reply was expected of her.

"I'm sorry, Mom, but I just thought of something I need to go take care of real quick. I'll be right back."

It wasn't great, but her mom nodded and Renee excused herself from the table. She needed a few minutes alone, and then she'd be able to handle the rest of the evening.

Renee made her way into and through the house, wanting nothing more than to flop on the bed, grab one of the pillows and breathe in the smell of it. Her body felt heavy, and she gave a sigh of relief once she finally made it to the top of the stairs.

She opened the door to her room and had taken a couple of steps before she registered that someone else was already there. Jeremiah was sitting on the edge of the bed, watching her with those deep brown eyes that threatened to swallow her whole. His presence was almost overwhelming, and she didn't know if she felt more anxious or relieved by his having him there.

She should ask him to leave. It was her room after all, at least for right now. Or she could just walk right back out and go somewhere else. Either option would be better than being in a room alone with him. She knew that. Instead, she closed the door behind her and walked farther into the room.

When he pulled her down to sit beside him on the bed, she did, and when he kissed her, all she could do was kiss him back. Her entire body was screaming out for her to be in his arms, and any little voice telling her it was a bad idea was shouted down. It felt so good to kiss him. She felt drunk from the sensation.

After a few seconds, he pulled away and rested his forehead against hers. "I've wanted to do that all evening. It's been torture being so near you and not kissing you," he said.

"You looked like you were having fun dancing," Renee said, trying to sound casual.

Jeremiah smirked and she knew he saw right through her. She flushed with embarrassment.

"That was Kiki, Aaron's cousin. She asked me to dance with her so she could get away from her mother."

Relief flooded her. "Not an ex-girlfriend," she said.

"Well, yeah, that, too."

The relief turned icy in her veins, but then Jeremiah laughed. "We dated for about a week when we were thirteen."

He pushed the hair away from her face, sending tendrils of desire through her. Her heart pounded in her chest. "So, not exactly the romance of the century?"

He smirked at her again. She wasn't sure if she wanted to punch his arm or kiss the look right off his face. Perhaps both in quick succession. "No," he answered, shifting even closer to her, making it difficult for her to breathe. "Aaron was so pissed when I broke up with her and made her cry. That's when I learned not to fool around with his family."

She stared at him, waiting for him to hear what he'd just said. His smile didn't change. "What about me?" she finally asked.

He touched her fingers lightly with his own, then moved them slowly up her arm. "Doesn't count."

She didn't know exactly what he meant, but she didn't care. All her attention was focused on his soft caress. All the resolutions she had made such a short time ago melted under those warm hands.

Jeremiah knew this was his one opportunity to convince her to give them a chance. He had to tell her the whole truth before she remembered that she wanted nothing to do with him. He took a deep breath. "I've always tried to go for the things I want. It's been kind of a life philosophy—"

"That explains why you ever thought it was a good idea to ask out that supermodel," Renee mumbled, almost as if she was talking to herself.

He stopped talking, thrown off by her comment. How did she know about that?

"Aaron told us the whole story," she explained. "I'm pretty

sure he tells it to everyone. It's pretty funny. How long was it until you were able to walk normally again?"

"Over a month," he grumbled, making her laugh.

"Anyway," he began again, trying to get back on track. He needed to just say it, so he plunged in headlong. "I'm in love with you, Renee."

She stilled and stared at him. Jeremiah, always so confident, had never felt less sure of himself. He might have just ruined any chance of easing her into a relationship, but after what Kiki had told him, and how he'd felt when he thought there was a possibility she had feelings for him, he knew he needed to tell her the truth. He'd been in love with her since he first saw her, and now she finally knew.

Silence stretched between them.

At last, Renee opened her mouth. Jeremiah held his breath, waiting for her response. "It's…a joke, right?"

He'd never felt more serious in his life, and as he realized that this conversation was not going to end the way he hoped, all he wanted was for it to be over. For a second, he considered lying and pretending he'd been kidding, but he couldn't do it, even if it would save him embarrassment. Renee deserved only honesty. "No joke," he said, trying to smile and shrug.

Renee covered her face with her hands and shook her head. "I can't," she said, her voice muffled by her hands.

Jeremiah stood.

He took out the small object that had been weighing down his chest pocket and set it on the bed where he had just been sitting. "For your shoe box apartment," he said.

Then he turned and walked out of the room, shutting the door behind him.

Twelve

The rehearsal dinner was winding down, and most people had gone home. Jeremiah stood outside the circle of lights, away from the merriment. Renee hadn't come back down to the party after their disastrous talk, and he wasn't sure if that was a relief or not.

Kiki walked up to him and gave him a hug. "It's good to see you, Jeremiah."

"Good to see you, too, Kiki. I'm glad you're back."

"Your talk with the bridesmaid didn't work out, I take it?"

There was no point to asking how she knew. He was sure it was pretty obvious that something was wrong with him; he just couldn't force himself to pretend to be his normal happy-go-lucky self when he felt anything but. She shook her head in sympathy. "If there's any way I can help, let me know. I'll be in town for a while. You know where to find me." She gave him one last hug and left, her mother chattering beside her.

Aaron came up to Jeremiah after Kiki had disappeared and slapped his shoulder. "You ready to go?" he asked.

Jeremiah had never been more ready for anything in his life. "Let's go," he said.

They went to Jeremiah's car, where Jessica was waiting. Aaron's overnight bag was sitting on the ground by her feet.

Aaron pulled her into an embrace. "I'll see you tomorrow, wifey."

Jeremiah got into his truck, allowing the couple their private goodbye. After a couple of minutes, Aaron climbed into the passenger seat and Jeremiah turned the key. Aaron rolled down the window and planted one last kiss on his bride-to-be, and then they were on their way.

Jeremiah tried to behave normally, for his friend's sake. "What made you two decide to do the whole 'night apart' thing? I didn't think you would be able to tear yourselves away from each other for that long."

"You only get married once. Or, at least, I do. So we're doing it right."

Jeremiah nodded and tried to think of something to say. Before he could think of anything, Aaron said, "So, you're still not going to talk to me about what's going on with you until after tomorrow?"

"Yep."

Then he would tell Aaron the truth about the whole thing. But until Renee was back in New York and Jessica was a happily married woman, he was keeping mum.

"Well, let me just say that whatever's happening, you need to fix it so you can get back to being your normal self. I've never seen you this tense and unhappy. It's not like you."

Why can't I be unhappy sometimes? Do I always have to be the jokester? Jeremiah kept the thoughts to himself. He couldn't snap at Aaron like that the night before his wedding. And he knew that he wasn't even annoyed at Aaron; he was annoyed with himself and the universe that would let him fall so hard for someone who refused to love him back.

Aaron said, "I don't expect you to be funny all the time or anything, I just want you to not be perpetually bummed out."

Jeremiah wasn't surprised that Aaron knew what he was thinking. They had been best friends for thirty years, after all. But he still didn't want to talk. "Why don't you tell me about the honeymoon?"

There was a beat of silence, and Jeremiah waited for Aaron to point out that he already knew about the honeymoon, but Aaron didn't. Instead, he filled the rest of the drive with the honeymoon itinerary. As they pulled into Jeremiah's driveway, he said, "I can't believe the flight is the day after tomorrow."

Jeremiah tried to muster up as much enthusiasm for Aaron as he could. "You're getting married tomorrow. I hope you're ready."

By the goofy grin on his friend's face, Jeremiah was sure his friend was more than ready.

Renee opened her eyes and squinted at the rectangle of light coming in her bedroom door, not moving from her prone position on the bed. Jessica was standing there, looking concerned. "I wondered where you had disappeared to."

Renee sat up with a sigh. She hadn't been asleep, but at least in the quiet darkness of her room, she'd been able to pretend she was back in New York, away from everything that was so confusing.

She ran her hand through her hair, trying to pull herself together, not an easy feat under her sister's unwavering gaze. "Sorry I left the party early. I was tired."

"Still not ready to talk about it with me, huh?" Jessica asked as she stepped into the room, sitting on the bed where Jeremiah had sat not very long before.

Renee thought about it. For a moment, she considered spilling everything to her sister, telling her everything that had happened. But she couldn't do that the night before the wedding.

What if Jessica was mad at her? Renee couldn't be the one to ruin the wedding.

Or worse, what if Jessica pushed her to talk to Jeremiah again? Renee didn't think she was strong enough to say no again. Not with those wonderful eyes staring at her, through her, as if they knew everything she wanted—

"Renee?" Jessica's voice cut into her thoughts.

She turned her attention back to her sister. "We can talk after the wedding."

Once she was back in New York and far away from Jeremiah's dangerously inviting arms.

Jessica still didn't look convinced. Renee smiled at her sister's stubborn nature. "I promise. We'll have a sisterly heart-to-heart when all this is done. Until then, all I want to do is celebrate your wedding with you. Okay?"

Jessica nodded and gave her a small smile back. "Fine. I won't ask you again until after the wedding. Now get some sleep. Tomorrow's the big day, you know."

With that, Jessica stood and walked out the door, closing it behind her. Renee was left in the dark. She reached over to the bedside table and felt around until her fingers landed on cold metal. It was the small piece of artwork Jeremiah had given her. She couldn't see it in the darkness, but the image was vivid and clear in her mind. It was only two inches tall, with copper and silver encircling each other in what could only be described as an intimate embrace. She ran her thumb along the curves of the design as she thought.

Jeremiah and Aaron sat at the kitchen table, where they'd been sitting since arriving hours ago. The time had passed in a mix of marriage talk and silence. Jeremiah didn't feel anywhere close to normal, but it was nice to spend a little time with his friend, and to see him so happy.

Aaron stood up with a groan. "It's late. I need to get some sleep. See you tomorrow?"

Jeremiah nodded. "It's a big day. I'll make you a special wedding-day breakfast."

He tried not to think about Renee sitting at this same table, eating the food he'd made for her. She had looked so cute. He stood up, too, though he couldn't imagine trying to sleep with his mind such a jumble.

Aaron seemed to sense his friend's thoughts. "What are you going to do?"

Jeremiah shrugged. "I think I'll go for a walk."

A walk would clear his thoughts. It was worth a shot, at least. Then maybe he'd be able to get some sleep.

Aaron picked up his overnight bag and headed for the stairs. "Don't stay out too late. As the best man, you're not allowed to take a nap during the ceremony. And I expect my breakfast bright and early. You can make it wearing that apron I noticed in the pantry, which looks suspiciously similar—"

"Another word and you won't get your matching hot pads," Jeremiah said, cutting him off.

"Fair enough," Aaron said, disappearing into the hallway.

Jeremiah's lips twitched. Then Aaron was gone and Jeremiah was alone in the big empty kitchen.

He shrugged on his jacket and headed out into the cold dark night, the sky above him bright with stars. He walked down along his property, every tree and building nothing more than dark shapes in the moonlight.

He had lived on this land all his life and could walk it blindfolded. It didn't give him any comfort on this night, though. Wherever he went, Renee was still there. He walked out into the brush, letting the cool air seep under his skin. But nothing helped.

His grandparents had bought the land when they were newlyweds. It had been their dream to own a ranch, and they'd worked it for fifty years, the last thirty as a family business with their grown son and his wife, Jeremiah's parents.

When Jeremiah's grandparents died, his parents moved to

Florida, leaving him to keep the land going if he wanted. Now that he looked around, though, he realized that he didn't really enjoy the ranching life. He'd just done it because he couldn't think of anything else to do. And even when he'd found something he truly loved to do, he didn't believe it could be a legitimate vocation.

But why couldn't it? He felt the need for some advice, and it couldn't wait.

He jogged back into the house and up the stairs to the guest room where Aaron was staying and banged on the door. "Aaron, get up. I want to talk to you about something. It's important."

Aaron opened the door, his hair a mess and his eyes bleary. "This better be good."

Jeremiah had been so intent on his own thoughts that he'd forgotten his friend was getting married the next day. "Sorry to wake you, but it'll only take a second. Come on."

Jeremiah led Aaron out to his work shed, Aaron muttering about how late it was the whole way. When Jeremiah opened the door and turned on the lights, though, the grumbling stopped. Aaron stared quietly at the sculptures filling the room. Jeremiah waited.

"You made these?" Aaron asked.

Jeremiah nodded.

Aaron slapped him on the back. "You're an artist. That's cool. You going to sell them?"

"Actually, I was thinking. What if I moved away from the ranch and did this full-time?"

Aaron thought about it for a second. "It would be weird to not have you nearby, but these are good, and if it makes you happy, then you should do that."

Jeremiah felt some of the weight on his chest lift. "So you don't think it's a crazy idea?"

"Way less crazy than waking me up in the middle of the night before my wedding day to show me a bunch of art. I'm going to bed now."

Aaron left, and Jeremiah looked around at his pieces, the possibilities open before him.

He knew he wouldn't be able to sleep, and the warring feelings inside him made his fingers itch. He stepped into the shed and got to work.

Renee opened her eyes. The sky outside her window was still dark, but she had been tossing and turning for so long that dawn couldn't be that far off. She checked her phone.

It was just a few minutes before five o'clock. She considered trying to go back to sleep, but after a few moments she stood and stretched. There was no point closing her eyes when all she saw was the way Jeremiah's face looked as he'd left her last night. Better to get up and have some coffee, maybe even try to get some more work done—though she had a feeling she knew how that would go.

She opened her door carefully, trying not to make any noise. As she walked down the stairs, she saw light streaming through the kitchen doorway. Someone had beaten her to the punch this morning, it seemed.

Renee entered the kitchen and found Jessica sitting at the table, a mug between her hands. "You're up early. Nervous?" Renee asked her.

Jessica shook her head. "Excited."

Renee got her own mug and sat down beside her sister, who would be getting married in ten hours. Jessica's eyes were sparkling, her cheeks rosy, and a little smile seemed permanently glued to her lips.

Renee couldn't think of a time when she'd felt as happy as her sister looked, except for a few glorious moments in Jeremiah's arms.

Renee tried not to let the heaviness she felt show. It was her sister's wedding day and she was *not* going to ruin it. "It seems like Stew won't ruin your wedding after all, right?"

Jessica sipped her coffee, looking over the rim at her. Renee thought she might return to the conversation topic from the night before, but she didn't. Instead, she rolled her eyes. "Fine, you were right. He's perfectly nice."

Renee tried to feel good about her sister's rare admission of fault, but she couldn't bring herself to gloat. "Is there anything we need to do this morning?"

Jessica nodded. "We need to put the centerpieces on the table and make our bouquets. We've got plenty of time, though."

Renee stood. She needed to feel busy. Idle time led to thinking, and she didn't want to think right now. Not about her job, not about Jeremiah. She went over to the buckets of flowers sitting in the corner of the kitchen and pulled out a handful of roses. "I'll just start getting the thorns off the roses. One less thing to do later."

Before Jessica could comment, her phone buzzed, for which Renee was grateful. She didn't need any lectures right now.

Jessica said, "Good morning, husband-to-be. Why are you up so early?"

He's probably just as excited as she is, Renee thought. She turned and focused on the flowers in her hands. She was happy for them, but that didn't mean she wanted to see Jessica's gooey look again.

"Really? Sculpting? It's weird that he never told us."

Renee smiled. Jeremiah had finally told Aaron about his artwork. When Jessica hung up, she wanted to ask about it, but stopped herself. It wasn't her concern.

That thought killed the smile on her lips and she turned back to the flowers.

"You ready?"

Jeremiah looked down at the rings and nodded.

Aaron fixed his tie one last time. "Don't be nervous."

"You're the one getting married, remember?"

Aaron smiled at the best man. "I've got the easy part. If something happens to those rings, Jessica will kill you."

Jeremiah put the rings inside his breast pocket and patted it. "Safe as can be."

"Then let's get out there."

Jeremiah followed Aaron to the far corner of the barn, where the decorated arch stood, waiting. They took their places and the music changed. Cindy, Jessica's best friend, came down first, with Renee following shortly after. Jeremiah kept his eyes off her, but it didn't stop his heart from pounding. Still, he ignored it and kept thoughts of her and their adventures in the nearby loft out of his head. This was about Aaron and Jessica.

Jeremiah heard Aaron let out a long breath and looked up to see Jessica in the barn doorway. She radiated joy as she walked toward Aaron and married life. Jeremiah couldn't stop himself from glancing at Renee. Her eyes were filled with tears as she watched her sister walk down the aisle.

Jeremiah wasn't sure if he hoped some of those tears were for him.

By the time Jessica had reached Aaron and was holding his hand, Jeremiah had torn his gaze away from the beautiful bridesmaid, determined not to look her way again, no matter how much he wanted to.

Renee leaned against the outer wall of the barn and breathed a sigh of relief. The ceremony had been difficult—forcing herself not to stare at Jeremiah the entire time was one of the hardest things she'd ever had to do, and it felt like her heart was tearing out of her chest the entire time. When Jessica had come down the aisle, the thought of what Renee might have given up made her want to cry.

But she wasn't Meg Ryan, and this wasn't some chick flick where everything worked out. Her life was too different from Jeremiah's, and that was all there was to it. And she was so close to being done with this whole mess. If she could avoid him for a couple more hours during the reception, she would be able to go hide in her room for the rest of the evening. After that, she just needed to sit tight until her flight Sunday morning, and then she'd be home free. For the time being, she would spend her hours looking forward to getting back to New York and going to work on Monday instead of mooning over Jeremiah.

The thought wasn't as appealing as she wanted it to be, but that was all the more reason to get out while she still could. Another day in his arms, losing herself in his eyes, and she wasn't sure she'd be able to leave. But for now, she could and she would, and it was really the best thing.

She didn't need anything but work to make her happy. Really.

Renee was thankfully pulled out of her thoughts by her mother's voice. "Renee! There you are! We have a problem."

At first Renee assumed it was about Stew's orange suit. "Did Jessica say something? Does Stew need to go find a different suit or something?"

By the look on her mom's face and the way she was glancing around as if she was worried someone was listening, Renee knew that whatever was going on was going to be worse than just the suit. She braced herself for something Jessica-freak-out bad.

The older woman didn't keep her in suspense. "There's no cake."

"What?" Renee asked, not sure she had heard correctly. As bad as Renee had guessed it would be, she hadn't imagined it would be *that* bad.

"The cake never showed. I just called the shop, and they lost the order or something, and now there isn't time to make one. You need to tell Jessica that she doesn't have a cake and find out what she wants us to do."

"*I* have to tell her? Why me?" This was really not Renee's best day ever.

"I know you can break the news to her calmly. Go on, the sooner the better. There isn't much time."

Renee dropped her head back against the wood behind her, then stood up straight. The reception was starting in ten minutes, and she was supposed to tell her sister that there wasn't going to be a cake. How the hell was she going to do that?

Renee forced herself to leave her mother's side and walked over to where Jessica and Aaron were taking pictures. They looked so happy staring into each other's eyes while the photographer's camera clicked over and over again.

Renee waited until there was a lull while the photographer set up for the next shot, then walked over to the happy couple. "So, funny story," she said, but then paused.

She wasn't sure how to say what needed to be said.

"What's going on?" Jessica asked immediately, her eyes narrowing.

Renee froze like a deer in headlights.

"Is it about Stew's suit? I know you tried to hide that from me, but I saw it and I'm okay. Worse things have happened."

Truer words were never spoken.

It was clear Renee wasn't doing a good job of easing into the bad news. At this point it was best to just come out with it. She said it all in a rush, as if that would soften the blow somehow. "The cake never showed, and apparently it's not going to make it."

Jessica's mouth opened into an O of surprise. "There's no cake?" she asked softly.

Aaron put his arm around her and squeezed. Renee felt guilty for some reason and kept talking to fill the silence. "Mom called the shop, and apparently there was an issue and your order wasn't filled. I'm sure you'll get your money back," she finished lamely.

Jessica kept staring at Renee, and Renee quietly waited for the meltdown. Aaron wrapped his arms around his new wife and tugged her close. Once her eyes moved away from Renee and focused on him, he kissed her lightly. "I'm sorry, babe. Tell me what I can do to help fix this so you can be happy on our wedding day."

Jessica's look softened as she stared into her husband's eyes, and Renee's heart, still raw from all it had been through, ached. Jessica took a deep breath and turned to her sister. "We'll survive. Ask Mom to MacGyver something for the cake cutting, but if we can't find anything in time, we'll just do without."

Renee was dumbfounded. Had she heard correctly? "*Mac-Gyver* something?"

Jessica nodded. "You know, pull something together. Preferably using a paper clip and some duct tape." She laughed at her own joke.

Renee couldn't believe this. "I know what it means to MacGyver something, I just don't understand. You're not going to freak out? What about needing everything to be perfect?"

Jessica looked at Aaron again. "Everything *is* perfect, with or without a cake."

Aaron rubbed his hand along her jaw and nodded, and they leaned in for a kiss so passionate it made Renee blush.

When they finally came up for air, Jessica broke away from Aaron, whispering in his ear. He nodded and walked out of earshot.

"We need to talk privately," Jessica told her sister.

Renee felt strangely relieved. "You really are freaking out. You just didn't want Aaron to know."

Jessica shook her head. "Nope. I really don't care about the cake. I'm sure Mom will figure out something that'll be fine." She put her hands on her hips and gave Renee a very big-sister look. "No, I wanted to talk to you alone so you could tell me what's going on with you. You've been mopey for days, and you promised you'd talk to me about it after the wedding. Well, it's after the wedding now. Spill."

"You know I meant later than this."

"Yes, but we have time right now and I want to help my little sister with whatever's going on. Let me help. Start talking."

Renee didn't want to tarnish her sister's wedding day by explaining exactly what she'd been up to that week. Even if Jessica was somehow magically okay with not having a cake, her little sister sleeping with the best man could send her over the edge into full-blown hysteria. Still, Renee needed to talk to somebody she could trust, and Jessica didn't seem like she was about to take no for an answer. Renee took a deep breath and chose her words carefully.

"I've been seeing somebody lately, but things got too serious and I had to break it off. I'm just trying to recover. It's no big deal, really."

"Why did you break it off?"

That was the question Renee had been answering in her mind over and over again. "I can't be in the kind of a relationship he wants. Not with this new job starting."

Jessica shook her head, her curls bouncing elegantly around her shoulders. "No, Renee. It's time you stop hiding behind your job."

Renee was about to argue, but Jessica continued, "Ever since Dad died, you've thrown yourself into your work and distanced yourself from everyone. It's true, so don't argue. I think you're afraid to fall in love and then lose someone."

Renee felt dumbstruck for the second time in less than ten minutes. Was that what she'd been doing? She didn't know for sure, but the idea made her stomach feel queasy. She pushed it to the side to examine later. She grasped for the train of thought Jessica had derailed. "Well, there are other problems. He doesn't live in New York, for one—"

"—and I'm guessing you didn't even talk to him about how to work around that," Jessica interrupted. "Go on, what else?"

Renee sighed, exasperated with her sister's know-it-all attitude. She seemed so sure everything was fixable, but she didn't understand and Renee couldn't explain it without telling her secret. "It's not that easy, Jess. I can't just move and give up my job and everything I am for a guy."

There was a silence as Jessica absorbed what she had said.

"That's what you think I did, isn't it?" Jessica asked, her hands flat against the front of her gown.

Renee didn't answer.

"I didn't give up my identity, Renee," Jessica said, her voice quiet but firm. She put one hand on Renee's arm and looked her straight in the eye, as if trying to get her to listen carefully to what she had to say. "I found a guy and a place that matched my identity. I was never New York. I like animals and trees and jeans, and living here suits me. I was always Texas—I just didn't know it."

Renee looked down at Jessica's hand. The new wedding ring sparkled, and she thought about how happy her sister seemed. Maybe there was a way to have that, too. Jessica continued, "I'm still editing, which I love, but I'm also taking time to be happy and enjoy life with someone I love. That's what's important. Really, the only issue is whether or not you love this guy. If you do, you can figure out the rest of that stuff. You're a smart woman."

Renee didn't know what to say. "I need to go talk to Mom about the cake."

Jessica nodded. "Think about what I said. And don't stress about the cake. You worry too much."

With that, Jessica turned and flounced away in her beautiful wedding dress. Back to taking pictures, back to the man she loved. Renee sighed and went to find her mom and pass on the message to "MacGyver something."

As she walked, she opened her silver clutch purse and pulled out the small metal piece of artwork Jeremiah had given her. She stroked the copper and silver curves, then put it back in her purse just as her mother scurried up.

"Is she okay? What did she say?"

Renee shrugged. "She's fine. She just said to figure something out and that it wasn't a big deal." Her mom looked confused, so Renee added, "She's just happy to be married to Aaron, I guess."

The older woman gave Renee a watery smile. "When I married your dad, I was so happy I wouldn't have noticed if the roof collapsed on top of us."

The thought of how much her dad loved her mom made Renee ache inside. She didn't know what to say.

Stew walked up at that moment in his terrible suit and wrapped his arm around her mother's waist. "Did you speak to Jessica, Gloria?"

Renee watched her mom as she explained about Jessica's reaction, and recognized the look on her face. She loved Stew. Her husband had died and she was willing to love again, even if it meant she might get hurt.

Stew nodded as her mother finished. "You stay here. I think I saw a shop in town that might work. I'll take Aaron's truck and be back in a jiffy."

With that he kissed Renee's mom on the cheek and hustled away. "He's a nice man," Renee said.

Her mom nodded, watching him go.

Jeremiah felt worn-out, but he tried not to show it. He hadn't gotten much sleep the night before, and the glare of the lights in the tent was making his head ache. He had a new piece of art to show for his long, sleepless night, at least. It was full of sharp edges and deep cuts.

If he could just get through a few hours of this reception, he'd be free to do whatever he wanted for the next, well, forever. His empty calendar yawned in front of him. He could keep himself busy trying to sell his pieces and figuring out where to go, what to do next.

Jeremiah brought himself back to the present, to the wedding reception going on all around him. He looked down at the paper in front of him again, a frown creasing his brow. In less than an hour, he would need to make his best man speech. The problem was, he'd written it days ago, and it was funny and light and happy, three things he definitely wasn't feeling.

He needed to rewrite it—that was for sure. Although what

to say completely eluded him. Still, the idea of changing his speech at least gave him an excuse to slip away from all the merriment and avoid being around all those people. Especially that one person, the woman whom he constantly saw out of the corner of his eye.

He went over to where Aaron sat, looking so damn happy it was annoying, and said, "I'm going to head up to the house for a minute. I need to make some quick tweaks to my speech. I've got time, right?"

Aaron studied his friend for a minute before nodding. "Speeches aren't for a half hour or so. Are you going to tell me what's wrong yet?"

Jeremiah thought for a second, but he already knew the answer. "I will, but not today. For multiple reasons."

Aaron seemed to accept that, and Jeremiah exited the tent and made his way toward Jessica and Aaron's house. Inside, he grabbed a pen and one of Jessica's many pads of paper and sat down on the couch to write, grateful for the silence.

He quickly wrote a new draft of his speech, then ripped off the page and started again as soon as he reread it. He couldn't read something that fake and generic at Aaron's wedding, but what could he say that was honest without bringing down the whole party?

It would just need to be something sincere. Just because Renee didn't want to be with him didn't make Jessica and Aaron's love any less special. He started writing again.

"Hey, Jeremiah."

The sound of her voice made him jump, sending a squiggle of ink down the page. He turned and looked straight at Renee, something he'd managed to avoid the entire day. God, she looked beautiful in her bridesmaid dress.

She seemed to be waiting for him to say something, but what was he supposed to say? Hi? Good to see you? Remember that time when I told you I loved you and all you could do was shake your head?

Better not to say anything. After a few seconds, she sat down. Her eyes never left his, and he couldn't have pulled his away if he wanted to. She said, "I'm sorry about yesterday. The truth is I'm scared. But I don't want to lose you because—"

She hesitated, and hope rushed through him like a wildfire. He tried to tamp it down, but it was impossible. "Because," he prompted.

"Because I love you, too," she finished, a flush deepening the color of her cheeks.

For a second he wondered if this was a delusion created by too-little sleep. His hand slid up her arm and cupped her cheek. She was real all right.

A giddiness took over, and before he knew what was happening, he leaned in and took her mouth with his, feeling the pleasure of her lips erase all the tension that had built up in his body.

He wanted to laugh, to pick her up and whirl her around, to kiss every inch of her until she came again and again.

He opted for the third one. He'd do the others later, but a man had to have priorities.

Now that she'd said it, the truth of her words left her feeling light and free. She kissed him back enthusiastically, and when they finally broke apart for air, she said them again. "I love you, Jeremiah."

He gave her his wonderful lopsided smile. "What took you so long?"

She shook her head. "I don't know. I was scared. I can be pretty stupid sometimes."

He pushed the hair out of her eyes. "You're wonderful, Renee."

He pulled her closer and his mouth went to her ear. With a nibble at her earlobe that made her shiver with delight, he said, "I love you, too."

Jeremiah's lips and tongue moved slowly down her throat. Renee continued with her prepared speech, even as his touches drove all thoughts from her mind. "You should know I don't care about ranches and horses and chickens."

"Good," Jeremiah answered, his hot breath on the wet trail he'd made causing her to gasp. "I hate chickens. They're horrible devil-beasts."

He slid her down on the couch so he loomed over her, then moved on to teasing her nipples. Even through the dress, his touch made her moan deep in her throat as her nipples hardened into tight nubbins. "What about the ranches and horses?" she managed to get out while she unbuttoned his pants, eager to touch him.

He growled as her fingers grasped his dick, sliding a condom along his length. She had felt silly at first when she'd gone up to her room and grabbed one before searching for Jeremiah, but now she was extremely grateful to her past self. When Jeremiah spoke again, his voice was ragged. "You know, I've never really loved being a rancher. I think I'm going to like living in the city."

Her stomach fluttered at the words. He was going to come to New York to be with her. She still hadn't absorbed the idea that he would leave Texas to be with her.

"We still need to do the Vegas rodeo, though," he added.

She could live with that. "I'll even wear a cowboy hat."

She saw fire dancing in his eyes as his hands roved over her. "I've seen you in a cowboy hat. It's a good look."

He slid her skirt up, revealing her thong. In seconds, it was pushed to the side and his fingers were playing her like a musical instrument. She arched her back against the couch, pulling him fully on top of her. She bit at his lower lip.

He positioned himself against her, making her squirm with delight. "I think I'll spend some time working on my art. Maybe do some shows or something."

She nodded, her eyes closed, nearly all her control gone. She could hardly keep the thread of the conversation going, but there was still more to say. "I'll help you. I'll have more free time, since I'm going to try working only normal hours for a change. Now that I have a reason to be home, it seems like a good time to try to work like a person who has a life outside of the office."

With that, he kissed her deeply as he buried himself inside her, making her cry out with the pleasure of it all. He groaned. "Yeah, I'm definitely going to love New York. It'll be like a movie. *A Cowboy in New York City*."

She couldn't respond with anything more than his name as he rode her toward oblivion.

After, they rearranged their clothing and went back to the reception, giddy with the emotions of the last half hour. They walked to the tent hand in hand. As they entered, Jeremiah looked at her, as if waiting to see what she would do. Instead of letting go, she squeezed his hand and kept it in hers. "I suppose we should go tell them, now that we're planning on a long-term relationship."

That idea sent a thrill through her, and his wide grin suggested that he felt the same. They strode together toward where Jessica and Aaron sat. Jessica eyed their clasped hands.

Before her sister could say anything, Renee said, "Jessica, remember how you're not freaking out, even when there's no cake?"

Jessica seemed suspicious, but only said, "There's cake. Stew went to a store in town called *Nothing Bundt Cake,* so now we'll be doing a Bundt cake cutting. He saved the day, even if his suit is a bad color."

Renee wanted to comment on the fantastic shop name, but there were more important things to focus on. "Well, you didn't freak out about that, so I'm sure you won't freak out about this, either. Jeremiah and I are a couple."

Jessica rolled her eyes. "Yeah, we know."

"You know?"

"Of course. You two weren't exactly all that good at hiding what was going on," Jessica said, smirking. "I mean, you're really not that subtle. That day you two were putting up the lights, you were making out right next to the door. You really didn't think I saw you? And your footsie under the table bordered on pornographic."

Renee was amazed. "You saw us? And you didn't say anything?"

Jessica shook her head. "Nope. We wanted to give you two a chance to make it happen on your own before stepping in with an added push or two. Remember how I said I owed you for your help with the wedding? Well, now we're even."

A realization swept over Renee and she slapped her head, feeling incredibly stupid. "There was no burst pipe." It wasn't a question.

Jessica laughed so hard she couldn't speak. Aaron took over, "I was so sure you two would figure that one out and see what we were up to, but Jessica said she could pull it off. I'm still surprised neither of you saw through that. I lost a bet there."

"What did you bet?" Jeremiah asked.

Aaron didn't answer, but his smirk and the way Jessica blushed said it was something inappropriate to discuss in public.

Renee narrowed her eyes. "Wait. If you wanted us to get together enough to come up with a reason to kick me out of your house, and you knew what was going on the whole time, then why did you keep barging in on us?"

Jessica said, "Oh, that was just because it was more fun that way. Watching you two pretend to be innocent and trying to act cool when it was so obvious was absolutely hilarious."

Renee couldn't believe her sister. She'd been set up and had had no idea. Jessica seemed so proud of herself.

Jeremiah wrapped his arm around her waist and turned to the newly married couple. "I'm going to kill both of you, you know that, right?" he said, but his mouth was spread in a wide grin.

Renee smiled, too. They'd been tricked, but she had to admit, it was the best trick of her life.

Jessica stood. "It's time for the cake cutting now. Are you

ready to watch us cut a very beautiful last-minute Bundt cake? I'm sure it's going to be delicious."

Jessica looked at them as if daring anyone to disagree.

Nobody did, and everyone watched as Jessica and Aaron sliced into their last-minute cake.

Everyone except for Renee and Jeremiah. They were too busy staring at each other to see anything else.

Epilogue

"I just got off the phone with the bakery. The cake is now on its way to the reception hall." Jessica said as she strode into the room.

Renee looked at her sister in disbelief. "You called them again? I told you to leave them alone the last time you called a half hour ago."

Jessica looked at herself in the mirror, adjusting her midnight-blue bridesmaid dress so it fell perfectly over her rounded stomach. "I know, but I just wanted to double-check."

"Double-checking was at least five calls ago. At this point I wouldn't be surprised if they didn't deliver my cake out of spite."

"Oh, you'll have cake. They know exactly how important it is that there's cake at your reception. I made it very clear to them."

Renee didn't want to think about what Jessica might have said to the poor woman who owned the bakery. "I'm going to hope they think you're a crazy pregnant lady and don't charge me extra for the annoyance."

Jessica waved her hand in the air, as if it was ridiculous to think that anyone would mind being repeatedly called and threatened over the delivery of a baked good. "I'm your maid of honor. It's my job to make sure everything's perfect."

It really wasn't, but Renee didn't say anything. She had known Jessica would become the ultimate wedding planner before she even asked her sister to be the maid of honor. If she hadn't, she wouldn't be Jessica. So there was nothing she could do but let her sister indulge in some of her more neurotic traits and relax, knowing that everything was in good hands.

"Thanks, Jessica," she said. "I know you've got it under control. Nothing will go wrong, I'm sure."

Jessica was about to respond when her phone buzzed with an incoming text. Worry lines appeared on Jessica's forehead as she read whatever it said, and Renee waited for whatever bad news her sister had gotten. "Did I speak too soon?" she asked.

Jessica looked up and gave the bride a tight smile. "Don't worry. I can take care of this. I'll be back in ten minutes."

With that, she started to rush toward the door. "The ceremony starts in fifteen!" Renee called after her sister, but by the time she finished, the door was already closed and she was alone, wondering what had happened. Whatever it was, she doubted it was anywhere near as bad as Jessica thought it was.

With a few minutes alone in the little bridal room that adjoined the chapel, Renee sank into the couch in the corner, her skirt poufing up as she did so. She chuckled to herself, amazed once more that she'd ended up in a poufy white gown covered in sparkly rhinestones. Who would have guessed?

Someone knocked on the door. She assumed it was her mom, coming to tell her what Jessica was dealing with. "Come in," she called, not moving from her spot.

Jeremiah poked his head into the room. "Is Jessica gone?"

Renee felt a rush of affection as her husband-to-be walked in, a giant smile on his face. "I wanted us to have a couple of minutes alone before the ceremony," he said, sitting beside her on the couch.

She looked him up and down, enjoying the way his suit

hugged his body. "You look amazing," she said, reminding herself that she couldn't undress him at that exact moment.

He wrapped an arm around her bare shoulders. "You, too. This is the dress I've heard so much about but wasn't allowed to see, huh? Wow. Worth the wait."

It was only then that she remembered she was in her wedding dress. "You weren't supposed to see me before the ceremony, you know."

He gave her his lopsided grin. "I know. Jessica wouldn't have let me in."

Realization dawned on Renee. "You sent that text." He didn't deny it. "What did you tell her?"

"I said that Aaron couldn't find the boutonnieres."

She glanced at the flower pinned to his breast pocket. "She's going to kill you when she figures out it was a lie."

Jeremiah shrugged. "She can't kill me. It would ruin the wedding, which is her main priority today."

His logic was infallible—she had to give him that. She snuggled closer to him, shoving sections of her dress out of her way to do so. "Another woman asked about my ring this morning. The lady at the hair salon wanted to know if you would be making more of them. I gave her your number."

She glanced down at the delicate golden band wrapped around her left ring finger. The intricate details still amazed her, and she couldn't imagine how much time and work Jeremiah had put into secretly creating it before he proposed. It was truly a thing of beauty.

He squeezed her closer. "I'll think about that after the honeymoon. Right now, there are other things on my mind than building up a new business."

"So you're ready to give up your bachelorhood in about ten minutes and settle down as an old married couple?" she asked, looking up at him.

His eyes roved over her body again, making her skin tingle.

"If it means I get to see what you're wearing under this dress later tonight, then absolutely."

She gave him a seductive smile. "Not much."

He leaned in, his lips inches from hers. "My favorite," he whispered, tugging at a loose strand of her hair.

She lost herself in his eyes as he closed the gap between them.

Just as their lips touched, Jessica's voice broke into the moment, forcing them apart. "No! Hair, makeup, dress! You're going to ruin all of it!"

They both looked at the angry pregnant lady towering over them. "You're not even supposed to be in here, Jeremiah. You need to get up to the altar."

She shook her head at him. "Do you have any idea how worried I was when I got your text?"

Renee tried to stifle her laugh at her sister's serious manner, but she couldn't stop herself from giggling. "Jess, you need to calm down. Everything's fine. You've done a great job. Now relax a smidge and let me enjoy my wedding."

Jessica looked as if she might give some sort of a retort, but then she took a deep, calming breath. "Okay. It's your wedding—you do what you want. But Jeremiah, you need to be out of this room in forty-five seconds if we're going to keep to the schedule."

Jeremiah nodded solemnly, but his eyes sparkled. "Thanks for being so relaxed about everything."

Jessica either missed or chose to ignore his sarcasm, because she just smiled and nodded at him.

Renee waited for a second, then realized her sister was going to keep standing there unless she said something. "You might want to turn around if you don't want to watch us making out for the next forty-five seconds."

Jessica rolled her eyes and turned her back. "Thirty-five."

Renee's gaze went to her husband-to-be. "We better make this time count," she said.

He didn't need any more prompting than that, pulling her

close and pressing his lips to hers. The world disappeared as she savored the moment.

It took three tries for Jessica to pull them apart. "Okay, now you really are behind schedule," she told them.

Jeremiah leaned his forehead against Renee's as they caught their breath. "Are you ready?"

She smiled up at him. "I am."

He shook his head. "It's 'I do.' You might want to practice before you get up there."

Renee rolled her eyes. "You better get out of here before Jessica has a meltdown. I'll see you in a minute."

He gave her one more kiss, then left.

Renee stood, and Jessica fussed around her for a few moments before declaring everything perfect. Then Jessica handed Renee her bouquet. "Love you, little sis. Let's go get you married."

Renee nodded, unable to speak, and followed her sister out the door. Her heart was too full for words as she walked out to join the man of her dreams.

* * * * *

Keep reading for an excerpt of
Heart Like A Cowboy
by Delores Fossen,
out now!

CHAPTER ONE

THAT WHOLE DEAL about bad news coming in threes? Well, it was a crock. Lieutenant Colonel Egan Donnelly now had proof of it.

First, there'd been the unexpected visitor, AKA the messenger, who'd started the whole bad-news ball rolling. That'd teach him to open his frickin' door before he'd even finished his frickin' coffee.

Then, there was the so-called celebration that would stir up the worst of his past and serve it up to him on a silver platter. Or rather on a disposable paper plate, anyway.

Then, a letter from his ex, which he figured was never a good sign. Who the heck actually wanted to hear from their cheating ex? Not him, that was for sure.

Those were the three things—count them: one, two, three—that was supposed to have been the final tally of bad crap even if for only a day, but apparently the creator of that old saying had no credibility whatsoever. Then again, Egan had known firsthand that bad news didn't have limited quantities.

Or expiration dates.

Now he was faced with ironclad confirmation that those other three things were piddly-ass drops in the proverbial bucket compared to bad-news number four.

And now, everything in his world was crashing and burning.

Again.

Thirty Minutes Earlier

IN THE DREAM, Lieutenant Colonel Egan Donnelly saved his best friend's life. In the dream, the explosion didn't happen. It didn't blast through the scorched, airless night. Didn't tear apart the transport vehicle.

Didn't leave blood on the bleached sand.

Didn't kill.

In the dream, Egan was the hero that so many people proclaimed he was. He made just the right decisions to save everyone, including Jack. *Especially Jack.*

Egan didn't fight tooth and nail to come out of this dream—unlike the ones that were basically a blow-by-blow account of what had actually happened that god-awful night nearly three years ago. Those dreams were pits of the darkest level of hell where everything spun and bashed, stomping him down deeper and deeper into the real nightmare. Those dreams he fought.

Had to.

Because Egan had learned the hard way if he let those dreams play out, then it was a damn hard struggle to come back from them. Heck, he was still trying to come back from them.

Despite wanting to linger in this particular dream where he got to play hero, it didn't happen, thanks to his phone dinging with a text. He frowned, noticing that it was barely six in the morning. Texts at this hour usually were not good. Considering that all three of his siblings were on active duty, *not good* could be really bad.

He saw his father's name on the screen, and the worry instantly tightened Egan's gut. His dad had just turned sixty so while he wasn't in the "one foot in the grave" stage, he wasn't the proverbial spring chicken, either. Added to that, his dad still ran the day-to-day operation of Saddlebrook, the family's ranch in Emerald Creek, Texas. The ranch that'd been in the Donnelly family for over a hundred years and had grown and grown and grown with each succeeding generation. All that growth required hours of upkeep and work.

Found this when I was going through some old photo albums, his dad had texted.

What the heck? That gut tightness eased up, some, when Egan saw it was a slightly off-center image taken in front of the main barn on the ranch. His dad had obviously used his phone to take a picture of the old photo. Emphasis on *old*.

It was a shot that his grandmother, Effie, had snapped thirty years ago on Egan's eighth birthday. His brother, Cal, would have been six. His sister, Remi, a two-year-old toddler, and his other brother, Blue, was just four. Stairsteps, people called them, since they'd all been born just two years apart.

In the photo, his dad, looking lean, fit and young, was in the center, flanked by Egan and Remi on the right, and Cal and Blue on the left. Remi and Blue were both grinning big toothy grins. Cal and Egan weren't. Probably because they'd been old enough to understand that life as they'd known it was over.

Their lives hadn't exactly gone to hell in a handbasket,

but this particular shot had been taken only a couple of weeks after their mother had died from cancer. A long agonizing death that had left their dad the widower of four young kids. Still, his dad was eking out a smile in the picture, and he'd managed to gather all four of them in his outstretched arms.

Bittersweet times.

That's when their mom's mom, Grammy Effie, had come to Saddlebrook for what was supposed to have been a couple of months, until his dad got his footing. Effie was still living on the ranch thirty years later and had obviously put down roots as deep as his father's.

Egan was wondering what had prompted his dad to go digging through old family albums when his phone dinged again. It was another text from his dad, another photo. It was an image that Egan also knew well, and he mentally referred to it as the start of phase two of his life.

The first phase had been with a loving mother that sadly he now couldn't even remember. That had ended with her death. Phase two had begun when his dad had gotten remarried four years later to a young fresh-faced Captain Audrey Granger, who'd then been stationed at the very base in San Antonio where Egan was now. It was an hour's commute to the ranch that Audrey had diligently made.

For a while, anyway.

In this shot, his dad and new bride dressed in blue were in the center, and both were flashing giddy smiles. Ditto for Remi and Blue. Again, no smiles for Cal and Egan since they'd been ten and twelve respectively and were no doubt holding back on the glee to see how life with their stepmom would all play out.

It hadn't played out especially well.

But then, it also hadn't hit anywhere near the "hell in a handbasket" mark, either.

If there'd been a family photo taken just two years later, though, Audrey probably wouldn't have been in it. By then, she'd been in Germany. Or maybe England. Instead of an hour commute, she'd come "home" to the ranch a couple of times a year. Then, as her career had blossomed, the visits had gotten further and further apart. These days, Brigadier General Audrey Donnelly only came home on Christmas. If that.

Egan sent his dad a thumbs-up emoji to let him know he'd seen the pictures, and he was considering an actual reply to ask if all was well, but his alarm went off. He got up, mentally going through his schedule for the day. As the commander of the Fighter Training Squadron at Randolph AFB, Texas, there'd be the usual paperwork, going over some stats for the pilots in training, and then in the afternoon, he'd get to do one of the things he loved most.

Fly.

Of course, it would be under the guise of a training mission in the T-38C Talon jet, not the F-16 that Egan used to pilot, but it would still give him that hit of adrenaline. Still give him the reminder of why he'd first joined the Navy and then had transferred to the Air Force so he could continue to stay in the cockpit.

Egan showered, put on his flight suit, read through his emails on his phone and was about halfway through his first cup of coffee when his doorbell rang. He had the same reaction to it as he had the earlier text. A punch of dread that something was wrong. It wasn't even seven o'clock yet and hardly the time for visitors. Especially since he lived in base housing and therefore wasn't on the traditional beaten path for friends or family to just drop by.

Frowning, he went to the door. And Egan frowned some more when he looked through the peephole at the visitor on his porch. A woman with pulled back dark blond hair and vivid green eyes. At first glance, he thought it was his ex-wife, Colleen, someone he definitely didn't want to see, but this was a slightly younger, taller version of the woman who'd left him for another man.

Alana Davidson, Colleen's sister.

"Yes, I know it's early," Alana sighed and said loud enough for him to hear while she looked directly at the peephole. "Sorry about that."

Wondering what the heck this was all about, he opened the door and got an immediate blast of heat. Texas in June started out hot as hell and got even hotter. Today was apparently no exception. He also got another immediate blast of concern because there was nothing about Alana's expression that indicated this was a social visit.

Then again, Alana and he never had social visits.

Never.

Just too much old baggage, old wounds and old everything else between them. Ironic, since she'd been married to his best friend. Now, she was his dead best friend's widow and bore that strong resemblance to his cheating ex-wife who'd left him just days before Jack's death.

Egan was no doubt an unwelcome sight for her, too. He was the man who'd not only failed to keep her husband alive, but he was also the reason Jack had been in that transport vehicle in the first place.

So, yeah, old baggage galore.

"Sorry," Alana repeated, looking up at him. Not looking

at him for long, though. Like their avoidance of social visits, they didn't do a lot of eye contact, either. "But I have an appointment at the base hospital in an hour, and I wanted to catch you before you went into work."

"The hospital?" he automatically questioned.

She waved it off, clearly picking up on his concern that something might be medically wrong with her. "I'm consulting with a colleague on a chief master sergeant who's being medically retired and moving to Emerald Creek. I'll be working with the chief to come up with some lifestyle changes."

Alana made that seem like her norm, and maybe it was. She was a dietitian, and because as Jack's widow she still had a military ID card so she wouldn't have had any trouble getting onto the base. Added to that, Emerald Creek was a haven for retirees and veterans since it was so close to three large military installations. There were almost as many combat boots as cowboy boots in Emerald Creek.

"How'd you know where I live?" he asked.

"I got your address from your grandmother." She glanced over her shoulder at the street of houses. "I occasionally have consults here, but it's the first time I've been to this part of the base."

Yeah, his particular house wasn't near the hospital, commissary or base exchange store where Alana would be more apt to go. Added to that, Jack had never been stationed here, which meant Alana had never lived here, either.

"Full disclosure," she said the moment he shut the door. "You aren't going to like any of what I have to say."

Now it was Egan who sighed and braced himself for Alana to finally do something he'd expected her to do for three years. Scream and yell at him for allowing Jack to die.

But there was no raised voice or obvious surge of anger. Instead, she took out a piece of paper from her sizeable handbag and thrust it at him.

"It's a mock-up of a flyer that Jack's mom intends to have printed up and sent to everyone in her known universe," Alana explained.

At first glance, he saw that the edges of the flyer had little pictures of barbecue grills, fireworks, the American flag and military insignia. Egan intended to just scan it to get the gist of what it was about, but the scanning came to a stumbling slow crawl as he tried to take in what he was reading.

"Join us for a Life Celebration for Major Jack Connor Davidson, July Fourth, at the Emerald Creek City Park. It'll be an afternoon of food, festivities and remembrance as a celebratory memorial painting for Jack will be unveiled by our own Top Gun hometown hero, Lieutenant Colonel Egan Donnelly."

Well, hell. Both sentences were full-on gut punches and thick gobs of emotional baggage. Memorial. Life celebration. Remembrances. The icing on that gob was the last part.

Top Gun hometown hero.

Egan was, indeed, a former Top Gun. He'd won the competition a dozen years ago when he'd been a navy lieutenant flying F-16s. The hometown part was accurate, too, since he'd been born and raised in Emerald Creek, but that *hero* was the biggest of big-assed lies.

"I can't go," Egan heard himself say once he'd managed to clear the lump in his throat.

She nodded as if that were the exact answer she'd expected. "I'm guessing you'll be on duty?"

He'd make damn sure he was, but wasn't it ironic that the memorial celebration would fall on the one weekend of the month he usually went home to help his dad on the family ranch? Maybe Jack's mom knew that, or maybe the woman just believed that such an event would be a good fit for the Fourth of July.

It wasn't.

Barbecue, hot dogs, beer and such didn't go well with the crapload of memories something like that would stir. He didn't need a memorial or a life celebration to remember Jack. Egan remembered him daily, hourly even, and after three years, the grief and guilt hadn't lost any steam.

"I'll let Tilly know you can't be there," Alana said, referring to Jack's mother. "She's mentioned contacting your stepmom to see if she could be there for the unveiling."

"Good luck with that," he muttered, and Alana's sound of agreement confirmed that she understood it was a long shot.

What would likely end up happening was that his brother Cal would get roped into doing the "honors." He'd known Jack, and Cal's need to do the right thing would have him stepping in.

"The last time I ran into Tilly, she didn't want to discuss anything involving Jack's death," Egan recalled.

Alana nodded. "That's still true. Nothing about how he died, et cetera. She only wants to chat about the things he did when he was alive."

"So, why do a *memorial* painting?" Egan wanted to know.

"I'm not sure, but it's possible the painting will be another life celebration deal that she'll want hung in some prominent part of town like city hall or the library. In other words, maybe the painting will have nothing to do with Jack even being in the military. Tilly was proud of him," she quickly added. "But she's never fully wrapped her mind around losing him."

That made sense. The one time he'd tried to talk to her about Jack's death, she'd shut him down. As if not talking about his death would somehow breathe some life back into him.

"There's one more thing," Alana went on, and this time she took a pale yellow envelope from her purse and handed it to him. "It's a letter from Colleen."

Egan had already reached for it but yanked back his hand as if the envelope were a coiled rattler ready to sink its fangs into his flesh. The mention of his ex-wife tended to do that. Memories of Colleen didn't fall into the "hell on steroids" category like Jack's. More like the "don't let the door hit your cheating ass" category. Colleen had obviously liked that direction just fine since she hadn't spoken a word to him since the divorce.

He glanced at the envelope, scowled. "A letter? Is it some kind of twelve-step deal about making amends or something?" he asked.

Alana shook her head. "No, I think it's a living will of sorts."

That erased his scowl. "Is Colleen dying?"

"Not that I know of, but she apparently decided she wanted to make her last wishes known. She sent letters for me, our aunt and your dad. I have his if you want to give it to him."

Egan reached out again to stop her from retrieving it, and Alana used the opportunity to put the letter for him in his hand. "I don't want this," he insisted.

"Totally understand. I read mine," she admitted. "Along with spelling out her end-of-life wishes—cremation, no funeral, no headstone—she wants us to have some sister time, like a vacation or something."

Egan had no idea how much contact Alana and Colleen had with each other these days, but it was possible when Colleen had walked out on him, she'd also walked out on Alana. He thought he detected some animosity in Alana's tone and expression.

He went straight to the trash can in the adjoining kitchen and tossed the envelope on top of the oozing heap of the sticky chicken rice bowl that had been at least a week past its prime when he'd dumped it the night before.

"I'm not interested in wife time with her," he muttered, knowing he sounded bitter and hating that he still was.

Unlike what he was still going through with Jack, though, his grief and anger with Colleen had trickled down to almost nothing. *Almost.* He now just considered her a mistake and was glad she was out of his life. Some days, he could even hope that she was happy with the Mr. Wonderful artist that she'd left him for.

When he turned back to Alana, he saw she had watched the letter trashing, and she was now combing those jeweled green eyes over his face as if trying to suss out what was going on in his head. Egan decided to diffuse that with a question that fell into the polite small talk that would have happened had this been a normal visit.

"Uh, how are you doing?" he asked. On the surface, that didn't seem to be a safe area of conversation since it could lead to that screaming rant over his huge part in her husband's death. But Egan realized he would welcome the rant.

Because he deserved it.

Alana took a deep breath. "Well, despite nearly everyone in town deciding I should live out the rest of my life as a widow, I've started dating again."

That got his attention. Not because he hadn't known

about the town's feelings. And not because he believed she shouldn't have a second chance at romance. But Egan had thought she didn't want such a chance, that she was still as buried in the past as he was. Apparently not.

"I'm only doing virtual dating for now," she went on, not sounding especially thrilled with that. "Last week, I had a virtual date with a guy who has six goats and eleven chickens in his one-bedroom apartment in Houston."

Egan didn't especially want to smile, but he did, anyway. "Sounds like a prize catch. You'd never have to buy eggs again. Or fertilizer."

She shrugged. "He was a prize compared to the one I had the week before. Within the first minute of conversation, he wanted to know the circumference of my nipples." Alana stopped, her eyes widening as if she hadn't expected to share that.

Egan smiled again, but this one was forced. He hadn't wanted Alana to think he was shocked or offended, though he was indeed shocked. He'd never considered nipple size one way or another.

He'd especially never considered anything about Alana's nipples.

And he hated that was now in his head. That kind of stuff could mess with things that already had a shaky status quo.

"Dating at thirty-five isn't as much a 'fish in the sea' situation as it is more of a, uh, well, swamp," Alana explained. "Think scaly critters, slithery, that sort of thing, with the potential and hope that some actual fish lingering about will eventually come out of hiding."

That didn't sound appealing at all, but then he hadn't had to hit any of the dating sites. He could thank the eternal string of matchmakers for that. Unlike the widowed

Alana, apparently everyone thought a divorced guy in his thirties shouldn't be solo. Especially a guy who'd had his "heart broken" when his wife had walked out on him right before his best friend had been killed.

"How about you?" she asked, clearly aiming for a change of subject and her own shot at small talk. "Have you jumped into dating waters?"

He shook his head. "Too busy."

She broke their unwritten rule by locking her gaze with his for a second or two. "Yeah. Busy," she repeated. And it sounded as if that were code for a whole bunch of things. For instance, wounded. Damaged. Guarded. Guilty.

All of the above applied to him.

It was hard for Egan to think about his happiness when he'd robbed Jack of his. *Busy*, though, was a much safer term for it.

"Well, I gotta go," Alana said when the silence turned awkward, as it always did between them. "I'll let Tilly know you won't be at the life celebration so she can find someone else to do the unveiling."

Egan frowned when a thought occurred to him. "She won't ask you to do it, will she?" Because he couldn't imagine that it'd be any easier for Alana than it would be for him.

"No." Another sigh went with that. "Tilly still has me firmly in the 'grieving widow' category, which apparently will preclude me from lifting a veil on a painting and doing other things such as dating or appearing too happy when I'm in public."

He wanted to ask, *Aren't you still a grieving widow?* But that would go well beyond small talk. It could lead to an actual conversation that would drag feelings and emotions to the surface. No way did he want to deal with that.

Obviously, Alana wasn't on board for such a chat, either, because she headed for the door, giving him a forced smile and a quick glance before she left and went to her car. Egan watched her, doling out his own forced smile and what had to be a stupid-looking wave.

Since he didn't want to stand around and think about this visit, Colleen's trashed letter—or Alana's nipples—he grabbed his flight cap and keys so he could go to his truck. He barely made it a step, though, before his phone dinged with another text.

Great. Another photo trip down memory lane.

But it wasn't.

It was his father's name on the screen, but there was no picture. Only six words that sent Egan's heart to his knees.

Get to Emerald Creek Hospital now.